The LOST ISLAND *of* TAMARIND

NADIA AGUIAR

SQUARE
FISH

FEIWEL AND FRIENDS
NEW YORK

SQUARE
FISH

An imprint of Macmillan Publishing Group, LLC
175 Fifth Avenue
New York, NY 10010
mackids.com

Our books may be purchased in bulk for promotional, educational, or
business use. Please contact your local bookseller or the Macmillan Corporate and
Premium Sales Department at (800) 221-7945 ext. 5442 or by e-mail at
MacmillanSpecialMarkets@macmillan.com.

Library of Congress Cataloging-in-Publication Data

Aguiar, Nadia.
    The lost island of Tamarind / by Nadia Aguiar.
      p. cm.
    Summary: Thirteen-year-old Maya, who has spent her life at sea with her marine bi-
ologist parents, yearns for a normal life, but when a storm washes her parents overboard, life becomes anything but normal for Maya, her younger brother and baby
sister, as they land at a mysterious, uncharted island filled with danger.
ISBN 978-1-250-10391-8 (paperback)   ISBN 978-1-42991-811-4 (ebook)
    [1. Adventure and adventurers—Fiction. 2. Islands—Fiction. 3. Magic—Fiction.
4. Brothers and sisters—Fiction. 5. Pirates—Fiction. 6. Giants—Fiction. 7.
War—Fiction.]   I. Title.
    PZ7.A26876Los 2008
    [Fic]—dc22   2008005623

Originally published in the United States by Feiwel and Friends
First Square Fish edition: 2010
This Square Fish edition: 2017
Map illustration copyright © 2008 by Jeffrey L. Ward
Book designed by Barbara Grzeslo
Square Fish logo designed by Filomena Tuosto

10 9 8 7 6 5 4

AR: 5.8 / LEXILE: 880L

It is not down in any map; true places never are.
—*Moby-Dick,* Herman Melville

to Bermuda

Bembao

Only Blue House in Bembao

The Ravaged Straits

The Black Cross

Lopez-Marcanzo

Four Palms

The Lesser Islands

Limmermor Beachs

Overview of Greater Tamarind

THE NORTH

NEGLECTED PROVINCES

EASTERN LANDS

THE SOUTH

Maracairol

GREATER TAMARIND

THE NORTH

Opera Shell

Nero Jungle

Abandoned
Ophalla Mines

Cloud Forest Village

...se and Maria's
...House

THE SOUTH

NEGLECTED PROVINCES

Nailanda River

Giant's Road

Señor Tecumbo's villa

...athilde's tin shack

Port Town

©2008 Jeffrey L. Ward

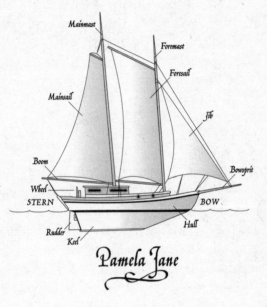

Mainmast

Foremast

Foresail

Mainsail

Jib

Boom

Bowsprit

Wheel

STERN

BOW

Rudder

Hull

Keel

Pamela Jane

❊ CHAPTER ONE ❊

Maya's Dilemma ❊
Granny Pearl ❊ *The PAMELA JANE* ❊ *"A long time ago, near the
equator"* ❊ *A Mysterious Octopus* ❊ *A Sinister Visitor*

Dolphins had been riding in the bow waves of the *Pamela
Jane* all morning. They were plump and shiny and they played
like children and spoke to each other in their strangely human
language of squeaks and whistles. Usually Maya loved when
dolphins swam with the boat, but today she barely noticed
them. She was sitting on the bow, leaning against the cabin
wall, out of sight of the main deck, which is where she went
when she wanted to be alone. When she heard her mother calling her she frowned more deeply and tucked her legs up so that
she couldn't be seen.

"Maya!"

She didn't answer.

The warm Atlantic rushed blue and strong over the hull of
the *Pamela Jane* and stretched flatly to the horizon where white
clouds bloomed. Maya's parents had collected the last of the

algae samples they needed early that morning and within a few hours they would be sailing into port at St. Alban's, where they would drop off the samples at the Marine Station.

Her mother's voice grew muffled as she went into the cabin, and then her footsteps thumped on the steps as she came back on deck. Her shadow appeared over Maya a few moments later.

"Didn't you hear me calling you?"

"Sorry," Maya said. She rested her chin on her knees and trained her gaze on the horizon. The boat rose and fell gently on the swells. Her mother refolded her scarf and tied it over her hair and sat down beside her.

"What is it?" she asked.

Maya felt tears rise to her eyes again but she blinked them away and glared out at the sea.

"You know what it is," she whispered. "I don't want to live on the boat anymore."

Suddenly Maya felt more angry than sad. Frowning, she picked ruthlessly at a scab on her ankle. "Everyone's always on top of me," she said. "I don't have any *privacy.*"

Her mother considered.

"It's a big ocean," she said. "It's lucky that we're all together on it."

"I don't want to *be* on the ocean," said Maya. "I want to be on land. I want to live at Granny Pearl's and go to school. I want to be like everyone else. I want to know people my own age. I want *friends.*"

Here Maya felt tears welling again.

"You have Simon."

Maya scowled. "He doesn't count."

She picked at her ankle and didn't look at her mother. It

2

wasn't Simon's fault. He was perfectly happy. He was always sweet and cheerful and even if he was annoying sometimes, people always liked to have him around because he was so good-natured. Maya didn't *want* to be so unpleasant all the time. She loved her family. It just seemed like she couldn't help her bad mood these days. She felt her mother watching her.

The boat eased on the waves. A nurse shark that had been following the boat for a couple of days reappeared and Maya watched it, just a few feet below the surface off the lee of the boat. It must have scared off the dolphins and now the sea was quiet except for the sound of the water breaking against the *Pamela Jane*'s hull.

"I'll talk to your father," her mother said finally. "Meanwhile, we'll be in Bermuda in a week. Try to enjoy that thought, okay? We can talk about all this when we get there."

She leaned forward onto one knee and kissed Maya's head.

"It will all be all right," she said.

She left and Maya was by herself with the lonely clatter of the halyards on the mast.

Maya's parents, marine biologists Marisol and Peter Nelson, had one quick stop to make at the Marine Station in St. Alban's to drop off samples of sea creatures they had collected, and then they would be on their way for their summer visit to Granny Pearl in Bermuda.

Granny Pearl was Peter's mother. She lived in a little blue cottage that faced out to sea. She had soft brown skin and gentle wrinkles. She smelled like warm soil and ginger and sundried laundry. Sugar snap peas grew in her garden, as well as cassava, parsley, and odd-shaped green squash. She kept a patch of milkweed for the monarch butterflies. She had a great love of bats and would often sit out on her porch on summer evenings, watching their soft black flickers across the heavy night sky. On the stone railing of her porch she kept a conch shell that she would lift to the children's ears so that they could hear the soft sigh of the ocean inside the shell. *Do you hear?* she would whisper. *When you're out on the ocean, this is how I know where you are.*

It was to the cove at Granny Pearl's house that the *Pamela Jane* had first drifted, abandoned, back before Maya had even been born. Granny Pearl had looked out through the kitchen window and had seen the crewless schooner coming into the cove as if she knew exactly where she was going. She had been encrusted in strange, jewel-like barnacles, her sails had been ghostly tatters, and her cabin had been almost entirely empty, scoured bare by the wind and waves. When Maya's parents plied the barnacles free from the wood, they found the boat's name written on the bow: *Pamela Jane*. The only thing left in her cabin was a book with blank ivory pages and a red leather cover, which Maya's parents found in a drawer sealed shut by humidity. They posted notices in shipping journals all over the world, but when no one had claimed the *Pamela*, the Nelsons had freshened her paint and refitted her sails and she had belonged to them ever since. They had even installed a very small laboratory in her cabin where they could store samples they took from the sea.

Maya was thirteen and she had lived on the *Pamela Jane* her whole life, first with just her parents and then with her brother, Simon, who was nine now, and later their baby sister, Penny, who was eight months old. Their parents were marine biologists who worked for the Marine Stations. For a long time

Maya had believed that there was nothing better than life on the open ocean, sailing from port to port on the warm trade winds that blew across the Atlantic Ocean.

She had seen silver-flippered seals that barked like happy dogs, fleets of menacing purple Portuguese men-o'-war balloons blown along by northerly winds, and magnificent swordfish that leaped out of the sea and sailed clean over the deck of the *Pamela Jane*. Simon had once even touched the barnacled side of a whale. His father had lifted him over the edge of the starboard railing as the great gray flank surfaced and rolled back under. The creature's unfathomable eye, big as an oil well, had looked right at Simon. Like most people who lived on the sea, they knew the map of the stars by heart and could navigate by them at night. Often Maya and her mother would lie on their backs on the deck under the big velvety sky, and her mother would point out the constellations: Andromeda, Lyra, Orion, and the most graceful of them all, Cassiopeia, her arms jointed like an insect's against the night sky. On stormy nights they watched Saint Elmo's fire dancing high on the mast, leaping between the lines.

Each year they followed the Gulf Stream from the coast of South America into the Caribbean and up to Bermuda and then back down again. The children's parents tracked the breeding seasons of schools of parrot fish and amber jacks, recorded algae levels on the equator, studied the migration patterns of Capricorn whales, and many other mysterious things. They made stops at ports along the way. Each port was different. In Tulomso there were giant sea-pumpkins that grew along the beaches, in Port Cardina great albatrosses with snowy white beards nested in the cliffs, and in the waters around St. Malan's glowworms rose to the surface in whirling lights on the third night after each full moon. Near Trinidad and Tobago were massive oil tankers whose horns had great deep bellows. They would call to each other as they passed in the shipping lanes. The *Pamela Jane* would chase playful schools of whales to farther Patagonia at the south of the continent, where Maya and Simon could see haunting white ice floes bobbing in the distance, vapors of steam dancing around them before they would turn, the *Pamela Jane* rushing back to warmer waters.

Since they were always moving from port to port, Maya and Simon didn't go to school like most children did. But every morning their mother gave them lessons, on the deck when the weather was good, and down in the cabin when it was foul. The pages of their schoolbooks were damp and curled from the sea air. Maya had always been proud that she and Simon knew things that land children didn't: how to tell the difference between a jacknose and a barracuda, how to tell how quickly a squall on the horizon would strike, if at all, and how to rig a fifty-two-foot schooner. They could read the machinery of the GPS, the boat's navigation system, which told them what their latitude and longitude was, and the radar, which told them what vessels were near them, and if there was bad weather up ahead. They could each cook a meal on a gyroscopic stove in the galley, which was what the kitchen on a boat is called. Simon was an expert in knots and could tie fisherman's bends, spider hitches, surgeon's loops, and blood-knot line joiners, along with hundreds of others. He had read a book on it and now knew more knots than their father. There were even a few that he was sure he had invented himself.

But lately the magic had gone out of life on the sea for Maya.

She didn't know how it had happened, but sometime in the past year living on the *Pamela Jane* had become unbearable. The journeys between landfalls stretched out dully. Simon got on her nerves constantly. And even with her family around her, she found that sometimes she was so lonely she would cry by herself on her top bunk in the cabin. She longed to be in one place, in a proper house that wasn't always floating from one place to the next, with a backyard instead of a deck and windows instead of portholes. She was tired of five of them being crammed into such a tiny space together, and it had only gotten worse since Penny had come along almost a year ago. Maya and Simon shared a narrow bunk bed in the room that doubled as the family's living room, and Penny slept there, too, in a hanging cot in the middle of the room that swayed as the boat moved through the water and rocked her to sleep. Maya had no space to call her own. If she went up to the stern, someone was there, if she snuck back down into the cabin, someone undoubtedly would come barging through shouting, "Maya, Maya, where are you, Maya?"

Their stops in ports were no better. There were no other boat children her age. She was too old to play games on the dock with the little kids but too young to go to the cabanas along the beaches where calypso music played and local teenagers hung out. "*Far* too young," said her father. While her parents were busy at the Marine Station in each port, Maya could easily have disobeyed them and gone inside the cabanas, of course. And it wasn't that she wouldn't have disobeyed them—it was that she was too shy. She was scared that she'd go inside and have no one to talk to and everyone would see that she was there alone. That would have been mortifying—too mortifying to risk. Simon, if he'd had any interest, would have been able to walk right in and make friends with everyone there. Simon, their mother said, could talk the ear off a snail.

Simon was the one people liked. Sometimes the Nelsons

would cross paths with people they had met for just an afternoon two years ago, and the people would still remember a conversation they'd had with Simon. Their mother said he was special that way. But Simon didn't care about the cabanas. He was still happy to run around on the beach and the docks and could spend hours talking to crusty old sailors or young biologists from the Marine Stations. Once these things had made Maya perfectly happy, too. But somehow, she didn't know how or why or even when it had begun to happen, the joy was gone.

For months now she had been begging her parents to let her stay behind when they left this time. She had even written them letters: *Dear Mami and Papi, I think the time has come for me to go to school like a normal person my age. I'm sure that Granny Pearl will be happy to have me live with her. . . .* And finally, finally, they had relented, and said that they would talk with Granny Pearl when they reached Bermuda. But Maya was still nervous. If they didn't sort everything out soon she would miss the start of the school year and she'd have to stay on the boat for another year. Another whole year—Maya couldn't bear to think about it.

🐬 🐬 🐬

"Maya!"

Someone else, again! Maya felt a shadow fall across her again. Her family couldn't give her any space—they even had to put their shadows on her! She opened her eyes and saw Simon standing over her.

"What?" she asked sharply.

"Papi's going to tell me the story about the island," he said. "If you want to come hear."

"That's okay," Maya said. "Thanks. I'll stay here."

"Later, do you want to play cards?"

"I don't know," she said. "I'm busy thinking right now. Sometimes I just need time to *think*. By myself."

"What are you thinking about?"

"About being somewhere where everyone can't bother me every two minutes," Maya muttered.

"Later on, we could trade shells," offered Simon. "I could give you the milk moon snail of mine that you wanted. Or the red triton."

Maya sighed. Simon was nine. He was at that age when sometimes he acted grown-up and sometimes he was as irritating as a seven-year-old.

"I'm not talking anymore," said Maya, closing her eyes. "I'm just thinking."

"But . . ." began Simon.

"Shhh!" said Maya loudly. "Thinking!"

Simon lingered a minute more and then she heard him trudging back to the main deck. As soon as he was gone she felt a pang of remorse. It wasn't Simon's fault that things weren't how they used to be. A moment later, her father's voice drifted to her on the breeze.

"A long time ago, near the equator, there was a mysterious sea. Storms brewed around its edges and no boats could sail into it. In the middle of this sea was an island. Since no boats could reach it or leave from it, it was entirely cut off from the Outside World. Different life-forms sprang up and flourished. Fish the color of jewels flashed through the waters. There were villages built in the tops of ancient trees and mythical creatures and the strangest plants you've ever seen. It was an incredible place."

"And there was a giant," Simon interrupted.

"*There were lots of giants,*" their father said.

"*And they sang.*"

"*Yes, all the giants were singers.*"

"*What was the island called?*" asked Simon.

"*It had a lot of different names,*" said their father. "*So I couldn't really tell you for sure.*"

"*And how big was it?*" Simon asked.

"*It could be as big or as small as you wanted,*" their father replied. "*It always seemed to be changing sizes, you see.*"

"*No way,*" said Simon. "*That couldn't happen.*"

"*That's where you're wrong,*" said their father. "*Almost anything can happen.*"

Maya sighed. She had heard it all before.

Maya went down into the cabin and, checking the passageway quickly to make sure that no one saw her, slipped into the tiny laboratory where her parents kept the marine samples. Shades were drawn over the portholes and the room was dim. Salt-water tanks lined the walls. If they hadn't been covered with black canvas, Maya would have seen dozens of odd sea creatures drifting inside them: pale sea horses, crustaceans with dappled shells, alien moon jellies pulsing toward the surface. One tank was anchored to the table in the middle of the room where the microscopes were, and this was the one Maya approached. She had been there earlier when her father had drawn what was inside it up from the sea. She slid the canvas aside and slowly raised the lid; it opened up like the top of a treasure chest. Suddenly brilliant, blue-tinged rays of light shot out from the tank.

It took Maya's eyes a moment to adjust. The light dimmed a little and she watched as the tiny octopus floated slowly through the water. It was as clear as glass, with fine neon filaments. *It's so weird,* she thought. All the sea creatures her parents collected these days were peculiar. It was as small as Maya's thumb, but the power of the light it emitted was astonishing. Looking into the tank was like standing in a window with moonlight flooding in. Maya's thoughts wandered back to the problem of life on the boat. She sniffled and a tear fell into the tank. The tiny octopus recoiled, its neon tentacles collapsing. A moment later it rose to the surface as if it was curious. Maya saw its eyes, luminous, with inky violet pupils, looking up at her. She sniffled again and wiped the back of her hand over her cheek.

Maya heard footsteps in the hall pass the laboratory door. She knew in a moment someone would be back that way and would pop their head in and find her. Quickly she drew down the lid of the tank and the light in the laboratory dimmed. She lingered a moment, a few rays of the octopus's light shooting through the gap and dancing on the wall behind her. Then she closed the lid firmly. She slipped quickly back to the passage-way, pulling the door shut behind her. She ran up the stairs and onto the deck.

The dolphins and nurse shark were gone now and the *Pamela Jane*'s white sails were blinding in the sun. Her father was standing at the wheel, writing in the ship's log. She wanted to talk to him about school and Granny Pearl, and about the curious, glowing octopus, too, but she would have to wait.

The logbook was full of boring stuff—their coordinates, the wind direction and speed, the weather conditions, sightings of other ships, and notes about unusual things, such as the large cargo ship buoy that they had had to tack to avoid earlier that morning. Her father recorded these things diligently at regular intervals each day. The idea was that if anything unforeseen happened out at sea, such as a storm that blew them off course, or if the mechanical navigation equipment broke for any reason and they were lost, they could consult the ship's log. From the facts that had been recorded in it, they could piece together a good estimate of where they were and where they needed to go. *Basically, a ship's log is to help you find your way if you got lost*, their father always said. Every seafaring vessel had one. He had taught both Maya and Simon how to use the information that was in it. Simon knew far more about the particulars of it than she did.

Usually their parents used the same pale blue canvas books that they bought each year in port, but a few months ago they had run out of pages in an old book while out at sea. Her father began to use the book that had been on the *Pamela Jane* since they had found her. Kept for sentimental reasons, for a long time it had sat forgotten on a top shelf among volumes about coral reefs and intertidal zone crustaceans and other similar titles in the cabin. It was impressive, large, and old-looking, its red leather cover decorated with a fine gold pattern, parts of which had been rubbed away.

Simon had caught something in a net and was examining it in a bucket of seawater, which he now lugged over to them.

"Hey, look what I found," he said. Inside was a small creature with soft purple spines. When he reached his hand into the bucket it shrank away from him. "What is it?" he asked their father.

"It's a purple maginot," said their father, closing the logbook. "And you should probably leave it be. They don't like company much."

"Ouch!" Simon cried, snatching his hand out of the water. "It stung me. It has prickles."

"Told you," said their father. "They're quite antisocial."

"It reminds me of Maya," said Simon. "They should call it a Maya maginot."

Maya saw her father look away so that she wouldn't see him smile.

"Why don't we give your sister a break, and why don't you set that thing free back in the ocean?" he said to Simon, squeezing Maya's shoulder. "St. Alban's is right up ahead, anyway—see?"

"I see it!" Simon shouted, pointing to a green speck in the distance. "We're there!"

As they watched, the green speck grew palm trees and sandy beaches and houses. The warm air rushed over the *Pamela Jane*, filling her sails, and the water broke icy-white around her bow.

"This is a short visit, right?" Maya grumbled.

"Yes," her father said. "We'll be in and out within a few hours. We just need to drop off the samples."

Usually Maya loved stopping at St. Alban's. The head marine biologist, Dr. Fitzsimmons, was an old friend of her parents, from the days when they had all been students together at the Oceanic Institute. He had a tufty red beard and weak blue eyes and freckles that blended together across his cheeks. Whenever they had a few days in St. Alban's, the Nelsons would go to dinner at the home he shared with his wife, who made an excellent mussel pie and always made sure there was plenty of hot water so that the Nelsons could take proper showers. Maya loved to sit at a real table in a real house that didn't rock and sway. On the bookshelves were rows of marine science journals that her parents and Dr. Fitzsimmons had published articles in. And the St. Alban's laboratory was superb, with state-of-the-art equipment and friendly junior marine biologists who worked for Dr. Fitzsimmons. Recently Dr. Fitzsimmons had been hired by the Red Coral Project, which was studying the effects of pollution on certain types of coral. He had brought the Nelsons on board and they had been collecting samples for the project for nearly a year now. In the beginning everything had seemed like business as usual, but in the past months they had been discovering unusual, glowing sea creatures like the octopus.

Dr. Fitzsimmons was waiting for them on the dock when they arrived. He waved to them and offered them all a hand onto the dock. As usual, Maya was the first one off the boat, and she realized instantly that Dr. Fitzsimmons didn't seem like himself. Usually a friendly, furry man, he seemed strangely nervous, and when he pulled her up he grasped her arm roughly and barely seemed to see her.

A man who Maya had never seen before was standing behind him, off to the side. He didn't seem to notice her either, so she was able to take a long, curious look at him. He wore an eggplant-colored wool hat, even though the sun was out, and it was pulled down over his craggy brow, which jutted out over a pair of very deep-set amber eyes. Wiry white hair sprouted from his chin and his ears. His nose was purplish and it had bulbous growths all over it that reminded her of the eyes on a potato. He was not looking at her, but was staring so intensely at the boat behind her that Maya felt as if she was in a cold shadow. Then

14

Simon scrambled up behind her and then her whole family was there and the dock was suddenly noisy and full of people.

Her father handed up the tanks with the marine samples. In one of them the moon octopus was in his small dark cage, sloshing gently from side to side. Her father hoisted himself onto the dock after them.

"Wait until you see these," he said to Dr. Fitzsimmons. Then he caught sight of the stranger.

"Let me introduce you to Dr. Izquierdo," said Dr. Fitzsimmons. "Dr. Hábil Izquierdo. He's working on the Red Coral Project, too. Dr. Izquierdo, these are the Nelsons, Dr. Nelson and Dr. Nelson and Maya and Simon and Penelope."

But the stranger barely seemed to notice them. Instead he was staring at the *Pamela Jane*, rocking gently on her moorings behind them. His eyes traveled over her sunny yellow hull, crisply furled white sails, freshly scrubbed deck, and neatly coiled lines.

"She has good speed for a boat her size," he said. "How many feet is she?"

"Fifty-two," said Maya's father.

"And a half," added the stranger, almost to himself.

"Yes," said Maya's father, surprised. "You have a good eye. She's actually fifty-two and a half feet from bow to stern."

"Still a beauty," said the stranger, again almost to himself.

Then abruptly he turned and began walking past all of the moored boats toward the end of the dock. Maya noticed that one of his shoes made a peculiar clicking sound on the dock.

"All right," said Dr. Fitzsimmons quickly. "Why don't we get these samples up to the lab?" He helped Maya's father carry the tanks of samples and they started up the hill to the Marine Station.

"Strange old guy," said Maya's father.

"He was a weirdo," said Simon.

"Simon," said their mother warningly.

"He *is* different," said Dr. Fitzsimmons. "I'll grant you that. The Red Coral people sent him over for a few days. But now tell me . . ." And he changed the subject.

Maya glanced back over her shoulder but the man was gone and the dock was empty.

By the time they reached the Marine Station she had forgotten about the odd visitor. Her parents left her to watch Penny outside in the garden while they went into the lab with Dr. Fitzsimmons. A lazy breeze rustled through the big poinciana tree and red petals fluttered loose. Simon wandered off to talk to a student biologist who was feeding the turtles in the outdoor aquarium. Maya sat there with Penny in her lap, her thoughts drifting off to Bermuda and the friends she would make at her new school, if only she was allowed to go. What Maya really wanted, though, was just one friend, better than all the others. A best friend. Maya had imagined this friend for so long now that she felt she knew her very well. She imagined them eating lunch together at school every day and taking the bus home together (because, of course, her best friend would live on the same road as Granny Pearl), and having long conversations about everything under the sun while they sat on Granny Pearl's porch in the evenings. It was going to be wonderful, Maya had no doubt.

Through the open window of the laboratory she could see her parents and Dr. Fitzsimmons talking. Their conversation drifted out to her.

"Because of the presence of the cobaltmoravia, we believe

that it's coming from deep in an equatorial jungle," her father was saying. "It's most likely that the mineral is being carried downriver and that's how it's entering the sea. . . ."

"Peter," said Dr. Fitzsimmons. "The Project wants this to stop here. You've already gone far, far beyond what you were hired to do. You aren't authorized to undertake independent research in this area. I've been instructed to warn you that . . ."

At this point Dr. Fitzsimmons walked across the room and closed the window and the rest of the conversation was lost to Maya. She felt a brief moment of alarm—what on earth were they talking about? But then Penny pulled a daisy out of the ground and began chewing it and Maya had to take it away from her, and by the time she had taken all the bits out of Penny's clenched fists, her parents were walking out of the laboratory with Dr. Fitzsimmons.

The adults made idle conversation as Dr. Fitzsimmons walked with them back down to the *Pamela Jane*, but Maya thought it seemed strained. Simon ran ahead of everyone. He reached the boat first and leaped on board and ran down into the cabin. His bloodcurdling shout a few moments later made Maya's heart leap into her throat.

In a few strides Maya's father was down on the dock, just as Simon emerged in a hurry back onto the deck. Dr. Izquierdo appeared quickly behind him.

"What's going on?" asked Maya's father angrily.

"I was just taking a look," growled Dr. Izquierdo.

"You could have asked to come aboard," said Maya's father, an edge to his voice. "I'd have been happy to show you around."

"He was trying to take the logbook," said Simon.

"I was only looking at it," said Dr. Izquierdo, glowering.

Simon was holding tightly on to the logbook, its strong red cover shining.

Dr. Izquierdo looked shiftily down the length of the dock. His hooded eyes were barely visible. *He's not a marine biologist at all*, Maya thought suddenly. He did not apologize, but instead his face grew stormy. He looked sullenly at Dr. Fitzsimmons before turning and walking briskly toward the steps leading up the hill to the Marine Station. A hollow echo bounced off the stone dock with every other step he took.

"I'm sorry about that," said Dr. Fitzsimmons as they watched Dr. Izquierdo, his figure receding as he went up the stairs on the hillside.

"Well . . . no harm done," said Maya's father. Maya could tell he was still annoyed but was trying to be polite.

As they stood there, a breeze came off the sea and at once the day turned cool. Maya glanced out over the water. The wind had stirred up white horses at the mouth of the harbor, and the water had become a chalky turquoise color. The *Pamela Jane* shifted on her moorings and her timbers creaked.

"Please, don't worry about it," said Maya's mother to Dr. Fitzsimmons. "It's not your fault he went onto the boat. No harm done, like Peter said. We should get going now, but next time we'll be able to stay longer and see you and Emily properly. And maybe we can talk more about the project then."

The Nelsons climbed aboard the *Pamela Jane* then and a few minutes later they were motoring away through the harbor, out toward the open sea. Maya and Simon stood at the stern to wave to Dr. Fitzsimmons. He was still standing on the dock, growing smaller as they drew farther away. Maya scanned the hillside above the harbor and caught sight of the figure in the eggplant-colored hat. He had paused on the road to the Marine Station and he, too, was watching them as they sailed away. Suddenly a shiver ran through her and she felt afraid. Dr. Fitzsimmons seemed forlorn and vulnerable there on the dock. Then both figures shrank and were lost to sight as the *Pamela Jane* reached open water.

❖ Chapter Two ❖

More of the Story ❖ *The Blue Line* ❖
Footsteps in a Storm

Once they were sailing again, Maya's parents were too busy to talk about Dr. Izquierdo or Dr. Fitzsimmons. Her father had checked the cabin quickly but everything seemed to be fine. He flipped through the pages of the logbook and glanced at the children's mother. The kind of glance that was supposed to go over the children's heads, but didn't.

"He was just a strange old guy," he said to Maya. "No need to have another thought about him, sweetie."

But Maya still had a bad feeling, and so did Simon. They leaned over the railing and watched as St. Alban's receded into a green spot on the horizon.

"He wasn't a marine biologist at all," Maya said. "I wonder what he was doing in St. Alban's. And why did he want the logbook?"

"I don't know," said Simon. "But do you think Dr. Fitzsimmons will be okay?"

"Who knows?" said Maya darkly. Something strange was going on—the scrap of the conversation she had heard between her father and Dr. Fitzsimmons ran through her mind again. What had it been about?

"Earth to Maya," said Simon.

Maya blinked. St. Alban's was no longer visible on the horizon. They were alone at sea again. She sighed.

"I'm sure he'll be fine," she said. When Simon looked reassured she added, "Maybe."

She turned around and leaned with her back to the railing. Her father was standing by the wheel, making notes in the logbook. The wind ruffled the pages, turning them quickly, and her father finished what he was writing and closed it. The evening sun glowed on the gold patterned cover. Maya heard her mother calling her then, and she went to the galley to help bring dinner onto the deck. The family sat down to eat outside as the clouds turned pink and orange and the water reflected the ruddy glow of the sky. Maya felt a slight pang when she thought that if everything worked out how she hoped it would, this might be one of the last dinners she'd have on the deck of the *Pamela Jane* for a while. Soon she might be sitting down to dinner at a real table at Granny Pearl's each night.

Later, Maya left her family still sitting on the deck and went down into the cabin. The sooner she went to bed, the sooner it would be morning and the sooner they would be in Bermuda. She put on her pajamas and climbed up to her top bunk and opened her history textbook. She read studiously because if she went to school she didn't want to be behind her classmates. She was still reading when her family came down off the deck for the night. Simon came barreling ahead of the rest of them and burst into the cabin.

"Guess what!" he shouted. "We just saw a spotted whale shark calf!"

"Can you imagine?" asked Maya's mother, coming into the cabin. "A spotted whale shark calf this far south? Isn't it the strangest thing? At this time of year?"

"Hmm," Maya said, turning back to her book. If she never saw another spotted whale shark calf in her life it would be fine with her.

Simon got ready for bed and settled noisily into the lower bunk to wait for their father, who always read to him at night. It had gotten dark since Maya had first come down below and only a faint bluish light came in through the portholes, so she switched on the lightbulb over her bunk and picked up her textbook again. Instead of being read to, Simon asked to hear more of the story that their father had been telling him that afternoon. Maya concentrated on her book and tried to ignore them, but it was hard not to listen in.

"*And what about when you sail into the sea?*" Simon asked. "*What happens then?*"

"*Well,*" said their father. "*They say that first you see a dark line in the water, a straight line, dark blue, going from east to west. The Blue Line. It's almost exactly on the equator. And when you cross it your boat rocks a bit, as if you'd sailed into something solid.*"

"*But we've sailed over the equator,*" said Simon. "*Lots of times. You know it doesn't do that. And you don't see a line either.*"

"*Well,*" said their father. "*Maybe in some places you do. Maybe just in the place where the magical sea is. It's like the gateway. And once you sail through the gateway you're in the sea.*"

"*And then what happens?*" Simon asked.

"*And then you see bubbles here and there on the surface of the water.*"

"*Why?*"

"*Because there are deep trenches in the earth beneath the sea, the deepest anywhere in the world, and they release steam that bubbles up, so the sea looks like a cauldron just starting to boil."*

"That's cool," said Simon.

"Very," said their father. *"And in the middle of the sea is the island, of course. But hardly anyone from the Outside knows that the island even exists. The few who know about it don't know how to reach it. When they try, storms throw their ships and planes off course and when the storms are over, the people find that all their navigation equipment—anything magnetic or mechanical—has been ruined. The only people who have ever found the island are those who stumble upon it by accident."*

"What about the people who live there?" Simon asked. "Do they ever leave it?"

"Oh," said their father. *"Perhaps a few. Just a very few ever have. And only a few ever got in from the Outside. And once you cross over, in either direction, you can never go back."*

"Never?"

"Well, almost never," said their father. *"It would be very difficult. Very difficult. You would have quite a story to tell if you managed it, let's put it that way."*

$\backsim$ $\backsim$ $\backsim$

Maya must have fallen asleep listening to Simon and her father, because she woke up to find that someone had turned off the light over her bunk and folded the page in her book and tucked it under the edge of her pillow. She sat up, rubbing her eyes. She hadn't even felt herself drifting off to sleep. And now it was too early to be waking up. Something was wrong. Then she realized that the *Pamela Jane* was heaving from side to side in the waves, and rain was hammering on the deck above.

Her father came into the children's cabin and waited by the

ladder up to the deck. He had on one of the safety harnesses that had to be worn when going up onto the deck during a storm. Maya's mother appeared a moment later.

"We've sailed into some weather," Maya's father said to her when he saw that she was awake.

The *Pamela Jane* rolled uneasily on another wave, and her father put his hand on the wall to steady himself and waited for Maya's mother to finish fastening the clasp of her harness. Maya was still half asleep and disoriented as she watched her mother reaching forward to tighten the strap on Maya's father's harness.

"Where are you going?" she asked, getting her voice back and feeling more awake now.

"The forestay is loose," her mother said. "We're going to secure it. We'll be right back, seashell. Try to fall back asleep."

As she went past Maya's bunk she paused for a moment and reached up and squeezed Maya's ankle. Then she followed Maya's father to the companionway. The boat nearly broached in the next wave, but when she righted, Maya's father cracked the hatch and he and Maya's mother disappeared on deck. The hatch slammed shut behind them.

Maya was wide awake now. She lay in her bunk, alert and tense, and listened to the sound of their footsteps on the deck through the whistling wind and rain. Maya called Simon's name but as usual he was sleeping like a log. Maya told herself not to be worried. Squalls at sea often came out of nowhere. They had been in hundreds of them before and there would usually be something on deck that needed to be retied or battened down and her parents would have to go up onto the deck. There was a game that Maya played when this happened. As she lay huddled on her bunk she would count their footsteps on the deck. She told herself that as long as she could keep counting, everything would be okay. She had done this for as long as she could remember. *One, two, three, four, five* . . . Usually by the time Maya got to about sixty-three they would be back in the cabin, water streaming from their foul weather gear, their hair wild and stiff with salt, their cheeks bright from the wind. The highest she had ever had to go was eighty-four.

Maya propped herself up on her elbow to check on Penny. She was still asleep, swaddled snugly in the hanging cot that, though it was cross-tied, swung back and forth slightly with each wave. Maya lay back down again and concentrated on hearing the muffled sounds of the footsteps on the deck. *Thirty-two, thirty-three, thirty-four* . . . The torrential rain and the roar of the waves made it almost impossible to hear anything else. She counted any thump or thud as a step. Below her in the next bunk she heard Simon stirring.

"Maya?"

"It's all right," she said. "It's a storm. Mami and Papi went onto the deck to fix the forestay."

"There weren't any storms on the radar when we went to bed," said Simon.

"Well, there's one now," said Maya. "Do you want me to come and sit in your bunk with you?"

"Okay," said Simon.

Maya climbed quickly into Simon's bunk. They sat at either end, bracing themselves against the bars so that when the boat heaved they wouldn't fall out. Penny woke up and started to cry, but Maya thought she'd be safer in the hanging cot than if she tried to hold her, so she left her there.

"It's all right, Penny," she called as soothingly as she could. The storm was scaring Maya, too, but she tried not to let her voice quaver.

"What number are you on?" Simon asked. Maya couldn't see him in the dark.

"Thirty-five," she said. "But it's so loud out there I think I missed some."

"I think I heard a step," he said. "Thirty-six."

Thirty-seven, thirty-eight, thirty-nine . . . They went all the way up to sixty-four before they lost the sound of the steps again.

Outside the cabin the wind howled through the black void and fierce waves pummeled the sides of the *Pamela Jane*, whose beams creaked and moaned and sounded as if they would snap. It was all Maya and Simon could do to hang on and not be flung from the bunk when the boat pitched in the waves. Maya was relieved that she hadn't taken Penny out of her cot. Waves crashed over the deck, and the children watched as water seeped in through the hatch and rolled across the floor whenever the boat listed.

When the thunder and rain eased a little, Maya strained her ears to hear her parents. But the footsteps had vanished. All that was left was the wail of the wind and the drumming of rain, steady now, and an odd wave that washed over the deck.

"Simon," she said in the darkness, "I'm going to see if they need the hatch opened—it may be stuck or something. Stay here."

Holding tight to the railing of the bunk, Maya stood up to go to the companionway but when the boat lurched again she fell forward onto her knees. She had to crawl through the water on the floor the rest of the way. When she reached the steps she clung to them for a minute to get her balance before she climbed to the top. She forced the hatch open and salt water dumped down her neck. She stuck her head out and in a flash of lightning she looked both ways up and down the deck but it was empty.

Their parents were nowhere to be seen.

Great black walls of water stood over the boat, and the sea was still surging over the railing. Frantically Maya looked up and down the deck again but there was nothing but giant, inky mountains and valleys of ocean all around them. A monstrous swell was lifting the schooner to its crest as if they were nothing but a bit of foam. The icy rain lashed her furiously and she began to shiver. She heard Simon calling her, then another wave struck the *Pamela Jane,* and the boat pitched suddenly, throwing her off the steps and back into the cabin. The hatch slammed shut with a bang and they were in darkness again.

Shaking uncontrollably, Maya was fumbling her way back to the bunk when a wave struck, sending her flying across the cabin. She screamed and closed her eyes. The wave had thrown Simon out of his bunk, too, and they collided on the floor in a jumble of limbs. A deafening boom of thunder filled the cabin and it seemed that it would split the *Pamela Jane* into pieces of driftwood. Pain shot through Maya's head and limbs and she no longer knew which way was up. As Maya and Simon struggled to untangle themselves, the boat pitched to starboard, and the deck tilted at such a steep slant that they began rolling across it. Maya felt sure the *Pamela Jane* was capsizing. But almost immediately, another wave sent the boat rolling in the opposite direction. Maya and Simon tumbled across the deck, and Maya felt her head strike something hard. Numbness spread through her body and the world was snuffed out.

❧ Chapter Three ❧

The Day After

When Maya awoke, her head was throbbing and Penny was crying. Sunlight streamed in the hatch, which was knocking brokenly against the deck, one of its hinges missing. Maya wriggled her fingers and toes. Everything was stiff and sore, but it worked. From on deck, she could hear the sound of the breeze through tattered sails. Simon was lying on the floor near her.

"Simon," she whispered, shaking his shoulder until his eyes opened.

He sat up and looked groggily around him as the events of the previous night flooded back to him. Maya picked Penny up from the hanging crib and went down the hall to her parents' cabin. Simon followed her. They looked in the doorway but no one was there. Objects had been tossed around during the storm and the floor was strewn with paper and clothes. They looked into each cabin but they were all empty. Her step quickening, Maya went back through the cabin and up the companionway to the deck. The sun was bright and she had to hold her hand over her eyes to protect them from the glare off the wet boards. The sea was calm and flat. Their parents were nowhere in sight.

Simon ran back down to check the cabin again but came right back up, an astonished look on his face. "They're gone," he said.

He walked to the railing and gazed out over the water in disbelief.

Maya walked forward a few steps, up to the closed chock where the line from the safety harnesses would have been fastened. There was only a stump of the line left—after that the fibers were shredded. The rope holding their parents to the deck had snapped. A sharp cold feeling came over her.

The sea looked sweet, docile, the light dazzling off points of tiny waves. Maya's eyes hurt from searching it. The boat rocked slowly and a metal clip on one of the halyards clacked forlornly against the mast. The ocean had never looked so vast and empty. Her throat and chest began to tighten and she felt her limbs going numb and the world blackening around her. Her head still hurt from where she had struck it the night before. She had not been sick during the storm but now she felt dizzy and ill. Afraid she would fall with Penny in her arms, she sat down for a moment.

"We have to radio for help," she said to Simon when the blackness receded. Her voice felt like it was coming from very far away.

They went back down into the main cabin, and Maya put Penny back in the hanging crib. Maya followed Simon into the captain's quarters. The first thing that she noticed was that the GPS screen was black and lifeless. She pressed the reset button but nothing happened. And nothing happened when she pressed other buttons on it either. From the corner of her eye she caught sight of the old compass. A thousand spidery cracks blurred its glass face. Beneath the glass the needle had snapped in half. Maya looked over at Simon. He had his ear to the radio and was turning its knob. But there was no familiar crackle of static. It was silent.

"It's dead," he said. "Everything here is broken."

In a daze they went back on deck. Maya felt the blackness seeping in around the corners of her vision again, but just then she noticed that the rowboat was missing. She turned to her brother.

"They've got the rowboat," she said. "They're okay."

Her words were swallowed into the blue void of sky and sea.

"They've got the rowboat, they're okay," she repeated loudly as if to ward off any creeping thought that they were not. "They're probably not even that far away from us."

The two children could not have said how long they stood there. The sun reflecting off the sea scalded Maya's eyes. There was only a faint touch of a breeze now and then. The ocean was deserted. For miles around them there was nothing, not the smudge of another boat on the horizon, not a school of flying fish being chased by a bigger fish, not the friendly squeak of a dolphin.

They were completely alone.

Simon sat down cross-legged and stared out bleakly.

Maya wanted to sit down, too, to sit down and not move and pretend that what was happening wasn't happening, that there had never been a storm, that there were still five people instead of only three on the *Pamela Jane*.

Simon had begun to cry very softly.

"Wait," Maya said finally. Her throat was dry and her voice felt rusty, almost as if it were someone else's voice and not her own. She paused, sorting out her thoughts. Her brain seemed to be working more slowly than usual. "They were wearing life jackets—I saw them putting them on before they went on deck. And they have the rowboat. And we know they're both strong swimmers. They're probably in the rowboat right now, waiting for help."

As she spoke, Maya began to feel more convinced that everything really might still be alright.

"Right?" she said. "We have every reason to think they're okay. We just have to figure out what to do now."

Simon sniffled and wiped his eyes with the back of his hand.

"Since the radio is broken and we can't call for help, we're going to have to sail to land ourselves so that we can have rescue boats sent out for them," Maya said. "Okay?"

But neither of them wanted to move. Maya's head ached. From the cabin they heard Penny begin to cry. The sound of her baby sister brought Maya out of her fog.

"Simon," she said firmly. "You start rigging the sails. I'm going to feed Penny and then I'll be out to help you." She stood up. Simon slowly began to get to his feet. Maya stopped before she went down the ladder into the cabin and looked back at him. "If it were us who'd gotten swept overboard, would they just sit here?" she asked. "No—they'd do something to find us!" she answered triumphantly. "So get going."

Maya heated a bottle of formula on the stove and fed Penny. When she came back out, Simon was finishing rigging the mainsail. Even though their parents had fitted the *Pamela Jane* with winches and levers so that the children could do everything on it themselves, the sail was still heavy enough that it took both of them to hoist it. They each grabbed the main halyard and began to pull, sinking all their weight into it. The runner whined as it slid up the mast and slowly the sail began to lift. They didn't think about anything else for the next few minutes as they worked. The sail sounded like thunder as it rose and then with one last haul it was up, brilliant white and standing seventy feet above them.

Beads of sweat had sprung up on Maya's brow. She stood

back, heart pounding, and wiped the sweat off with her shirt. The physical exertion had given her new energy.

"Maybe we won't even make it to land before we find them," she said. "We'll be sailing and we'll see them in the water. The storm couldn't have blown us that far away from one another. And even if we don't find them ourselves, it's just a matter of getting to land so that search boats can go out to pick them up."

Looking out at the endless fathoms of blue encircling them, Simon could have said that Maya was crazy. But instead he nodded.

"I'll get the logbook," said Simon. "So we can figure out where we are."

They had been drifting, hardly moving at all, when out of the blue the wind shifted and a shiver passed over the water. Maya felt a surge of adrenaline—or perhaps it was hope—course through her arms and legs. She looked at Simon and she saw that he had felt it, too. For a moment in the distance they both thought they saw a dark blue line in the ocean, stretching from one horizon to another. They thought of the Blue Line in the story that their father had been telling them just a few short hours ago, and they felt their hearts squeeze for a moment. When they blinked the line was gone.

Back on the deck, Simon sat down and rested the logbook in front of him. He looked at it for a moment before he opened it. The pages inside were creamy white and their edges were gilt. The log entries began several months ago, and his father's handwriting filled the book with notes about the weather and their position at sea. Simon turned the pages and then he stopped, frowning.

"Maya," he said. "Take a look at this."

"What?" asked Maya. She was at the bow, rigging the jib and keeping an eye on the horizon, but she left what she was doing and came and looked over Simon's shoulder.

"It's weird," he said. "It isn't an ordinary ship's log. Papi's written all kinds of things in here. And drawn pictures."

Simon turned the pages slowly and slowly the starched, neatly recorded logbook entries gave way to a surreal catalog of sea creatures. Sketches of sea life had been drawn in colored pencils: pale lavender jellyfish with dark purple eggs sat on the tops of the pages, their tentacles flowing down and getting entangled in the writing. One-eyed fish with subtly shining scales peered out at Maya and Simon. Ornate sea fans and rubbery anemones hugged the seafloor at the bottoms of the pages. Sea horses drifted through records of weather conditions and sightings of other ships. Beside each creature were long lists of cryptic numbers and notes and equations and records of the coordinates at which each animal had been found. On one page the depths of the sea itself had been drawn, shading from a sunny turquoise surface into emerald and then through grades of blue, from sapphire to a deep midnight black above the ocean floor. There was a chart for recording luminescence. Names of elements and chemical compounds and mysterious, evocative words floated like bubbles through the pages.

Simon began to turn the pages quicker. Schools of sinewy question marks, seductive, perplexing, moved silently through the margins in search of something. Their parents seemed to be working on some type of problem. Their mother had left notes beside their father's, answering his questions, posing new ones. Some things were crossed out. Some phrases appeared again

33

and again, as if their parents were musing through a puzzle that they had yet to solve: *Origin of substance? Location of epicenter? Probable source?* The children could make no sense of it. And then the entries came to an abrupt end. The last record was made right before their parents had gone onto the deck in the storm: a simple note about the storm, and that they were going on deck to fix the forestay. After that the pages were blank, as seemingly lifeless as the bottom of the ocean. Simon turned quickly back to a page where they could see their parents' handwriting. It made both of the children feel better to see it there. Simon reached out and touched one of the pages.

"It doesn't make sense," said Simon. "Why would they have drawn all of this? You're only supposed to record coordinates and what the weather is and what other boats you see."

"Can it still help us?" asked Maya.

Simon nodded. "I think so," he said. "All the coordinates are still here. But I wonder what all the rest of this stuff is about."

Simon pored over the logbook and began reconstructing the path the *Pamela Jane* had been on before the storm. Later he could wonder about the purpose of the mysterious drawings. Right now they had to focus all their attention on getting to land.

"We've been sailing northwest since we left St. Alban's," he said. "According to this, we were sailing northwest at 6 knots at 11 degrees north latitude, 52 degrees west longitude when the storm struck," he said. "The storm was blowing from the north and we were caught in it for about six hours, would you say?"

"I don't know," Maya said. "At least."

"Well, let's see," said Simon. "Papi notes that there were

34

signs the storm was approaching at twenty-four hundred hours last night. He made a note here that he and Mami were going onto the deck at oh one hundred hours. You were awake then and I woke up right after—we know the storm was pretty bad by then. By the time we woke up this morning, at seven hundred hours, the storm had probably passed about two hours earlier, which would mean the storm winds were blowing us south for six hours, which, I think, would probably put us somewhere near here. . . . Now if the sun is here . . ."

Maya found it hard to pay attention. The whole thing was too much like a math problem for her. Maya didn't like charts and numbers and calculations so she just watched as Simon worked.

"If my calculations are correct," he said finally. "We should sail due west. That's our closest point to land." He smiled triumphantly at Maya.

"Great," she said. "Thank you. Now, I'm going to start cleaning up the cabin. Can you get us on course?"

"Aye, aye," said Simon.

After Maya had gone below deck, the *Pamela Jane* rolled suddenly from starboard to port, and the pencil Simon had been using flew out of his hand and rolled across the deck. When he went to get it, for a moment he thought he saw the strange blue line again, this time on the other side of them, receding swiftly into the distance.

🐬 🐬 🐬

The jib mast had been damaged in the storm and some sheets needed to be replaced so for the next hours Maya and Simon worked to repair everything and keep the *Pamela Jane* on course. They took turns on watch. The one off watch sat with Penny and mended torn sails. Penny seemed puzzled that their parents weren't there and she kept looking around the deck for them. Every time she did, Maya felt a lump rise in her throat.

Simon caught a red snapper and cooked it for their lunch. When Penny was hungry, they fed her tinned milk and brought her out to sit in the shade. Simon complained, but Maya wouldn't let him have any of the milk so that she could save it for the baby. When a swell caught her off balance and she spilled half of it on the deck he sighed and made a big production of the whole thing. Maya had to grit her teeth to stop herself from getting into an argument.

In the evening, Maya tucked Penny into her little hanging cot in the cabin and sang to her until she fell asleep. On her way back to the deck, she stopped in the doorway to her parents' quarters. She could only bear to look in their room for a moment, but she took one of her mother's sweaters and put it on, less because she was cold than she thought it would be comforting. Outside, an orange glow was seeping through the water, sinking into the ocean depths. Darkness came suddenly and then they were moving along beneath a tapestry of stars, new ones popping out every minute. She pulled the sweater more tightly around her.

"We'll have to take turns on watch tonight," she said.

Simon nodded and they sat there quietly, staring into the darkness.

"Wait," said Simon excitedly. Something had occurred to him that might be able to help. "We forgot about the flares!"

"Right!" said Maya. She felt excited, too. The flares could be seen for miles—maybe a nearby ship would see their distress signal and they would be rescued.

They had never shot distress flares before, but their parents had taught them how in case there was ever an emergency. Simon found the flares and brought them onto the deck. He lit the first one and stood back as it rocketed into the sky, leaving a train of sparks that were quickly snuffed out by the damp air. A couple of hundred feet up they exploded, illuminating the *Pamela Jane* and the sea around her. The sky and the water blazed orange for a moment, and the dark backs of fish were visible beneath the surface of the sea. Then the salty blackness swallowed the flare, and Maya and Simon stood there on the gently rolling deck, waiting for their eyes to adjust again after the brief, sudden brilliance.

They waited a while before they lit the second flare, turning and squinting at the horizon all around them in hopes of seeing a ship's light or an answering flare. But there was nothing, just the sound of a fish jumping out of the water. They fired the second flare, but still there was nothing. The smell of smoke lingered in the air, and Maya's disappointment as she scanned the darkness was bitter.

They sat in silence for a while.

"I could stay up with you," offered Simon.

Maya shook her head. "Get some sleep. We'll switch in a few hours. There's no point in both of us trying to stay awake at the same time and then falling asleep and missing seeing a ship. Or land."

Simon sat there for a few minutes before he went below deck. Without him, sitting in the darkness, a keen sense of aloneness overwhelmed Maya. She missed her parents sharply, as she had not when she had been busy all day. She felt the enormity of the sea around her. Her little brother and sister were in the cabin, young and in need of her protection. She was the eldest; she was in charge. She was responsible for them until they found their parents. Until they found their parents . . . Maya felt another stab of fear. She had no idea where they were or where they were sailing. If they didn't find land in a day or two they would be out of food for Penny. What were they going to do? The night was hot and humid but Maya shivered. She was so deep in her thoughts that she didn't see Simon until he was standing right in front of her, holding a blanket and pillow.

"I checked on Penny," he said. "She's still sleeping. I thought I would come and sleep out here with you. For the fresh air."

"Oh," said Maya. "All right." She was touched—she knew that Simon knew that she would be lonely and afraid out there by herself. Tears burned her eyes. She was happy that he couldn't see them in the dark. She wanted to say something, anything to him, about the day, about how frightened she had been and how glad she was that he had been there with her.

"I think we're making good time," she said instead.

"Yes," said Simon from beneath the blanket. "The wind has really picked up. We'll definitely reach land by tomorrow."

Maya murmured affirmatively, as if of course this was true.

"Maya?"

"Go to sleep."

Simon sighed.

"Good night, Maya."

"Good night."

Soon Simon was asleep. Maya sat awake on watch. She was an experienced sailor, and she kept her eye on the horizon for the lights of land or another ship, and she got up to adjust the sails every now and then. But as fine a sailor as she was, she was too preoccupied to notice that they were veering ever so slightly off course, just a few degrees with every mile of ocean they left behind. With her brother asleep beside her and her sister safely tucked in in the cabin below, Maya struggled to keep her eyes open as the *Pamela Jane*—her yellow hull and crisp white sails illuminated in the moonlight—plowed through the warm sea.

❦ Chapter Four ❦

A Peculiar Shell ❋ *A Visit from a Green Parrot* ❋ *Land Ho!* ❋
Ashore on an Unknown Island ❋ *The Disappearance*
of the PAMELA JANE ❋ *Into the Jungle*

It was late the next morning when the green parrot lighted on the bow, rising and falling with the waves, ruffling its green crest. A bird meant that land couldn't be far off! The children looked eagerly at the sea all around them, but there was no sign of shore. The parrot cracked a lustrous shell in its sharp beak, one half of it clattering onto the deck.

Simon bent down to pick it up. He held it up to the sky and ran his fingers over its nubby ridges. On first glance it was unremarkable. It was a yellowed ivory color with deep grooves whorled on its surface. Its inside was polished smooth as marble. In its center was an iridescent blotch typical of that seen on the inside of a common oyster, somewhere between deep cobalt blue and bottle green in color. It could have been any shell. Simon was about to toss it overboard when something caught his eye.

The blotch seemed to be glowing faintly. It was hard to tell, as it would be hard to see a lamp turned on in a room flooded with sunlight. Simon cupped his hands over it and peered into the darkness and then pulled his head back in surprise. It *was* glowing! Though there was no living creature left in it, somehow the shell itself seemed alive.

"Maya, look at this," he said, holding it out to her. "I've never seen a shell like this before. Have you?"

She glanced at it quickly. "I don't know," she said. "But right now you're only supposed to be on watch. We don't want to miss land."

Simon looked back down at the shell. As he watched, the light in it seemed to be fading and then it died completely. The shell lay extinguished in the palm of his hand. Frowning, Simon put it in his pocket. He looked back up at the parrot, sitting high in the rigging, and then he went to keep watch at the bow.

"We may be able to see land from here," said Maya. "I'm going to look out from the top. Watch Penny."

The bosun's chair was like a swing-set seat with a seat belt. It was connected to the mast with a pulley. The person sitting in it could hoist herself up the height of the mast, which Maya did, sweating by the time she reached the top. She felt dizzy when she looked straight down the mast to the deck, so she kept her gaze out to sea. The top of the mast added a few miles to her sight, but still the horizon was empty. Off to starboard a few miles out, a shaggy golden pasture of sargasso seaweed rose and fell on the swells, and off the stern Maya could see the dark backs of a school of bonitos racing through the cool water. She rested her cheek on the mast and felt the gentle sway of the waves and let her thoughts wander. Maybe if she stayed there for long enough, by the time she came back down her mother and father would be back, her mother down in the laboratory, her father making notes in the logbook as he kept watch.

She was startled by a shadow silhouetted on the other side of the topsail. The green parrot appeared above the sail, hovering in the wind for a moment and watching her, before dipping down and coasting through the rigging and perching atop the jib mast.

What are you up to? she thought as she watched it sway stiffly to keep its balance. There was something strange about the bird's interest in them.

"Well?" Simon called up to her.

"Nothing," she answered. "Not a thing in sight."

After one final look around, Maya loosened the line and began lowering the bosun's chair. On the deck, she tied it back in its place and went and sat beside Simon on the bow.

"I'm hungry," he said.

"We have to conserve food," she said. "And you ate an hour ago."

"But I'm growing. I need food."

"We'll eat as soon as we catch something."

"Well, if I can't eat, I might nap," said Simon.

"All right, you nap. I'll keep watch for a while."

🐬 🐬 🐬

The green parrot ticked back and forth on the jib mast as the morning wore on. Simon was napping in the cabin, and Penny was drowsing under her frilly white parasol so Maya was the first one to sight land—soft, boiling mists lifting over hills in the distance.

"Simon!" she shouted. "Come quick!"

Simon scrambled on deck and ran to the railing. They gazed at an island as it came into view. Green mountains loomed over pink sand beaches. Here and there the land fell away in sheer cliffs where flowers fluttered in cascading mats of vines. Green cushions of vegetation padded the hills. The smell of cinnamon, cloves, and other spices wafted over the water, and sugarcane fields lay flat and silver in the breeze. The sight held Maya and Simon transfixed and then they began to dance wildly around on the deck.

"Land ho!" shouted Simon, sprinting to the bow and back to the stern.

When she was younger, Maya had been able to turn fifteen cartwheels from the bow to the stern of the *Pamela Jane*. Forgetting that she was too old to cartwheel anymore, she turned eleven of them before she fell and sat there out of breath, grinning, watching the beautiful sweep of land coming closer. Then she got to her feet.

"We'll sail around the coast until we see a town," she said. "Come on!"

Maya and Simon wanted to get to the leeward side of the island, where bringing the *Pamela Jane* to shore would be safest. At first everything went smoothly. Simon stood at the bow and watched for reefs, and Maya stayed at the wheel and a mild wind drove them easily westward around the island. The parrot dropped from the top of the mast and squawked once and took flight toward land. But as it did, suddenly, out of nowhere, a brisk crosswind rose and the *Pamela Jane* began picking up speed—too much speed when they didn't know where they were going or what lay ahead in the water. They reefed the mainsail but the wind only seemed to grow more intense.

"Tack!" Maya cried, and the boom swung across the deck and the *Pamela Jane* veered from starboard to port. Still they were being pushed swiftly toward shore. Simon abandoned the bow and helped Maya to drop the sails, and for the next few minutes they yelled orders to each other, shouting to be heard over the wind, but despite their best efforts they were rapidly drawing close to shore. A tidy cove and lick of white beach came into view and they were heading straight for it.

"I can't do anything!" Maya shouted. "We'll just have to go in!"

The wind died once they were inside the sheltered arms of the cove. Maya and Simon began dropping the jib sail as the current gently drew in the *Pamela Jane*. The water was crystal clear down to a white sand seafloor. When it was shallow enough, Maya called for the anchor to be dropped. It took both of them to turn the winch before the heavy steel anchor splashed into the water and sank, dragging the chain with it as it went. After a moment it held fast.

"Well," Simon said. "What do we do now?"

It was a good question. Maya didn't have an answer. It had seemed like a triumph finding land—but now that they were there, what should they do? She was hoping that the wind would drop soon and they would be able to sail out of the cove and around the island until they saw a town. But the wind might not die down until the evening and the whole long afternoon sprawled in front of them. She couldn't bear the thought of sitting there doing nothing that whole time. She gazed up at the great green hills rising steeply above the beach.

"I think we should climb those hills and get a good view of the whole island," she said. "Maybe we'll be able to see a town from there."

"Hmm," said Simon, looking skeptically at the hills. "I was thinking we could build a signal fire on the beach."

"And just sit here and wait for some ship to *maybe* come by, *maybe* in a few weeks or months?" said Maya impatiently. "We have to go and find help for Mami and Papi. We can't just sit here."

"Do you see the size of those hills?" Simon asked.

"Fine," Maya said. "You stay here and build your signal fire, mullet head. You can keep Penny with you, too. Less for me to carry."

Simon considered. "Mami would probably say that splitting up wasn't wise."

"You're just scared to stay by yourself for an afternoon."

"I am not! You're just so slow that you could never make it to the top of a hill and back in an afternoon. I'd be an old man before you'd get back here. An old, old man." Simon stood and walked around in a circle slowly, his back stooped, his hand trembling on the knob of an imaginary cane.

Maya rolled her eyes.

"Well, I'm not waiting here and doing nothing. And it's even possible that the same winds and current that carried us here brought them here, too. Who knows—they could even be on the next beach over right now and if we sit here we'd never know it."

"And we could climb one of those hills and all we'd see is other hills, and a ship would come by and sail right past without us, and—" Simon said.

"And nothing. You stay here then, if that's what you want."

"I—"

But Simon stopped and began picking a splinter from one of the planks on the deck. A dark, brooding look descended over his face. Their parents called it his Maya face.

They sat there quietly for a while, the breeze rustling the green palms and the wavelets lapping the sand. The waves sounded like laughter. The jungle exhaled a loamy, vegetable smell. Maya wondered how big the island was and what she would see if she did climb to the top of one of the hills. She was afraid. What if there was nothing?

"Maya," Simon asked, staring through the mouth of the cove and out to sea. "Do you really think they're okay?"

Maya's shoulders stiffened. "They had the rowboat," she said. "They're fine."

"I guess," Simon said, squinting at the horizon. He was quiet. "But what if . . ."

A lump rose in Maya's throat. "Enough wasting time," she said. "We're going to climb a hill and find help and then you can stop bothering me with dumb questions."

She stood up and offered Simon her hand.

"It might take us a few hours," she said. "We should pack a few things that we might need."

"Good idea," agreed Simon.

Just then the parrot that had been on the boat reappeared and flew down low over them and then disappeared back into the jungle.

"That bird is weird," said Maya. "It's like it's watching us."

With a last look at the parrot, Maya went down to the cabin. She found her old backpack and took the remaining food in the kitchen, bottles of water, diapers for Penny. . . . What else would they need? It might take most of the afternoon to reach the top of the hills. Better to take too much than too little. She looked around the galley. Can opener, matches, lighter, pocketknife, canteens, a bottle, and tinned milk for Penny. A small pot in case they had to boil water before they drank it—it would probably come in handy. The first aid kit! Good thing she thought of that. What else? She caught sight of her mother's calendar tacked to the wall. It had been two days since they had seen their parents. They had been due in port in Bermuda tomorrow—her mother had circled the date on the calendar. Maya drew some comfort from the thought that very soon people would be wondering where they were.

She went to look for Simon and found him stuffing his backpack with books.

"Simon! You can't take those. We can't carry them."

"They're Papi's books," Simon said. "We have to take them. I'll carry them."

"You can't," said Maya. "I need you to help me carry the rest of the stuff—the stuff we DO need."

Simon's mouth tightened into a thin line. He kept squeezing books into the backpack.

"*Tropical Marine Ecosystems*?" Maya read on one of the covers. "How is that going to help us?"

"You never know," said Simon. "You never know what's going to be useful."

"Oh, jeez," Maya said. "Look, if you want to carry *Tropical Marine Ecosystems* to the top of a mountain, that's fine. But I'm going to split all the stuff that we do need to take between us. Whatever you can fit in your pack after that is your business. But remember, I'll have to carry Penny, too, so you have to take a lot of the heavy stuff."

She went back to the galley and divided the supplies, dumping Simon's half on his bunk.

"And hurry up," she said. "We want to try to get there and back before dark."

Maya finished packing her own backpack and then she found the baby sling her mother used to carry Penny in. She made her bed—if her mother found the *Pamela Jane* she'd want to see the beds made—and she tidied up the galley, and then she went on deck to wait for Simon. She waited for a while, listening to him pack and repack his bag.

"Hurry UP, Simon!" she called.

Finally he emerged. It was clear that he had decided not to take the books, but Maya prudently decided not to say she'd told him so. They decided to inflate the spare rubber dinghy and paddle to shore in it so that the packs wouldn't get wet, and then Simon would paddle back and leave the dinghy on the *Pamela Jane* and swim back to shore.

Before they got into the dinghy they paused to look over the boat.

"Good-bye for now, *Pamela Jane*," said Simon. "We'll see you soon."

Yes, good-bye for just a little while, thought Maya, feeling surprisingly sad. Even though they would be gone for only a few hours, it was hard to leave the boat. She turned to climb carefully down the ladder, Penny in one arm.

Before he climbed down the ladder after Maya, Simon suddenly clipped his heels together and saluted the *Pamela Jane*, her furled white sails and sunny yellow hull and freshly scrubbed deck, and then he clambered into the dinghy and they began to paddle to shore.

Once there, Maya scrambled happily onto the beach. It felt good to be on solid land! While she waited for Simon to take the dinghy back and return, Maya adjusted the straps of the sling so that it fit her, and she lifted Penny into it. Now that she was on the shore looking up at them, she wasn't sure that they would be able to reach the top of one of the hills—they looked steep and treacherous. But what was the point in waiting on the beach? None, as far as Maya could see. Maya was not someone who could sit and wait patiently, anyway.

Simon splashed to shore and joined Maya. Maya turned around for one last look at the boat before their hike and that's when her eye caught motion on the opposite shore of the cove. She didn't believe her eyes at first, so she squinted and took a few steps closer to the water. Simon had seen it now, too: a single green vine that was coming out of the jungle and moving, arched and waving through the air over the water toward the *Pamela Jane*.

As the children watched, mouths hanging open, the vine reached the boat and began to coil itself around the mast as if it were the trunk of a tree. Other vines, seeming to move of their own volition, were coming down out of the jungle, and the air began to thicken with green cords. Still others rustled out of the undergrowth and slithered across the surface of the cove. Soon the deck was carpeted in a green, cushiony mat, and vines hugged the hull like creeping ivy. For a moment Maya feared that the vines would snap the mast in two or cause the whole boat to capsize. The children gazed in stunned silence as the vines drew the *Pamela Jane* slowly through the water toward the shore, where she came to rest. Then, wrapped snugly around the vessel, they stopped moving.

"Maya . . ." said Simon, a slight quaver in his voice.

But Maya was speechless. She strained her eyes to see the contours of the *Pamela Jane* beneath the glossy green leaves. A chill spread through her. She felt truly afraid now. They were lost and alone, and instead of finding help, they had arrived on a strange and dangerous island. She tried to think. As much as she hated to see the *Pamela Jane* that way, even if they could cut all the vines free—and she wasn't sure if they could, with just the pocketknife they had—the wind didn't favor leaving the cove. It could stay like this overnight, or even for a few days. And, if she was honest with herself, she was worried about taking the boat back into open waters. She and Simon were experienced sailors, but they were still just kids. With a small baby to take care of, no less.

"I think," she said, still looking at the place where she knew the *Pamela Jane* was. "We should stick to our plan. We can come back later with help."

Simon lingered for a moment, but Maya turned and began walking down the beach, heading toward the jungle. It looked like an impenetrable green wall. Simon, lagging behind and less than eager to go on a long hike, was surprised when Maya turned her shoulders and slipped in between the leaves and disappeared. For a moment he was alone on the beach, then he hurried to follow his sister. In a moment the white beach was empty and still again, a little frill of turquoise water nuzzling it, the white sand blinding in the sun. Anyone arriving in the cove would never have even known a boat was there.

⚜ CHAPTER FIVE ⚜

Flying Fish ✳ *The Green Parrot Returns* ✳
The Logbook ✳ *A Face* ✳ *Penny Vanishes* ✳ *Carnivore Vines* ✳
Enter Helix ✳ *"People blowing in from the outside"*

Inside the jungle the air had a gloomy green glow and smelled like rotting vegetables. Penny, wide awake now, gnashed her bald gums into Maya's shoulder and hummed monotonously. Maya tried to convince herself that the vines that had taken the *Pamela Jane* were just some bizarre tropical species she had never heard of before—it seemed more and more possible the farther they got from the boat. Before long Maya's legs were scratched and thick brown goop glopped up to her ankles. She had to watch each step, parting branches and vines with her hands and making sure she didn't step right into the deepest of the murky puddles. Behind her, Simon was deliberately making his shoes squelch and splatter the mud.

"Don't get your clothes dirty," Maya said without turning around.

"You're worried about me getting my clothes dirty *now*?" Simon asked incredulously.

In another hour, Maya's shoulders were aching from Penny's weight and they seemed to have made little progress. Though that was hard to judge, because everywhere she turned everything looked the same. She even saw green when she closed her eyes. The trees formed a thick canopy overhead and she had no idea where the hills were that had seemed so towering just a little while ago from the beach.

"My signal fire isn't seeming like such a bad idea anymore, is it?" Simon asked from the back. Maya ignored him and tramped on through the tangled undergrowth.

Maya thought the first of the silver darts that flashed past was just her eyes playing tricks on her. But then there was another, and another. A rumbling sound rolled toward them through the thick green air and they turned to look all around them but couldn't tell where the sound was coming from. Flashes of silver streaked past them on all sides. Maya had fainted once, and right before she had collapsed she had seen tiny sparks fly around the edges of her vision. It was like that now. *No, no, no*, she thought. *Please don't let me pass out*. But it was obvious that Simon and Penny could see the silver sparks, too. Maya's mouth dropped open when she saw the first fish dash past her, fins beating furiously, slices of gills opening and closing. And behind it came a whole school of silver flying fish, hurtling from out of nowhere. The children could not duck in time, and were caught in the middle of them and forced along the jungle floor.

"It tickles," Simon cried. The fish were nibbling his neck and one had gotten caught under his collar and now its tail slapped back and forth across his chin.

As quickly as they had appeared, the fish disappeared, swerving off the path and pattering into a long pond that ran alongside the path, so covered in spongy mosses and lilies that until then Maya and Simon hadn't noticed it. Its surface was broken for a moment and then the green sealed over again and was nearly still, the lilies turning slowly on a slack current.

"What the heck WAS that?" Simon breathed.

"Sometimes schools of fish fly like that," Maya said. "You've seen them, out at sea."

"That's out at sea," said Simon. "Not on land. And these were doing more than just jumping out of the water for a few seconds—they were bombing through here. They were out of the water for a while."

"Well, they weren't really on land," said Maya haltingly. "They came out of the pond, or whatever it is, there. And they were going so fast that they probably weren't even out of the water for that long."

"Whatever," said Simon. "It was weird."

Maya looked all around them and caught sight of a parrot, watching them from a branch a few yards away. It was the same parrot that had been on the boat, she was sure of it. It had a silver fish in its mouth and as Maya watched, the bird dove off the branch and flew off into the undergrowth.

"What's weird is that parrot who keeps following us," she said. "It's giving me the creeps."

"I don't see it now," said Simon, looking all around.

"It went off with one of the fish in its beak," Maya said.

"Well, I guess we should keep going," said Simon, shifting his backpack higher on his back.

In a few more yards, the path—for there seemed to be some sort of rough path worn into the vegetation—swung away from the pond and cut deeper into the jungle. The children followed it.

"Simon," Maya asked. "Do parrots even EAT fish?"

"I didn't think so," Simon said cautiously. "But I guess they do here."

"Wherever *here* is," Maya muttered.

They walked in silence for a while. Maya had the uncomfortable sensation that she was being watched. She glanced behind her from time to time—quickly—in hopes of catching whatever it was, but there was never anything but more and more jungle pressing in on itself, fighting for space. Once she thought she saw a face through the trees, held very still watching them, and her heart leaped into her throat. But before she could say anything she looked again and saw that what she had seen was in fact a funny-shaped knot on a tree that, in the weak light, had looked for a moment like a face.

They stopped to rest in a clearing of banana plants. Maya peeled a banana halfway down and broke off pieces for Penny. She had two tins of milk, but she wanted to save them.

"The insects are huge here," she said. "And so is the fruit. Look at that breadfruit up there." She swatted an insect off her arm. Above them in the clearing a yellow butterfly, large as a bat, floated in the hot mass of air.

All around them the jungle vibrated nearly imperceptibly. A lizard sprang between branches, shaking the leaves ever so slightly. Peculiar birds swooped high above in the canopy or sat on low branches, watching the children and blinking every few minutes. Flowers seemed to be growing even as Maya watched them, but she blinked away sweat and told herself it was just the heat playing tricks on her eyes.

Simon was quiet for a few minutes, thinking, before he spoke.

"Maya," he said.

"Yes."

"Remember that shell the parrot brought?"

In her mind, Maya could still hear it clatter on the deck.

"Have you ever seen a shell like that before?" Simon asked.

He took his backpack off and fished around in it and withdrew the shell. "I mean, anything like it at all?"

"No," said Maya shortly.

Simon reached into the backpack and took out the logbook from the *Pamela Jane*. When she saw it, Maya opened her mouth to berate Simon for carrying it with them, but then she decided that an argument wasn't worth it. He already had it with him now, anyway, and he was the one who was going to have to carry it. And it was comforting to see something from the *Pamela Jane*. Simon found the page he was looking for and turned the book around so Maya could see it.

"I found this right before we sighted land," he said.

Maya looked down at the page. One of their parents had made a pencil sketch of the same type of shell that the parrot had brought to the *Pamela Jane*. Maya felt the hairs on the back of her neck go up.

"It isn't just this one," he said. "Maya, all the things they drew in the logbook—I've never seen any of them before. You know that we know every kind of shell and animal in the ocean all around here. The things they've drawn just don't exist. They're close to real things, but they're not the same."

"The shell is just a coincidence," Maya said, cutting him off.

"No, Maya, there's something weird here. Why would Papi have written about all of these things in the logbook? You're only supposed to record coordinates and what the weather is and what other boats you see. What's all the rest of this for?"

Simon turned a few more pages.

"Maybe these things are clues to help us figure out more about this place," he said thoughtfully. "Papi always said that the logbook was to help you find your way when you get lost."

"Yes, but it's to help you find where you are when you're

still out at sea," Maya said. "We're not out at sea anymore, Simon. And even when we were, the logbook didn't help us much, did it? If it had, we'd know where we are right now."

Maya glanced quickly at the book and saw the sketches and diagrams and notes written in her parents' familiar scrawl. Suddenly she felt deeply afraid. She feared what the writing in the logbook might mean and she didn't want to look at it. The feeling that they were not anywhere ordinary had been growing and gnawing at her as the day went on, but she still desperately wanted to believe that they were just on the uninhabited side of some known island, and that if they could just get to help, everything would be okay. She just couldn't think about the logbook right now. She stood up and tossed the banana peels into the trees, then lifted Penny back into the sling.

"We just have to keep going" said Maya. "Even if the things they wrote had anything to do with this place, we still need to get to a town," said Maya.

"But," said Simon.

Maya began walking but Simon didn't follow. Exasperated, she sighed and turned around to look back at him.

"Okay," she said. "Okay, okay. I'll look at the logbook later, all right? I promise. But right now we need to concentrate on finding help. Then they can tell you all about the book themselves, okay? Come on, let's start moving again."

"We don't even know where we're going," Simon muttered, getting to his feet. "We've been walking in circles." But he put the logbook back in his backpack and, glaring at Maya's back, he trotted to catch up with her.

"I'll go in front for a while," he said, overtaking her.

Maya let him go because something had distracted her. The

face. There it was again. Just off the side of the path, watching them from between thick leaves. Maya blinked and it was gone.

🐬 🐬 🐬

Both annoyed with each other, Maya and Simon walked in silence for a while. But then the bad feeling passed and they fell into a rhythm, singing sea songs and counting to one hundred in as many languages as they knew. Simon tied a spare shirt around his forehead and broke off a walking stick and pretended that he was one of the old explorers discovering a new continent. Maya played along and her spirits lifted. Suddenly even the pack on her back with Penny in it felt lighter. She felt a rush of love for Simon and Penny. Anytime now they would walk into a town where they would be able to get help—they may even be reunited with their parents by later that day. She reached her arm behind her head to grasp Penny's pudgy little fist to give it a squeeze, but her fingers just sailed through the air without touching her sister.

Maya gasped and stopped in her tracks.

"Simon!" she cried. "Simon, Penny's gone!"

"What do you mean, gone?" he asked from up ahead on the path.

"I mean, she's *gone!*"

Simon came charging back through the trees as Maya pulled the empty baby sling over her shoulder, holding it limply in front of her. She met Simon's eyes, fearful of his reproach. Simon stared at the empty sling.

"How do you lose a whole baby?" he asked incredulously.

Maya shook her head slowly and her eyes filled with tears that spilled over.

How had this happened? One moment Penny was there, the

next she wasn't. Maya tried to remember when she had noticed that the sling felt lighter. It was only in the past minute or two. *Think, think, think,* she told herself. But all she could think was that her baby sister was missing and it was all her fault. She no longer knew what to do next.

Simon frowned and swallowed. "All right," he said. "It's all right. We'll just retrace our steps and find her. Let's go!"

Maya stumbled blindly after him back along the path, except the path they had been walking on seemed to have grown over as soon as they'd left it. After a few minutes Simon stopped and turned slowly in a circle, surveying the jungle.

Maya sank into a crouch and closed her eyes and put her face on her knees. "It's all my fault," she said. "I'm the eldest. She was my responsibility." She started to cry softly. "Don't, Simon, don't," she said, pushing him away when he came to sit next to her. "Leave me alone."

She heard him tramp a ways into the jungle and stop. After a moment, from the cracks between her fingers she could see shadows passing evenly back and forth in front of her and she heard the creaky sound that a rope swing makes when it rubs against the polished part of a branch. Something was touching her forehead. She hung her head lower, burying her face in the crook of her elbow and brushing the leaf or bug or whatever it was away with her other hand.

When she heard the baby gurgle only a few inches away from her she nearly leaped out of her skin. She shouted and jumped to her feet just in time to see a thick green vine, curled over into a cradle, sweep Penny back up away from her. Maya gasped but was struck dumb when the vine rose up slowly and swayed. There was no breeze in the jungle, so the vine was moving on its own.

Like the vines that had enveloped the *Pamela Jane,* vines all around Maya were growing, right before her very eyes. Green and muscular, they advanced like snakes. In the curl of the vine that held her, Penny giggled. The vine seemed to be tickling her. Simon ran back through the jungle toward his sisters and stopped and stared in shock when he saw Penny. Maya jumped up to try to grasp the baby, but Penny was just out of her reach.

"Quick!" said Simon. "Lift me up and I'll grab her!"

But Simon was too heavy for Maya and they both toppled over. As she scrambled to her feet, Maya heard the sound of tinkling chimes and in the distance through the trees she saw another school of flying fish zipping past.

Just then a whistling sound came through the air above the children's heads and an arrow struck the vine just above where it held Penny. Then more appeared, whizzing through the air, all coming from the same direction, and struck the vine. Wounded, the vine released Penny and she dropped into Maya's arms. Maya fell to the ground, struggling to catch her breath, staring at the vine as it slunk away back into the jungle, arrows protruding brokenly from its skin. She held Penny close and looked her over quickly but the baby seemed to be unhurt. Maya and Simon looked in the direction from which the arrows had come but no one was there.

Slowly the realization crept over Maya that earlier, when she had seen the face, her eyes hadn't been playing tricks on her after all. Someone *was* out there.

"Come out!" she called, getting her voice back.

"I don't like this. . . ." whispered Simon, his voice trembling.

"Come out!" Maya called again. Her heart beat painfully against her ribs.

Maya and Simon stood close together and Maya held Penny tightly. They gazed into the darkness of the jungle but could see nothing.

Around them, thick, fleshy vines were waving slowly. Every now and then one of them shivered violently, as if it had sneezed. One swiveled a little as if it was observing Simon. Then quick as a snake, it whipped down and coiled around his ankles and hoisted him upside down ten feet off the ground. One minute he was standing next to Maya, the next he was gone. He was too surprised to make a sound, but Maya screamed.

She looked up to see him in the air above her, a large green vine coiled around his middle. From the corners of her eyes, Maya could see more vines advancing, some of them crawling along the jungle floor, others dropping down from branches high above, some moving straight through the air like the heads of snakes about to strike. Thinking she was about to be taken, too, Maya clutched Penny to her and began to scream. And when Maya began to scream, so of course did Penny. She did that thing that babies do: She took a huge breath in and hollered until her face turned purple.

The vine had pinned Simon's arms to his sides and was inching toward his neck as he struggled to free himself. Penny was crying at the top of her lungs. The vine on the ground near Maya had almost reached her. She kicked it furiously, but more were coming at her from other directions.

"Help!" she shrieked. "Help!"

And then, out of nowhere, a boy dropped down onto the path in front of her. He landed in a crouch, touching the ground as silently as a cat and steadying himself with one hand for a moment before he rose in a fighting stance, holding a spear in front of him. Arrows bristled from a loop in his belt. Maya knew at once that his was the face she had seen twice that day already. His skin was painted with camouflage and his hair was wild; no wonder he had blended into the undergrowth. Maya stopped screaming and stared.

"What are you doing here?" asked the boy. He held the spear clenched in his fist. Its tip glinted hard and bright as a diamond.

Maya's mouth hung open but she couldn't speak.

"Boat," shouted Simon. "Boat, boat, boat! We came on a boat!"

Maya leaped to one side to avoid a vine that had snuck up behind her. Then she was dancing from foot to foot as the vines crisscrossed the path, gliding over one another and reaching for her. Overhead, the vine that had Simon began to lift him higher into the trees.

"Do something!" Maya cried.

The stranger swung onto the low branch of a nearby tree and, with a flourish, raised his spear toward Simon. Maya screamed and closed her eyes, opening them just in time to see the stranger make a few swift strokes across the vine, which bled a bluish sap and wilted, easing Simon to the jungle floor. The rest of the vines began to retreat, as if they were being sucked slowly back to where they had come from. They rattled through the leaves on the ground and knocked flowers loose. Then they were gone and the jungle around the children was still.

"What were they?" Maya breathed.

"Carnivore vines," said the boy, putting the knife back in his belt. "Some plants are flesh eaters, you know. They'll grab you and squeeze you to death and then have you for lunch." He turned to Simon and helped him up.

"Thank you," said Simon.

"No problem," said the boy.

Maya and Simon looked at him in amazement. A necklace of shark's teeth rested on his bare chest. His ragged pants were held up by a rope tied around his waist. A lumpy scar was all that remained of his left ear. Though he couldn't have been much older than Maya, the tattoos on his arms were already faded. The green parrot from earlier, invisible until then, sailed down from the canopy and landed on his shoulder. Penny's sobs had subsided into hiccups and she was looking curiously at him.

"What are you doing here?" said the boy. "You obviously don't know anything if you think it's safe to walk through here. Especially with that baby."

"Well, it wasn't exactly by choice," said Maya a bit haughtily. The boy had saved them from the vines, but he had also been following them for hours before, maybe since they had reached the island, and she didn't think he was to be trusted.

"We just got here," explained Simon. "We were in a storm and our boat was blown off course—we don't really know where we are."

"I watched you sail in," said the boy. "But what I want to know is why you were sailing in the first place."

"We were on our way to Bermuda," said Maya.

"Bermuda?" said the boy. "Never heard of it."

"Look," said Maya. "Please, we need to get to a radio or phone. We have to get help."

"No, *you* look," said the boy. His tone had changed and he no longer sounded so pleasant. Maya held Penny tightly to her. "There's nowhere on this whole island—North or South—

that's called Bermuda. And nobody just sails around—the only people on the water are the pirates. Where are you really from and who sent you? Are you spies from the North?"

Maya and Simon were dumbfounded. He didn't believe them? And spies? They were just kids—how could they be spies?

"The North?" Maya asked, clearing her throat.

The strange boy narrowed his eyes. "If you want to play games, I can leave you to find your way out of here yourselves," he said. He turned and swung his spear over his back and began walking away.

"Wait!" Simon cried. "Please don't go! We're telling the truth! Our parents were lost overboard in the storm and we sailed here, but we don't know where we are. We left our boat so that we could climb one of the hills to see better. Please, we're telling the truth!"

The boy stopped in his tracks and then he turned to face them.

"You're telling me you're from the Outside?" he asked, watching them closely.

"We're from the *Pamela Jane*," said Simon helplessly.

Maya felt the seconds tick by thickly as the boy stared at them. She realized she was holding her breath. Finally the boy dropped his gaze.

"Maybe you are telling the truth," he said. He seemed amazed by this. "It does happen sometimes, people blowing in from the Outside," he said almost to himself as he levered his spear back down. He studied the children, his eyes bright with curiosity. "I've seen a few of them before."

"I knew it," Simon whispered to Maya, his eyes lighting up. "This is the place from Papi's story. I knew we were here."

Maya felt amazed.

"Where *are* we?" she asked the boy.

"Where are you?" the boy asked, raising his spear over his head. He twirled it around with a flourish and planted it firmly in the earth in front of them. He smiled.

"You're in Greater Tamarind."

❧ CHAPTER SIX ❧

Greater and Lesser Tamarind ✳
Seagrape ✳ *An Enchanted Banyan Grove* ✳ *Sleeping Jaguars*

*G*reater Tamarind.

When they heard the name, a strange feeling came over both Maya and Simon. They had been sailing around this part of the ocean all their lives and knew the name of every island and inlet, beach and cove, but Greater Tamarind was nowhere they had ever heard of before. It was a mysteriously powerful name, and Maya repeated it several times in her mind.

"Welcome," the boy added wryly. "Right now we're actually just on one of the tiny Lesser Islands. Greater Tamarind is just to our east. There's just a tiny channel separating Greater Tamarind from the Lesser Islands."

Suddenly Maya felt angry. She didn't want this to be happening. She wanted to have come to shore in an ordinary place, where they could get to the authorities, who would send out search boats to look for their parents. No one had ever heard of Greater Tamarind—it wasn't a real place! It didn't exist. They must be just on the uninhabited side of some Atlantic island. This boy, whatever his name was, was playing a cruel joke. Exhausted from the ordeal of the storm, her feet blistered, her heart heavy from the burden of trying to find their parents, her pulse still racing from the scare of the vines, Maya began to get angrier and angrier. If this boy had wanted to help them, he would have done so first thing that morning, instead of following them all day. He wasn't to be trusted. She narrowed her eyes at him.

"We can't wait here anymore," she said. "We have to keep going."

The strange boy laughed. "Going? You have no idea where you're going. I've been following you for hours. You've been walking in circles."

"Told you," said Simon to Maya. He was gazing at the boy's shark's teeth necklace admiringly.

"We're going to climb one of the hills," Maya said. "To see where we are. So we can get help."

"You can't climb these hills," said the boy. "They're way too steep. Even I couldn't do it. And your parents wouldn't be on this island, anyway, even if they were here. Like I said, this is one of the Lesser Islands. Nothing here but flesh-eating plants, flying fish, and jaguars."

"Jaguars?" asked Simon.

"There's hundreds of them," the stranger said.

"Then how come you're here?" Maya challenged.

The boy smiled and tapped his bow. "I'm a hunter," he said.

Maya looked at the glinting tips of the arrows. He had been tracking them all morning as if they had been prey. She saw a shadow flicker in the canopy high above them and she shuddered. What if the boy was right? What if there were jaguars?

The boy seemed to make a decision. "Look," he said. "If your parents are here, they're most likely on the main island, Greater Tamarind. I can take you there."

"But we can't just leave our boat," said Maya.

"It will be safe where it is," said the stranger. "The vines will hide it. And even if you could cut them free, if you try sailing around the island the pirates will get you. There are fleets sailing around the coast all the time. It was just luck that you didn't run into one on your way in. You wouldn't be so lucky again."

"Pirates?" asked Simon, his eyes shining.

"Yup," said the stranger. "The waters around here are teeming with them. Because of the war."

"What war?" asked Simon.

"The War Between North and South," said the boy. "It's been going on since before most people here were born." When Maya and Simon looked at him blankly, he shook his head. "Look, you'd better stick with me. I'll take you to Port Town. It's the nearest town and the safest place in Tamarind. You'll be okay there."

Maya hesitated. She didn't know what to do. She believed the boy that the hills were too steep for them to climb—they were barely making any headway through the flat part of the jungle where they were now. But how could they just leave the *Pamela Jane*! Then again, what if he was telling the truth— what if there *were* pirates? She could tell that Simon wanted to go with the boy—maybe her brother was right. She took a deep breath.

"All right," she said. "We'll go with you."

"Who are you?" asked Simon. Maya could see he was in awe of the older boy, with the camouflage paint on his face and the tattoos on his shoulders and the sharp silver arrows gleaming from his belt.

"My name is Helix," said the boy. "Come on."

"Wait," said Simon, hurrying after him. "Don't you want to know our names?"

"I already do," said the boy over his shoulder. "You're Simon, she's Maya, and the baby is Penny. You're all very loud.

I've been listening to you all afternoon. Did you think you were the only ones in this jungle?"

Helix moved quickly, slicing a path through the tangled undergrowth, and Maya and Simon had to hurry to keep up. Maya had moved the sling from her back to her front so that she could keep a protective hand on Penny's sleeping back while they walked. The green parrot stayed a little ahead of them, coasting from branch to branch.

"That's the parrot that came on our boat this morning," said Simon. "Even before we saw land."

"That's Seagrape," said Helix. "She disappeared earlier. I didn't know where she went but then she came to get me and brought me to the beach. That's how I saw your boat coming in."

Maya struggled after the boys, going as quickly as she could with Penny. Helix and Simon kept up a lively conversation but Maya didn't join in. Instead she fretted. She didn't like Helix or their situation one bit. Who knew where he was really taking them? They had no idea where they were going, not really. But Maya didn't know what else they could do. She kept her eyes peeled for the jaguars Helix had talked about but she saw no sign of one.

Finally Helix stopped and put his finger to his lips.

"From here on we're going to have to be totally quiet," he said. "I mean it. Don't say anything and watch where you walk. Don't step on a twig even."

"Why?" whispered Simon.

"Because in a minute we're going to come out into a grove of banyan trees and that's where the jaguars will be. They'll all be napping at this hour."

"Then why are we going this way?" asked Maya. "Shouldn't we be *avoiding* the jaguars?"

68

"We can't," said Helix. "They're on the shore all around here and my raft happens to be on the other side of those trees. Because of the way the currents run, this is the only point at which you can get to Greater Tamarind from the Lesser Islands. All the other currents drag you *toward* the Lesser Islands— that's probably why you ended up landing here. You have to know the waters really well not to get sucked into a current. The winds are bad, too. We don't have any choice but to go past the jaguars."

"Come on, Maya, we have to do what he says," said Simon.

Maya pressed her lips together. She didn't say anything but she began following Helix, keeping one eye on the path in front of her so that she didn't step on anything that might make a noise. She hoped that Penny wouldn't wake up. When they got to the banyan trees, Maya and Simon stopped in their tracks and stared.

They were looking into a vast, magnificent, and spooky grove of gigantic trunks, covered in a shaggy hide of mottled green lichen. Their roots stood above the ground, forming dark, cathedral-like hollows large enough for the children to have hidden inside. Ropy vines with hairy tassels of roots stretched down from the branches to burrow into the earth and form new trunks, until over time the whole grove had become interconnected, and the canopy of leaves was so dense that little sunshine could get through and the light beneath the canopy was just a murky green gloom. But it was not the banyans themselves that Maya and Simon could not take their eyes off of, it was what lay beneath them.

Lying napping beneath the majestic trees were forty or so jaguars.

The jaguars had thick, soft, honey-colored fur with black

spots. Beneath the green glow of the trees, each animal looked like a pool of light with tiny blots of black shadow. Vines swept soothingly back and forth over their backs in a fine breeze and rumbling purring rose from the creatures.

"Don't worry," said Helix in a very soft whisper. "These vines aren't like the others. They're just sweeper vines—they put the cats to sleep. They'll only nab you if you move too quickly. Just don't make a sound and we'll be fine."

He put his finger to his lips and motioned them to follow him as he began tiptoeing lightly through the grove. Simon went after him and a moment later, Maya took a deep breath and followed them. She watched where she put her feet, stepping gingerly so that not a single leaf would rustle nor twig would snap and disturb the cats' slumber. Though it would have been difficult for the creatures to hear them over the roar of feline snoring. By the time the children got to the middle of the grove the sound was almost deafening. A tiny branch broke against Maya's arm when she brushed past it and she froze in her tracks and waited, not daring to breathe, but the cats lay perfectly still, the vines sweeping in long, even strokes over their backs. The children crossed the halfway mark. Up ahead Maya could see water shimmering through the trees. They would get to the raft and then they'd be safe. Cats hated water, after all. The water got brighter and brighter with each step toward it. Maya tried to clear her mind of anything but where to put her feet. The right foot on a patch of soft ferns, the left foot balancing on a root sticking out of the earth, right foot in the quiet muddy place right there, left foot down just between those two rotting sticks . . .

Then the worst thing happened.

Penny woke.

And began to wail.

It was unlike Penny to wake from a nap crying but perhaps she had sensed the danger around them in her sleep. Horrified, Maya stiffened. Helix and Simon stopped, too, and looked over their shoulders at her. She looked back at them helplessly. Around them the cats began to wake. Whatever spell the vines had put them under couldn't withstand the cries of an eight-month-old infant.

A fat yellow paw slapped down on the ground in front of Maya's feet. Her breath caught in her throat and she looked into the furry, spotted face of a sleepy jaguar. The cat was stretching and yawning, its muscular jaw stretching out nearly in a straight line, its eyes rolling back in their sockets. When it opened its eyes again it leaped up, startled. Its lips and whiskers drew back in a snarl, and it lifted one of its great yellow paws to strike. Maya looked at the enormous, dirty claws and imagined what they were about to do to her, but could not seem to make herself move. Her feet felt rooted to the earth. And even though she was petrified, she was able to think quite calmly that even if she did begin to run, the giant cat would catch up with her in a heartbeat.

She took a deep breath, preparing for the strike, but just as the jaguar's paw descended in a death blow, from the corner of her eye she saw Helix swing his bow down from over his shoulder and withdraw an arrow from his belt.

But Helix's arrow sailed through the air without striking its target, because suddenly a long dark vine came swinging across and flew right under the jaguar's ribs and lifted it up in the air. It hung, swinging slightly to and fro, twenty feet off the ground.

71

The creature let out a surprised and outraged yowl that woke any cats that had still been sleeping. Suddenly all the jaguars were on their feet, snarling, ears flattened, tails dancing like flames. Several cats leaped for the children at the same time and as they did, other vines dropped down and looped around their middles and hauled them into the air, where they swung back and forth, howling in fury.

"Don't move suddenly!" Helix shouted to Maya and Simon. "Or the vines will grab you, too!"

Maya had been about to make a mad dash for the water but she stopped and stood absolutely still.

"Very slowly," Helix said. "Very slowly we're going to keep walking until we get to the raft, okay?"

"Okay," said Simon. He and Maya began following Helix again, and they walked through the rest of the grove, looking up in amazement at the jaguars swinging slowly back and forth overhead.

They only started running when they left the grove and neared the shore. Maya breathed a sigh of relief to be back out in the sunshine again. But they stopped short when they realized that Helix's raft couldn't fit all of them. Growling noises still coming menacingly from inside the jungle, Maya hurried to collect driftwood and Helix sliced a few thin, rubbery vines from the edge of the forest and began tying the driftwood to the raft to make it bigger.

"I can do that better," said Simon.

"It's true," said Maya. "He's the knot expert."

Working quickly, Simon tied a series of knots that bound the driftwood to the raft.

"Impressive," said Helix.

As Helix pushed the raft into the water and they clambered

onto it, Maya looked nervously over the water. The channel separating the tiny island they were on from the bigger island was narrow, but the current flowed treacherously.

"Are you sure this is safe?" she asked.

"You can stay here if you like," Helix said. "The vines will let the jaguars back down in a few minutes and I'm sure there'll be a big fight over who gets to have you for lunch."

That was it, Maya did *not* like Helix. She gritted her teeth and crawled onto the raft.

"Fine," she said. "I'd rather drown than be eaten."

❖ Chapter Seven ❖

On the Way to Port Town ❖ *A Dirty*
Diaper ❖ *Pirates!* ❖ *Maya Has an Idea* ❖
A Voice from the Beach

The crossing was rough and the current played wickedly with the flimsy raft. Twice they almost capsized. Almost as soon as they reached the shore, the raft split apart and the current pulled the pieces out to sea. When Maya looked back she could see the vines swarming around the edges of the small island they had left behind.

"Don't worry," said Helix. "That kind of vine only survives on the Lesser Islands. Which is a good thing, since there are enough problems here without having to worry about flesh-eating vines."

Maya and Simon looked at each other.

"What do you mean?" Maya asked.

"You'll find out," said Helix, but that was all he would say about it. He had already started to walk quickly into the jungle, and the children hurried to follow him.

"How big is Tamarind?" asked Simon.

"Big," Helix answered. "Huge. Even I haven't been over all of it."

The boys took the lead and Maya struggled along in the rear with Penny.

"They'd slow down a bit if they had to carry you," she muttered to the baby.

Maya half listened as Simon continued to ask Helix questions, and Helix began to tell him all sorts of wild stories about encounters with gorgeous mermaids who sang to him and hair-raising sea battles between pirates and surviving for weeks on end by himself in the depths of the jungle when he went hunting. Maya didn't believe any of it for an instant. She did gather, though, that Tamarind was quite vast, and they had only seen a tiny southwestern corner of it so far, and that there was a war going on that prevented most people from traveling much. She hoped they would reach Port Town by early afternoon. She thought she could make it until then. Her stomach was starting to growl and her feet beginning to hurt badly, but she didn't want to be the one to ask to take a rest. Finally they paused to catch their breath. Helix looked at Penny and wrinkled his nose.

"Um, I think she needs her diaper changed," he said.

Maya had to agree. She took Penny out of the sling and set her on a large flat leaf and took out a fresh diaper—good thing she had remembered to bring *those* from the ship. Taking a deep breath, she took off the dirty diaper and wrapped it up.

"Oh, sick!" said Simon.

"Oh, knock it off," said Maya. "Do you think I *like* doing this? Simon, it's your turn next time."

"No way," said Simon. "That's a girl's job."

Not knowing what else to do with it, Maya put the dirty diaper under a stone in the undergrowth. She cleaned Penny up as best she could, thinking evil thoughts about Simon. He never made a big deal of dirty diapers—it was all for Helix's benefit. Penny babbled away about something while Maya pulled her shirt back down. *What on earth are you saying?* she thought. She wished her mother were there. Maya had often helped her with Penny, but she had never had to take care of the baby all by herself before—how was she supposed to know what Penny needed? She only had a few more store-bought diapers left—after that, she would have to switch to the cloth diapers her mother sometimes used. She sat the baby back upright and sighed. Maybe they would reach the town before the real diapers ran out.

They were on a coral path that ran along a few feet from the edge of cliffs. The cliffs dropped steeply down to where the surf broke icy white at their base hundreds of feet below. The children sat in the shade of tropical thorn plums and looked out to the glittering sea. There was not a ship in sight. A giant white albatross wheeled in the air.

Helix went off to forage for lunch for them, and Simon started to recount Helix's stories to Maya in vivid—and often bloody—detail.

"Did you hear how he got that scar on his ear?" he began. "He was in a fight with a pirate and the pirate sliced it right off and then he made Helix watch while he used it as bait and then he reeled in this huge barracuda and . . . !"

Maya interrupted him. "Look," she said in a low voice. "Don't believe everything he tells you. We don't know anything about him."

Simon frowned at his sister. "Just because you don't like him doesn't mean I don't have to," he said. "You never like *anybody*." Simon looked broodingly down at his blistered feet. "Anyway," he said, "if it wasn't for him you'd still be making us walk around in circles, waiting for the vines to eat us!"

They heard rustling in the trees, and Helix returned carrying papayas.

"How long before we get to Port Town?" Maya asked him.

"At this rate," said Helix, taking out his knife and slicing a papaya. "About four days."

"*Four days!*" Maya cried, dismayed.

"Well," said Helix. "Give or take. It's slower because of the baby."

"I can't carry Penny for four days," Maya said. "Isn't there a faster way? Or a closer town?"

Helix shook his head.

Simon, hearing the note of despair in his sister's voice immediately said, "I can help carry Penny."

"No," said Maya. "I'm bigger than you and she's heavy for me."

"I can carry her for a while," said Helix.

Maya looked at the arrows bristling from the bag on his back and at the sharp point of his spear and didn't think it was a good idea to let him hold Penny. Plus, Penny was her responsibility, and since their scare with the vines she didn't want to let the baby out of her arms.

"Even if we didn't have Penny, I don't think we could keep going for four days," she said. "We've only walked for a few hours so far, and—" She looked down miserably at the ground. Blood had dried on scratches on her legs and flies buzzed around the cuts. Her feet were so blistered now that each step was painful. Why hadn't she asked how far away Port Town was earlier? She didn't know what to do next—she had been sure they would be able to reach a town that same day. She blinked away a few hot tears and closed her eyes tightly until the feeling passed. There would be nothing more mortifying than crying in front of Helix. She suddenly felt furious at him—it was his fault they had left the boat. The poor *Pamela Jane,* alone in the cove, with those horrible vines choking her! They should have cut her free and sailed away then and there. Maybe it wasn't too late—maybe they could still turn around and walk back the way they had come. It was a much shorter distance back to the cove than it was to Port Town. They could swim back to the boat and—a loud boom sounded, interrupting Maya's thoughts.

The children didn't know where the sound was coming from at first, but then Helix motioned for them to duck. They crawled to the cliff's edge on their stomachs and looked out between the bushes and listened as another boom, this one closer now, ricocheted off the cliffs. Tiny pebbles rattled down to the sea below, and the great white albatross wheeled in the air. A puff of gunsmoke drifted around the curve of the coast and then a ship appeared, sails billowing strong in the wind. Maya and Simon and Helix watched in silence as others rounded the coast behind it.

"Pirates," breathed Simon.

Helix nodded.

Maya's knees turned to jelly.

From the children's perch high on the cliffs the men on the decks of the ships were just tiny dark figures. The fleet sailed close together, like hornets in flight, their cannons glinting dangerously in the sun. The albatross began climbing high in the air, as if to draw them away from its nest. From one of the decks below Maya saw a sudden burst of fire through the bright air and heard a pistol crack. Then there was another and another and then the albatross cried out—it had been struck!

It began to fall out of the sky, heavy as a stone, past the edge of the cliff where the children lay, and pinwheeled down toward the white surf breaking at the foot of the cliffs. There it vanished.

Maya looked gravely down at the sea. A new fear began to spread through her as she realized that this part of Helix's story had been true—there *were* pirates. Did that mean he was telling the truth about other things, too?

"Come on," said Helix. "Before we become firing practice." Still crouching, the children followed him swiftly off the coastal path and back into the trees.

〜 〜 〜

The children had been so frightened by the pirates that even though they were tired, for a while after they left the cliffs they didn't want to stop walking. They were thirsty and their canteens were empty, so Helix said he would take them to a nearby freshwater river. They walked in silence. Even Simon had stopped chattering and after a while Maya noticed his pace beginning to lag. He plodded along with his head down. Maya was relieved when they left the high jungle and began to walk downhill. At the bottom of the hill they met up with a trail that ran through the trees just above a long and desolate row of beaches. Every now and then the children caught a glimpse of the sand and sea. They heard the river before they saw it. It was away from the beaches, farther into the jungle. They went through the trees until they reached a little glade along its shore.

Maya lifted Penny out of the sling and set her down on the soft emerald grass. She was fussing and Maya couldn't seem to do anything to quiet her. Then Penny began to cry properly.

Maya picked her up and rocked her. "What's wrong?" she murmured. "What is it?"

"It would be better if she could talk to us," said Simon, patting Penny's hand.

At a loss, Maya opened one of the two tins of milk and filled Penny's bottle. It did the trick—Penny took the bottle and guzzled the milk, making soft noises as she gazed up at her siblings with her big dark eyes. Maya realized with dismay that Penny wouldn't be able to drink all of it, and that they had no way to save the rest, and after that there was only one tin left. If they didn't find another source of milk, Penny was going to only have water and whatever soft foods they could find for her.

Penny content for now, Maya knelt by the river and drank deeply and splashed water over her face. The current was too strong for swimming, but she and Simon took off their shoes and peeled off their socks—their feet had bled right through them—and sat with their feet dangling into the cool water. Maya flexed her toes and grimaced as she looked at her feet.

"I don't think I can even put my shoes back on," said Simon.

Maya could hear a faint whining tone creeping into his voice.

The thought of hours and days of hiking unspooling before them seemed impossible to contemplate. There was now no question that they could not return to the *Pamela Jane*. Even if they did succeed in cutting the boat free, they could sail out of the cove and right into the clutches of the pirates. Maya didn't know what to do. It was late in the afternoon now—the days were short here. The river was already turning a deep murky green and the first shadows were gathering beneath the trees. How could they possibly walk anymore tomorrow? Dragonflies hummed in the hot air. She closed her eyes and lay back, listening to the river as it murmured against the muddy banks.

She sat up suddenly. "Where does the river go?" she asked.

A funny expression passed over Helix's face. "Eventually it comes out near Port Town," he said. "But it travels deep into the jungle first."

"Is there any way of traveling along it?" asked Maya. "I don't think we can go much farther like this."

Helix looked uneasy. "This is the Nallanda River," he said. "It goes through the Nero Jungle. You don't want to go there, trust me."

"Why not?" asked Simon. "What's so bad about it?"

Helix didn't answer. Maya's eye wandered to his scarred ear and she looked quickly away.

"I don't know what other choice we really have," she said. "Maybe we can build some sort of raft. Or do boats ever come along? Maybe they'd take us with them."

"Barges come along sometimes," Helix said reluctantly. "The traders carry supplies up and down. But, really—it's very dangerous. I think you should stay with me—I can get you to Port Town safely."

Maya looked at Simon. She could tell that he had decided that he wasn't going to act like a baby in front of Helix, but she could also see that his feet were rubbed raw and he was already exhausted.

"I think we're going to have to wait for a barge," she said. "I think it's our best option."

"You're making a mistake," Helix said.

"Can't you come with us on the river?" Simon asked Helix.

Helix shook his head. "I won't go near the Nero Jungle," he said. "And if you were smart, you wouldn't either."

Maya opened her mouth to speak but just then she heard a voice coming from the beach that was just beyond the fringe of jungle. The others heard it, too.

"Someone's there," Maya said urgently, gathering up Penny and scrambling to her feet. "Simon, come on, I hear someone out there, I'm sure I do! Let's go!"

"Wait!" said Helix. "Don't go out there."

Maya grabbed Simon's arm but he pulled away. He stood wavering between Maya and Helix.

"Oh, come on," Maya cried. "Before whoever it is is gone!"

"Why shouldn't we go out there?" Simon asked Helix.

"There is someone there," Helix said. "But he's not going to be able to help you."

"I don't know what you're talking about," said Maya. "But I heard someone out there and we have to go! Come on, Simon, *now*!"

Simon turned to Helix and shrugged. "She's my sister," he said. "I have to go with her."

With that, Maya went crashing through the undergrowth toward the voice. She could hear Simon behind her. In a moment she burst out onto a beach and stopped. All up and down it were hundreds of giant turtles. On land the creatures moved so slowly that they barely seemed to move at all, like a scene from a dream. Some were swimming in on the tide, their dark heads bobbing in points of blackness on the blue. When they reached the shore they scrambled up the beach, their pebbly legs scouring the sand, leaving faint, windswept etchings in their wake. The others already sat high up on the dry sand, basking in the sun, which shone on the tiles of their vegetable-green backs.

And in the midst of them a man with wild white hair had frozen in his tracks and was staring at Maya.

A grown-up! thought Maya. Finally they were saved!

❊ Chapter Eight ❊

The Mad Zoologist ❊ *Limmermor Turtles* ❊
Strange Coincidences ❊ *Singing Sand* ❊
Down by the Tide Pools

Maya and Penny, Simon just a few paces behind them, jogged towards the figure, but the man just stared at them in horror. Not knowing what to do, the children stopped and stared back at him. He wore a limp white hat. Beneath its brim the skin around his very light blue eyes was crinkled from years of squinting at the glare from the sand and sea. He was very pale—the kind of profoundly pale person who should never really be out in the sun—but he had been, anyway, and in consequence, his neck and hands had grown thick and leathery and had a permanent ruddy burn. Time and exposure to the elements had leached the color from his threadbare clothes. He was holding a small turtle in his hands and the turtle was cycling its legs through the air, trying to get away. When he put it down the creature trundled off down the shore and joined others who were basking on the hot sand.

"You can't be here," the white-haired man said finally. "You'll have to find another beach for yourselves." When they stood there motionless he waved a hand at them. "Go on, go, back the way you came."

Maya was taken aback, but she thought that if she could just explain their situation, he could help them. Before she could get very far, the old man interrupted her.

"I can't help you," he said. "I can't, I can't, I can't!"

"Please," pleaded Maya, beginning to feel desperate. "Do you at least have a radio or telephone?"

"None of that here," said the man, sweeping his hand down the beach. Maya looked past him and he certainly seemed to be telling the truth. Aside from the slumbering turtles and a ramshackle hut thatched with palm leaves, there were no signs of life. The man turned and began walking away. It was as if he hoped that if he couldn't see the children, they wouldn't really be there. He mumbled to himself as he went.

Simon had been looking at the turtles lumbering inelegantly out of the sea. The only time they reached any speed was on the rush of the final wave that carried them up onto the sand. Simon had an idea. He could always figure out how to get people talking.

"We're here to ask you about the turtles," he called out suddenly.

The man stopped and turned back around. For the first time he looked at them with some interest.

"Limmermors," he said, eyeing the children keenly. "They're Limmermor turtles. You won't have heard of them—no one has yet. They won't until I get back one day. I'm a zoologist—Dr. Limmermor, you may have heard of me—my boat sank in a storm—I'm sure there would have been newspaper stories. . . ."

He paused a moment but the children looked at him blankly.

"Oh, well, you're all awfully young, perhaps it was before your time. At any rate, I didn't know it then, but it was my great good fortune that the storm happened. It's how I discovered the Limmermor turtle right here, on this beach. In the zoology directory under turtles it should go between the leatherback and the loggerhead. When I go back one day they'll have to publish a new edition of the directory to include it. It's going to take the zoology world by storm. It's priceless, you know. Years and years of research on an unknown species in a pristine environment—how many scientists can say they've had that opportunity? Limmermors are unique, you know," he said, looking at the turtles. "Their eggs—" He stopped and changed the subject abruptly.

"A pristine environment," he repeated. "This beach. So I'm going to have to ask that you leave nicely now, just the way you came. I can't have the turtles disturbed."

Maya, feeling quite desperate now, opened her mouth to speak, but the man cut her off.

"No, no, no!" he said. "No more! Please go! This is very bad for the turtles. You'll all have to go and figure things out for yourselves," he said, turning and shuffling away from them. "No visitors for years and now five at once," he mumbled to himself.

Visitors. Five? But there are just three of us, thought Maya—her and Simon and Penny. Who were the other two? She looked at Simon. No, it was too much of a coincidence. . . . But it was *possible,* wasn't it? Simon seemed to think so.

"Wait!" he cried breathlessly, running after Dr. Limmermor. "Who else has been here?"

Dr. Limmermor shied away as Simon reached him.

"Alone!" he said. "Leave me alone!" He closed his eyes and when he opened them he seemed pained to find that they were still there.

"I'll tell you what I told them and then you have to leave!" he said, distressed. "Stay out of the jungle, it's full of soldiers; stay out of the sea, it's full of pirates. Find a quiet corner for yourself somewhere where you can live peacefully. A beach—but not this one, it's taken. Now, please, leave us alone!"

"But . . ." said Simon.

Maya caught up with Simon.

"The people who were here—maybe they were our parents," Maya said urgently. "What did they say? Where were they going?"

Dr. Limmermor waved his hand vaguely in the direction of the jungle.

Simon tried to ask another question but Dr. Limmermor put his hands over his ears and bellowed, "No more questions! Good night!" He began striding quickly away on the soft sand, mumbling "no, no, no" over and over to himself.

The light had begun to fade swiftly and the turtles had become just dark bumps on the sand. In the last light the children watched the zoologist, like a blot of salt spray whipped up by the wind, spinning ethereally down the shoreline.

Maya stood there helplessly. The zoologist was mad. And now evening was falling and the jungle was beginning to get dark. A tear slid down her cheek. They were supposed to have found people by now—people who could help them. They were supposed to have sounded the alarm and rescue boats were supposed to be out searching for their parents right now. And instead, here they were stranded who knew where and of the only two people they had met so far, one she didn't trust and the other was plainly crazy.

Simon looked up at the dark hills of the jungle.

"Mami!" he shouted, a note of desperation in his voice. "Papi!"

Maya joined in and for a few minutes they called as loudly as they could. Finally they fell silent, holding their breath and listening. Their shouts had scared a few birds, who flew up out of the trees and farther down the beach, but that was all. Except for the chirping of frogs and insects and the purr of the sea, all was quiet. Maya could hardly bear it. She felt so alone. The jungle loomed solid and dark over the beach. Could their parents be out there somewhere? She looked down at the sand for their footprints, but even as she watched, a breeze was rippling the beach into small dunes. Any footprints from the day before would have dissolved long ago.

Just then a soft noise nearby caught Maya's attention. Between two nearby dunes was a turtle, digging in the sand to bury her eggs. What startled her were the eggs themselves. There were seven or eight of them and they glowed faintly. *Strange,* thought Maya.

Before Maya could think about it further, there was a crackle at the edge of the jungle. The children jumped.

"Helix," Simon cried. "You stayed!"

"I tried to tell you," Helix said. "He's been on this beach practically forever. He thinks he's from the Outside. He's crazy."

"What do we do now?" Simon asked.

"If you would like, that is, if *Maya* would like," said Helix, "I can take you just over these rocks to the next beach and we can sleep there tonight."

🐬　🐬　🐬

From the new beach on the other side of the low rocks they could see Dr. Limmermor and the Limmermor turtles in the distance. Inside the jungle it was already pitch-black, but the white sand of the beach held the light longer. The first thing the children did was to gather driftwood and soon a fire was crackling merrily. They caught a fish and roasted it on a makeshift spit over the fire, and Helix returned from the fringe of the jungle with a shirt full of avocados that they ate with the fish. Reluctantly, Maya heated the last tin of milk for Penny. From then on she would have to eat grown-up food. When dinner was finished, Helix went down to wash in the sea, which, in a trick of the tides, was as still as a mirror except for a fine lace of white foam that trembled slightly along the edge of the shore.

Simon sat cross-legged in a patch of sea daisies. The logbook was open in his lap, and he was studying it intently by the light of the fire. Finally he sighed and closed it and held it in his lap.

"Maya," Simon said slowly. "Do you think it was Mami and Papi that Dr. Limmermor saw?"

Maya wondered the same thing. How many people just washed up by storms could there be on the island? It could have been their parents. If it was, where had they gone?

"I don't know," she said. "I hope so. It would mean we're going the right way."

The children fell quiet. The jungle behind them and the sea before them were both pitch-black and when a cool breeze blew over them, they felt lost and lonely.

"I wish Mami were here," said Simon softly.

Maya did, too. Her heart ached. She looked over the rocks, down Limmermor beach, and saw Dr. Limmermor down by the water. A funny sound began to come from the edges of the darkness, from where the palms leaned over the beach and the shadows multiplied. A high, singing sound, like thousands of delicate crystal chimes, so beautiful it held the children transfixed. After a moment Maya noticed that the sand was shifting around them. A fine surface layer was rolling over itself. It was the particles of sand rubbing against one another that made the singing sound.

"Musical sand," she whispered. "Papi told me about it, that in some places in the world the sand sings." Tears welled up in her eyes at the thought of her father.

Helix returned from bathing in the sea and suddenly Maya and Simon both felt more cheerful. He had washed the camouflage off of his face, and Maya was startled to see that without it he looked completely different—he looked quite nice, in fact. He sat down by the fire. Penny was fast asleep already. Lulled by the singing sand, Simon was heavy-eyed and he yawned and nestled down in the sand, his head on his backpack.

Eventually the breeze died away, and the muggy breath of the jungle descended onto the beach. The sand lay silent in little hillocks of moonlight. Down by the shore, moonlight shone in the tide pools.

"Come see the pools," Helix said to Maya. "We won't be far away—we'll be able to see your brother and sister the whole time."

Still moved by the beauty of the singing sand, Maya felt happy for a moment that Helix had asked. She nodded and they walked down to the tide pools. The pools stretched out down the beach, and each one of them contained a reflection of the moon, nearly full now and already quite high in the sky, so that there were dozens of moons glimmering before Maya and Helix. Maya knelt down to look into one of the pools. As she watched, the reflection of the moon began to recede and a light inside the pool grew brighter and began to rise through the shallows, shattering the moon into dozens of soft, jagged pieces. It was some sort of sea creature that was casting the light, but it was still impossible to see the animal clearly beneath the rippling surface. Maya looked up and saw that other bright lights were surfacing in tide pools all the way down the beach.

When she looked back down at the tide pool, the surface of the water had settled and she could see the creature clearly. Her heart skipped a beat. A tiny, perfect octopus, just like the one that her parents had collected from the sea and taken to St. Alban's on their last day together, was looking up at Maya with its familiar indigo eye. Its tentacles glowed so brightly they outshone the moon. Then Maya realized that there were dozens of creatures just like it in tide pools up and down the beach. The lights in the pools grew more intense, until the beach seemed almost as bright as day, and then together they began to dim and the pools fell back into darkness. Maya once again found herself looking at the reflection of the moon.

Was this where all the strange, glowing sea creatures that her parents had been collecting came from? Maybe it wasn't an accident that the children had landed in Tamarind. Could their parents have been looking for the island? Did these creatures have something to do with the Red Coral Project?

Helix reached into the water and a polyp crawled up his hand and wrist, tiny red tentacles flowing in the gentle current. Past the tide pools, the waves sizzled white around the boiler reefs. Maya glanced behind them. Except for them, the strip of beach was deserted. She snuck a sideways glance at Helix. Maybe she had judged him too quickly. Maybe he wasn't so bad. He was almost handsome, in a way. His curly hair was bleached from sun and salt and ropy veins crossed the muscles on his arms. He was probably only a couple of years older than she was. Maya looked bashfully down at her hands and picked at her nails.

"I didn't want to tell you earlier," he said. "In front of your brother. But you may as well know, whether you take the river or come with me on foot, you aren't going to be able to find help in Port Town. Not the kind of help you're looking for. There's no one who can help you on Greater Tamarind."

"What do you mean?" asked Maya. The good mood she had been in a moment before abruptly slipped away. "Somebody has to be able to help us."

"You don't know much about this place yet," said Helix. "But I know it isn't anything like where you came from. If I were you . . ." he said. He paused. "If I were you, I'd try to start forgetting everything in your life before and get used to being here."

"We're going to find our parents," Maya said coolly.

"Well," said Helix. "You'll see."

Maya didn't know what she had been thinking. Helix wasn't nice-looking, and he certainly wasn't nice. The earlier mistrust she had felt for him flooded back. She looked at him angrily.

"What do you know?" she asked. "You aren't much older than I am. Who are you to tell me we won't find our parents? And why are you out here by yourself, anyway?"

Helix didn't answer and Maya grew angrier.

"Oh, forget it," she said, beginning to climb down the rocks, so quickly that she scraped her knees. She couldn't wait until she never had to see Helix again. "I don't care what you say, anyway. We're going to find our parents, I'm going to make sure of it. And now I'm tired. Good *night*."

Back with the others, Maya lay down in the sand so that Penny was sheltered between her and Simon. *Forget about Helix,* she thought. *Think about something else. Name the constellations.* That very bright star, the brightest in the sky, it was Betelgeuse, part of Orion. And there was Taurus. And Pisces, the fish. She could see its scales, just faintly. Those were just the big constellations, though there were hundreds and hundreds of others; she had memorized them, sitting wrapped in a blanket with her mother on nights on the *Pamela Jane*. Lying on the sand, Maya started with the constellations in the east and let her eyes travel west and read them across the sky as tiredness overtook her. Farther down the beach the phosphorescent glimmer of the tide pools glowed on and she fell into a troubled sleep.

Later she thought she half woke, to see Helix sitting close to the fire for light, intently studying the pages of the logbook. She wanted to stop him—he had no right to be looking at their book—but sleep was too powerful and it pulled her back under before she could resist.

❧ Chapter Nine ❧

Good-bye ＊ *More from the Logbook* ＊ *The*
Ghostly Barge ＊ *A Map for the Children* ＊ *Frightening Cargo*

The following morning Maya woke in the early breeze
coming off the sea, gently rattling the palms. Over the rocks
on the next beach, the Limmermor turtles were trundling
down from the dunes toward the shore. All around them the
sand was smooth and cool and white and the ocean was calm.
Maya woke Simon as Helix was returning from the edge of
the jungle with fruit for their breakfast. The logbook had been
returned to Simon's backpack, and Maya wondered if perhaps
she had only dreamed she had seen Helix reading it the night
before. She bathed and changed Penny, noting with some alarm
that the diaper supply was dwindling and would likely not last
the day.

The children ate breakfast and tossed the fruit peels to an
inquisitive turtle who had come and was waiting a few feet away
and then they were off, leaving the beach behind and heading
back into the jungle. They were headed farther down the river,
to where Helix said there was a dock. Maya's shoes were damp.
They chafed her feet and she winced with each step. The
children walked even slower than they had the day before. Only
Penny, riding in the sling and babbling away, seemed cheerful.
Maya told Simon about the creatures they had seen in the tide
pools the night before and he listened with interest, frowning
slightly as he thought. The sun climbed and in a short while it

was brutally hot. Maya tried not to think about how much her feet hurt. She was having a hard time putting the memory of the evening before at the tide pools with Helix out of her mind, though she couldn't say why it was making her feel so strange. She was still cross at him, and worried about what he had said. She would be happy when he was gone and they were on their own again.

In an hour they had reached a dilapidated wooden dock on the river's edge. The dock and the stretch of the river were deserted.

"This is as far as I go," Helix said. "A boat should be by here sometime today."

Maya and Simon looked down the brown curve of the river, rippling over deadheads and stones here and there.

"Are you sure you won't come with me?" Helix asked.

Maya nodded.

Helix looked worried. He sighed, then he whistled for Seagrape and the bird coasted down out of the trees and landed on his shoulder. In one swift motion, Helix yanked out several of her long green tail feathers. The parrot squawked in protest and nipped Helix's cheek. She flew up and perched on a branch, where she grumbled and ruffled her feathers.

"Sorry," Helix called up to her. Then he cut a thin string of animal hide from his bag of arrows and he quickly tied the feathers to the string and then knotted the two ends together. He handed the necklace to Simon.

"Keep this on all the time," he said. "It will help protect you. And you take this," he said to Maya, passing her his spear. "Don't be afraid to use it."

Maya took it in surprise. It was heavy and a sharp steel blade was fitted to its end. She propped it on the ground, blade in the air, and tried holding it as a walking stick, like Helix did. Simon slipped the leather necklace over his neck and touched the smooth green feathers.

"Thank you," he said. "But protected from what?"

"From some things, not others," said Helix. He looked like he was about to say something else, but then he didn't.

"Well, good-bye," he said finally. "Maybe we'll meet again."

Maya smiled stiffly. "Thank you for your help," she said. "Good-bye."

Helix turned and vanished into the soft blackness of the jungle. Seagrape circled the river a few times and then swooped, screeching as she flew over the children's heads, and then disappeared after Helix. The children were alone again.

Simon was quite dashed by Helix's departure.

"I liked him," he said morosely. "He was fun."

Maya shrugged. "It's better now, just the three of us again. Now we'll find Mami and Papi. Helix was only going to get us into trouble."

"So what do we do now?"

"Wait, I guess. He said a boat would be by sometime later on."

Simon wandered down the edge of the river a little and dug for worms on the muddy banks. Occasionally he tossed pebbles into the river. Penny fell asleep in the shade of a banana plant. Maya made herself comfortable on the grass and tried to stop her thoughts from turning to Helix. She tried to make herself think about her usual daydream, of living at Granny Pearl's and going to school. But it was hard to hold the daydream in her mind this time. When she was sure that Simon was too far down the riverbank and too absorbed in whatever was living in the mud there to see her, she reached for his backpack and took out the logbook from the *Pamela Jane*.

She turned its pages slowly. The first few were blank, except for the very first, at the bottom of which was a red wax seal. She'd never noticed it before. She couldn't make out what the insignia was. She ran her finger over the raised edges of the seal and turned the page. Her parents had made all sorts of notes, most of them in shorthand. The cryptic words, scrawled hastily, yielded no wisdom. But in her current predicament, the possibility of any slight glimmer of communication with her parents took on special, secretive weight. She looked again at the complicated mathematical equations, notations of water temperature and salinity, measurements of fish, diagrams of unusual shells, charts showing the progress of peculiar weather systems, and illustrations of extraordinary marine life.

She noticed that on almost every page he had written things about something called Element X. *High density of Element X present in crouching oysters found at 13 degrees south, location surprising, contradicts earlier findings . . . Element X, still unidentifiable . . . Structure of Element X determined unstable . . . High concentrations of bioluminescence in creatures found in the Tropical Kala Stream . . . Origin of Element X???* What were her parents pursuing? Was this part of their work for the Red Coral Project? Maya wondered if it had something to do with their argument with Dr. Fitzsimmons.

Maya's eye stopped on a page with sketches of the three children. They were drawn in her father's hand—she would know it anywhere—and a lump rose in her throat.

The first was of her, Maya. Look at how his pencil had lifted her hair as though a breeze had caught it! She was sitting there, chin in one hand, gazing broodingly out to sea. She looked so glum! Was that how she looked to them all? Who would want to be around such a misery? He had drawn in the tiny white scar on her temple and her ear where it showed through her hair. Such loving attention to detail. Maya studied the picture closely. The only mirror on the *Pamela Jane* had a jagged diagonal crack through the middle of it, and the tin on the back was peeling off and the glass was fogged with scratches. So try as she might, craning her neck and peering sideways, she had never been able to see herself clearly. But she was pretty, how he had drawn her.

She turned the page and found a sketch of Simon. It was Simon, but not just Simon, it was Simon the way her father saw him. He was squinting and looking up from where he was crouched on the deck, examining what looked to be a spiny lobster. It was so exactly Simon that Maya laughed a little bit. Her father was quite a good artist—he had not only drawn their physical likenesses, but had captured their personalities, too, which only someone who loved them as much as he did could have done.

And then, on the next page, a pencil sketch of Penny, sleeping in the crib her father had carved for her from driftwood. Penny was barely visible beneath a light blanket. There was the fat curve of her cheek, her sweetly closed eyes, and the angelic ruff of curls on the top of her otherwise bald head. But a shell on the deck beside her crib was drawn with more detail, more intricacy. Penny's face was still too young, changing too quickly, to be captured in something as still as a drawing.

A shiver went through Maya. If she didn't find their father, Penny would never know him and he would never know Penny.

Simon was plodding slowly down the riverbank toward her,

so Maya closed the logbook and slipped it back into his backpack. She lay back and closed her eyes and pretended to be sleeping so that he wouldn't talk to her. She felt too strange and emotional right then—filled with so much love for her family she thought she might weep—but if he spoke to her she was afraid she would snap at him. Why was it like that with family?

She heard him sit down near her on the grass. In a little while, when the weepy feeling had passed, Maya sat up. Simon was idly flipping the pages of the logbook.

Simon stopped reading.

"What is it *about*?" he asked. "And what's it all doing in our ship's log?" Perplexed, he turned back to start at the beginning again. "Hey," he said after a while. "There's something funny. Look at this—see?"

He tilted the book so that the light caught it at different angles.

"The first few pages of Papi's notes have funny shiny squiggles on them—on the paper. I didn't notice them before."

"Maybe something spilled on the pages," Maya said. She wandered to the jungle's edge and climbed a guava tree and began tossing the fruit to the ground below.

When Simon looked up again he saw a wooden barge appearing around the bend in the river, traveling slowly toward them on the current. Maya caught sight of it then, too, and she jumped down from the tree to join Simon. She had to blink several times to be sure she was really seeing it. Its wood was bleached ghostly by the elements, and except for a few coils of rotting rope, its deck was bare. It looked as if it was a wreck dredged up from the deep—it seemed remarkable that it was even afloat. A faded blue tarpaulin was stretched over the middeck to provide shade. It was empty except for its captain, a sunburned older man with dark skin and a blue cap pulled down over his shiny black hair.

"Hello!" Simon called, waving.

The man seemed surprised to see three children there and he stared at them as he cut the engine and the barge glided alongside them. They had gathered up Penny and their belongings and were waiting for him. Maya smiled politely as the barge came to rest against the dock.

"Hello, sir," she said. "Would you please be able to give us a ride down the river?"

"You're all alone?" the bargeman asked, baffled. He looked past them into the jungle, but of course there was no one there.

"Yes," said Maya. "We're trying to get to Port Town."

"To Port Town?" the bargeman repeated. He lifted his cap for a moment to scratch his forehead. "That's miles and miles away. And this river goes deep into the jungle—very deep into the jungle—before it gets to Port Town. It isn't safe for children."

"That's okay," said Simon cheerfully. "We aren't scared."

"If you'll take us, we can explain," said Maya. She didn't want to lose any more time standing on the edge of the river when they could already be on their way to Port Town. She had studied the bargeman quickly and decided that she could trust him. He had kind eyes.

"Please," she said. "It's urgent that we get there as soon as possible."

A branch cracked loudly in the jungle behind the children and they jumped, startled. The bargeman's eyes flew quickly to the wall of trees, and Maya was alarmed to see fear in them. She suddenly felt very vulnerable standing there exposed on the riverbank and she badly wanted to be on the barge and moving.

"Well," said the bargeman. He seemed to be agonizing about what to do. "I can't just leave you here like this. . . ."

Something rustled in the trees and the bargeman made his decision. He reached out a hand for the children to grab.

"Come on," he said. "Hop on."

Simon jumped onto the barge first and turned to smile at Maya. Maya hesitated for a moment—*was* this the right thing to be doing? But when the bargeman reached out his hand to her she grabbed it and, holding Penny tightly, leaped onto the barge. The captain started the engine again and the barge left the dock, a fan of surf in its wake, and they were off. Maya looked behind her and saw that the sound had come from a gentle, snub-nosed agouti that had come down to the river to drink. She leaned back against the railing and breathed a sigh of relief. The bargeman retrieved a small wooden box from the cabin and put a blanket in it, and Maya rested Penny down gratefully.

"Who are you?" the bargeman asked. "And what are you doing out here on your own?"

"I'm Maya, this is Simon, and this is our little sister, Penny," said Maya.

"We're looking for our parents," said Simon, quickly describing them for him. "Have you seen them?"

The bargeman shook his head, frowning. "I'm sorry," he said. "I haven't."

The children had been hopeful for a second, but at his answer they sighed. They explained their story to the bargeman, who told them his name was Rodrigo. He listened in amazement and when they had finished, he looked at them from beneath his blue cap, his eyes dark and serious.

"I've seen strange things out here," he said. "But nothing

that looked quite so out of place as the three of you. You gave me a real shock when I came around the bend and saw you. You're very lucky, you know. Children don't usually survive long in the jungle."

~ ~ ~

Rodrigo was calm and gentle and Maya felt safe with him. He told them that Helix had been right and Port Town was the best place for them to go. Maya began to relax and believe that in a short time they would reach help. Everything would be fine after all. The children listened as Rodrigo talked to them about Tamarind. He told them that they were in the South, on the Nallanda River. The river began in the mountains in the North and looped around until it finally emptied out into the sea near Port Town. He explained that he was a trader and brought goods back and forth from Port Town to the people in the jungle.

Simon had an idea. "Would you draw us a map of the island?" he asked. He withdrew a stubby pencil from his pocket and handed the logbook to Rodrigo.

Rodrigo glanced ahead of them but the river was calm and wide, so he let Simon take the wheel. Balancing the logbook in one hand, with the other he drew the island. It was shaped like a fat oval, and was longest from east to west. Then he drew a wavy line—the river they were on, presumably—which began in the middle of the island and struck out boldly across the interior before making a loop and again heading south, where it emptied into the sea. At its point of origin, Rodrigo scribbled a huddle of triangles, a range of mountains that divided the island in half. In the waters off the west of the main island he drew a few small blotches.

"These are the Lesser Islands," he said, "where it sounds like you landed. And all this here on the main island—" The pencil made scratching noises against the paper. "Is jungle." Rodrigo drew in more rivers and then began putting points along the southern coast of the map, drawing in one point on the southwest coast more heavily than the others.

"Maracairol," he said. "The capital of Greater Tamarind."

"How do you know the island so well?" Simon asked, impressed. He loved maps.

"I used to be a schoolteacher," Rodrigo said, smiling. "A long time ago." He began to sketch a few other features, but the river they were on, the real river, had narrowed and he handed the logbook back to Simon and took the wheel again. Maya looked at him with new interest. Unlike most people her age, Maya had never had a real schoolteacher before and so she was eager to know everything she could about school. But she felt shy suddenly and didn't know what to ask.

"Maya wants to go to school on land," said Simon.

"There aren't any schools left on Greater Tamarind," said Rodrigo. "Now, you'll have to let me concentrate for a moment, the currents are tricky here and this barge has seen better days."

Rodrigo kept his eyes on the river ahead of them, and the barge took the tiny series of rapids smoothly and then they were out of the white water. Simon studied the map and then put the logbook back into his backpack and watched as the green walls of the jungle slid by.

Though a barge on a river is not the same thing as a sail-boat on the open sea, there was something comforting about being on the water again. They glided along, bright blue parrots flying overhead and hummingbirds coming out over the boat, their tiny wings whirring. Animals came to the river to drink water, and the children saw all sorts of wildlife: a mother ocelot and her cubs; hairy-toed sloths clinging to branches on the fringes of the jungle (Simon counted seven of them in total); enormous yellow butterflies (each of them was bigger than Penny); and hundreds of birds—toucans, parakeets, scarlet macaws, and snowy-white egrets, who stood in the shallows on their stilt legs and watched as the barge slipped past. As Rodrigo had promised, Simon saw monkeys coming down to drink and the barge even nosed through a family of alligators floating in the middle of the river, basking in the sun.

Simon sighed happily. The world made sense to him at that moment. They were on their way to the place where they would be able to find help for their parents, and at some point soon they would all be reunited and everything would be fine. Better than fine, in fact. Their lives would actually be better than they had been before, because now they had survived the evil Lesser Islands with their man-eating vines, they had made two new friends (Rodrigo and Helix, even though Helix was gone now), and they were on a thrillingly creaky old boat on a river in the middle of a jungle and they had seen monkeys and alligators.

"May I explore the deck?" he asked Rodrigo.

Rodrigo nodded and Simon ran off to the bow. He stayed up there for a while, looking out for wild animals up ahead on the riverbanks before he returned to the main deck, pausing to crouch down and peer inside the cabin.

Rodrigo came to life then.

"Don't go in there!" he shouted, but it was too late.

Simon stepped back up onto the deck, his face pale.

"You have guns," he said. He stared at Rodrigo, betrayed.

Maya could just see into the grimy windows of the cabin, where there were crates stacked with all sorts of guns, black and vicious, sticking out at all angles. There must have been hundreds of them. And around them were crates of grenades and wires and explosives. What kind of man would be carrying guns down a river? She looked at Rodrigo fearfully.

The rest happened quickly. The river narrowed and turned a bend and Rodrigo had to pay attention to steering the barge. Maya saw a flicker of movement in the jungle up ahead and then they rounded the bend and came face-to-face with a group of soldiers standing on the banks of the river, a thorny nest of rifles pointed at the crew of the barge.

❊ CHAPTER TEN ❊

Ambush! ❊
Rodrigo's Story ❊ *A Change in Plans* ❊
On the River at Night

Don't shoot!" Rodrigo cried. "I'll bring her alongside the shore!"

He began turning the wheel and the barge spun slowly around and headed into the soft muddy bank. "You two get down and stay down," he said under his breath. "Keep the baby quiet. Do whatever I tell you, the instant I tell you, do you understand?"

Maya and Simon flattened themselves on the deck of the barge, shielding Penny. They felt the barge rock as the first of the soldiers boarded, and they heard them shouting at Rodrigo. Maya heard what she was sure was the sound of a rifle butt hitting him. She turned her head and watched the soldiers. They were wearing camouflage uniforms and they had black bands tied around their foreheads and masks of charcoal painted around their eyes. One kept his gun aimed at Rodrigo, who stood there with his hands over his head. Another soldier went down into the cabin and returned a moment later. He shouted to the men on shore, and several more soldiers boarded the barge and began carrying cases of guns and ammunition out of the cabin and passing them up onto the bank.

"Who are they?" Maya heard one of the soldiers ask.

"They're my nieces and nephew," Rodrigo said. "They're just children."

"What about the boy?" asked the soldier.

"He's too young!" said Rodrigo. "When he's older, he'll be a soldier. But now—please—leave him be for another few years."

"Do you think we need more mouths to feed?" said the soldier. Maya watched as ten pairs of boots stamped over the deck and jumped from the railing back onto the riverbank.

"Keep moving," one soldier called. "You never saw us!"

"I never did," said Rodrigo, stumbling back to the wheel. The whole thing had happened so fast. The soldiers had probably been on board the barge for less than a minute. Maya and Simon stayed where they were until finally Rodrigo said they could get up again. Maya looked behind them. The riverbank where the soldiers had been was deserted now, and receding in the distance. She turned to look at Rodrigo. A trickle of blood ran down from a cut over his eye where the soldiers had struck him. Simon watched him fearfully.

"I'm sorry, children," said Rodrigo finally.

"Who were those men?" Simon asked. He still felt quite shaky.

"Soldiers," said Rodrigo. "The jungle around here is full of them."

Maya and Simon peered nervously around them. The jungle that moments before had been full of amazing animals once again looked menacing.

"When will this terrible war be over?" said Rodrigo, sighing deeply.

The war began over ophalla many years ago, Rodrigo told them. It was a stone, bluish white, as bright as diamond. It was found deep underground in some places in Tamarind. Legend said the earliest people in Tamarind had built their first cities from it, and those people were said to live for hundreds of years. It seemed true that ophalla must have had some sort of miraculous healing power. It had always been considered very precious, but it was thought that the last of it had been discovered and mined long ago. But then a vast new source was found in the jungles in the middle of the western end of Tamarind. There was a mad rush to seize it, and the Council of Old Families that had ruled Tamarind for generations began claiming all land that it thought contained ophalla. The problem was that the Council was in the South and was mainly made up of people from southern Tamarind, but most of the ophalla was found in the North.

"The Council began kicking people in the North off their land—land that had belonged to their families for generations," Rodrigo said, keeping an eye on the river ahead as he spoke. "The people in the North protested, of course. Many of their men began going into hiding in the jungle, where they lived in camps and staged raids on the South. That only made the southern soldiers behave more brutally. Soon civil war had broken out. In the early days there was violence almost constantly. There were battles in the jungles and in the mountains. All the boats and ships on this side were forced into service, carrying men and supplies for the government. They were frequently attacked by boats from the other side. Even river barges carrying potatoes to a market in town were attacked and sunk. Meanwhile, soldiers were sneaking into the towns and setting off bombs. There was death and hunger everywhere.

"The war raged on long after the new ophalla mines had dried up, though. The same thing happened that happens in every war. With every person killed, more people were inspired to join the soldiers or the rebels to avenge the deaths of their loved ones and the cycle continued and the war grew bigger.

"Eventually the towns and cities had all been so badly ravaged that there was no one left in power anymore and Tamarind fell into anarchy. It's remained that way ever since. It began to separate into tiny areas, with each little town cut off from every other town, and jungle cut off from coast, and the mountains dividing the island into two. Bands of rebel soldiers roam the jungles and terrorize the towns. The seas are run by men of the old war fleets who have turned into nothing more than pirates. No one is safe. People disappear all the time. They're kidnapped or killed in revenge attacks. Young men have no choice but to become soldiers. Everyone lives in fear."

The river narrowed for a stretch and dappled light from the overhanging trees slid over the barge. Then they left the sun altogether and were moving along in shadows. The muddy water swished around the hull of the barge. Maya could smell the damp, mulchy smell of the jungle pressing in on them.

Rodrigo wasn't looking at them at all now. His hands gripped the wheel, keeping the barge in the middle of the gloomy stretch of the river. His face grew dark. When he spoke again his voice was bitter.

"My wife was killed one day, in an explosion in the town we lived in. She had been a teacher, too. We had always planned to have children, but now, when I see what Tamarind has become, I'm grateful that I didn't bring new life into it."

Maya and Simon were silent, not knowing what to do or say. Maya wanted to be off that barge more than she had ever wanted anything. Rodrigo seemed to have forgotten them and was staring with black, angry eyes at the river ahead of them.

But just then Penny woke and began to cry, and with that peculiar and magnificent power that infants have, she made everyone forget everything else but how to make her happy again. Maya picked her up and rocked her, and Simon danced on one foot with his hand on his head making funny faces, and Rodrigo, looking completely surprised for a moment, then began whistling a tune so vigorously that Penny hiccuped once and her tears stopped as quickly as they started.

The river widened and the barge came out of shadows and back into a sunny stretch. Finally Rodrigo cleared his throat.

"I'm sorry, children," he said. "Life isn't that bad—you're here. I shouldn't have said what I did. But we have a problem now. It would have been fine for you to come all the way to Port Town with me, but I was supposed to deliver that cargo to a rebel camp about half a day upstream. When I get there and they find I don't have it, there's going to be trouble. I can't have you there for that."

"But what will we do?" asked Simon. He and Maya looked out at the dark jungle on either side of them. They were in the middle of nowhere.

"Don't worry," said Rodrigo quickly. "I have a cousin who lives with his wife a few miles downstream. You'll be safe with them until I come back. I can take you to Port Town then, when things have calmed down."

"We can't wait," said Maya at once. "We have to get to Port Town as soon as possible! We can't just wait here—"

"I won't take you with me any farther," said Rodrigo firmly, a sharp edge entering his voice. "Not now."

Maya recoiled, and Simon, too, seemed to shrink as Rodrigo spoke. It was no use arguing. Rodrigo had made up his mind. The sky darkened and Maya could smell rain on the air. The jungle oozed down to the river's edge, where clotted masses of foul-smelling flowers hung from low branches, trailing in the water. A snake wriggled down the muddy riverbank and swam alongside the boat for a moment. It began to rain, slowly at first. The children stared gloomily out at the river, dimpled beneath the drops. Fretful thoughts circled in Maya's mind. How long would she and Simon and Penny have to wait for Rodrigo to return?

To try to cheer them up, Rodrigo got a pair of hammocks from the cabin and shook the spiders out over the edge of the barge, then strung the hammocks between the beams under the tarpaulin. Being in a hammock put Simon in a better mood and he sat happily cocooned in it, watching the river slide past, the jungle dissolving in the mist. Maya climbed into hers and Penny fell asleep in her lap. Maya and Simon fell asleep, too, and when they woke it was dusk and the rain had tapered off.

Night fell swiftly and the moon rose above the palms and soon they were gliding along beneath its light. They passed tiny villages of just a few rows of wooden houses on stilts that sat on small crescent beaches, ivory in the moonlight. Music from strange instruments drifted out over the water. Loose seeds rattled in pods and dry grasses brushed together and animal-hide drums beat steadily. All along the shores of the river they could smell the robust odor of cassava and smoke. Sometimes the children could see people dancing around the fires. They left the camps behind, the fires shrinking to glowing orange embers in the distance, and ventured farther down the river, where the only sounds were the symphony of frogs and the occasional splash of fruit falling.

They reached a faded wooden house on stilts, standing by itself on the edge of the river, and Rodrigo moored the barge alongside it.

Maya and Simon had no choice. This was where Rodrigo would leave them.

❧ CHAPTER ELEVEN ❧

*The Wooden House on Stilts * Sojourn *
Rodrigo's Gift * Borrowing a Canoe*

The first couple of days that the children were with Rodrigo's cousin, Jose, and Jose's wife, Maria, it did nothing but rain, which was just as well, since Maya's and Simon's feet were blistered badly and needed time to heal. Maria made herbal poultices and wrapped their feet in them. They did a lot of eating and sleeping. Maria took care of Penny, singing to her in the kitchen as she worked in the days and rocking her to sleep each night. Maya had run out of diapers for Penny, but Maria showed her how to use a special type of soft jungle moss inside a diaper. She also showed Maya an abundant, plum-sized red fruit, which she said was what people in the jungle fed infants. It was good to have her sister taken care of by someone competent and kind, and Maya was grateful to have a rest. They were all exhausted.

After the first couple of days, between rain showers she and Simon would help with chores: feeding the pigs that snuffled in a pen down near the river; scything the undergrowth in Jose's cassava fields, which undulated in a green sea to hills in the distance; peeling ripe fruit to make juice; and raking cooking cassava on the outdoor stove. In the evenings Jose would paddle in one of the canoes to the middle of the river, where the drinking water was purest, and Maya and Simon would wait and help to carry the buckets back up to the house.

"You're very strong!" Maria told Maya, taking the bucket from her one day. "What a brave girl you are, to take care of your brother and sister like you do. Your mother would be very proud of you."

When rain kept the children inside the house, Maya's thoughts would turn worriedly to the question of what they would do if Rodrigo didn't come back. What if he had gotten into worse trouble than he thought when he had arrived at the rebel camp without the cargo? And even if he was okay, it would take another couple of weeks before he said he would be able to return for them. It seemed like an eternity.

It had become too painful for the children to look at the logbook, so it sat untouched in Simon's backpack until one afternoon during a break in the rain, when Maya took it down to the riverbank. She sat by herself turning its pages. An idea had occurred to her the evening before and she was looking for something in particular on the map. She turned to the page that Rodrigo had drawn and looked at it in amazement. A whole miraculous world had sprung to life. Simon had only given him a pencil, but somehow he had filled it in with pigments. He must have finished it during the rainstorm, without them knowing—his gift to them.

Mountain peaks shone dazzlingly in a jagged line across the island, and rivers spilled out of their heights and roared through vast green swaths of jungle. Tiny threads of streams wove through shaded valleys, and here and there lakes sat blue and placid. Harbors and inlets were etched precisely, and fleets of ships sailed around the coast. The map was populated with tribal camps, villages, and coastal towns. The capital city, marked by a star, beckoned on the southwest coast. Animals were drawn in miniature here and there, along with mysterious, intricate symbols that Maya could not decipher. Wavy roads followed the coastline and connected towns. A tiny crop of islands—Lesser Tamarind—sat off Greater Tamarind's western shore. Thick green vines waved from them. The waters around the island—the bays and harbors and reefs and currents and the mouths of rivers—were labeled, too, with strangely beautiful names: Zallalona River, Crooked River, First Hope River. Mermaids frolicked in the waters off the coast, and here and there were what appeared to be giants. An island with giants—it sounded like the island in her father's story. Could they have found the island of Papi's tales? But Maya thought all those stories had been made up to entertain them during the long trips between ports. Maya forced her attention back to the map in hopes that it would yield some clue about their predicament. Her eye roved over the page. It was only the western bump of Greater Tamarind that was colored in, the rest stretched out in an arid, tawny desert, without signposts of any kind.

Her eye fell on the Nallanda River and she found the spot where Rodrigo had told them they were. And there, just a little way down the Nallanda River, she saw what she was looking for: fine blue tributaries that branched off the main river and trickled off into the jungle. The tributaries bisected the vast green space and rejoined the Nallanda later, miles closer to Port Town. The barge would have been too big to travel on one of the tributaries, but not a smaller boat. A smaller boat like one of Jose's canoes. It would be possible, she thought, tracing her finger over the thin blue thread, to take a shortcut to Port Town on a tributary and cut out miles and miles of jungle. They would pass the outskirts of the abandoned ophalla mines and a smoking triangle that Rodrigo had drawn, whatever it was, but they would not have to go near them. Maya closed the book and looked out the window at Jose's canoes moored on the riverbank nearby. Each thin wooden boat was narrow and lightweight, and curved like an incisor. One of them would do it, she decided. They could take food with them, and she still had Helix's spear, which the soldiers who had ambushed the barge had not taken. She could use it for protection. They just couldn't afford to wait for Rodrigo any longer.

She waited until late that evening to tell Simon—she knew they had to leave without Maria or Jose knowing, since they would try to stop them, and she didn't want him to blurt out their secret.

"But that's *stealing*, Maya. . . ." he said.

"It isn't stealing if you really need it," Maya said. She was counting on her elder sister authority to convince him. "And, anyway, they have several of them. Don't be a baby, Simon."

Calling Simon a baby would always get him. Reluctantly he agreed that they would leave the next morning.

When the first milky light of dawn arrived, Maya was on her feet quickly. She woke Simon and managed to lift Penny up without waking her. Then, grabbing her backpack, which was already packed and ready, she left the note she had written for Maria in the middle of the room, and she and Simon crept silently from the house on stilts. They walked on tiptoe down to the river's edge, the grass still pearly with dew, and untied one of the canoes. They settled gingerly into it, small silver walls of water pouring in over the gunnels, and they pushed out over the river.

Scared that Jose or Maria would stir and discover that they were gone, Maya paddled quickly. But it wasn't as easy as it looked. Small silver waterfalls rushed in over the gunnels and soon the canoe was sitting low in the water. Simon turned to look behind them and the canoe nearly capsized.

"Simon!" Maya exclaimed. "I need you to concentrate! This thing isn't exactly seaworthy."

The canoe righted itself and before long the sun had risen, turning the river from orange to muddy brown, and the little wooden house on stilts was far behind them. Penny sat snugly in the sling on Maya's back. After a while, Maya saw the first of the tributaries coming up ahead on the left. Which one should they take? Before she could decide, the river had picked up speed and they glided right past the first one. The river was deceptively powerful and Maya realized in alarm that she didn't know if she was strong enough to get them off it. Sweat breaking out on her forehead, she began to paddle as hard as she could toward the river's edge, where they were approaching another tributary. The strength of the current was going to carry them straight past it!

"BAIL, Simon!" she shouted.

Maya paddled furiously and Simon bailed with a wooden bowl and at the last moment the tributary current caught them. They left the main river behind and headed into the narrow green gloom. Maya sighed in relief and rested, letting the water carry them along. The tributary felt safer and less exposed than the Nallanda River.

Maya felt the strength return to her arms and she began to paddle again, more slowly this time. The paddle splashed rhythmically and the canoe skimmed along. The jungle burbled and chirped around them. The children saw a monkey leaning down from a branch to drink from the river. Countless furry spiders scuttled to the other side of the tree trunks they passed and bright birds twitched overhead. Happily, the children were oblivious to the black snakes coiled on branches overhanging the river and the chomping piranhas circling beneath the boat, as well as the alligator that they glided right past, its two eyes like yellow lamps just inches from their elbows.

After some time they noticed that the water was growing shallower and finally it reached a dead end. Maya looked in dismay at the jungle around them. This wasn't on the map! She had thought they would meet the larger river again. They must have taken one of the tributaries that didn't go all the way through the jungle. What were they going to do? They consulted the map, but there was nothing that could help them take their bearings. They were lost.

"We're all alone," said Simon.

Since they couldn't paddle back against the current and they couldn't go any farther in the canoe, they would have to go on foot, heading, they hoped, toward the Nallanda River on the other side of the jungle. They spent the next few hours marching deeper into the jungle, where woolly spiders huddled in the crannies of trees and even the air seemed green.

❧ Chapter Twelve ❧

The Cloud Forest Village *
Valerie and Pascal * *A Volcanologist* *
The Last French Chanson

The children stumbled into the village—or rather, *under* the village—without realizing it. They would have walked right on through, noticing nothing, but Maya paused to shift Penny's weight in the sling and when she did, from the corner of her eye she saw a rope being drawn quickly up into a tree. She grabbed Simon and pointed above them.

Built between the branches of an enormously tall tree was a wooden house. The house had windows and doors and a porch with a railing. Its roof was thatched with palm leaves. To Maya's amazement, she saw another house in the next tree, and another after that. The houses were built high up in the cloud forest, the misty top layer of the jungle, and as the clouds shifted, some tree houses disappeared and others appeared. It was incredibly beautiful and Maya was speechless. A web of ropes and footbridges and ladders connected the houses. The sight was like standing on the deck of a tall ship and looking up into the rigging. People were running deftly along tightropes and bridges, and baskets were being passed back and forth along a pulley system.

When the people in the trees saw that the three newcomers on the ground had seen them they froze. Children stood stock-still on hanging bridges, and the baskets being passed between the huts ceased moving and rested there like great birds' nests. A murmur passed through the people in the treetops and then Maya and Simon saw a woman being lowered down to them in a chair connected to ropes from a branch high above—it was almost like the bosun's seat on the *Pamela Jane,* Maya thought. When the woman reached the ground she stepped out of it and stood staring at the children.

She was much older than their mother, but it was impossible to tell exactly what age she was. She didn't look like the rest of the people in the trees. Her skin was lighter and she seemed bigger, though it was hard to tell since everyone else was so high up that they appeared quite small. Her eyes were pale, pale green and her lips were colorless. She wore a faded green dress, on which Maya could just make out the faintest etchings of a long-ago pattern. Her hair was almost colorless, too. She didn't look scary, she looked worn out.

"Hello," Maya ventured finally.

The woman stared at them.

"Hello," Maya repeated. "Can you help us?"

A strange expression passed over the woman's face. "Pardon you must me. You must to pardon me," she said. "I am very rust with the old languages."

She seemed to be fumbling for the next thing to say. "Valerie Tétine," she said, putting her hand to her chest. "I am her."

With this pronouncement, a large smile broke over her face and tears filled her eyes.

"You must to pardon me," she said again. "I am amazement. To you. It has been so long to see anyone here. The lookouts did not see you until you were already under the village. But give me patience. The old languages will come back at me. Who are you? Why are you here?"

"My name is Maya, and this is my brother, Simon, and our sister, Penny," said Maya. "We're looking for our parents. They got swept overboard in a storm and we sailed to Tamarind."

Maya had been so focused on the woman that she didn't realize that the whole camp had begun to climb down the trees on rope ladders and chairs and were now suspended at different heights through the forest watching them. A few children had come right down onto the ground and gathered in a circle around Valerie and Maya, Simon, and Penny. They all wore skirts made of soft green leaves and they had shiny black hair and dark eyes.

"I was right," whispered Valerie. "You are from the Outside." She gazed at the children. "I think that you must to come with I and we can talk proper. And we must leave the ground before the bad creatures come!" Her gaze fell on Penny and stayed there for a moment. "Ah, beautiful, yes, the baby?"

She turned to the people gathered around and spoke to them in a language the children couldn't understand. A sympathetic whisper traveled up through the trees. A few women came forward, leaf skirts rustling, and patted the children on their heads. Then everyone began to melt back into the trees, climbing ropes and vines and standing on wooden platforms that were lifted like elevators up into the clouds.

"Do you think they're going to roast us?" Simon whispered to Maya.

"Hopefully they'll roast you first," Maya whispered back. "It's too bad you're so skinny."

"You're the biggest," said Simon. "If they roast anyone first, it'll be you. Unless they want just a little nibble, then they'll roast Penny first."

Penny gurgled.

"Enough," Maya whispered to Simon. "Keep your wits about you."

"Move with me," Valerie said. "Don't be fright, they won't to hurt you."

She started walking and the small crowd that had come down out of the tree parted. Maya and Simon and Penny followed Valerie. Other children ran behind them, talking excitedly to one another. One little girl ran up behind Simon and pinched him on the arm and ran off giggling with her friends.

Valerie took them to the foot of the great tall tree that she had come from. She tugged on a rope and a rope ladder fell down. She began to climb and Simon and Maya, with Penny in the sling, followed her. They climbed and climbed, past plump, spotted mushrooms that grew from knots in the trunk; past giant red moths, folded into soft triangles against the bark; past lines of leaf-cutter ants marching in a column to the base of the tree, crunching loudly on leaves just inches from the children's ears; past deep cushions of emerald moss and coiled vines and the silvery undersides of leaves; past a hollow in the tree trunk from which a round-faced owl peered out at them with yellow eyes; all the way to a wooden platform that turned out to be the porch of Valerie's house. Valerie offered them a hand up and they stood there, looking all around them and blinking in amazement.

Around them, stretching far into the jungle on all sides, were hundreds of tree houses, connected by ropes and ladders and footbridges. It was a whole village in the treetops. Pristine white clouds nosed their way through the village, sometimes passing right through one doorway of a house and out another. The whole village was forever vanishing and reappearing as the clouds rolled through.

"You must to meet my husband, Pascal," said Valerie. "Pascal!" she called, going into the house. "*Ou étes vous? Pascal!*"

The children waited. There was a sound of shuffling inside. Valerie reemerged, chattering away to a tall, broad-shouldered man with steely gray hair. He was an old man, but he had thick muscles in his arms and a rugged jaw. He was carrying a tiny metal instrument and when he saw the children he lifted his shaggy silver eyebrows for a moment. He questioned Valerie, who responded impatiently. Then he made a grumbling noise that Maya took to mean, "Oh, well, children are quite ordinary, even ones found wandering alone in the heart of the jungle. Now let me get back to my work."

Muttering in a deep gravelly voice, he went back inside and drew a curtain behind him. Alone on the porch again, Valerie smiled at the children.

"Um," said Maya. "Where *are* we?"

"That is a very big question," said Valerie, studying her. "Me, I don't ask that question. But right here is where the Cloud Forest People live. Look, listen, *écoutez,* we all have many questions, yes? You for I, and I for you? But you must have hunger! So, how about we have some food and we get to know each the other. And we ask the questions then, when my English comes back to me better. It's been so long since I spoke in the English, so long, so long . . ."

Her voice trailed off and again her eyes filled with tears.

"You *enfants* sit here. I'll be back with the dinner for us. Okay, yes?"

"Yes," said Simon, taking off his backpack and plunking down. "Come on, Maya," he said. "I'm tired. And we haven't had a real meal since dinner last night."

Dinner last night—they had still been with Maria and Jose

then. Maya felt a pang. The light was beginning to fade in the jungle. Simon was right, all they'd had to eat all day were bananas and mangoes they had picked along the way, and the cassava bread she had taken from Maria's kitchen. She sat down, taking Penny out of the sling and laying her down on the ground on her stomach. Penny was able to lift herself up onto her hands and knees in a crouch now. She didn't actually crawl or anything yet, she just wobbled around a bit. But still, she had only started doing that in the past few days. Maya sighed. She had to get Penny back to their mother.

Valerie went inside to fix dinner, and the children were left alone on the deck. From there they could see the activity across the village. Realizing Maya and Simon weren't a threat, people had gone back to doing whatever they were doing before the strangers had arrived. The treetops were bustling. There was a constant procession of woven baskets traveling between tree houses on a complex system of levers and pulleys. The baskets began empty and were hoisted almost out of sight in the heights of the trees and then were returned and transported from house to house, each basket brimming with a white foam of flowers, some of which trickled over the edges and drifted to the earth below, where the smallest Cloud Forest Children scurried about collecting them. A delicate, luxurious scent drifted through the trees.

"This place is amazing," breathed Simon. "*Real* tree houses! Where people *live*!"

Maya could tell how awed Simon was by the treetop village and she didn't want him getting any ideas about prolonging their time there. "We'll stay right now and eat and we'll ask if we can spend the night here," she whispered. "Maybe Mami and Papi came by this way, too. We'll find out what we can about Tamarind from Valerie—maybe she can tell us something useful. But we have to leave right away in the morning. Understand?"

Simon ignored her and tiptoed to the window of the tree house and was peeking through a break in the curtains.

"Come back," Maya hissed.

"Shhh," said Simon. "Come look."

Her curiosity getting the better of her, Maya knelt beside him and peered into the Tétines' tree house. Through the doorway to what must be the kitchen they could hear things clattering around and see the back of Valerie's pale green dress. Another doorway opened into what looked like the bedroom, with a dried grass mat on the floor. The main room, though, the one they were looking directly into, appeared to be a type of study or office. Pascal was leaning over a table spread with all sorts of copper instruments. He held a bell-shaped instrument to his ear, listening, and he was scribbling in a notebook. Maya noticed heaps of similar notebooks stacked on the far wall. Whatever Pascal was recording, he was serious about it. Just then he looked up, and Maya and Simon ducked quickly out of sight. Maya's heart pounded. She found Pascal alarming. She and Simon went and sat down at the other end of the porch. Simon was frowning.

"All those instruments on the table," he whispered. "I've seen them before—not those exact ones, but ones like them. They're what people used to use to study volcanoes—to tell when they were going to erupt."

"How do you know that?"

"When we were in Suriname last time, Papi took me to the museum there and they had a room all about volcanoes. You didn't come with us that day, you were in a bad mood."

Maya rolled her eyes.

"Wait!" exclaimed Simon. "I just remembered something."

Simon opened his backpack and withdrew the logbook and turned the pages briskly until he reached Rodrigo's map. His finger roved over the page until he found what he was looking for and then he brought it down, right next to one of Rodrigo's tiny drawings: a triangle with what looked like smoke pouring from its top.

"A volcano!" he said triumphantly. "Now we know where we are."

Maya looked eagerly at the map. She felt a great deal better knowing where they were. Now they had a chance of finding their way back to the river and on to Port Town. But a volcano? That was all they needed. Simon was frowning.

"Something's off," he said. "Those instruments that Pascal has are what people *used* to use to study volcanoes a long, long time ago. No one uses them anymore. Now there are machines that do everything for you. So why would he be using such old things?"

Maya didn't know—things were weird in Tamarind. Before she could respond, Valerie came back outside, arguing over her shoulder with Pascal. She set down a pot on the deck.

"He and his volcanoes!" she said to the children. "That's all he does—think about his silly volcanoes, that's how we ended to this place. He's a, how you say it? Volcanologist? He studies the volcanoes. It was his job. That is how we come to this place in the beginning. And now I have not stepped my foot on the ground in so many years, until I see you today. I tell Pascal that the only thing that will make me leave the cloud forest—to go to the bad place out there—" She motioned vaguely to the jungle. "Is if the volcano, it, how do you say—erupts one day. It is the only thing. Until then, we stay here, where we are safe."

She filled bowls with the contents of the pot: a thick yellow porridge with tender meat and vegetables. Hungry, the children dug in and fell into silence, their questions put aside. Valerie gazed at them happily.

Out over the tree house village, work seemed to be ending for the night. The baskets returning from the heights of the trees weren't sent back up again, and people looked like they were beginning to make their ways back to their tree houses. The aroma of cooking vegetables and spices from other houses began to fill the air. Valerie's gaze fell on Penny, who was chewing on the edge of Maya's wooden bowl. Valerie's eyes grew moist and luminous.

"You are too young to take care of baby," she said to Maya.

"No," said Maya firmly.

A slight shadow of a scowl crossed Valerie's face but then she brightened.

"May I hold the child?" she asked. Maya hesitated for a moment but then she passed Penny to Valerie, but the baby began to cry and Maya had to take her back.

"It is all right," said Valerie. "She will get used to me in time."

In time, thought Maya, trying to hide her surprise. How long did Valerie think they would be there?

Simon had been studying Valerie.

"You and Pascal don't look like the other people here," he said.

Valerie's gaze softened when she turned to him.

"Oh, *mon petit,*" she said. "We are not Cloud Forest People. We came here long, long ago. It is a far story. I mean it

127

is a long story. I will tell to you, but first, I wish to hear about you. Poor *enfants*—without parents!"

Suddenly and violently, Valerie began to weep. She hid her face in her hands. Maya and Simon felt horribly uncomfortable, and they looked guiltily at the floor of the deck.

"I am sorry," Valerie said, sniffling. "*Je suis désolée.* It is emotion, you see. You must to *excusez moi*! You are the first people here in all this time who are not from this place." She dabbed her eyes and took a few deep breaths. "But you must finish to eat. You are hungry! Me, I am too, how do you say? I am too overcome to eat. It is the emotion, you know. I have not seen other faces than Pascal and the Cloud Forest People for so long."

She dabbed her eyes again and then she looked at Penny and she smiled.

"We will have a treat," she said. "I will play the music for you, yes?"

She went inside and carried an old phonograph to sit in the doorway. She wound its handle and its gears made a whirring noise. She gingerly withdrew a brittle old record from a thin paper sleeve, yellow with age, and placed it carefully on the phonograph. The record began to turn and crackle like a fire just catching and then a scratchy song in French came through the shell-shaped speaker. Maya and Simon could tell that it was a very old song.

"It is old French *chanson*," Valerie said, turning up the volume on the phonograph. "The phonograph is from our boat. It belonged to my mother and I take it with me when we leave Paris. It was my gift from her. Now all the records break, though. This is the last one I have. It was the most popular song when we leave Paris. When it break, too, then, poof—all gone. No more of the old music. So I take very good care of it."

Her eyes filled with tears again.

A kernel of horror began to grow icily in Maya's stomach about Valerie and Pascal, about just how long they had been in Greater Tamarind. She remembered the mad zoologist on the beach. He had been from the Outside, too. Did no one who came from the Outside ever leave? The Outside! Maya was alarmed that she was already beginning to think of the world beyond Tamarind as the Outside World. If no one who arrived here ever left, how were she and Simon and Penny going to find their way home?

"Please to tell me," Valerie said, smiling and sniffling. "You said you came to here on a boat? How?"

Maya told her the story as briefly as possible. Valerie closed her eyes. "So sad," she whispered. "Poor children, poor children."

Maya and Simon looked down. It *was* so sad.

"But we think they might be here, in Tamarind," said Maya. "We met someone who may have seen our parents."

Something in Valerie's eyes worried Maya. It was a sad, knowing look.

"Have you seen our parents?" Maya asked. "Have they been here?"

"No, they haven't," said Valerie. "Oh, children, children," she sighed sadly. "This place—" She swept a hand over the dimming forest. "This place is strange and wild. *Strangement,* you know? You cannot fathom it. I cannot, Pascal cannot, the Cloud Forest People cannot, and you cannot. We are safe here. The Cloud Forest People are peaceful, but beyond . . . it is darkness."

And certainly darkness did seem to be creeping in all around them, thickening like smoke. No Cloud Forest People were left on the ground, all had retired to their tree houses for the night. There were no lights in the homes and one by one in the distance they slipped into darkness in the canopy. A faint bit of moonlight reached the porch where the children sat.

"Didn't you ever try to go home?" Maya asked.

Valerie seemed far off in her own thoughts.

"We tried," she said, her gaze returning to Maya and Simon. "Once. But there is nowhere to go," she said. "Children, *enfants*. There is no escape from this place."

Valerie told them that she had been a young woman when she arrived in Tamarind from the Outside. Pascal had been sent to study volcanoes in the Caribbean when a storm came, blowing them off course and grounding their ship on reefs. They rowed to shore, bringing with them what belongings they could, and by the time they reached the beach, their ship had slipped beneath the surface and was gone. Monkeys and parrots climbed and flew at the edge of the jungle above the beach, and the sultry green hills rose above them. They did not know it yet, but they were in Tamarind.

They decided that they would explore until they found a town. There were seven of them to begin with, and they followed a freshwater stream. At night Valerie wrote letters to her sister by the light of their campfire, still thinking that it wouldn't be long before they would reach civilization. Then the stream they had been following went underground and the jungle grew denser and they had to slow down. Their knives grew dull and it was difficult to cut their way through the tough vines. The first one of their company who they buried was the ship's cook, who had been bitten by a strange spider and did not wake up one morning.

The next one to disappear was the man who had been walking at the back of the line. At first they stopped and waited, thinking that he would come along. They shouted and shouted, and turned and retraced their steps, but they never saw him again. By then they were hungry and thirsty. They tried to drink the moisture in the cups of leaves, but it was not enough.

"Now I would know how to catch water, of course," said Valerie. "We learned everything from the Cloud Forest People. But then we were thirsty and frightened and we didn't know where we were, or even how to get back to the beach."

Valerie seemed to be sinking into memory and as she did her English improved.

"There were five of us. Me, my husband, Pascal, our old friend Pierre who studied volcanoes with Pascal, another passenger from the ship named Thomas, and the cabin boy, Louis. But then Louis started to complain that he was having trouble seeing, and when he woke up one morning he was blind. I can still hear him scream when he woke up and everything was dark. He was so terrified, poor boy. We took turns leading him through the jungle, but he began to come down with a fever and before long he was too ill to move. He was burning up. We laid him down and tried to comfort him, but there was nothing we could do. We had no medicine. He died and we bury him as best we could.

"We were very thin and hungry then and we thought we would die in the jungle, too. At night there were strange, tiny blue lights in the air all around us. I wondered if it was ghosts, spirits, black magic—and I was very afraid. Now I know it was only lighted bugs, jungle fireflies that—what is your word for it? Pollinate? That pollinate the cloud orchids. The lights were beautiful but they terrify us. We were so deep in the jungle that there was little change between night and day, but night was very most black. *Noir*. It seemed to press on our throats." Valerie lifted her hands to her throat. "Complete black darkness and then these little blue lights turn on and off.

"And then one day we realize that a man is following us. We never see him but we know he is there. He follows with us for three or four days. One night we fell asleep around our fire. I feel someone watching me in my sleep and I open my eyes and he is there, standing, looking down on us. I shouted and shouted and the others woke up and he disappeared. Pascal said that I had just had a nightmare.

"The next morning when we wake up, there is a pile of fruit left beside us for us to eat. We look all around and then we see a man jump down from a tree. I knew he was not going to kill us because he had stood over us when we were sleeping and if he wanted to kill us he do it then. He took the cupuaçu fruit from the pile and he split it on a rock and he comes to us with the pieces. Oh, my hand trembles when I took it from him! We did not take our eyes off him, but we eat the fruit and then we follow him and that evening we arrive here, at the Cloud Forest People camp.

"You can imagine our shock when we see the sight of all the tree houses and bridges and ladders and ropes—a whole world above our heads. All the Cloud Forest People came out to see us and they took us up the ladders into the trees and we spent the night up here and we have been here ever since. The Cloud Forest People adopt us. They gave us a tree house to live in. We moved to this tree later, when we knew how to build better. They taught us how to farm the cloud orchids. In time we learned the language. Pierre, God rest him, never really learned it. Until he died two years ago he was always gripe, gripe, gripe."

Valerie pointed to the house in a nearby tree that stood empty and dark.

"I write letters to my sister every week since the shipwreck, even now. I keep them all. She was my younger sister, but she'll be *une vieille,* an old woman now, if still she is alive. If she had children, they would be grown up. I try to picture what she would look like, where she lives. But sometimes I just tell myself I will not think of this—I won't see her again, so what does it matter?"

Valerie sighed deeply.

"Most of the time, I feel like I am one of the Cloud Forest People. But seeing you, speaking European languages, so many memories are brought back to me. But those memories I have, they are from a long-ago time. It is gone. If even we could get back now it would all be change. All be different."

"But you said you tried to leave once," said Maya. "You tried to go back home?"

"Once," said Valerie. She paused, her face hidden in the shadows. "It was a mistake."

Moonlight sifted through the trees, and Maya and Simon waited quietly for Valerie to speak.

"We had been here perhaps for several months," she began. "Pascal, Pierre, Thomas, and I took food to last several days and we left on foot. We had been walking for three days when we got close to civilization. We heard guns and cannons and we could smell smoke far up ahead. The next day we came across a group of people who were fleeing from their town. They were wounded and hungry. They looked like ghosts walking to us through the trees. They carried a child who would not wake up. Soon we passed others like them. There was a war, they said. They were fleeing and we traveled with them for some days.

"At night when the fireflies came out they were all terrified.

134

They believed the fireflies were evil spirits who would steal their souls. And it seemed like there must be evil spirits here, to make these people look as they did, so hungry and scared. We kept going and we found bodies rotting in the jungle, left where they had fallen. We thought that maybe another part of the island would be safer, so we changed our direction, but everywhere it was these fleeing ghosts. So many of them. There was no place safe. And then finally we were attacked by soldiers. Thomas and some others were killed. Pascal, Pierre, and I escape, and we come back here to the Cloud Forest Village, to the peaceful tribe, who live high up, where the air is pure.

"I tell Pascal I will never go out there again. Out there it is bad, here it is safe. It was time to give up our hope to return home. Here is home now. All that will make us leave is if that volcano goes up in fire—the volcano is the only thing worse than facing what is out there. But until then, we stay."

The phonograph had wound down and was silent. Valerie looked out over the darkness before she spoke again.

"And so, we are froze here," she said. "Froze, in the middle of the hot jungle."

🐬 🐬 🐬

Valerie set up grass mats for Maya and Simon on the deck that night. She offered to take Penny inside to sleep in a cot, but Maya said that she would keep her sister with her. Valerie seemed disappointed. Maya was glad when Valerie left them and she was alone with Simon and Penny again. Greater Tamarind was such a strange place, full of so many people with dark, secret sadnesses. Maya felt grateful that she had her brother and her sister with her and that at least this part of their family was still together.

"Maya?" Simon whispered.

"Yeah?"

"How long do you think that Valerie Volcano has been here?"

"I don't know," whispered Maya. "A long, long time." She paused. "Wait a minute," she said. "What did you just call her?"

"Valerie Volcano," repeated Simon.

"Valerie Volcano," said Maya. She began to giggle.

It was not just the name, but the serious way that Simon said it that seemed so funny to Maya. And they were both exhausted and their nerves were frayed, so it didn't take much to set them off into a fit of giggles. When the giggles started to subside, all one of them would have to say was "Val" and the other would snort and then they would lie there laughing help-lessly for the next few minutes, their hands clamped over their mouths.

"Okay," Maya said finally. "We should sleep now. We're going to have a long walk ahead of us tomorrow."

"We could stay a little longer," said Simon. "To explore the village."

"No way," said Maya. "We leave first thing."

They were quiet for a few minutes.

"Hey, Maya, look!"

"Shhh," whispered Maya. "It's time to sleep."

"No, look, for real!" whispered Simon. "I think it's those lights Valerie was telling us about, the jungle fireflies!"

Maya opened her eyes.

There were indeed sparks of mysterious blue light, blinking on and off in the darkness beneath the canopy. There were a couple, far across in the next tree, then there was one, twinkling in the air just over the deck where the children lay. As it came close Maya could see the clear shell of its body and the luminous filaments of its insides. More appeared and filled the air, until the children could see them gathered thickly as stars all across the Cloud Forest Village, all the way into the distance where they were just pale glimmers, trembling like distant galaxies.

✤ CHAPTER FOURTEEN ✤

Charge of the Piganos ✳ *Penny in
Danger* ✳ *Simon Explores the Cloud
Forest Village* ✳ *Vertigo* ✳ *Netti and
Bongo* ✳ *Rebels* ✳ *Vanishing Village* ✳
The Child Stealer!

Valerie had warned the children the night before about the morning charge of the piganos. Still, when Maya and Simon were jolted out of sleep by the thundering roar of the approaching herd, their hearts pounded and it took them a moment to remember where they were. They crawled to the edge of the deck in time to look down through the milky dawn light to see a herd of pig-like creatures stampeding below the village. They were ferociously ugly animals, with great saber tusks and giant snouts and stunted little legs. Even the females had woolly beards. The odor rising from their hides was foul.

The herd galloped beneath the village and their thundering hooves faded into the distance. Maya hoped that they would be far away before she and Simon and Penny left that morning. The horrible smell dissipated and she looked out through the clouds of mist billowing through the treetops and soft wet leaves and the sweet-smelling white flowers. The treetop village was coming to life. Villagers, mere shadows in the cloudy light, were climbing high into the branches to pick the flowers and there was the faint squeak of ropes as empty baskets made their way into the heights. Penny had woken and begun to cry. Babies have all sorts of different cries, and this one alerted Maya instantly. It sounded distressed.

Thinking that she must be hot, Maya lifted the light sheet lying over Penny. Her breath caught in her throat as she saw the rash, red as strawberries, blooming puffily over Penny's stomach and back, her arms and legs. Even her toes. Maya saw at once that it wasn't an ordinary rash that babies get. It was something strange and ferocious. The blood in Maya's veins turned cold and she tried to stop herself from panicking. *Penny can't be sick,* she thought, terrified. *She can't be.* She felt Penny's forehead with the back of her hand, as their mother used to do. It felt hot. But was it? Maya had never felt Penny's forehead like that before and she wasn't sure. Maybe it was always like that. What was she supposed to do? Maya desperately wanted her mother. Penny began to cry in earnest and Maya picked her up and began to rock her. It took all of Maya's might to stop herself from crying, too.

Valerie came out and when she saw the rash her eyes widened and she disappeared immediately down the tree, promising to be back in a few moments. Maya knelt rocking Penny, murmuring soothing things. Simon sat silently, his eyes large with fear.

Valerie returned with a brown root in the pocket of her dress, which she took to the kitchen and boiled and mashed into a pulp. When it cooled she smoothed the paste over the baby's skin with a damp cloth. She spoke to herself in French as she worked. Before the children's eyes, the welts began to subside and Penny's sobs tapered off. Soon she was resting quietly in Maya's arms. Maya took a shuddery breath.

"Will she be okay?" she asked.

"*Oui,*" said Valerie. "Not to worry. It is from a plant that must have brushed against her. But she will be fine."

"From a plant?" asked Maya hoarsely. "Then why didn't Simon and I get it, too?"

"Oh, you are too tall," said Valerie.

"Too tall?" asked Maya.

"She means we're too old, probably," said Simon. "Maybe it only affects babies."

"*Enfant* is fine, yes," said Valerie. "But we must watch her. The thing, how do you say? The rash, it can come back with a very bad fever for a few days. After that, no rash, *enfant* is okay." She gazed down at Penny. "She is very precious, yes?"

"Yes," whispered Maya.

Maya did not want to chance moving on until they knew for sure that Penny would not get a fever, so she agreed to stay in the Cloud Forest Village for the next few days. Simon went off on his own to explore the village—Valerie assured Maya it was fine, as long as he stayed in the treetops and didn't go down to the jungle floor below. Valerie urged her to go with him, but Maya refused. She was too shaken to let Penny out of her sight. She spent the morning on the platform porch, amusing Penny with flowers and twigs and her spare shirt, which she tied into a rag doll. Pascal came out a few times and glanced down at them from beneath his bushy silver eyebrows before shambling back inside. She could hear the clatter of copper instruments from inside the hut.

Later, when Penny napped, Maya leaned back and watched the lacy green leaves above her shuffle in a fine breeze. The breeze loosened stray orchids and they drifted past, white and cool as clouds. She had nothing else to do, so she took the log-book from Simon's backpack and turned to the map. If they were near the volcano that Rodrigo had drawn, then they had not come nearly as far as she had hoped they had. The best thing they could do, she thought, once Penny was well, was to keep heading east until they found the river again. Even if they had to walk along the Nallanda River all the way to Port Town, it was still a shorter route than they would have taken with Helix. Though she couldn't help but reflect on the thought that if they had stayed with Helix, they would have been there already.

That settled, there was nothing else to do but turn the pages, looking at the dreamy pageant of sea life floating across its pages. Suddenly a phrase returned to her, from the conversation overheard in St. Alban's. Her father's voice: *from deep in an equatorial jungle*. He had said something about something coming from an equatorial jungle . . . what was it? Maya struggled to remember but his words escaped her. She wondered if it was part of the puzzle somehow.

By the afternoon she was bored and Penny was sleeping peacefully so she was happy to see Simon return. As usual, he seemed to have made friends with everyone already. An entourage of children jogged across the bridge with him and waited, smiling and waving at Maya. The girls made sympathetic faces, nodding to Penny. Simon had found nothing out about their parents, but he was full of interesting details about the workings of the camp.

"Want me to stay with Penny for a bit, so you can explore?" he asked.

Maya shook her head. "It's all right," she said. "I'll stay."

"No, no," said Valerie, coming out onto the porch. "You go to see the village. Play with the other children! I stay with baby." She squeezed Penny's pudgy little hand between her fingers. Before Maya could protest, Valerie had scooped the baby up out of her arms.

"Come on, Maya!" said Simon. "Come with us!"

Maya looked worriedly at Penny, but she seemed fine and did not appear to be bothered by Valerie holding her. Valerie gazed down at her, rapt.

"All right," said Maya finally. "Just for a little while, though."

"Yay!" cried Simon. "Come and meet everybody. This is Bongo, he's been showing me around. Everyone else is with him."

A smiling, black-haired boy waved to Maya, and Maya waved back. A necklace with a nutshell at the end of it rested on his neck.

"He has an older sister," said Simon. "They live right over there, see, just a few houses away."

Maya looked through the trees to the tree house Simon was pointing to. A girl standing in the doorway ducked quickly inside.

Maya suddenly felt free—she looked at the treetop village spreading out before her, waiting to be explored. It *was* amazing, and it would be so fun to be with other children. She smiled shyly and went to join them. But as soon as she stepped foot on the hanging bridge and felt it wobble beneath her, she was overwhelmed by dizziness. The earth below seemed extraordinarily far away and the spotted light through the canopy felt crawly on her skin. What was wrong with her? She used to climb the rigging of the *Pamela Jane* without batting an eye.

"Come on," said Simon. "It isn't that bad. You'll get used to it!"

The Cloud Forest Children waved her on encouragingly. Gripping the rope railings, Maya inched forward until she was several paces out over the hanging bridge that connected Valerie's porch with the rest of the village, but then she glanced down and her stomach felt as if it dropped to her feet and the earth heaved below her as if it were an ocean. She couldn't go any farther—there was no way. She wouldn't be exploring the village or playing with the other children after all. She felt bitterly disappointed.

"Go ahead," she said to Simon through clenched teeth. "I'll stay here."

"Just put one foot in front of the other," said Simon.

"Simon, *go*," said Maya irritably. "It's not going to help if you're watching."

"You know what Mami always tells you," said Simon. "You're going to miss out!"

He dodged around her and pattered across the bridge to the other side. The Cloud Forest Children waited behind her smiling, motioning her to go forward. One took a few steps out onto the bridge in front of her and tried to take her hand. Maya shook her head violently and clung to the guard rope.

Simon trotted back over the bridge toward her.

"Look," he said. "No hands!"

"Don't come crying to me when you fall and kill yourself," she said.

"I can't come crying to you if I'm killed!" he called cheerfully. He stopped and bounced up and down a few times.

"Oh, STOP," Maya said. "You're making it jig!" She glared at him.

Simon laughed and ran off, the small band of Cloud Forest Children following after him.

Fine, Maya thought. Just fine. That rat. He'd be lucky if a pigano didn't eat him. He'd be lucky if Maya didn't FEED him to a pigano, actually.

Angry with herself, Maya felt determined that she would make it across just this one bridge, then she could turn around and go back to Valerie's. "Don't look down," she muttered to herself. Inching along gingerly, she made it a few feet farther before she snuck a glance down to the ground and the world began to spin. She squeezed her eyes shut for a moment and waited for the feeling to pass before she started again. When she reached the end of the bridge she gasped and leaped onto a platform, hugging the tree trunk. She looked ahead through the trees and she saw the girl who she had seen before, Bongo's sister, still watching her. Maya waved and the girl ducked back behind the door again, but then she looked back out and returned the wave. Simon and the rest of the Cloud Forest Children were nowhere in sight. A tear slid down Maya's cheek. It was always so easy for Simon. She wiped it away quickly when she heard a bridge squeaking and looked up to see the girl approaching her. The girl walked lightly over the bridge, unafraid. She stopped at the edge of the platform and looked at Maya shyly.

"Hello," said Maya.

～ ～ ～

Bongo's sister's name was Netti, and by counting on their fingers, Maya and she figured out that they were the same age. Netti was a thin girl, with dark shiny eyes like her brother's. She had knobby knees and elbows and she wore a dress stitched together from soft leaves. She knotted together a dozen cloud orchids into a type of scarf and draped them over Maya's

144

shoulders. They blocked Maya's view down to the ground, and Maya found she was able to walk across the bridges without being afraid. Netti took her to explore the village and later, when the flowers wilted and the scarf fell apart, Maya realized she had gotten used to running over the bridges and she didn't need it anymore.

The Cloud Forest Village was vast and everyone they met on the bridges and in the huts was friendly and gentle. Emerald snakes glided down tree trunks and rainbow-colored parakeets flitted between branches. Netti told Maya the names of things in her language and Maya repeated them diligently. Maya and Netti met Simon and Bongo and the other children and they raced over bridges together and spent hours swinging from ropes between tree houses, the green jungle passing in a blur, soft plants batting their arms.

Maya discovered a lot about the village. She learned that food was abundant in the trees: juicy red berries from curling vines; lichen that looked like spinach; crowds of giant mushrooms; even a type of amber beetle that the Cloud Forest People would pluck from the bark and pop into their mouths. In soil-filled hollows in the trunks they farmed different types of nuts. The main food was the cloud orchids themselves. Most work in the village went to gathering them from the lofty heights of the canopy, then separating the petals from the stamens. The meaty stamens were fried or roasted or left raw, and served with every meal. Water was hoisted up in buckets from a stream below and carried throughout the village.

Through hand gestures Netti told Maya about the volcano, and then took her up one of the elevators to the volcano viewing platform. They rose up, up, up through the leaves, the ropes of the elevator squeaking, and then broke out of the canopy into the light. Maya found herself in the middle of a bright blue sky, a few puffy clouds skating along, miles of jungle sprawling all around them and then there, to the north, the volcano. It was green at its base and climbed up into purplebrown rock. Thin steam rose from it, like a kettle. It had been so long since she had been in fresh, dry air that Maya breathed it in deeply, feeling the sun hot on her hair.

Maya and Netti went back to check on Penny a few times, but it was not until dusk that Maya returned for the night. Penny's rash was far better and Valerie was feeding her when Maya ran back across the bridge, out of breath and happy. It felt like such a long time since she had had a carefree afternoon!

They stayed in the Cloud Forest Village for the next few days, while they waited to make sure that Penny's rash wasn't going to worsen, and Maya escaped happily each morning to run and climb and play with Netti and the other children. She told herself that they couldn't do anything until they were sure that Penny was okay, and in the meantime, why shouldn't she be out with her new friends? After all, when had she really ever had a friend before? It wasn't fair that she had to be responsible for her siblings all the time, and for getting them all back to their parents. She knew that Penny was safe with Valerie, so when her worries intruded, Maya pushed them out of her mind as forcefully as she could. She would grab onto a vine and go hurtling through the air or scamper on ropes to the very tops of the trees where the orchid pickers worked, and by the time she reached the top, she would be so out of breath that the only thing in her mind was the sound of her pounding heart.

The one threat to Maya's enjoyment of those days was Valerie. Maya didn't like her very much. When Maya and Simon returned for meals, Valerie chattered to them about things they must beware of in the jungle: poisonous plants, piganos, soldiers, and, most dangerous of all, the Child Stealer. Valerie would usually wait until dusk to talk about the Child Stealer, as if she wanted to make Maya and Simon as scared as possible. Her face would pale and she would drop her voice to a whisper, as if she feared being overheard.

"They call her the Lady Who Rides the Jaguar," she'd whisper. "She kidnaps children who stray too far and she makes them her slaves."

But it was hard, with food in their stomachs and a safe place to sleep, and the promise of another day of swinging from vines and journeying deeper into the wondrous cloud forest, for Maya and Simon to feel much fear. They felt safer here than they ever had in Tamarind. The logbook lay untouched in Simon's backpack and they did not think beyond their days in the trees. After Valerie would go to bed, Maya would wait until the jungle fireflies came out and then she'd catch as many of them as she could in a large orchid she had plucked earlier. When the rest of the fireflies moved on into the jungle, she would kneel at the edge of the porch with the ones she had cupped in the flower, their electric bodies glowing through the translucent petals. She would wave the flower back and forth until, from several tree houses away, she would see an answering light from Netti's house. They would communicate in long and short flashes of light, a complicated sequence of Morse code that meant nothing except that they would see each other in the morning. After a while they would tire and release the petals. The fireflies would lift up and hover

like tiny sparks before dispersing and fading singly off into the
night.

~ ~ ~

Maya was returning to Valerie's one evening when she heard a
sharp, insistent birdcall and became aware that something was
happening across the Cloud Forest Village. People were reeling
in the last of the orchid baskets and dashing into their homes.
As she watched, they tossed what looked like sheets of leaves,
stitched together, out of their windows, camouflaging their
houses. It was as if the village was vanishing before her very
eyes. Just then Maya felt the bridge she was on begin to shake
and Simon, Bongo, and a couple of other children appeared.

"Run, Maya," Simon whispered. "Back to Valerie's! I don't
know what's going on but someone's coming!"

The birdcall still sounding, Simon grabbed her hand and
they ran over the last part of the bridge into the Tétines' tree
house. Pascal was throwing the sheets of leaves out the windows, and Valerie was sitting in the middle of the floor in the
house, rocking Penny back and forth and trying to stop her crying. She looked at Maya in relief when she came in and handed
the baby up to her.

"Please," she whispered imploringly, wiping tears from the
corners of her eyes. "You must make her to be quiet!"

Maya held Penny close to her and murmured in her ear until Penny stopped crying.

Pascal shut the door of the house and they all sat down in
the semidarkness. The piercing cry of the warning birdcall
ended and the Cloud Forest Village fell silent. Maya was eye
level with a crack in the wall and from it she looked out over the
village, except that it was as if there had never been a village

there. The rope ladders and suspension bridges had all been taken in, and the houses were invisible through shaggy masses of leaves. Then from the earth below, Maya heard the sound of feet approaching. Twigs snapped and leaves rustled. It wasn't just one pair of feet, it was many. And they sounded like they were in boots.

Pascal sat in the dimness, looking angry as usual, and Valerie's cheeks were pale. Bongo and his friends sat silently, but Bongo smiled reassuringly at Maya when she looked at him. The footsteps were getting closer. Simon tapped Maya's shoulder and pointed to a knot in the floor, through which they could see down to a small area of the ground below. As they watched, soldiers in uniform passed below. Maya kept absolutely silent. The soldiers wore different uniforms than those worn by the soldiers who had ambushed the barge. Their uniforms were olive green, not black, and even from up high Maya could tell that the fabric was frayed and patched and caked with dirt. They had rifles slung over their shoulders, the muzzles pointing unknowingly up into the treetops. They weren't making a great effort to be quiet, so they must have felt quite safe. They seemed tired. One picked up a fallen cloud orchid and twirled it between his fingers before dropping it, where it was crushed underfoot by soldiers marching behind him.

Maya glanced at Penny, who was looking watchfully at everyone around her. Thank goodness she was quiet now, Maya thought. She looked back down through the knot in the floor, but there were no more soldiers passing beneath. The footsteps seemed to be getting fainter. Swishing leaves and cracking twigs could be heard in the distance. Everyone in the tree houses stayed where they were for some time after the soldiers could no longer be heard.

"It was just soldiers," said Valerie, brushing her hair back with a trembling hand. "At least it was not her."

The Cloud Forest Village was just beginning to stir again. People were slowly opening their doors and coming out onto their porches. Valerie took Penny from Maya, and Maya went outside. The sheets of leaves were withdrawn into the windows and the bridges were hung between the trunks again. The climbing ropes were tossed back down and the baskets began squeaking on their pulleys back up into the lofty heights of the canopy. Maya ventured out onto the porch, the others following after her, when suddenly the warning birdcall pierced the air again. Maya turned in time to see Valerie grab all the children she could reach and pull them back into the tree house. Maya crouched down and froze, her heart hammering in fear.

In a few moments, without moving her head, she lowered her gaze to the jungle floor and then she saw, right below her, the largest jaguar she had ever seen. Sitting on the jaguar was a cloaked female figure whose face was hidden. The jungle all around had fallen deathly silent. Maya had never heard it like that before. The frogs and the crickets and all of the myriad chirping, whistling, whirring, buzzing, singing insects were silent. The woman held a lamp in front of her, lit by a strange white stone. Maya felt that the figure below must be able to hear her heart beating. She looked back to the tree house and met Valerie's gaze. Valerie's face was pale as a ghost's and her eyes were dark with fear.

Maya looked back down and when she did she saw that the figure on the jaguar was looking up now, directly at her, but a clump of leaves hid most of her face and all that Maya could see was a smile, a woman's smile, with curved lips, and sharp, straight teeth. Maya stopped breathing. Had the woman seen her? And then the woman lowered her head and the cloak hid her once again. The jaguar began moving and in seconds Maya could neither see the spotted orange fur of the immense creature nor hear the tread of its giant padded feet. The cat and the woman were gone.

Maya couldn't move. Still crouching, her legs were turning numb. Finally, she stumbled back to the door of Valerie's tree house.

"Who was that?" Simon asked Valerie.

Valerie brushed her hair back, her hand still trembling. Her voice shook as she spoke.

"The Lady Who Rides the Jaguar," she whispered. "She was looking for a child to steal."

"Why doesn't somebody stop her?" Simon asked, a quiver coming into his voice. "Make her go away?"

"You cannot stop evil," Valerie whispered. "You never can. You just have to hide from it so it does not get you!"

Simon shifted closer to Maya. But Maya was frightened, too.

"You must be very careful now, Simon, Maya," said Valerie, her face pale but her eyes frighteningly bright. "She will come back!"

Simon had shrunk into a little ball.

"She will come back until she has taken a child," said Valerie. "She will—"

"Stop!" Maya cried. "Stop telling us these things! You're just scaring us!"

"Children must be scared!" said Valerie, her cheeks flushing.

"It is the only way to keep them safe! You must be afraid of everything, children! Everything in the world wants to hurt you! And *enfants,* you are so precious! Children are so precious. You must be kept safe!"

Maya put her arm around Simon and she hugged Penny close to her with her other arm. *I will keep them safe,* she thought.

❧ CHAPTER FIFTEEN ❧

A Very Sad Event ✳ *Simon Wants to Stay* ✳
The Big Dark

Maya's frightening glimpse of the Child Stealer jolted her. She realized that she had let time slip past, and she regretted that they had lost many valuable days in the search for their parents. Penny was healthy again and they could move on. But even as Maya was deciding this, something terrible happened. The morning after the Child Stealer had been seen, while Maya and Simon were having breakfast, commotion broke out in the village. Valerie dashed outside and stood at the railing of the deck.

"What is it?" asked Simon. "What happened?"

Valerie listened to the shouts from the trees and then she bowed her head sorrowfully.

"The Child Stealer," she said. "She returned. Two children have been taken."

Cloud Forest Men, armed with bows and arrows, swung down on the ropes and jumped onto the floor of the jungle. They split into different groups and took off running in all directions. Whistles and birdcalls passed among the tree houses and echoed across the jungle.

"Who was taken?" Maya asked. "Which children?"

Valerie paused. "I am sorry," she said. "It was Bongo. And Netti. They think that Bongo was taken first, and Netti found out and she went after him."

Maya felt something catch in her heart. Netti! Her friend!

Her first friend. And Bongo! Sweet little Bongo! With his shiny black hair and twinkling eyes.

"Will they get them back?" she asked hoarsely.

Valerie lowered her gaze.

Simon looked shocked.

"That's why you children mustn't stray," said Valerie, wiping her eyes. "It's very bad out there. I have *told* you," she added, looking sternly at Maya.

The sky darkened then and the light in the jungle dimmed. Rain began, rustling on the thatched roofs. Tiny ferns growing from the trunk of the tree trembled in the drizzle. A cockatoo sitting on a nearby branch ducked its head into its chest to stay dry. Then from the houses drumming began. The drums were made with the hide of piganos, stretched across hollowed-out tree stumps. They beat in rhythm, deeply and loudly through the rain. If Netti and Bongo were out there, if there was even the slimmest chance that they had escaped from the Child Stealer and were wandering lost in the jungle, the booming drums would guide them home. No one in the village believed they were still out there, but the drums beat on, anyway.

Before Maya knew it, tears were spilling down Simon's cheeks and he had begun to sob. It distressed her to see him this way, and she put her arm around him.

"It's all right, Simon," she said. "They'll find them and bring them back."

Inside the house, the vine chair squeaked as Valerie rocked back and forth, holding Penny close and singing softly.

The drumming never ceased, even as the morning turned into afternoon, and afternoon to evening, and evening to darkest night. When a drummer grew exhausted, another came to take his or her place, and the villagers kept the drums beating throughout the night. They kept them beating until evening of the second day, when one of the search parties returned with the nutshell necklace that had belonged to Bongo, which they had found in the mud half a day's walk from the village. There was no sign of Netti. Weary and defeated, the searchers climbed to the treetops. People came out to watch them return, and the drummers lowered their heads sorrowfully and put their instruments down. The village was quiet except for the sound of weeping from the home of Netti and Bongo's family.

🐬 🐬 🐬

Maya woke up the next morning feeling miserable. Her friends were gone. All joy had left life in the Cloud Forest Village. Children were kept inside the tree houses, and people moved somberly about their tasks. Now that there was no more running around playing and exploring the leafy green heights of the village, Maya realized how attached Valerie had become to Penny. Valerie tried to take Penny away from her a few times and when Maya refused, Valerie sulked. It made Maya furious—just because Valerie didn't have any children of her own didn't mean that she could have Penny. She wasn't Penny's mother, and she didn't know how to take better care of her than Maya! No, Penny belonged to Maya and Simon until they found their parents again.

Maya knew they had to leave. She just wanted to make sure that the Child Stealer was long gone before they set out. But things between Valerie and Maya were growing tenser. They quarreled one morning and Valerie finally left in a huff to gather food, leaving the children behind. Pascal was not around and as soon as Valerie was gone, Maya stormed into the tree house to get the logbook. She wanted to consult the map so that she could plan their escape, but she couldn't find it in Simon's backpack or anywhere else. Simon was sitting on the porch, staring out across the village. Since Bongo had disappeared, he hadn't ventured far from Valerie and Pascal's tree house. He absently stroked Seagrape's green feathers on the necklace Helix had given him, and Maya had to repeat his name several times before he heard her.

"Simon," she asked. "Where's the logbook?"

"Pascal has it," he said.

"Pascal?"

"He wanted to see it, so I gave it to him."

Feeling suddenly suspicious, Maya stood up and went inside. Neither Pascal nor Valerie was there, but she felt weird peering into Pascal's study, looking at all his things. She saw the logbook at the end of his table and went to get it. It was opened to a fresh page, which Pascal had already half covered with notes about the volcano. Why on earth was he recording his notes in their logbook? One of his own notebooks was lying on the table next to the logbook and Maya opened it gingerly. What she saw made her gasp.

She turned a few more pages quickly and her mouth dropped open. Every single millimeter of each page had been written on, so many times over that it was impossible to read anything he had written, or to make any sense of it at all. Maya flipped through the rest of the book and every page was solidly blackened with ink. But this was what Pascal sat working on every single day! Was there no point to it at all? Fearful of what she would find, she closed the notebook and went to the rest of Pascal's notebooks, which were stacked along a bench against the wall. Nervously she opened the first one. Then another. And another. They were all the same. Pascal had written over

156

his own writing so many times that the pages were just inky darkness. He must have run out of paper years, perhaps decades, ago and that was why he had asked to see the logbook.

Maya felt a cold fear spreading through her. She knew then that if they didn't leave soon they might never leave. With each day that passed, they would be less and less likely to go, until they had become like Valerie, kept prisoner by their fear, forever unable to reach what was most important to them. Well, Maya wouldn't allow it.

Hands shaking a little, she turned to Rodrigo's map. She judged that they had a two- or three-day hike ahead of them before they could reach the river again. Valerie had told them that once the Child Stealer had struck, she wouldn't return to the same place for a long time, so with luck the children would not run into her. Piganos were a concern but they would move quickly and keep their ears open and if they heard the beasts charging they would climb the nearest tree as fast as they could. They had become quite adept tree climbers during their time in the Cloud Forest Village and she was sure that they could make their way swiftly from the ground into the safety of high branches. The same went if they heard any soldiers coming. No matter what happened to them in the jungle, they had to try to find their parents. What if Mami and Papi were looking for them this very minute? They would leave at once. She had to tell Simon.

Maya jumped, startled, when Valerie appeared in the doorway. She must have left something behind and returned to get it.

"What are you do?" she asked in a high voice.

"Pascal borrowed our logbook," Maya said, forcing herself to sound cheerful. "I'm just taking it back. I want to thank you for everything you've done for us, but I'm packing up our things now because we're leaving."

Heart hammering, Maya took the logbook back outside onto the porch and put it in Simon's backpack. Valerie followed her out.

"Maya," she said. "Stay."

"We can't," said Maya. "We have to find our parents."

"I must implore you," said Valerie. "*Do not go into the jungle*. Maya, you are just a young girl, an *enfant*! You cannot take care of your brother and sister. Stay here with me and I will take care of you."

"No!" Maya shouted. "We already have a family! We already have parents!"

Valerie looked at her sadly.

Maya turned to Simon. He had been sitting with his legs dangling between the bars of the porch but now he looked up at them for the first time.

"I like living in a tree house," he whispered softly. "Maybe we should stay."

Valerie watched Maya carefully. "Your parents, you must let them go, Maya," she said. "They were lost in the storm. You must allow yourself to forget. Be happy you are here, where you are safe. Forget before, forget other things. You may stay with us, with Pascal and I. We have talked. One day, when you are older, we will build you your own houses in the trees. The Cloud Forest People will be your family. You'll be happy, you'll see."

Maya listened in horror. Forget the *Pamela Jane*, forget Granny Pearl in Bermuda, forget Mami and Papi, forget their lives? Never! She would not forget and she would not let her brother and sister forget either. She would not let them be like Dr. Limmermor and Rodrigo and Valerie Volcano and all the other people on Greater Tamarind who had let themselves forget. They had stayed there too long already.

Simon had been staring down at the ground below. Now he sat up, absently plucking a leaf and twirling it between his fingers and turned to Valerie.

"Can I have a house very high up, high enough to see the stars through the trees at night? With a rope swing all the way to the ground?"

Valerie smiled. "Of course, *mon cherie*. Anything you want for your house. After all, it will be yours."

"I want to talk to my brother," Maya told Valerie coldly. "Alone."

Valerie looked at her sadly but stood up, brushing her hands off on her dress.

"You talk," she said as she got up to leave. "You take some time to think about what is best, Maya. Best for Simon and Penny, and best for you, too, even if you can't see it now, *petite* Maya."

A hard, heavy silence sat between Maya and Simon. Around them, vines dripped with orchids and the subtle, dizzying perfume drifted through the canopy.

"We have to leave," she said in a low voice. "Even if it's dangerous. It would be worse to stay here—stuck here, like Valerie, because we were too afraid to ever try."

Simon wrapped his arms around his knees. He turned his head away from Maya and put his cheek on his knees and did not answer her.

She opened the logbook and turned to the map. She pointed

to where they were and traced her finger on a path through the jungle, skirting the volcano and farther on, the abandoned ophalla mines, and ending back at the Nallanda River.

"We'll go east until we reach the river again," she said. "Then we'll build a raft and take the river to Port Town."

"And what happens when we get there?" Simon asked, suddenly loud. He glared at her bitterly. The force of his anger surprised Maya. "There's nowhere here where we can get help, not really—everyone's told us that."

Maya faltered. What if he was right? What if help was never going to be found, and going into the jungle was just taking them into great danger? A stubborn blankness descended over Simon's face, making it impossible for Maya to read what he was thinking. She wavered for a moment but then she knew that whatever lay ahead, they had to go meet it. There was nothing for them in the Cloud Forest Village.

"Simon," she said, her voice low and urgent. "We can't just *stay.* What about our parents? You want to be with Valerie instead of Mami?"

Simon put his chin back down on his knees and looked at the deck.

Hot tears sprang to Maya's eyes. She shook her head.

"They're gone, Maya," Simon whispered. "You know they are. It was a big storm."

Maya stared at him, shocked. She felt sick. She pinched her arm, hard, so she wouldn't burst into tears. Simon had always been the optimist about everything, but ever since Bongo and Netti had disappeared, he hadn't been himself. Maya could hardly bear to see him this way.

"We don't know that!" she said.

They sat there in silence, Simon still turned away.

"Fine," said Maya finally, getting to her feet. There was a horrible lump in her throat. "You stay here. I'm leaving tomorrow, first thing in the morning. And I'm taking Penny with me."

"No, you won't."

"Oh, yeah? You'll see when you wake up tomorrow and I'm gone."

"You should leave Penny here," called Simon as Maya stalked off back into the tree house. "Valerie Volcano will take care of her better than you can."

Maya didn't look back, but her face burned at that last comment. She *had* taken good care of Penny. In the house she went to Valerie's room. Penny was lying awake in her cot, watching a hummingbird hovering in the window. Maya picked her up and squeezed her close.

"I'm sorry, Penny," she whispered. "I'm going to get you back to Mami."

～ ～ ～

Maya had left the logbook on the porch beside Simon and when she was gone he looked down at the map, at the blue loop of the river running through endless miles of jungle, and at the volcano, smoke pouring from its mouth. He didn't care about the map anymore. He didn't want to think about the rest of Tamarind, or about his parents, or about anything but staying where they were, safe in the Cloud Forest Village. Maya could do what she liked. Simon would stay with Valerie, forever if he had to. But then his eye stopped in the middle of the jungle, across which, in block capitals, at a slant going up from left to right, Rodrigo had written

ABANDONED OPHALLA MINES

Suddenly Simon knew.

He grasped the logbook in both hands and stared at the map in amazement. The mute parade of sea creatures rolling softly through its pages seemed to have voices now. The creatures seemed to smile up at him, light glittering through their bodies. He had discovered their secret.

It had been staring them in the face all along. How had he not seen it before?

Just then a tremor ran through the floor beneath his feet and a deep rumbling began in the distance. The trees themselves looked like they were trembling. A thunderstorm must be approaching. Simon ran into the tree house and met Maya in the doorway, where he practically shoved the book into her hands.

"Ophalla!" he shouted. "I figured it out! It's ophalla!"

"What are you talking about?" she asked.

"Ophalla is what's making the creatures in the water glow!" Simon cried.

Ophalla. Maya's thoughts began to swirl. All at once the world began to darken and the rumbling grew louder.

"Rodrigo told us ophalla was a bluish-white stone," said Simon. "That *glowed*. All the creatures Mami and Papi were finding, they have ophalla in them! It's in the water somehow."

Maya felt a flash of recognition. In her mind's eye she saw the luminescent octopus again, the one her parents had culled from the sea, and the multitudes of others like it she had seen in the tide pools that night with Helix. There were the turtle eggs that glowed, too, and the jungle fireflies, and who knew what else in Tamarind? Was the same thing causing all of them to glow? Her father's voice returned to her again from the last day in St. Alban's. *From deep in an equatorial jungle* . . . What had he said after that? It was there, just out of her reach. . . . Something about a river . . . What was it? Then she remembered. *It's most likely that the mineral is being carried downriver and that's how it's entering the sea. . . .*

"It's coming from the abandoned ophalla mines," said Maya, stepping forward and peering at the map. "Particles could have washed down the river into the sea around Tamarind. . . ."

"And somehow it got into the creatures in the Tamarind Sea," said Simon. The throaty growl of the storm sounded closer now.

"Some of those animals were getting through the Blue Line into the outside ocean, our ocean," Maya continued.

"And that's what Mami and Papi were finding," said Simon. "Except they didn't know what was causing the animals to glow—that's what they were trying to figure out. What it was and where it was from. That's what all the notes and drawings in the logbook were about!"

"But we do know," said Maya. She looked back at the map, at the words ABANDONED OPHALLA MINES sitting on a stretch of rocky jungle marked by Rodrigo.

"They don't look very far from here," she said. "Probably just a few days' walk."

The two children looked at each other, their faces pale. They were both thinking the same thing: If they found what their parents had been searching for, it might somehow help lead them to their parents. The possibility filled Simon with new hope. Maybe they were closer than they had imagined to filling in the missing pieces of the puzzle.

They would go to the abandoned ophalla mines.

While they had been talking, the light had dimmed further and now it was nearly dark. The children became aware that there was a frenzy of activity happening around them in the

Cloud Forest Village. Simon detected the scent of ash in the air and he realized something else.

"It isn't a storm!" he cried. "It's the volcano!"

Maya's heart skipped a beat.

"We have to get out of here *now*," she said.

↬ ↬ ↬

Pascal had been on the ground when the rumbling started but now he appeared on the rope ladder and stepped onto the porch. His great gray eyebrows bristled over his eyes, which shone in the sudden dusk that had descended over the jungle. He looked wild. Soft gray ash had begun to fall from the sky, trickling soundlessly down through the leaves and coating them in a fine silver film. Pascal reached his hands out, palms upward, catching the ash and rubbing it between his fingers. Then he shouted joyfully.

"The big dark! It has come!" He turned and hurried into the tree house.

A fine silt of ash was covering the surface of the jungle, turning it gray. Like a furnace, the volcano was pumping out thick black smoke that choked the sun. As the children watched, the jungle grew dimmer. It was like the twilight before a very great storm. Across the Cloud Forest Village, people were sealing their windows and door frames with leaves and strips of bark to keep out the ash.

Valerie came running back over the footbridge to the tree house.

"Hurry, children!" she cried. "The day has come! The volcano will erupt!"

She ran into the tree house, calling for Pascal, and emerged a moment later with a small suitcase. It was so ancient that the

164

strap broke, rotted through from the humidity, and Valerie and Pascal's few faded possessions, kept there in preparation for this moment, spilled out onto the deck.

"No matter," she said. "No matter, no matter. Soon there will be new things. Soon we will go back home. We will go to the coast, a boat will find us!"

Maya had never seen Valerie like this before. She was terrified and excited at the same time. Her cheeks were crimson and her eyes were luminous, as if she had a fever.

"Let me carry the baby," she said.

"No!" said Maya, turning her body so that Valerie couldn't reach Penny. Valerie ran back inside, chattering to Pascal. Copper instruments clattered.

"We just have to go," said Maya, and Simon nodded.

"Wait!" called Valerie as the children began to climb down the tree. "I am coming with you. Pascal, he will follow!" She hesitated, looking down at the children, her eyes large with fear.

First Simon and then Maya—holding Penny tightly—climbed down the rope to the ground. A fine layer of ash covered the bark and the tops of the leaves and the ferns and the caps of mushrooms that grew in the hollows of the tree's trunk. The air was thick with it. Valerie came after them, but halfway down, she froze. Her face was pale and her hands were trembling.

"Wait," she cried. "We must stay. It is bad out there! I was wrong, children, come back! Stay!"

"We have to go!" Maya shouted back up to her, shading her eyes from the ash to look up at Valerie Volcano's frightened face. Ash drifted silently down between the trees.

"No," Valerie cried, clutching the rope ladder. "I am too scared. I cannot leave! You children, stay, please!" she begged. "Please, children, stay with me! Come back!"

Tears ran down Maya's cheeks, leaving paths in the ash that was slowly coating her skin. It was awful to see the terror in Valerie Volcano's eyes. Ash had settled on Valerie's hair and shoulders and limbs and for a moment she looked to Maya as if she was already half buried.

"Keep going," she said to Simon, gritting her teeth. "We can't stop."

They slid down the end of the rope. On the ground, Maya grabbed Simon's hand and they began to run as fast as they could, far away from Valerie and Pascal and the sad final days in the treetops. As they ran, the air thickened with ash and the lofty heights of the Cloud Forest Village were lost behind them.

✴ CHAPTER SIXTEEN ✴

The Earth's Lungs ✴ *1,000 Bottles of Beer on the Wall* ✴
Nearing the Mines ✴ *A Horrible Little Man* ✴ *Witchwood Road*

Over the next days Maya and Simon, taking turns carrying Penny, went as fast as they could to get as far away from the volcano as possible. But they heard no more rumblings and no surge of molten lava came, crushing the jungle behind them. They believed that the volcano must not have erupted, after all. Only a faint smell of ash lingered in the air.

"Remember what Papi said?" said Maya. "That jungles are like the earth's lungs? The air will be best in here."

Maya had not realized how oppressive Valerie and the sadness of the disappearance of Netti and Bongo had become. Though they were alone in the jungle, she felt happier than she had in some time. They ate bananas and guarana and cupuaçu and found a tiny trickle of a stream to drink from. They followed the stream for days. Simon fashioned a slingshot out of a forked stick and a rubbery vine and he kept it always at the ready, but no piganos bothered them. It was as if the rumblings of the volcano had sent them all scurrying to their lairs, as animals do when disaster threatens. Maya carried Helix's spear with them, but she never had to use it, except to reach fruit on high branches, when it came in very handy. Simon still wore the necklace of Seagrape's feathers.

They kept an eye out, but never saw any sign of Bongo or Netti. As they hiked they sang songs. They sang "One Thousand

Bottles of Beer on the Wall" from the beginning to the end. They counted as high as they could in as many languages as they could: French, Spanish, Portuguese, Dutch. They were much stronger and more used to hiking than they had been when they first arrived in Tamarind, and at times it all felt like a great adventure.

"When Penny's older, do you think she'll remember any of this?" Simon asked.

"I don't know," said Maya. "She's not even a year old. I don't know if I can remember anything that far back."

The hill they were walking up got quite steep then and it was too difficult to talk, so the children fell into silence and just concentrated on putting one foot in front of the other.

"I think she'll remember some stuff," Simon said after the path had leveled again and they caught their breath. "Maybe she'll remember without really knowing what she's remembering. Like, when she's older she'll smell orchids or she'll taste cupuaçu, things she doesn't have all the time, and she'll remember it somewhere in her mind, even if she doesn't know where it's from."

"Maybe," nodded Maya.

By the end of a week the air was free of even the faintest trace of ash and there were no longer any cloud orchids overhead or trickling down to the jungle floor. The foliage changed. Tree trunks broadened and leaves became thicker and darker and grew closer together. Ferocious red flowers—dark in the low light—bloomed in the hollows of branches and sprang onto the children's path. Sometimes the children passed evidence of life: messy nests in the crooks of high branches, holes that led into dark burrows in the earth, roots that had been gnawed by jungle creatures, but they never saw anything other than birds and lizards and insects. They found ever stranger new fruits to eat. Each night they chose a tree and slept in a huddle at the foot of it. The jungle was too thick to see the sky, so there was no sun or stars to tell them which way they were going, but for stretches of each day they felt surprisingly brave and were not unhappy.

The first clue that they were going the right way was that here and there on the jungle floor they began to see traces of a powder that glowed in the dark. They knew that they must be nearing the mines.

⌒ ⌒ ⌒

After days of ducking under branches and clambering over tree stumps on no real trail, one morning the children found a narrow footpath. They walked along it for some time. When they stopped to rest, the foliage was so thick that there was nowhere to sit but right in the middle of the path, which is what they did. That's where they were when a gnarled little man, coming from the opposite direction, nearly stumbled into them.

The children scrambled to their feet, hearts pounding. The little man—he was less than four feet tall—froze in his tracks and stared at them in horror. He was so still that for a moment he seemed to blend in with the undergrowth.

"Lord save me," he whispered. "Spirits. They've come for me."

"We aren't spirits," Maya said, afraid that he would faint with fear. "I'm sorry. We'd just stopped to rest. We'll get out of your way."

"Can you tell us where this road goes?" Simon asked.

The little man looked around him, as if expecting more strange children to appear from all sides. Through the gloom

169

of the jungle his skin was eerily pale, as if it had never seen sun. His eyes were set far apart, like those of a reptile, and the irises were light as sand. His bare feet were covered in calluses thick as boots and he carried a sack over his shoulder. His eyes glittered suspiciously.

"No children walk freely through here," he said. "Who are you? Why hasn't she found you yet?"

"Who?" Simon asked.

"You know who," the little man said ominously. He lowered the sack from his shoulder and rested it on the ground. Maya squinted to see what was inside it, but it was too dark to tell.

"Please," asked Maya. "We're trying to get to the old ophalla mines. Can you tell us which way this path goes?"

"The old ophalla mines," said the little man slowly, an ill-tempered glint appearing in his yellow eyes. Maya noticed that though he was short, he looked immensely strong.

"What's in the bag?" asked Simon, peering at it and taking a step forward.

The little man reached for the sack greedily, as if he didn't even want Simon to look at it, but as he did so, his short little leg kicked it. Its contents rattled together and then something slipped out and rolled across the path to the children, stopping only when it hit Simon's toe. Maya and Simon recoiled in horror.

It was a skull—a very small, round skull, with great hollow eye sockets and a hinged jaw and set of wobbly brown teeth grinning up at them. Without thinking, Maya kicked it hard, back to the little man, who seized it and tossed it into the sack and drew the string tight.

Maya and Simon trembled and could not speak.

"War skulls," said the little man. "The earth is still giving them up. Soldiers, people who fled from the towns and hid out in here. The jungle is full of their bones. Sometimes I find whole skeletons hanging from trees, bodies blown there in explosions and left to rot, until I come across them all these years later. She finds uses for them, so I take them to her."

He moved the sack behind him on the path as if he was afraid that the children would steal it.

"Who *are* you?" she breathed.

"Who are YOU?" the little man asked. He was growing increasingly bold and unpleasant. "What are you doing here?"

"We're looking for . . ." began Maya. She didn't want to say her beloved parents' names in front of the stranger.

"Looking for someone?" the little man asked, digging a grimy finger into his hair to scratch his scalp. "Whoever you're looking for, you won't find. Unless you want to look in here." He rattled the bag of skulls, and Maya and Simon jumped back. The little man laughed.

For a moment Maya believed him, believed that somehow he could know that they would never see their parents again. He seemed to take pleasure in the stricken looks that passed over their faces. Then Maya noticed Simon's chin beginning to quiver and as scared as she was, she also felt a spark of rage kindle in her. Who was this horrible little man to upset her brother? Who was he to tell them anything? He couldn't know anything about their parents. Maya squeezed Penny to her protectively. Penny had been silent the entire time, as if she dared not make a peep. As she turned, Maya's foot slipped off the path and into the vegetation. A strange tingling sensation traveled up her leg. She hoped she hadn't touched some poisonous plant—that would be all they needed right now.

"The old ophalla mines are down that road," the man said, pointing to where Maya's foot had slipped.

"There's no road," said Simon, looking into a wall of green jungle.

"Oh, there's a road," the little man said. "That's Witchwood Road. You won't know it until you're already on it, but it's a road all right. It will take you straight to the mines."

The mines! Maya and Simon looked at each other.

The little man paused and lowered his voice. "They could tell you where it leads," he said, shaking the sack so the skulls knocked together. He grinned, revealing rotted stumps of teeth.

A macaw screeched and dove off a high branch and into the jungle, startling them. The man hoisted the sack over his shoulder. Maya and Simon squinted into the jungle where he had said a road was and thought they could almost make one out. It was overgrown and murky with shadows before it faded into blackness. It was strangely menacing. Did it really lead to the mines? And was the "she" the little man kept talking about the Child Stealer? They were both afraid of the new path. But they had set out to go to the mines . . . Simon looked at Maya and without speaking, they decided.

They would take Witchwood Road.

The little man saw it, too, and a smile curved up one side of his face.

"She'll find you now, anyway," said the little man gleefully. "It doesn't really matter which way you go."

Suddenly the little man caught sight of the necklace around Simon's neck. He froze, looking swiftly over the children's faces again.

"Who are you?" he whispered, and this time it was he who

seemed afraid of them. Holding the bag of skulls between himself and the children, he squeezed past and began hurrying away nervously. Soon he was gone from sight. The volume of the birds' and insects' chirping seemed to intensify as Simon and Maya stood there.

"What just happened?" Simon asked.

"I have no idea," said Maya, looking at Seagrape's green feathers. "It seemed like the feathers scared him. Come on, we should keep moving," she said.

The children began to make their way down Witchwood Road. Maya still felt her legs tingling. The undergrowth stirred as they passed and then closed around the place where they had stood. No one would ever have known that only a moment before three children had been there. A snake slid down a tree and over the patch where they had stood and went on its way. A tiny bright yellow bug, previously hidden from view, crawled out to the edge of a leaf and took flight, right into the paw of a giant red monkey who had been sitting motionless, camouflaged in the vegetation, unseen by the children. The monkey glanced down at the bug and then closed its fist around it. He lifted it to his mouth and, with an almost delicate flutter of his lips, swallowed it. Then he turned and began climbing to the top of the canopy. He swung silently and swiftly, arm over arm, in the direction that the children had gone.

CHAPTER SEVENTEEN

*The Monkey * Labyrinth * Terror*

The jungle was hot and airless. Only faint sunlight filtered through the thick canopy, and Maya and Simon had no way to tell what time it was. They lost their way sometimes, but then the narrow slip of a footpath would reappear, drawing them deeper into the jungle. Simon had been in the lead for a while when Maya noticed a blue butterfly perched on his backpack. She was going to tell him when she saw a second attach itself to his shoulder. Another had settled on Penny's foot. And then Maya and Simon and Penny were in the midst of a silent maelstrom of blue and yellow and red and emerald.

"They're so beautiful!" Maya cried.

Simon had turned to face her and they smiled at each other through the soft storm of color, mute as snow. Simon stretched out his arms so that butterflies landed on them, hanging upside down like bats or tiptoeing like ballerinas, flexing their wings slowly. There were hundreds of them, maybe thousands, lighting the dim jungle with a riot of color. They converged in a flock ahead of the children and the color grew dense, like a strange, magical vapor. A few stragglers fluttered around the children's heads. The children followed them until the butterflies began to fly too fast for them to keep up and then dissolved into the darkness up ahead.

"Oh," said Maya. "They're gone."

Mesmerized by the butterflies, she and Simon had left the path and this time it did not reappear. Softly glowing dust powdered the earth here and there, and they believed that they must be very near the mines. They stopped and looked all around them, trying to get their bearings. That's when they saw the first of the stone totem poles standing in the middle of the jungle. It was about twenty feet tall and five feet thick. Maya and Simon went closer so they could examine it. The stone was worn and cool to the touch. It was covered in a soft fur of moss.

"Where do you think it came from?" Simon whispered.

"I have no idea," said Maya, shaking her head slowly.

There were three more totems at intervals along a path and then the children came to a pink wall straddled with hanging vines. In the middle of the wall, almost totally obscured by vegetation, was an archway. Simon parted the vines and he and Maya peered cautiously into a walled courtyard. No one seemed to be there. Glancing one last time at the jungle behind them, they stepped inside. When Simon let the vines go, a green wall closed behind them. It was almost impossible to tell where the archway had even been.

The children stood looking all around them. They had a bad feeling about the place. There were white stone fountains and clusters of miniature palm trees. A footpath meandered through the flower beds, from which sprang a fury of startling jungle flowers of varieties the children had never seen before. At one time the courtyard must have been serene and beautiful. But now the foliage seemed to be devouring itself for space and the faint scent of rot crept through the air. Ferns taller than the children—taller than anyone—arched over the path, and spongy, spotted flowers grew close to the ground. The fountains were dry and the pink stone was crumbling. The air was curiously still.

The children were startled by a small brown monkey, who began chattering and dropping fast, arm over arm, down the trunk of a palm tree. It crouched on the path in front of them, releasing a torrent of chatter, but then it stopped talking and sat there, absently stroking the tip of its own tail. When Penny gurgled, the monkey bounced up on all fours towards the children and reached up and touched Penny's toes. Maya stepped back, holding Penny tightly to her, and the monkey spun in a circle, scolding. Penny giggled and kicked her arms and legs.

The monkey sprang forward on the path, still chattering, and turned back as if to wait for them.

"I think it wants us to follow it," whispered Simon.

"Do you think we should?" asked Maya.

Simon thought. "I don't know," he said. "But we've lost the path."

They were in some type of ruins. . . . Could this be the ophalla mines? They weren't sure they could find their way out now, and the desire to know what lay beyond the courtyard was powerful—both of them felt it. Could they be on the brink of discovering what their parents had been searching for? When the monkey beckoned them again they followed him.

The creature led them across the courtyard to a place in the wall where they had not seen a door, but it drew back the vines with its hairless little fingers, and the children entered another walled garden much like the first.

The day seemed to grow darker and a buzzing noise was coming from somewhere nearby. A few stray butterflies had appeared and were fluttering around them. As Maya watched, their wings changed color, darkening until they became almost black. The buzzing grew louder and was now coming from directly overhead. Maya saw with horror a thick cloud of insects hovering in the air above them, blotting out the sun. In the dimming afternoon, the light from the lamps stood out brighter. It was then that she realized that the lamps along the path were not ordinary lamps, but skulls on poles, with tiny flames lighting their eye sockets and glimmering between their teeth. Panic filled her.

A funny breeze stirred by the mass of insects lifted the vines overhanging the wall, and Maya saw that the wall beneath was built of skulls, too. They were in some type of sinister aboveground catacombs.

"Simon, this was a mistake," she whispered, grabbing his hand. "We have to get out of here."

Simon had seen the skulls now, too, and heard the buzz of the insects escalating overhead. The two children held hands and Maya clasped Penny tightly to her as they began to run back the way they had come. Except they didn't know which way that was—it all looked the same. Suddenly they realized they'd been led into a maze—there was no way out. They turned wildly down alleys and corners until they were hopelessly lost. Maya dropped Helix's spear and did not stop to pick it up. The insects descended and the volume of their buzzing rose. Then Maya spied a turning up ahead that looked familiar—yes, wasn't this where they had entered the maze? She recognized the pink flowers growing over some fallen stones. Just around the next bend would be the archway and the freedom of the jungle. They ran as hard as they could and rounded the turn and there they stopped dead in their tracks.

Standing now in the archway was something that made the children's eyes widen in fear and their limbs tremble. A giant jaguar, larger than any they had ever seen, stood blocking the exit, ears flattened, body braced to pounce, great claws flashing in the dim light. And astride the cat, her burning gaze fixed on the three children, was the woman Maya had seen that day in the Cloud Forest Village.

Maya, Simon, and Penny had come face-to-face with the Child Stealer.

❖ Chapter Eighteen ❖

In the Courtyard ✳ *Monkeys, Skulls, and Lampreys* ✳
An Unlikely Talisman

Run!" cried Maya.

The children turned to run, but they never had a chance. In a silent yellow blur, the jaguar pounced. At the last moment Maya clutched Penny to her and threw her free arm around Simon and closed her eyes. But instead of feeling the animal's claws rip into her insides, Maya felt a pair of strong arms scoop her up with the others and cocoon them inside a dark cape. Then they were galloping through the maze.

Finally they came to a halt. The woman opened her cape and the three children spilled out onto the ground. The Child Stealer dismounted and led the jaguar inside a crumbling old temple, where they both disappeared. Maya and Simon, breathless from the wild ride, scrambled to their feet. A brown ball of fur barreled toward them and they realized that it was the little monkey they had seen earlier. He turned in circles, berating them.

Maya huddled with Simon and Penny and looked around. They were in a courtyard. At the far end was the temple, where the Child Stealer and the jaguar had disappeared. Cracks forked like black lightning along its walls and tough weeds split the stone. Small fires burned on its steps. The firelight made the shadows of spiders loom large and wobbly-legged on the temple walls. Scattered around the bare yard were smoking black pits, and the air was acrid. There was a pond in the center and slippery-looking lampreys swarmed in masses just beneath the surface. There was no escape.

There was the *scrape, scrape, scrape* of a stick broom on stone, and Maya noticed that an old man had come around the corner and was sweeping the ground in front of the temple. When he saw the children he lay down his broom and began making his way over to them. Iron shackles bound his ankles and a chain ran between the shackles, preventing him from moving at more than a shuffling gait. Was he a slave? A prisoner? *Where on earth are we?* Maya thought. Simon nudged her and nodded at the far wall, where a row of large red monkeys sat on their heels, smoking long pipes and exhaling bluish smoke. They were all much bigger than the tiny brown monkey who had greeted the children, and they stared at the children with glassy eyes. One lumbered to his feet for a moment, then slouched back against the wall.

Maya and Simon saw the woman's shadow inside the temple and heard her tread on the steps before she actually reappeared. It was the first time they had gotten a good look at her. She was a tall, strapping woman, wearing a black tunic draped over one shoulder. Her long, black hair was sleek as oil and it glowed with a strange luster in the unnaturally faded light. Green-black jewelry glittered around her neck, on her wrists, and in her ears. As she stepped closer, Maya could see that the jewelry was made of beetles. There were hundreds of them— small and large, jointed limbs neatly folded, bodies bulbous— all preserved in shiny lacquer and strung together. When the woman moved, they shimmered in the dull light.

Her burning gaze still fixed on the children, the Child Stealer snapped her fingers and a tiny boy in ragged clothes appeared from behind what appeared to be a well. He ran forward with an upturned skull, which, bowing, he lifted up to the woman. She sipped from it slowly, never taking her eyes from the children. The child returned to the well, where he stood still as a statue. The woman had not blinked.

It dawned on Maya then that the skulls weren't monkey skulls, but the skulls of children. Shock and revulsion rooted her to the ground. Even as she stood there in the middle of the broiling-hot jungle, she felt her whole body turning cold. Just then the small brown monkey ran up to the woman and scampered up her robe, where it sat on her shoulder and scolded the children. It combed the hair back behind her ear with its tiny, human-like hands. Then the woman spoke in a low, level voice.

"The monkeys can have the little one," she said. "And the two big ones can go to the mines."

The monkeys could have Penny! Maya's knees turned to rubber. She looked at the monkeys and she noticed that as they sat there they were plucking butterflies from the air and tossing them into a simmering cauldron. The creatures' colored wings darkened as they absorbed the water and tiny squeals rose from the cauldron, which bubbled over now and then, its liquid hissing when it touched the hot stones. Seeing Maya watching them, the monkeys began to jeer.

The old man shuffled toward the children and reached out his arms to take Penny. Maya flinched and squeezed Penny tightly in terror. They all took a step backward and Simon's backpack knocked one of the lamp-skulls off its post. Its jaw came unhinged and the flame was snuffed out. The old man kept walking steadily toward them. The children were being backed up into the monkeys, who drew their lips away from their big yellow teeth and grimaced. Maya shuddered as she felt fur brushing the back of her leg. They could go no farther.

As the old man reached to take Penny, Maya could see the Child Stealer watching everything, the beetles glimmering around her neck.

Then Simon remembered something. Taking a deep breath and flinging one arm over his eyes, he stepped in front of his sisters, dropped to his knees, and with his free hand he held out Seagrape's green feathers, still attached to the cord around his neck.

The old man and the Child Stealer recoiled. Maya watched in disbelief as the color drained from the Child Stealer's face. The monkeys began to sniff the air and then they lumbered off to another corner of the courtyard, where they sat making mournful keening noises. Simon peeked out from beneath his arm, and Maya stood there in shock. What had just happened? Why were they all afraid of Seagrape's feathers?

From a safe distance, the old man watched them with new curiosity. The Child Stealer recovered herself. She was staring at Maya so piercingly that Maya was sure she could read her thoughts. Finally she spoke.

"Take them to the Egewa prison. Lock them up."

❖ CHAPTER NINETEEN ❖

A Horrifying Glimpse Underground ✳
Ice-White Stone ✳ *Child Slaves* ✳ *"No!"*

The old man took a few steps toward Maya and Simon, ankle chains rattling, and before they knew it he had slipped a rope around their wrists and bound them tightly. Maya pulled the rope but it just sawed her skin. There was no use fighting. The old man led them up the steps of the temple. Maya wanted to say something to comfort Simon but she was too terrified herself.

The air inside the temple was stagnant. Yellow mushrooms clustered in the moist corners and a vile stench rose from them. The angry growl of the unseen jaguar rose and fell threateningly from somewhere in the darkness. The old man opened a trapdoor in the floor and pushed the children ahead of him. Maya and Simon and Penny began to descend a seemingly endless flight of steep damp steps. When they finally reached the bottom, the old man unlocked a gate and led them through and locked it behind them. They were in a narrow tunnel cut into dank, dripping stone. Even though her hands were tied, Maya managed to give Simon's hand a squeeze.

There were sounds of banging and hammering and rattling wheels echoing up ahead. They began to walk down the tunnel, drawing closer to the noise. Curiously, the tunnel seemed to be growing brighter the deeper into the earth they went and as they turned a corner, at the end of the next passageway, the children saw an intense white light. They walked toward it, and it grew brighter and brighter and then they were standing in the entrance to a vast underground chamber, with walls and a cavernous ceiling of radiant, white-blue stone. Maya's mouth dropped open. Could this be . . . ?

"*Ophalla*," Simon whispered.

Gleaming white walls reached up to the soaring ceiling and cascaded down the other side, like ice that had melted and then frozen again. Tunnels broke away here and the children could see down into their opaque blue mouths, reaching deep into the earth. In some places the stone was too bright to look at. In others Maya and Simon saw that it was tinged with green, as if algae were trapped inside it, and in other places it was so clear and so deep that it became a piercing, polar blue. It looked as cold and refreshing as ice, though it was only an illusion. It was broiling in the chamber.

They were inside one of the old ophalla mines.

But this one wasn't abandoned.

It was full of hundreds of children, chiseling away at the dazzling stone with pickaxes. Bigger children worked chunks of the rock free and smaller children scooped them into wheelbarrows and jogged away with them into the tunnels. The stone's glow was reflected in the sweaty, grimy faces of the children.

And what children they were! Skin and bone, their eyes were huge and hollow, their clothes in rags. Some of them had limbs that looked as if they had been crippled from malnutrition, or bones that had broken and never been set properly. Long-haired red monkeys—the guards—were stationed here and there. As Maya and Simon watched, one of them suddenly howled and ran on all fours to a child who was so tired that he looked as if he was about to fall asleep standing up. The monkey knocked him down, but the child scrambled to his feet at once and began heaving larger chunks of the white-blue stone into a wheelbarrow, his frail legs quaking under the weight.

The old man waited while Maya and Simon took in their fill of the scene. The slave children paid no attention to the newcomers. When the old man moved on, Simon stumbled and fell but the old man simply yanked on the rope, and Simon was pulled back up and forced along. They crossed the chamber and turned down another tunnel and passed through another pair of locked gates. Maya realized that until then they had been descending, but now they were climbing back toward the surface of the earth.

They emerged, blinking in the daylight, out of the side of a hill. There was a large flat field, stripped of trees, and at one end of this stripped area a giant hole yawned in the earth. It appeared to be the main entrance to the mine. Children surfaced from its depths, pushing wheelbarrows gleaming with icy chunks of the strange stone. Sometimes two or three children were needed to force the heavy wheelbarrows up out of the crater. At the top, smaller children took over, and they pushed the wheelbarrows across the flat earth in a line heading into the jungle, where they disappeared from view. Squinting, Maya could make out hulking red monkeys posted at intervals around the hole in the earth to keep the children from escaping. The old man pulled Maya and Simon and Penny along and they entered a path back into the jungle and lost sight of the mine.

In a tiny clearing on the other side of the hill, he stopped before a strange wooden cage made of branches glistening with resin. The Egewa prison! When Maya realized that they were about to be locked inside it, she began to struggle violently. But the old man reached out and grabbed Penny, so Maya stopped resisting. She may not be able to stop the man from locking them up, but at least he wouldn't take Penny. She could hardly believe what was happening. The man swiftly sliced the knots that bound their wrists and shoved them inside. It was an awful sensation, looking out through the bars as the old man locked the cage. And now he was just walking away, leaving them there with no word about what was going to happen to them!

"*No!*" Maya screamed. She grabbed the bars and began shaking them.

Suddenly she felt a powerful need to sleep. She heard Simon's voice as if she were underwater, sinking swiftly, and he were on the surface calling to her. She sat down, hard, and tried to put her hand up to her face to rub her eyes but her arms felt too heavy and sluggish to move. Visions of the wicked red monkeys, the beetle jewelry glinting on the Child Stealer's neck, the multitudes of children in the mine, swirled in her mind as if they were all going down a great drain together. Maya felt as if there were something very important she must tell Simon, but then the images slipped down the drain, drawing her down into darkness with them.

✣ Chapter Twenty ✣

The Egewa Prison ✳ *The Ark* ✳ *Element X* ✳
Horatio the Jailer ✳ *"Ask her"* ✳ *Evondra*

Maya sat up slowly and looked all around the prison. Simon must have untied her shoelaces and taken off her shoes because they were sitting in the corner. He was sitting cross-legged, holding Penny in his lap. The logbook was open on the ground next to him.

"What happened?" Maya asked blearily.

"You touched the branches," said Simon. "At first I thought you were dead, but they just put you to sleep. It's the resin on them that does it. They're Egewa branches, from the Egewa tree."

"Egewa?" said Maya, swallowing. Her throat was so dry.

"The old man who brought us here told me," said Simon. "His name is Horatio. He came back this morning to give us breakfast. I saved some bread for you. Here, you should eat something."

"This morning?" Maya asked. "How long did I sleep for?"

"Since yesterday afternoon," said Simon. "But don't worry, I took care of Penny."

Penny gurgled and waved her fists and Maya picked her up and kissed her. With her free hand she took the stale hunk of bread. Her thoughts were cloudy and confused but as she sat there the events of the day before returned to her and once again, clearly before her, she saw the chamber of gleaming white stone and the hundreds of child slaves with gaunt faces

187

and lifeless eyes and limbs thin and brittle from hunger. This was where all the stolen children were taken. One of the old ophalla mines was in fact the Child Stealer's lair, and she and Simon and Penny had walked right into it.

"Netti and Bongo!" she said suddenly. "They could be here."

Simon nodded gravely.

As Maya's drowsiness wore off it was replaced with a growing sense of claustrophobia. Their prison was about ten feet by ten feet and was just tall enough for her to stand up in. The floor was dirt. The walls were made up of evenly spaced Egewa branches, and the roof was thatched with dried palm leaves blue with mildew. In one corner was a jug of water, and in another, concealed behind a palm leaf, a simple toilet had been dug into the ground. The prison sat alone in a small clearing on a hill. Dense green jungle rose on all sides around them. Maya could hear the sound of construction on the opposite hill, but could not see what was being built. She moved to the other side of the prison and what she saw made her think that she might still be dreaming: Lodged in the undergrowth on the hillside, listing to one side, was a giant wooden boat.

"It's an ark," said Simon, following her gaze. "All those kids we saw working in the mine, it's where they live. The old man comes and lets them out in the morning, then locks them back up at night."

"How did it get there?" Maya asked, trying to shake off the fuzziness.

"There's a little stream at the bottom of the hill here—you can just hear it. It probably used to be a proper river, but when the water level dropped the ark was stranded up here."

Maya gazed at the ark.

"I don't know why we're in here and the others are all out there," said Simon. "I think it has something to do with Seagrape's feathers—the Child Stealer seemed so scared of them—but I don't know why. And I don't know how we can get out of here either. We can't just kick down the bars. I studied the way the cage has been built and if we kick one branch down, the whole thing will fall on us. And if just touching the branches with your hands for a few seconds put you to sleep for nearly a whole day, then I'm afraid that if we had branches falling all over us it might actually put us to sleep. As in, for good."

As Maya watched, an insect tried to crawl across one of the branches and fell back in a dead swoon.

"And we can't dig under them," said Simon. "I tried—there's only a few inches of soil before it hits rock." He shifted and Maya saw that the contents of his backpack were spread out on the ground around him. "Right now I've been trying to see if we have anything here that can help us escape," he said. "You should always know what all of your tools are."

Unappetizing as it was, Maya broke off a piece of the bread and forced herself to eat it. Her brain needed nutrients if it was going to think properly. She had no idea what they were being held for, or for how long the Child Stealer intended to keep them, and she tried hard to quell her rising sense of panic. Simon was very calm as he focused on the objects on the ground. Even though he was her little brother, Maya found this reassuring. Taking a deep breath to steady herself, she turned her attention to the objects.

Quite a number of things that they had started out with when they left the *Pamela Jane* had been lost. What was left were: a bag of fishhooks; a spool of fishing line; a pocketknife; matches; a magnifying glass; now filthy spare shirts and socks; a small steel pot; a leaky pen and three stubby pencils; and, of course, the logbook, a little worse for wear but its red leather cover still somehow regal, the gold pattern still shimmering faintly. The pocketknife seemed the most promising tool, but even that didn't present any obvious path to escape without the whole structure collapsing on them. And the short, dull blade was hardly enough to threaten Horatio with when he came to bring them food. Disheartened, she let her eye wander over the objects. She could see no way that they could be of any help.

"There's one other thing," said Simon, looking around quickly to make sure that Horatio wasn't coming. "In the mine, when I pretended to fall, I picked this up and put it in my pocket."

He withdrew a white stone, the size of his palm. Even in the daylight it emitted a soft glow that grew intense, waned, and then grew stronger again.

Ophalla. Element X.

The elusive element that their parents had been searching for—they were holding it in their very hands. Maya took it and turned it over. One side was craggy and covered in mossy soil, the other half was crystal clear, like gemstone, deepening in its center into a fathomless blue-green. Tiny pockets of air, like air bubbles trapped in ice, were frozen in the middle. It was cool to the touch. Maya felt some mysterious power emanating from it. She felt as if she held something living in her hand.

"If it's so precious, we'd better keep it out of sight," she said. "In case anyone comes."

Penny began to fuss then and Maya turned her attention to

consoling her. Simon packed up everything but the logbook. He knew it was pretty hopeless, but it was still their most likely link to their parents. He turned the pages slowly. Some things were still unexplained, like those funny shiny squiggles in the first several pages, which Simon had first noticed when they were waiting on the riverbank for a barge to come along. He scratched at them with his nail but they remained. He discovered that Pascal had written a couple of pages of his own notes, all nearly indecipherable scientific observations about the volcano near the Cloud Forest Village. Nothing that was useful to them. The only new thing that Simon discovered was that, if he angled the book slightly in the light, he could see dozens of faintly shining fingerprints spotting the pages. He showed it to Maya and they realized that the fingerprints were his, and had come from touching the ophalla stone.

The hours dragged on fruitlessly. Boredom set in. On the opposite hillside, felled trees crashed through the undergrowth, hammers rained incessantly on wood and stone, and commands were barked in different languages. Maya and Simon thought that perhaps the Child Stealer would appear and that they would be sent to work in the mines. But nothing happened. The noise of construction droned on, the day blistered with heat, and Maya and Simon did their best to amuse Penny. They knotted the necklace with Seagrape's feathers in it and gave it to her to play with. By the time Horatio brought them fresh water and their dinner—bowls of bland, starchy gruel—Maya felt desperate.

"Please," she begged Horatio through the bars. "Why are we here?"

At first he refused to answer. He seemed, in fact, not to

have heard her at all. He was an old man with a creased, shiny head, and eyes that seemed to have sunken deep into his face. His clothes were ragged and his feet bare, his toenails rimmed with dirt.

"Please," Maya asked again. "Why is she keeping us here?"

Just as she thought Horatio was going to leave without saying anything, he nodded toward Penny.

"Ask her," he said. "She knows."

Perplexed, Maya looked down at Penny, sitting in Simon's lap. She wiped sweat off her brow with the back of her hand. *Ask Penny? What could he possibly mean?* Simon was puzzled, too. He stared down at Penny and then it dawned on him.

"I don't think he means Penny," he whispered. "He was looking at the feathers—he means Seagrape."

"That doesn't make any sense," Maya whispered back. "How can we ask Seagrape—she's a parrot! And she isn't even here. . . ."

Simon shrugged helplessly. Horatio was turning to leave.

"Wait!" Maya cried. "Don't go! Please, why is the Child Stealer keeping us here? At least tell us her name!"

Horatio paused, his back to them.

"Evondra," he said finally.

Evondra. It was a name that seemed to come from a dark, forgotten place. It made Maya think of the insects that seethed on the clammy undersides of rocks or strange, unseen creatures that lurked in the dark caves. She repeated it in her mind and a shiver crept over her skin. Horatio walked away.

Night had fallen and pitch blackness filled the children's world, shrinking it, and they huddled together. Questions, thick as jungle shadows, crowded around them in the Egewa prison.

What had Horatio meant when he had said to ask the parrot? Who was Evondra? Why had she been frightened of the feathers? How had Helix known to give them to the children?

Penny fell asleep and Maya took the necklace gently from her and stroked the soft, green feathers. What was their secret?

❧ CHAPTER TWENTY-ONE ❧

*Time Passes * Night Lights *
By the Fireside*

A human can never be happy in a cage of any kind.

The next few days passed in a tedious blur. Maya and Simon listened to the sounds of construction throughout the long, monotonous crawl of hours. It was hot and steamy and the insects were relentless. After she begged, Horatio brought moss so that Maya could change Penny's diapers. She made sure that the baby was bathed properly once a day, but there was never enough water for her and Simon to wash, too. Occasionally, instead of Horatio, different children brought them their meals and, though they looked at them with bright, curious eyes, none ever dared to speak. If Maya or Simon said anything, the child dropped his or her eyes and hurried away quickly.

Maya's thoughts returned often to what would have happened if they had gone with Helix, instead of waiting for the barge that morning. She wondered who he was, where he lived, what his life was like. She thought of how he had cautioned them repeatedly not to go into the jungle. Had he known about this place?

Occasionally the ugly red monkeys would show up and taunt them, throwing pebbles and bits of twigs and the pits of fruit into the Egewa prison. Penny was terrified of the monkeys and would always weep inconsolably, until finally Maya would cover her eyes whenever she heard them coming. Once, to their horror, the children heard sudden, bloodcurdling screaming coming from the courtyard, which stopped as suddenly as it began.

Evening brought with it no relief, only new voracious insects and frightening noises of unseen predators in the undergrowth. They slept lightly and uncomfortably, rocks digging into their backs. Maya woke up one night and saw a jaguar leap fluidly down from the branches of a tree, Evondra astride its broad, muscular back, a dark form that looked like a sleeping child slung across the cat's neck. The low orange glow of the jaguar and the silhouettes of its passengers faded into the jungle, back toward the courtyard gardens, and Maya drifted uneasily back to sleep.

They did make one heartening discovery, however. One night, from the corner of her eye, Maya saw a light flashing from a window of the ark. It was not an ordinary light, but more of a white glow. Her heart quickened—she knew that sequence of short and long flashes! She rummaged in Simon's backpack for the ophalla stone. Cupping it in her hands, she made the same code that she had used to signal to Netti with fireflies on nights in the Cloud Forest Village. Could it possibly be Netti? She waited, holding her breath, and then from the ark came an answering sequence of light and dark—the same sequence that Netti had used to say "sleep well, and see you in the morning." Maya's eyes filled with tears. She was sure it was Netti, and if Netti was there, Bongo would be with her. Horrible as it was to know that their friends were the Child Stealer's prisoners, too, it was a comfort that they were nearby. Each night after that, when Horatio had left, the Egewa prison and the ark would communicate with the light from ophalla stones, giving each other a small glimmer of cheer in an otherwise cheerless place.

⌒⌒ ⌒⌒ ⌒⌒

Every day they were trapped in the Egewa prison was a day lost in the search for their parents. The decision to go to the ophalla mines now seemed foolish and dangerous, and Maya regretted trying to solve a mystery that didn't seem like it would bring them any closer to her parents at all. She and Simon were sure now that their parents knew nothing about the ophalla mines.

The children barraged Horatio with questions each time they saw him, but he ignored them. Then Maya had the idea that perhaps if they could get him to like them somehow, he would be more likely to help, or at least reveal some clue that would let them find a way out of there. Simon thought it was a good idea. After he had given them dinner, Horatio had begun lighting a fire outside the Egewa prison to roast ticano nuts. So when he arrived that night, they began to tell him about the *Pamela Jane* and about the storm that had separated them from their parents.

Horatio leaned over and stirred the fire, and the flames leaped up, but still he didn't acknowledge them.

Maya and Simon did not give up. Each night when Horatio came, the children told stories about their life at sea. It helped to pass the time, and reminded Maya and Simon of who they were and what life beyond the prison was like.

They described friendly schools of dolphins who would travel alongside the boat for weeks, riding the waves off the bow; the bioluminescent creatures that shimmered in the water at nighttime; the swordfish, twelve feet long, that had leaped over the deck of the *Pamela Jane* one afternoon. In talking about it, Maya realized how deeply she loved the ocean. She believed that, though he pretended not to listen to them, Horatio enjoyed the stories, and that's why he came back each night.

Finally, after a night spent describing the eccentric migration patterns of silver lobsters, Maya leaned as close to the bars of the prison as she dared—the sap glowed dangerously in the firelight—and in a low, pleading voice, again asked Horatio who Evondra was and why all the children were in the camp—and why she and Simon and Penny were being kept in the Egewa prison.

Horatio said nothing for a minute. Maya ground her teeth in frustration, expecting that he would snuff out the fire and leave and once again they would have learned nothing.

But then he spoke. "Why would anyone want to hear such a story?" he muttered bitterly. A stick snapped in the fire and a tiny shower of orange sparks flew up and were snuffed out in the moist air.

Maya spoke cautiously in hopes that if she wasn't too demanding he would stay there long enough to answer her. "Please," she whispered. "Why are we here?"

The darkness seemed to close in all around them, and the firelight flickered on Horatio's face. He stared into the flames for a few minutes before he spoke.

"She didn't start out this way," he said softly. Then he took a breath and began.

❧ Chapter Twenty-Two ❧

*Evondra's Story * Ophalla Cities *
Dark Women * Evil in the Jungle *
Ruling the Stone*

In Tamarind those who are gifted with fine voices are considered special," Horatio told them. "In legends of long ago, it was the power of a songstress's voice that was said to keep Tamarind safe from invaders from afar and awaken the healing powers inside ophalla.

"In ancient Tamarind, there were cities built from ophalla—one of these cities was supposed to be located here, deep in the Nero Jungle. At the heart of each city was an outdoor opera house, built to look like a magnificent shell, where a songstress would sing, summoning the power of ophalla. In time the cities were destroyed by wars or natural disasters. For hundreds of years they were gone and forgotten. People believed that all of the ophalla had been mined already—there was none left. All that remained were a few pieces in old churches and the homes of wealthy men. Here and there, you could sometimes find small fragments that had been made into jewelry and ornaments and talismans. But the ophalla cities lived on only in stories passed down through the generations.

"Then, just fifty years ago, ophalla was rediscovered in the mountains that divided North and South Tamarind. There was a mad rush for it. At that time, Tamarind was ruled by the Council of Old Families. Evondra was the last child of one of these families. She was raised in the luxury typical of the Old Families. She was born in a grand house on the top of a hill on the coast. Every window had a view to the sea. There were dozens of servants. Evondra's mother had a beautiful voice—crystal clear—and people from the town used to walk up the hill and sit outside the gates just to hear her sing. She used to put Evondra in a cradle in the garden and sing to her. Evondra's parents adored her. They built a small zoo right there on the grounds, and they filled it with jaguars and giant snakes and peacocks, just for her. Naturally, she became a very spoiled child. She had a brush and comb made of pearl, and a little white pony with a snakeskin saddle, and a private tutor who lived at the villa and gave her singing lessons each day. Evondra was a wicked and mischievous child. But she turned out to have a voice that surpassed even her mother's. She could hold people spellbound with it.

"Fighting had begun in the mountains, but it had yet to reach the coast and most of Tamarind still enjoyed peace and prosperity. At first Evondra's father had made a great profit from the ophalla trade. He even decided to rebuild one of the ancient cities, deep in the Nero Jungle, in the oldest part of Tamarind. It was to be a symbol of his family's power and wealth, and link the ancient traditions of Tamarind with the present. At its center would be the opera house, in which his daughter would sing. If things had been allowed to proceed as they had been, Evondra would probably have grown up and become a spoiled young woman with a beautiful voice and that would have been the end of it.

"But instead . . ." Horatio paused, looking into the fire. "The war broke out. All stories become sad here.

"Evondra's father continued with his mad plan to build the

199

opera house in the Nero Jungle. He ordered great blocks of ophalla to be quarried to build the shell. The stage was to be made from the wood of rare trees hundreds of years old. He hired women in the towns to sew heavy red velvet curtains with tassels threaded with real gold. I could go on and on telling you about his crazy plans for his opera house. Two men died, crushed while carrying blocks of ophalla through the jungle, and others perished on the construction site. Everyone said he was crazy.

"Then a full-scale rebellion broke out in the North. The South thought they could quash the rebellion quickly, but it began to spread. Before long Tamarind was in civil war. Evondra's father's new ophalla city was attacked and destroyed and the ophalla was stolen and dispersed across the island. The town on the coast where Evondra's family lived was under siege. Her mother became gravely ill. Because of the blockades, no medicine could reach her in time and she died. Evondra's father nearly lost his mind with grief."

The fire was ebbing and Horatio prodded it with a stick, sending up a shower of sparks, and waited until the flames, which had risen higher, settled again before he spoke.

"One night, not long after her mother died, grief-stricken, when a regiment was just outside her town, Evondra cut her hair short and put on boy's clothes and she ran away and joined them. For a long time her father would only believe that she had been kidnapped. He hired his own men and sent them out after her. But Evondra was too clever for them and she was never caught. She became a great fighter for the South before it was even discovered that she was a girl. And when it was discovered—well, you can imagine the stir it caused. People everywhere talked about it—it was the beginning of the legend.

"But her father, poor man, was heartbroken when he finally had to admit that she had run away on her own and was not coming back. He wasn't yet an old man but his wife had died and now without his daughter, he lost all will to live. He died during a siege. In time, as the old leaders of the North and South were slain, the war descended into pure chaos. By then Evondra had lost everything. Her family, her old life. She had killed so many already and had been witness to such carnage—you cannot see so much death and remain untouched. Something snapped in her mind. She became a mercenary—she fought for whichever side paid her more. She was a menace. She terrorized people on both coasts and she attacked traders and raided jungle settlements. Soon neither side would have anything to do with her and she became a pariah.

"But Evondra had spent so long in the jungle that she was an expert in it. It didn't matter that both sides had orders to kill her if they caught her, she knew how to survive on her own. She could walk barefoot alone through the deepest jungle for months—and often did. She knew all the secrets of the ancient tribes. Which plants are medicinal. How to hunt, where to find freshwater. When people came after her, she disappeared deep into the heart of the Nero Jungle. When she was younger, when she had first joined the soldiers and began to see more of life outside her family's home, Evondra had dabbled in the Dark Arts. In those days it had been just to play pranks on the other soldiers in her regiment. But later, when she went into hiding she found one of the Dark Women.

"The Dark Women are the only ones who know the old arts, who know the secrets of ophalla. They live in hiding, far from the towns and villages. There are never more than three or four in Tamarind at a time. But Evondra found one of these women as she was dying, and she convinced her to pass down some of her secrets before she died. Through traders and soldiers, rumor reached the coast that Evondra had begun bewitching animals. People said she rode a jaguar and she kept an entourage of monkeys. They said she had returned to her father's ophalla city and was living in the ruins.

"Who knows how the idea occurred to her? In my heart I hope that the first children she captured were an accident. Perhaps she didn't hunt them, perhaps they were lost in the jungle and she found them and before she could do anything else she had thought of it. Children to rebuild her father's city. Child slaves. Children make the best ophalla miners. They're small so they can fit in tiny tunnels, and they can drag the carts on their hands and knees through even the narrowest passageways. And children are easy to control.

"After the first two children, more followed. She hunted them. Like animals. Years have passed. For years now children have been rebuilding the ancient opera house. Many have died, but she always finds more. Yes, that's what you hear every day, the sound of the opera house being rebuilt."

"But why?" Maya whispered. "Why rebuild it?"

"Because whoever sung the old songs in the ancient opera houses ruled the very stone that Tamarind is built on," said Horatio. "The songstress called forth the power inside the stone. Very few know anymore what ophalla's power truly is, but in the old legends, it is both wondrous and terrifying. Before she died, the old woman told Evondra some secret, which she has been waiting to use until the opera house is ready. It's almost finished now, and when it is, there will be a concert and something will happen to the ophalla—I don't know what, but it will be something terrible."

Maya sat, absorbing all of this. "How did *you* get here?" she asked after a moment.

"I had made a promise to Evondra's father and so I returned," said Horatio. "I had known the family a very long time. I was Evondra's mother's singing tutor, and then Evondra's. I knew Evondra when she wasn't even an hour old. When she was a little girl, Evondra was like a daughter to me, you see. I wasn't treated like an ordinary servant. I was part of the family. Before he died, Evondra's father asked me to wait for her, to take care of her if she ever returned. In the old days there was no higher post in the Old Families than that of a singing tutor. Although I was his servant, he had been my great friend. I had loved Evondra as if she were my own. So, I suppose you could say that I returned because of love.

"At first I hoped I could persuade her to come back to the coast with me. The towns were more peaceful then. I thought I could train her again and she could sing there. It was folly. When I arrived she had already taken the first of the children. She made me her slave, too, and I've worn these ever since." Horatio rattled the shackles around his ankles.

"For a while I thought of escaping. I'd dream about the sea air and the sunshine and the open skies on the coast—but then one day the dreams just went away."

Horatio paused and looked at Maya and Simon.

"Once you have loved a child, no matter what that child grows up and becomes, you will always look at them and remember that love."

They listened to the silence in the same dark air that earlier that day had been filled with the sound of hammers and saws and the great crunch of trees falling and crushing the undergrowth.

"Why doesn't anyone stop her?" Simon asked finally.

"People who live in the jungle, whose children are taken, why don't they get together and stop her?"

"Tribes have stories about Evondra," said Horatio. "They call her the Lady Who Rides the Jaguar, and they frighten their children into staying close to home by telling them stories about her—'If you stray too far, the Lady Who Rides the Jaguar will steal you!' But most people think she's just a story. There are so many things in the jungle that will endanger a child—piganos, paccas, jaguars, and soldiers who force young boys to join their armies—that tribes usually believe that their children are killed by these creatures or that the child strayed off too far and got lost. People don't want to believe that there is a place like this camp. It's too horrible to imagine and so they don't. They do nothing. That's how evil has always gone on."

Maya and Simon sat quietly. Firelight flickered over their faces.

"Has anyone ever escaped?" Simon asked, not really expecting a reply.

"Once," said Horatio slowly. "But it will never happen again."

A stick snapped in the fire. Horatio said no more. Maya and Simon sat absorbing all they had heard. Maya remembered Valerie Volcano and how fear had kept her living in the Cloud Forest Village, and she was struck by how it seemed that so many things, more than just bars and chains, could hold people prisoner—fear, and guilt, and even love.

Chapter Twenty-Three

A Bad Argument ✻ *A Creeping Thought* ✻
Fingerprints ✻ *Sound from the Sky*

The next day the children saw that the top of the opera shell was now visible over the treetops on the opposite hillside. The clanging and hammering went on late into the night. It must be nearly finished, they thought. Since Horatio had told them the story about Evondra he had not returned to light a fire and sit with them at night, and the hours of boredom were unbroken. The heat was unbearable, the insects maddening. Despair was creeping in on them.

Simon spent hours poring over the logbook, but Maya hated to look at it now. It just reminded her of her parents and made her sad. Any glimmer of hope she'd had that it could help them escape was gone.

"Simon, we've read the book a hundred times," Maya said, exasperated. "There's nothing there that can help us."

"You're wrong," he said. "I just have to find it."

"No, it won't!" said Maya. "Can't you see? The whole reason we're here right now is because we thought Mami and Papi were looking for ophalla—but look what happened! Now we're prisoners—and we don't know anything more! Just because ophalla glows doesn't mean it has anything to do with the sea creatures. We were wrong about everything. I never should have even let us leave the boat.

"Mami and Papi didn't really know anything about

Tamarind," she went on. "They studied animals in the ocean and reported what they found back to Marine Stations. That's what they told us they were doing, that's all they *should* have been doing! They were scientists, okay? That's all! They didn't know anything about Tamarind, not really, so nothing they wrote in the logbook can help us!" Maya said bitterly.

Simon stared at the book.

"You said 'were,'" he said quietly.

He would have walked away from Maya, just started walking and walking and left her behind for good, but there was nowhere to go. The Egewa bars glistened dangerously. He went as far away as he could, which was only a few feet, and turned around and stared into the jungle.

Maya turned around and faced the other way. The jungle, the prison, the sounds of the slave children at work all day—she couldn't stand it anymore. How long could they stay here like this? Each day blending into the next? It was too horrible to contemplate. She felt more miserable than she had the whole time since the storm, since she'd gone up onto the deck and realized that their parents were gone, since they'd left the *Pamela Jane* and trekked through the jungle. For the first time, she felt angry at her parents for having left them, and angry at herself for feeling this way, when she knew that the storm wasn't her parents' fault, and when she didn't even know if they were okay or not. She felt so awful that her whole body hurt.

She stared unhappily through the bars of the prison for a while, not moving. She shouldn't have been so mean to Simon. He was just a little kid, really. She turned around to talk to him and saw that he had left the logbook open on the ground between them. Drawing a shuddery breath, her eyes fell on the open page. In the margin she noticed a shopping list her mother had written for the next time they were in port.

LIMES
TINNED FRUIT
FRESH STRAWBERRIES
PEPPER
BATTERIES
SOAP

Maya began to cry.

It was from a day that summer, before the storm. They were supposed to arrive in port somewhere the following morning and her father had said he would get fresh strawberries for her there. Maya remembered that day as if it were something from a dream. She had been so bored on the *Pamela Jane* and so eager for her life to change that she felt she could hardly bear it. It felt like a lifetime away now. She had lain in her bunk bed with the curtain drawn over her, but it was too hot in the cabin, so she had come outside and sat on the foredeck, where if she kept her legs in, no one could see her. She was sick of eating food from tins, sick of eating fish, sick of having to flavor warm drinking water with wedges of lime. She hated Simon, she hated her parents, and she hated Penny, because since she had come along, there had been even less space in the boat.

But right now she would give almost anything to be back on the *Pamela Jane* that last day, her whole family there. Maya didn't tell herself that if she could just be back on the boat she would never complain again. She knew it wasn't true. She was growing up and it had been time for her to leave the boat and go to school on land. But she wouldn't have been so sullen so often, she wouldn't have gotten irritated at all of them so easily. Oh, what she would give if she could just return to things as they were before. A thought, a slimy, creeping thought wriggled around deep down in her mind, that if she hadn't said she hated living on the *Pamela Jane*, if she had been better and nicer, then perhaps her parents would never have been swept overboard in the storm. Perhaps it all really was her fault. Perhaps, just perhaps, her parents had even *wanted* to leave. This crazy idea was stuck in her mind, deep down as it was, and it weighed on her, and on this miserable afternoon, in the Egewa prison in the heart of the jungle, it came closer to the surface than it ever had before.

All the violence of Maya's emotion was gone and she felt deeply sorry. She wiped her eyes on the grubby hem of her shirt.

"I'm sorry, Simon," she said.

He didn't say anything but she saw his shoulders stiffen.

"I shouldn't have said what I said," said Maya. "I didn't mean it. We're going to get out of here and we're going to find them." She shifted closer to the middle of the prison near her brother. "We are."

"You don't believe that," said Simon, his voice muffled. He ducked his head so she couldn't look at him, but she could still see the side of his face, grimy with dirt and sweat. His hair, knotted and badly in need of a cut, was pasted to his neck. "I thought it was ophalla," he mumbled. "I thought it could help us find them." He buried his head in his knees and refused to look at Maya. Maya tried to touch his shoulder but he pulled away.

Penny began to fuss then, from the heat, no doubt—they were all greasy with sweat and light-headed. Maya had an idea.

She tore a blank page out of the logbook and folded it into a fan and began to fan Penny. Though her face was flushed, the baby began to quiet down as the breeze flowed over her.

"Is that better?" said Maya. "Poor baby. I should have thought of this before."

Maya decided to give Simon a little more time. Then suddenly she stopped fanning and sat stiffly, her gaze locked on the fan. The paper was folded at different angles and in the sunlight she could see that it was covered with shiny ophalla fingerprints—small ones, belonging to Simon. But that wasn't all. At the top of the fan, on the corner of the page, there was a larger, glowing print. A print belonging to a grown-up. Maya looked closer. It was a thumbprint with a jagged scar across its middle, causing a break in the print that appeared on the page. It was a scar that Maya happened to know had been caused by a fishhook. She had been there the day her father had reeled in the grouper that had fought on the deck as he was taking out the hook, and the hook had sliced his thumb. She had been only about three or four then, and she had cried because his thumb had bled.

It was her father's thumbprint here in the logbook, with ophalla on it, the same as hers and Simon's. Which could only mean . . .

"Simon!" Maya cried. "It *is* ophalla!"

Simon turned around then and Maya showed him the thumbprint on the fan.

"Papi must have been holding a shell or something that had ophalla on it," she said. "Look, his print is much lighter than ours, because he probably only touched a little of it, on a shell or something. But it's proof that he was in contact with it. It must have been what they were looking for."

Simon turned and looked at the page.

"This is important," Maya said. "We have to let them know."

Simon took a shuddery breath. "Do you really think we'll go home again?" he asked.

"I do," said Maya firmly, squeezing his shoulder. "You and Penny and me and Mami and Papi. We're all going to go home together."

That's how they were, on the brink of exhaustion, nearly despondent, listless and thin and dirty, trying valiantly to raise their courage, when they heard rumbling approaching in the sky. They listened hard. It sounded like . . . could it be . . . *a plane?* They leaped to their feet and peered frantically through the bars, trying to see. As the droning drew closer, their excitement grew. Could this be rescue? They caught a brief glimpse of a red, single-engine propeller plane as it flew overhead and began its descent over the trees. A moment later the noise stopped.

"It must be landing in the field outside the mines," said Simon breathlessly. "Where the earth is bare, remember?"

The plane seemed to have caused a flurry of activity in the camp. The great monkeys swung from tree to tree to see what was going on and a clamor rose from the slave children. Maya and Simon glimpsed Evondra walking quickly down the path toward the mines, several of the monkeys striding on all fours before her. Then she disappeared down the hill. A moment later the slave children's babble fell silent.

"What do you think's going on?" whispered Simon.

Maya shook her head. "I don't know," she said. "But it doesn't look like they were expecting the plane."

Neither of the children could bring themselves to say aloud what they hoped: that help had come. Neither of them took their eyes off the hillside. It was excruciating—waiting and not knowing. Who had been in the plane? What was happening now?

They didn't have much longer to wait. As they watched, a few of the monkeys, walking on their knuckles, appeared over the ridge and came toward the children's prison. Behind them walked a woman. She was wearing brown leather goggles pushed up on her forehead and a long silk scarf that wafted its length as she was marched along the path. Hearts sinking, Maya and Simon realized that, whoever she was, she was a prisoner now, too. Her hands were tied behind her back. A giant monkey led her along the path with a rope, and Evondra followed behind them, an entourage of monkeys surrounding her.

All hope of rescue draining away, Maya and Simon waited silently while Horatio unlocked the Egewa gate, cut the knots that bound the woman's wrists, and shoved her inside. Maya and Simon saw Evondra stop while she was still some distance away and stand waiting while Horatio locked the gate behind the captured woman. Evondra's face was hard as stone and her eyes, those deeply set, slightly slanted eyes, were black. In the heat of the jungle she emanated a coldness that made the sweat on Maya's skin feel icy. Then she turned and was gone, the odorous monkeys following her on the path.

❧ Chapter Twenty-Four ❧

Kate Shaw, Anthropologist

The woman wasn't old but she wasn't young. She was older than their mother, Maya was sure of that much. Her skin was leathery and creased from the elements, so it was hard to tell. She had bright blue eyes. She looked kind and very strong. Mud was crusted on her calf-high boots and she wore khaki pants and a loose white shirt. Her scarf, even though it was grubby and frayed, was made of pink silk. She saw Maya eyeing it.

"Friends gave this to me, before I left home," she said. "It used to be twice as long but I got bitten by a bossa bossa spider some time ago and it was all I had to dress the bite with so I had to cut half of it off."

She didn't seem at all surprised or particularly upset to be taken captive. When Horatio had shut the gate she had sunk down to her heels and now she shifted to a more comfortable posture. She smiled and extended her hand for them to shake.

"I'm Kate Shaw," she said. "The anthropologist. I'm with the Geo-Nautical Exploration Society and I've spent my life searching for the Mahala, the lost tribe. I believe I've come closer than ever to finding them, but now I seem to have gotten myself into some trouble. I saw a giant shell as I was flying over and I landed on some cleared land near what looks like some type of mine. What on earth *is* this place?"

Maya and Simon looked at each other—could this woman be from the Outside, too?

Since she was also a prisoner, they decided they could trust her, so quickly they told Kate about Evondra and how she kidnapped children and made them her slaves, and about the opera house that was nearly finished being built. Kate was horrified.

"How did you get here?" Simon asked.

Kate explained that she had been heading due south over the Lahari Stream, 50 miles north of the equator, when she hit a patch of turbulence. Before she knew it she was flying through a great storm that had come out of nowhere. She lost all radio signals and her compass went haywire. Within a few minutes, though, she had flown out of the bad weather, but she discovered that her plane's control board was broken—every instrument on it shot. Maya and Simon glanced at each other. It sounded like the same thing that had happened to the navigation equipment on the *Pamela Jane*. With no way to take her bearings, Kate was lost. She figured out roughly what direction she was going in from the sun, decided to fly due west, and after a couple of hours she spotted land in the distance.

"But what about you?" Kate asked. "What are you doing here? Even under all that dirt, in the state you're in, I knew as soon as I saw you that you weren't from here either."

"We're not from Tamarind and we didn't mean to come here," said Maya, sighing. "Our boat was blown off course in a storm and we ended up here—we don't even know where Tamarind is. Do you know where the island is, on a map?"

"On a map?" said Kate, looking faintly amused yet sympathetic. "Oh, my dears, this place isn't on any map. At least not one I've ever seen. We've wandered right off the map.

"You see," said Kate. "I was hired recently by an organization secretly investigating an island that has never appeared on any radar or satellite—it was unclear if it existed at all. Well, it does, and I seem to have found it."

A suspicion was occurring to Maya.

"The organization that hired you," she asked. "Was it the Red Coral Project?"

"Red Coral?" asked Kate. "No, that isn't it."

Deflated, Maya sat back. Simon looked at her.

"It could have different names," he said. "Especially if it's so secret. The organization would be harder to track down if it used different names."

"Aliases," said Maya.

"I don't understand," said Kate.

"Well . . ." began Maya, and she told Kate about their parents' work and the storm and everything that had happened to them since they had arrived on the island. Here and there Simon interjected when he thought that Maya had left out something important.

Kate sat silently when they finished, a slight frown creasing her brow.

"I don't quite know how to tell you children this," she said, hesitating. "It was some weeks ago . . . but I believe I've seen your father."

The world seemed to dissolve at the edges for a moment, as if Maya was about to faint. When she came back to her senses Simon had leaped up and was questioning Kate too quickly for her to respond.

"Shh," Maya said, tugging him back down to sit beside her.

"What do you mean, you think you've seen our father?" she asked.

"When I first got here," said Kate. "I landed in Port Town. I spent a few days wandering around, getting my bearings. One day a man stopped me in the street. He had seen me go by and because I didn't look like I was from here either, he followed me and asked if he could speak to me. He was looking for his children. Two girls and a boy, one of the girls was just a baby. He was a tall man. He had a beard."

"Papi doesn't have a beard," said Simon immediately.

"He might now," Maya said quietly.

"I'll try to be more specific," said Kate. Then she recounted details about their parents and the *Pamela Jane* that there was no way she could have known if she weren't telling the truth. She had, in fact, seen their father. Maya's head spun—their parents were here, they were *here,* somewhere in Tamarind. Simon suddenly looked brighter than he had in days.

"How is he?" Maya asked hoarsely.

"He was thin, but in good health," said Kate. "He was desperate to find you. I felt very badly for him."

"But he was by himself?" Maya asked, holding her breath.

Kate lowered her gaze.

"Yes," she said reluctantly. "He was definitely traveling alone. But I'm sorry, I didn't ask him anything and once he was sure that I hadn't seen any of you he didn't offer any more information. He thanked me and he continued on."

The children looked at Kate, suddenly devastated. Where was their mother?

"Maybe," began Maya. "Maybe they separated to find us. Or maybe they washed ashore at different parts of the island. It doesn't mean that Mami isn't out there, too," she said to Simon.

He nodded but he looked somber.

"He didn't say anything at all about our mother?" Maya asked Kate. "Are you sure?"

"I'm so sorry," Kate said. "When he found out that I hadn't seen you, he left. I didn't see him again."

"Did he say where he was going?" Maya asked.

Kate shook her head.

Maya's head began to ache. It was so cruel! A moment ago she had been brimming with joy at the knowledge that their father had survived the storm and was alive and well and on the very same island that they were on. And to hear the news in as unlikely a place as this—in a prison in the heart of the jungle—had made her feel giddy, as if anything was possible and at any moment their father might appear at the camp to take them home. And then immediately after that, to hear that their mother was not with him, to be left with no clue even as to whether she had made it safely to shore—it was too much. It had not even occurred to her before that their parents might not be together, so the knowledge that they were not shocked her to the core. Maya tried to collect her thoughts. "Kate," she asked. "If we escape, would you take us to the town where you saw our father?"

"Take you with me?"

"In your plane. We aren't very big. Simon and I could squash together in the backseat and I could hold Penny on my lap."

"Of course," said Kate. "Of course. And even if he isn't there anymore, you may find someone there who knows where he went. But the question is, how do we get out of here?"

❧ Chapter Twenty-Five ❧

Simon's Plan ✳ *Evondra, the Evil Opera Queen* ✳
Concert ✳ *Act of Daring* ✳ *A Great Rain*

How *would* they get out of there?

Maya didn't know the answer to that—their discussions with Horatio had left them none the wiser about how they might escape.

Later that afternoon, Horatio trudged up the hill to bring them cassava bread for lunch. The children didn't always get lunch and were happy to see him. Horatio passed the hunk of bread between the bars, and Simon took it and broke it into pieces for them to share. Horatio looked in at them.

"You'll be brought out tomorrow night," he said. "For the concert."

Maya's heart skipped a beat—freedom!

"And then you'll go back in," said Horatio, turning and shuffling off back down the hill, chain rattling.

Maya and Simon and Kate looked at each other, faces shining, barely able to contain their glee. Even Horatio's dismal parting comment could not dampen their spirits now. The prospect of freedom—even if it was only for the duration of the concert—energized them. Once they were out of the Egewa prison tomorrow night, they would somehow find a way to break away from whoever was guarding them. . . . They sat there pondering how when suddenly Simon's face lit up.

"The Egewa prison!" he whispered excitedly. "We can use the prison to help us escape!"

The following day dawned rainy and hot. Maya, Simon, Penny, and Kate huddled on the highest ground in the prison, but still puddles formed on the ground and the earth was soggy. They feared that the concert would be called off, but at nightfall the rain broke, the clouds began to clear, and moonlight shone on the wet earth and damp tiers of jungle. Maya and the others watched as, in the moonlight, the red monkeys escorted the slave children from the ark. They filed back out and over the hill to the opera shell.

Maya was on tenterhooks by the time Horatio arrived. He let them out of the cage one by one, tying their wrists together, then looping a chain between the three of them. The children stretched their legs and took their first deep breaths of almost-freedom—even the air itself seemed sweeter just outside the prison bars! Their limbs tingled as the blood rushed through them. Penny was snug in the sling on Maya's side. Maya was nervous about their plan and felt light-headed at the prospect of liberty. Horatio led them to the bottom of the hill, where they crossed a little footbridge—Simon had been right, there was a stream here. They climbed back up the hill on the opposite side and in the valley below they caught their first glimpse of what they had heard being built each day: the opera shell.

It was a staggering sight: a tremendous, fan-shaped shell, large and luminous as the moon, sitting in the middle of the jungle. It was built out of ice-white blocks of ophalla, carved and polished until they shone. In front of it, at its base, was a wooden stage. A few slave children were hanging from ropes, making final preparations. The rest were seated cross-legged on the ground in front of the stage. There were hundreds of them. Bulky, red-haired monkeys stood about the fringes of the crowd. Until then Maya had been so preoccupied with their escape that she had not thought much about the concert itself. But now, regarding the awesome shell, she felt a shiver of fear—what power in the ophalla was Evondra trying to unleash?

The only light beneath the jungle canopy came from the candles glowing in the skulls that stood on poles around the perimeter of the crowd. An orange glow lit the gaping eye sockets and leering jaws, and Maya cringed as they passed them. Horatio led Maya, Simon, Penny, and Kate down the hill and to the back of the audience, where he motioned them to sit down. A monkey at the front of the crowd cracked a whip and the hushed murmur rippling through the crowd faded. Silence descended. Another red monkey, scratching at fleas on its chest, walked past the children, its eyes roving the crowd. Maya met Simon's eyes. His face was pale. Their plan depended on him. It wasn't time yet, though.

Maya scanned the crowd but could not make out Netti or Bongo anywhere. Then all eyes turned as a figure emerged from the wings and walked out and stood in the center of the stage. The figure was silhouetted against the light of the shell, and though Maya assumed it was Evondra, she could not tell for sure. Maya glanced down at Penny. It was past the baby's bedtime and she was asleep, her breath soft against Maya's shoulder.

There was a rustling in the treetops overhead, and Maya saw that the slave children were pulling ropes tied to the highest branches in the canopy overhead. The canopy parted and a beam of moonlight, roiling soft as smoke through the clouds in the trees, fell like a spotlight on the figure in the middle of the stage. It was indeed Evondra. Her hair shone black as oil and her lips and cheeks were stained red with berries from the jungle. She wore a long gown, as purple as the flesh of piranhas. A dark green snake was coiled around her outstretched arm, its head turned and raised to face her, its forked tongue flickering like a flame in a breeze.

But there was no breeze in the jungle. The air was motionless and the clouds high up in the cloud forest moved so slowly they hardly seemed to be moving at all. Maya felt sweat pouring from her skin. It was almost too hot to breathe. The faces of all the children glowed dully in the moonlight.

A noise came from Evondra's throat, but it was not like singing. It was unlike anything Maya had ever heard. Her voice was clear as a bell and haunting. She sang only one note but it seemed less a note than a palpable vibration through the air. Slowly it seemed that all the creatures in the jungle ceased moving—the snakes stopped midway through their oily glide down tree trunks; the monkeys who had been munching fruit let the pits drop to the ground; the birds folded their wings and fell into reverent silence; even the tiniest ants and beetles stopped what they were doing as if to listen. As she sang, the ophalla shell behind her seemed to grow brighter. Maya watched nervously.

"The vibrations from her voice are doing something to the ophalla," whispered Kate.

Bubbles seemed to be rising in the ophalla, growing bright and clear.

The slave children and the animals of the jungle were transfixed. Then Evondra lifted her arm toward the crowd, and the children began to sing.

"She needs more voices," said Kate.

The children sang, their youthful voices lifting like a sweet breeze over the camp, holding a single note. Again Maya looked for Netti and Bongo, but there were too many children for her to make out individual faces.

Horatio left them and a different ugly red monkey came and took his place. Maya could feel its hot breath on her neck. There didn't seem to be any other creatures behind it though—they had all moved forward and were staring spellbound at the stage. Maya glanced at Simon. This was their moment.

Unbeknownst to Horatio or the monkeys, inside Simon's backpack was a stick of Egewa, taken from the bars of the prison and wrapped carefully in a spare T-shirt. The day before, Simon had cut several lengths of fishing line with the penknife. Without touching the bars, he had tied a complicated series of knots between two right angles of the prison, creating a nearly invisible web. The web held the prison walls intact for the next part: Moving carefully, Simon had used the pocketknife to saw free a four-inch length of a narrow Egewa branch. He had tied a piece of fishing line around the length, so instead of falling to the ground, it dropped only a few feet before the line caught it. It had dangled there, poisonous amber sap glistening, twirling gently as they all gazed at it, their key to escape.

The plan depended on Simon being quick. They wouldn't have a second chance.

Maya stared straight ahead and tried to breathe evenly so she wouldn't attract the monkey's attention. Beads of sweat clustered on her forehead. Slowly and without the monkey noticing, Simon, the knot expert, had untied his hands behind his back. Now he reached into his backpack. In one swift motion he withdrew the stick of Egewa, turned quickly, and shoved it in the monkey's mouth. The monkey bit down on it—it was a reflex—and quickly its eyes widened in horror. It spit it out, but it was too late. As the children watched, it slumped over; its eyelids grew heavy and then closed. Hands trembling, the children and Kate worked free the knots that bound their hands. Then crouching, they slipped back away from the crowd, through the shadows and into the jungle.

Now they just had to make it to the plane—and pray that it was still where Kate had left it. They ran as fast as they could, trying not to make too much noise. Maya held Penny to her tightly—she had woken but was too startled to cry. Kate was just in front and Maya could hear Simon breathing raggedly beside her. They reached the ridge and slipped quickly over to the other side, going faster now that they were running downhill. Maya began to think they would make it. Kate's plane should be in the field just beyond the next hill. It had begun to rain again, just a few scattered drops at first, then it picked up its tempo.

The strange singing behind them stopped suddenly and the jungle seemed to grow darker as the light from the ophalla shell dimmed. The rain came down violently now and the children could hardly see which way to go. If their absence hadn't been discovered already, it was sure to be at any minute, and they pressed on, gasping for air. They passed the Egewa prison and scrambled up the slope away from it. Maya looked over her shoulder and saw the walls of the prison collapse in a mud slide. Just like that, the place where they had spent so many long days as prisoners was gone in a wash of dirt and pebbles and tree branches.

Maya's heart raced as they stumbled along. It was hard to run with Penny and she was behind the others. Simon looked behind him and then grabbed her hand and pulled her along faster. The rain was coming down so hard that sometimes Maya could barely see a foot in front of her face. But there was the ark, just up ahead. Then through the curtain of water she could see the silhouettes of other monkeys galloping through the trees.

"They're looking for us," Maya gasped in a whisper. She felt like her heart was going to burst out of her chest. The monkeys screeched every now and then as they searched for the runaways. How were they going to get to the plane in time? The jungle was crawling with Evondra's monkeys. Farther down the hill, Maya could hear the rushing stream, already rising from the rain. She saw the slave children marching through the trees toward the ark—the rain must have stopped the concert, and the children were being sent back. Hoping to take advantage of the distraction, the children and Kate began moving in a crouch through the trees in the direction of the plane, when suddenly a great red monkey, his wiry fur slicked flat by the rain and his mouth peeled back in a grimace, dropped down from a tree in front of them. He threw his head back and howled. More monkeys were upon them in a moment, and the terrified children and Kate were forced back through the trees toward the ark. They were prisoners again! Maya's heart plunged—this couldn't be happening!

The monkeys jostled the children up the steps and pushed them inside. The door swung shut and they were in darkness.

The air inside the ark was foul. Nausea washed over Maya. Trembling, she leaned back against the side of the boat and waited for her eyes to adjust to the dimness. When slowly the scene before her became clear she held her breath and stared, horrified and speechless. The inside of the ark was like nothing she had ever seen. Children, their faces black with dirt from the mines, were crammed onto straw mats together. There weren't enough mats and many lay on the bare floorboards, where splinters drove into their bony hips. Everywhere was the dank, oppressive smell of human filth and despair. One hundred pairs of listless eyes watched Maya and Simon and Penny and Kate. As she looked around her, Maya knew that as awful as the past weeks in the Egewa prison had been, she and Simon and Penny had lived like kings and queens compared to these miserable children.

From a dark corner a small boy came bounding across the others, jabbering excitedly. The other children leaned out of his way but he had to hopscotch over the arms and legs that seemed to take up every inch of the floor. It wasn't until he reached Maya and Simon that they realized who it was.

"Bongo!" cried Simon joyfully. "It's you!"

Bongo wept tears of joy to see his friends.

"Simon!" he cried. "Maya! Penny!" He reached out and petted Penny's head gently.

Netti came running after him and she and Maya embraced. They all chattered excitedly; although they couldn't understand each other's words, the sentiment was clear. Netti wiped tears from her cheeks and smiled. But just then the ark lurched violently and a collective scream went up from the slave children.

"It's the rain," said Kate. "It's washing us down the hillside."

The ark slid a few more feet, and some of the younger children began to cry. Between the din of the rain on the deck above and the wailing in the hull, Maya could hardly think.

"We're going to slide down to the stream!" cried Simon. "And the water is rising—we'll float away!"

Kate eyed the rotting wooden beams overhead. "Who

knows how long this thing has been lying here like this—it could be rotted through. If there's a hole in it somewhere, the hull will fill with water and the ark will sink with all of us trapped inside. We'll all drown. We have to get out, now—we don't have any time!"

"We have to get to the deck," said Maya to Bongo and Netti. She pointed above them frantically.

The rain pounded down on the deck above them, deafeningly loud, and the boat slid another few feet. Then one of the boys said something and the others went off and returned a moment later with what looked like a beam that at some point in time must have fallen from the ceiling. The ends were rotting, but otherwise it looked sturdy. Standing evenly on either side of it and counting off, the boys then swung the end of the beam as hard as they could into the door that led to the deck. The force nearly knocked them over. The door shuddered but stood. Again the boys heaved the beam into it.

All the other children had gotten up and were crowded at the foot of the stairs. The boys with the beam swung it into the door again and again and again until finally the hinges snapped and the door burst open. Moonlight and rain poured in onto the dirty, upturned faces below. A cheer was raised and all the children began streaming up the steps to the deck. Maya, Simon, Penny, and Kate were forced along with them.

Slave children emerged out into the fresh, pure air. Clean, cold rain beat down and washed the grime from their skin. The ark was tipped to one side on the hillside, so the deck was at an awkward angle. They were nearly at the bottom of the hill now, and Maya could see that the little stream had swollen into a muddy, fast-moving river, and the water was still rising. Funnels of rainwater coursing down the hill had loosened the earth beneath the ark and it was sliding down the hill in fits and starts. Maya held on to Simon and Penny, afraid that the whole thing would roll over. A sudden mud slide brought it swiftly to the edge of the river and a collective scream went up from all the slave children, now massed on the deck. Silence followed as everyone waited, breath held, to see what would happen. The water rose over the keel and then—Maya held her breath—the ark began to float.

The red-haired monkeys saw the ark lift in the water and they came lumbering down the hillside to stop it. As the ark slid down the river beneath overhanging tree branches, a few monkeys dropped down, but the children tore off pieces of the railing and beat the creatures back with them, until they were forced overboard into the roaring white water below.

"My plane is on high ground," said Kate. "We've got to get to it."

"How?" asked Maya, tying Penny's sling more tightly to her waist. The ark was already beginning to pick up speed.

"We'll have to catch onto the next branch the ark goes under," said Kate.

Up ahead there were several branches overhanging the river. The ark was going so quickly now that timing a jump properly to catch onto a branch would be almost impossible.

"What about Bongo and Netti?" Maya shouted over the roar of the rain.

But Netti and Bongo were with other Cloud Forest Children. When they saw what Maya and Simon meant to do, they shook their heads. They would not come.

"It's now or never," shouted Kate as the ark passed beneath a low-hanging branch. "JUMP!"

But everything was happening too fast and Maya hesitated.

Through the torrential rain she watched as Kate caught onto a branch and the river swept the ark away without her.

"Maya!" Simon shouted through the rain.

Maya glanced back over her shoulder but Kate was already gone. She looked ahead and saw a high branch coming up. They could grab onto it and still catch up to Kate. They had to.

"We have to jump," she shouted. "Together—on the count of three."

She turned and, tears in her eyes, embraced Netti and Bongo.

"Good-bye," Simon shouted. "Good-bye!"

Maya shielded her eyes from the blazing rain and could just make out the branch, which was fast approaching.

"One, two, THREE!" she shouted, and they leaped.

Maya held on to the branch for dear life, praying that her fingers wouldn't slip free. Penny was jounced around in the sling on Maya's side, and Maya was terrified for a moment that she would fall out. The ark slipped away beneath them and they hung onto the end of the branch, suspended in thin air, the white water churning beneath them. They began to move, hand over hand like the monkeys did, toward the trunk of the tree, where they climbed down, grazing their hands and knees in their haste. The soggy earth sucked at their feet as they ran toward the clearing. The ark was already long gone down the fast river, and if they didn't reach Kate in time they would be stranded.

"Faster!" Maya cried. "Keep running!"

They reached the edge of the cleared land around the mine, but Maya couldn't see the plane. What if Kate had left without them? She scanned the scene and caught sight of the entrance to the ophalla mine, flooded with rainwater and sparkling like an ice-blue pond in the moonlight in the middle of the field. Monkeys congregated near the entrance. They spotted the children and a wild screeching went up through the tumult of the rain. Maya heard footsteps pounding behind them. When she glanced over her shoulder she saw monkeys dropped down on all fours and running pell-mell, their lips pulled back in threatening grimaces as they closed the distance. Maya saw Kate's plane at the other end of the field. Kate was standing beside it screaming at them to hurry. But Maya couldn't run any faster.

They reached the plane before the monkeys caught them. It was a two-seater, without a roof or windows, and Kate boosted the children into the backseat. Then she clambered into the front. Maya's heart caught in her throat while they waited for the engine to catch. It was still turning over and wheezing when the first rocks struck the side of the plane. More monkeys were coming into view, throwing ophalla stones at the plane as they ran. The monkeys were only strides away—how could the plane not be starting! Maya ducked down and pulled Simon with her and a stone whizzed directly over their heads. "Please just start, please just start," Maya repeated in a whisper and then, as if it heard her, finally the engine caught and the propeller began to whir. A moment later they were taxiing down the field, the plane bouncing and hopping on the uneven ground, the mud sucking at its wheels. Maya snuck a look behind them. The plane gathered speed. As the rain pounded down, one giant creature roared and increased his stride, his big burly shoulders rippling as he ran. He was nearly on them. But just then the plane's nose lifted off the ground and then the wheels left the earth and they were airborne, climbing quickly, nothing between them and the ground but sweet, pure air and rain.

It wasn't until they were safely up in the heights of the night sky, above the rain clouds, that Maya felt a sense of relief. She let the others put their heads up, and she looked out herself, gasping when she saw how high they were and she had to close her eyes until the dizziness passed. Then she looked down again.

The clouds broke and, from high above, in the moonlight they could see the ark floating down the river in the fast current, all the children on the deck jumping up and down and cheering and waving to them. Maya and Simon waved back furiously. On either side of the swollen river they saw Evondra's monkeys in the highest branches of trees, clinging on for dear life. That made them cheer louder. They caught sight of Evondra, fighting for space with a monkey on a skinny branch that bent precariously toward the rushing water. Then the water rose or the branch tipped too low, and she was suddenly in the violent river on her back, long black hair spread for a moment over the surface of the water as she spun in the current. Then the current pulled her under suddenly and she disappeared from sight. From the air, Maya and Simon could hear a new cheer go up from the ark. They sat there grinning at each other and then the plane began to climb more steeply and they left the boat behind. The children celebrating on the deck became as tiny as dots before a bend in the river concealed them completely from Maya and Simon's view.

Chapter Twenty-Six

View from Above ✳ *Into the Dawn*

The air up high was cool, and Maya's and Simon's clothes dried quickly.

"I haven't been cool in ages," Maya sighed in satisfaction.

Kate leaned back and shouted over her shoulder to them, "I'm taking us to the coast, to Port Town!"

"Where Papi was," Maya whispered to herself. "And where Helix lives."

"I wish Bongo and Netti could have come with us," said Simon, looking sad for a moment.

Maya considered. "No, this is better. They're not that far from the Cloud Forest Village. And there were other Cloud Forest Children who were prisoners. They can all go back together. If they had come with us, they would probably never get home. And who knows where we're going?"

Maya looked out of the plane. They had left the shining waters of the flood far behind them. The jungle spread out dark green below, so thick that they could only see the tops of the trees. Now and then there was just a twinkle of moonlight on rivers through the trees and then even those were gone. The jungle seemed endless.

"We could have been in there forever," said Simon.

Maya nodded soberly. Without speaking, the two children held hands. The plane roared on over the jungle, echoing off the roof of the trees, and then the river that they had seen from time to time widened and the plane followed it. Penny sat quietly in her lap and Maya held on to her tightly.

The children dozed off for a while and when they woke, dawn was breaking and the world was turning from gray to apricot and blue. After a while, Simon looked down and shouted.

"Look!"

There it was! The sea! Turquoise in the shallows where palms leaned into the water, dark blue out by the horizon. There wasn't a cloud in sight, just miles of blue sky, the air glassy with light.

Kate leaned back to say something but Maya and Simon couldn't hear her over the engine. Her scarf fluttered back in the breeze. She pointed out of the left side of the plane, and Maya and Simon watched as a seaside town came into view. Fishing boats tracked in around the reef line and sailing ships were docked in the harbor. A long, rickety-looking boardwalk jutted out into the sea, lined on either side with wooden shacks. The people walking on the boardwalk looked as tiny as ants.

They flew over the town and kept going until a flat, deserted strip of beach appeared. From high above it looked soft and white as a blanket. Kate brought the plane down gently. Maya's heart pounded as they touched down, the wall of the jungle rushing past on one side and the brilliant blue of the sea rushing past on the other. The plane fishtailed from side to side as the wheels spun in the sand. Maya and Simon grabbed on to each other until the plane slowed and came to a stop, the propellers still pulsing gently. Kate pushed her goggles up over her forehead and turned around in her seat to look at them.

"The town we flew over was Port Town," said Kate. "If you keep walking down this beach you'll get to it."

"Where are you going to go?" asked Simon.

"I have to find fuel," said Kate. "And I'll keep exploring. It's a once-in-a-lifetime chance, to see a place like this."

"Good luck," said Maya. She held out her hand to shake Kate's. "Thank you for everything."

Kate shook Maya's hand and then Simon's and then Penny's, too.

"Good luck to you as well," she said solemnly. "It was my great pleasure to meet you all, and I hope that you find your parents."

Penny gurgled and waved her fists. Before Maya hopped out of the plane, Kate spoke to just her. "You be careful," she said. Maya nodded.

Simon jumped down onto the sand first and stretched his legs, and Maya passed Penny down to him. Then she jumped down and knelt for a minute, pressing her palms into the sand. It was hot and dry. It felt so good to be out of the damp, moldy jungle. They waved to Kate as the plane began a crooked run down the sand then lifted, propellers droning, the sound bouncing off the wall of the jungle. For a moment Maya watched the pink scarf flying out behind Kate like the tail of a kite. Then the plane shrank to a tiny blot and vanished down the coast.

The children turned and started walking.

❧ CHAPTER TWENTY-SEVEN ❧

Port Town ✳ The Market ✳ A Gang
of Bullies ✳ Pirates' Den

The children were a raggedy company as they reached the end of the beach and joined a wide dirt road that led into Port Town.

The town was loud and colorful. Tin shacks alternated with stone houses painted vivid pinks and turquoises and oranges and greens. The stone houses had corrugated tin roofs and deep gloomy porches. In many of the porches, the children saw parrots shackled to railings. Hanging plants spilled out of windows and salted sardines were tied up on poles in dirt yards to dry in the sun. The streets were narrow and made of hard-packed dirt worn smooth under the wheels of carts. Barefoot young children played outside in the lanes. Funny-looking stray dogs of all shapes and sizes trotted in packs along the walls of the buildings, and goats bleated inside pens with chewed wooden fences. Carts carrying goods to a market rattled past the children: shiny purple eggplants, flurries of fluffy white chickens, ripe mangoes, hairy cupuaçu fruit, and plump watermelons. A watermelon fell out of a cart in front of Maya and Simon and Penny and split on the ground, and immediately children ran out from alleyways and fought over it, grabbing icy pink hunks.

There were dirty children running all over Port Town, and no one seemed to notice the three newcomers. Every now and then they passed a house that was boarded up or a space where it looked as if several houses had been demolished and now sat in ruins. There seemed to be no police station, no central authority, no one they could ask for help. They passed a burbling water fountain and stopped to drink, grateful for the cold, pure water.

"I don't know where to start," said Maya.

"That looks like a market in the center of town," said Simon. "Why don't we start there? We'll keep going until we find something."

Maya nodded and they began walking again. The sun beat down on their heads and the air was greasy with the heat. Music filtered out from porches where old men with sagging jowls sat on porches, playing cards. On the streets approaching the market, the children found people building stalls and stringing colored lights between the rooftops. It looked like preparations were under way for some type of party.

The market was reopening after siesta and sellers were withdrawing the fine nets covering the wares on tables. Rows of stalls wove around the square and each stall was covered with a roof of colored canvas. Diffused light shone through the roofs, tinting everything jewel colors. Palm weavers sat on their palm mats, weaving baskets and hats. Shell collectors arranged their wares in patterns on their tables—most were exotic shells Maya had never seen, but Simon pointed out shells like the one that Seagrape had brought to them on the boat after the storm, the same one that their father had sketched in the logbook. Flower sellers walked through the market with baskets filled with cut flowers hanging from straps around their necks. It was overwhelming. And then Maya smelled something familiar. A sweet delicate fragrance . . . and then she saw them, bunches of ivory cloud orchids in the flower sellers' stalls! The scent took them back to the Cloud Forest Village. For a moment, wandering aimlessly in the strange, sweltering town, Maya half regretted that they had ever left the cool green heights. They were jostled away from the flower sellers and farther into the market, toward food tables heaped with figs, mangoes, bananas, and damsons, and colorful jugs of tropical juices that sweated in the heat. In the center of the market was a giant barbecue and men in hats kneeled to turn the spits. The heat from it was scorching. Maya and Simon looked longingly at the food, their mouths watering. They hadn't eaten since the previous night.

When a pair of soldiers approached, Maya ducked quickly beneath a table stacked with guavas, pulling Simon with her. They watched their shabby boots go by and as they were about to lift the cloth and go back out into the market, Simon noticed something.

"Look," he said.

Maya followed his gaze to an empty wooden crate on the ground near their feet. On its side a word was stamped in bold block letters: HELIX.

"That's weird," said Simon.

Maya shrugged. It was probably just a strange coincidence. She looked out from beneath the cloth and when she saw that the soldiers were gone, the children stepped back out and began to walk back down the aisle between the stalls.

They kept going, past buildings that were half blasted away, half boarded up, and at one point they stopped and stood on tiptoe to peek in a broken window of what had been an old school. A powerful explosion had shattered the chalkboards and blown the desks to one corner of the room, where their metal legs sat in an ugly twisted tangle. Old schoolbooks, warped from the humidity, lay beneath thick cobwebs. Maya and Simon both thought of Rodrigo.

They left the blasted buildings and climbed the hill, stopping

235

halfway up to rest. At the top of the hill was a magnificent, coral-colored villa. On the outskirts of town was a big, flat-topped building with pipes and storehouses around it—an old factory, boarded up. A bell was tolling somewhere in the town below. Maya felt quite grave as she gazed down at the harbor. For so long she had just wanted to get to Port Town, but now that they were there, she didn't really know what to do. Masts of sailboats, sails furled, ticked back and forth in the breeze and the tide, and here and there people moved about on the decks. A few little rowboats brought people to shore from the boats moored farther out in the water. It was just like any port that they used to sail into with their parents. Maya felt a pang. Though they were too far away to see clearly, she saw a few children running down the dock. *That could be us,* she thought.

"Let's go to the port itself," said Simon. "Boat people always know other boat people. We have to start talking to people. Maybe someone will remember seeing Mami or Papi."

What Maya thought was no, there were too many people, too many boats, too many houses on too many streets in the town, and the task of finding their parents suddenly seemed more daunting there in the midst of civilization than it had when the three of them had been alone, marching through the jungle singing old sailor songs that Papi had taught them.

But she didn't say any of that. Instead she said, "I suppose it's as good a place to start as any."

So, lifting Penny back into the sling, they began to make their way to the dock.

From a distance the bay had looked like any ordinary bay with ordinary boats in it, but as they drew closer the children realized that it wasn't like any port they had ever been in. Aside from a few grungy fishing vessels wheezing on their faded

236

moorings, the ships all bore the same flag—a black flag with a violent red insignia in its center. The men walking on and off the slippery planks to the ships were great, brawny men with beefy arms and gold teeth flashing in the sun.

Kitchen slops were being dumped overboard into the already foul soup of fish skeletons, pig hooves, and garbage. Rotten cabbages bobbed like little ghoulish heads between the hulls of the boats. The shadows of sharks circled restlessly, their razor-sharp fins slicing through the debris. While Maya and Simon watched, a kerfuffle erupted on one of the planks leading from the dock to the ship. Live pigs were being carried, struggling, in a thick net onto the ship. But the plank was slick with fish guts, and a man slipped. As he caught his balance, one of the pigs slid squealing from the net and plunged into the water below, where it took only seconds before a frenzied mass of sharks devoured it, leaving behind a bloody cloud in the water.

Maya shuddered, a cold feeling in her stomach. Moments later she and Simon heard frantic squealing as the pigs were slaughtered on the deck of the ship. They kept walking, hoping to see someone who looked like they might be able to help. Farther down the dock, children were scooping jellyfish out of the sea and popping them beneath their tough bare feet. Simon was aghast. Why would they do something so cruel and pointless? A sailor came to the starboard railing of one of the ships and shouted down to the children with the jellyfish, who immediately began fighting and clawing one another for space on the edge of the dock, waving their hands in the air. The sailor tossed something down to them, but Maya couldn't make out what it was when it sailed through the air. It passed over all of their heads and landed on the ground between Maya, Simon, Penny, and the other children.

It was a freshly slaughtered pig's hoof, still attached to a bloody stump of the creature's ankle. The other children descended on the hoof, fighting for it, until one of them emerged from the pack with it raised triumphantly over his head. The heap of children rose disappointedly and brushed themselves off. As they did, one of the boys was shoved by one of the others and he bumped into Maya.

"Hey," he snarled. "What do you think you're doing here?"

He was around her age, Maya thought, but he had a hard, mean little face. He was about to run on after the others, who were leaving down the dock, but he stopped to catch his breath and stared at Maya and Simon. Then he took a step toward them, leering. They stepped back, dangerously close to the edge of the dock where the fins of the sharks circled in the water.

"I said, 'What do you think you're doing here?'" he repeated.

Maya froze and her palms began to sweat. Somehow an ordinary boy—not the terrifying soldiers who ambushed the barge, or an evil opera singer who kidnapped children, or the evil opera singer's monkey henchmen, or even a simmering volcano—just an ordinary bully not much older than herself—frightened Maya more than anything else had so far. She opened her mouth to speak but nothing came out. The boy took another step toward them and now their heels were teetering over the edge of the dock. Then, behind the boy, Maya caught sight of the poor deflated jellyfish, melting into shiny pools in the hot sun, and indignant anger welled in her.

"I've had *enough*!" she shouted.

There was a rotting gutted fish carcass on the dock next to her. It smelled putrid in the hot sun. As the boy took another step toward her, she kicked it hard. It flew through the air and struck him on the chin, leaving a greasy smear on his shirt. The boy looked shocked.

Maya smiled.

For a split second Simon was stunned at what Maya had done. Then he saw that the other children had noticed that something was happening and were coming back toward them down the dock. Much as he hated to back down, Simon knew that three (and one of them a baby) didn't stand a chance against ten. He had to get his sisters out of there fast. He grabbed Maya's elbow.

"Run for your life!" he shouted.

By then Maya had seen the other boys coming down the dock and had come to her senses. They ran as fast as they could, dodging fishermen and piles of nets heaped in the middle of the dock. Behind them they could hear that the pack of boys had broken into a run and were gaining on them fast, their bare feet thundering on the boards of the dock. Simon knew there was no way they could outrun them, especially with Maya carrying Penny. Leaving the dock, they ducked down a side street and for a moment they couldn't hear the boys behind them. Simon grabbed Maya and pulled her inside an open doorway and they held their breath. Seconds later they saw the boys charge past.

Sighing with relief, Maya and Simon turned to see that they were in one of the taverns, just a bare room with a long bar and round tables. The walls were stained with cooking grease and the smell from the kitchen turned Maya's stomach. The room was filled with men—dirty, sea-worn sailors with bristly beards and missing teeth, who looked as if they had not seen soap in years. Filthy scarves were tied around their heads. Several of them had ears stretched into big, yawning oh's by gold hoop earrings. As one of them lifted his arm to drain a pint glass, Maya saw that a blue sapphire sat in the place of a missing front tooth. Light reflected off the gun tucked into his belt. It hit Maya suddenly that these were not ordinary sailors. Simon realized it at the same time.

"Pirates," he breathed. His eyes shone.

All the men turned to look at the children.

CHAPTER TWENTY - EIGHT

Maya and Simon dashed out of the tavern and ran down another side street. Thankfully none of the pirates followed them. Their hearts were still thumping, but there was no sign of the boys anywhere.

"Those were real pirates in the tavern," Simon said. "A whole *nest* of them!"

Maya was not impressed at all by the thought of pirates. What were they were going to do now? She was deep in thought, trying to figure out what to do next, so at first she didn't know what was happening when Simon shouted and began running down the street after something.

"Simon, stop!" she shouted, and began running after him. What was he doing? There was no one behind them.

Simon turned down a tiny street, and Maya followed a few paces behind—it was hard to run holding Penny—and then she saw that he was chasing something, something that was flying in the air ahead of them. It was a green parrot. A green parrot! Seagrape? Could it be? Had she found them again? Maya began running faster. Simon was already halfway down the next narrow alley when she turned the corner and found him stopped in the middle, looking all around him.

"I've lost her!" he cried.

Panting, Maya caught up with him and they looked down all the side streets, but there was no sign of the bird. Then Maya glimpsed a flash of green from the corner of her eye and she grabbed Simon's arm and they began running down a narrow, crooked street after the parrot, who tilted her wings and soared neatly around another corner. The children had to slow down to make the turn, and as they came around the corner, they came face-to-face with Helix. He looked astonished to see them.

"Helix," cried Simon. "We found you!"

They heard footsteps coming. Maya didn't know if they belonged to the gang of boys, but she didn't want to find out.

"There are boys from the dock chasing us," she said urgently.

Helix glanced in the direction of the footsteps.

"All right," he said, turning to go the other way. "Follow me."

Helix took them down such a maze of paths and back alleys that Maya was thoroughly disoriented by the time they reached the little tin shack with blue curtains that he ushered them into. He shut the door behind them and quickly drew the curtains that faced the street.

"Phew!" said Simon.

"So," said Helix, smiling at the three children. "We meet again."

"I knew we would!" said Simon. "I kept telling Maya we'd find you again."

Maya was just starting to realize that they were with Helix. *Helix*. Again! The day they had arrived on the island, with the vines and the singing sand and Dr. Limmermor, seemed like a million years ago. He caught her staring at him and she looked away, embarrassed.

"Whose house is this?" she asked.

"Mathilde's," replied Helix.

"Who's Mathilde?" asked Simon.

"She used to take care of me, a long time ago," said Helix. "I still stay here when I'm in Port Town. Don't worry, she'll be happy to see us. She's a washerwoman—that's why there's so much laundry around here."

Maya began to relax. Maybe now they were safe. She looked around the room. The shack was just one room with a hard-packed dirt floor. Helix was right—there was laundry everywhere, heaped in piles to be washed, folded into crisply ironed stacks, and hanging to dry on a line outside the window. A big washtub stood in the center, and other tubs sat overturned in a corner. Off to one side a thin curtain parted the rest of the room from what looked to be someone's sleeping quarters. The back windows opened to a small yard on the hill where laundry fluttered in the breeze. Beyond the laundry was a view down to the harbor, where the pirate fleet was docked.

She jumped, startled, when something flew into the room, getting tangled for a moment in the curtains. But it was just Seagrape. The parrot strutted around the middle of the room, flapping her wings and sending bits of downy feathers flying on the breeze, before she hopped onto a perch near the door and sat there, looking down at the children unblinkingly.

"They can't find us here?" Maya asked, glancing back out the window.

Helix shook his head. "Nah. Just stay inside, and keep away from the window. You're lucky—it's market day today, there's lots of people around."

"Hey look!" cried Simon, pointing across the room to where what Maya had thought was one of the overturned washtubs had suddenly stuck out its head and began to trundle slowly across the room. "A tortoise!" Simon went up to the tortoise and patted his shell, which was made up of beautiful, dusty green tiles.

"Sit down if you want," Helix said to Maya. "Mathilde will be home soon."

Maya sat down and Penny fell asleep immediately, leaning against her shoulder. Slowly the panic of the minutes before began to ebb.

Helix smiled—he seemed happy to see them. "I want to hear what happened to you, after I left you at the river that day," he said. "I guess you found a barge that brought you here?"

The children told their story. When Helix heard about the soldiers who ambushed the barge he nodded gravely, but it was not until they reached the part about Evondra and the ophalla mines that Maya was sure she saw his face pale. But he said nothing and just kept listening. He seemed lost in his own thoughts as the story came to a close.

"They escaped?" he asked finally. "All of the children?"

"Yes," said Simon. "All of them."

"And that woman, she drowned? You're sure of that?"

"Yes," said Simon. "I'm sure she did—we could see her from the plane. We saw her go under."

"You had a lucky escape," said Helix seriously.

"Helix," asked Simon. "Were you there? Were you the boy who escaped? Did Seagrape do something to Evondra and now she's scared of you?"

"Nope," said Helix, suddenly breezy. "Sorry, kid. Wasn't me or Seagrape. Just a coincidence—there're lots of green parrots on this island."

"But why was Evondra scared of Seagrape's feathers?" Simon asked, frowning. Helix just shrugged.

Simon looked disappointed, but Maya could tell that he believed Helix. She didn't want to think about the jungle now, though. She had a million questions to ask Helix—chief among them, how they could go about finding their father—but while the children had been inside the shack, the clouds had risen from the jungle and rolled down the hill and settled in snugly over the town. The room grew darker and then the rain began, a low drumming on the tin rooftops that made it difficult to hear one another. Helix ran outside to retrieve the laundry from the line.

As he did, the front door opened. Startled, Maya spun around. But it was just an old woman with a bundle of laundry, a plastic scarf tied over her hair and her shoulders wet from the rain. She wiped her shoes on the mat, lowered the bundle to the ground, and propped up a faded old umbrella against the wall, a puddle soon forming beneath it. She didn't seem surprised to see the children and she beamed when she caught sight of Helix.

"There he is," she said. "There's my Helix come home and brought friends. Hello, little fishies."

Maya couldn't help smiling. There was something warm and kind about the old woman and she liked her instantly. She had a plain, worn face with bright eyes and cheeks flushed from walking quickly through the weather, and she wore an apron dress over her well-padded frame.

"This is Mathilde," said Helix, going over to kiss her on the cheek. "Mathilde, meet Maya, Simon, Penny."

"How d'you do, how d'you do?" Mathilde said, still beaming. "What beautiful little fishies! Thank you, Helix, for bringing them to visit me."

"Sorry not to give any warning," said Helix. "I just ran into them and they needed help so I brought them here. They're looking for their father—he may be in Port Town. They have to keep out of sight for a while and I was hoping they could stay with you here, just until I figure something else out."

"Of course, starfish, of course! Don't need to ask twice! But are they okay? Poor little ones, look at them! Good thing you've come here. Mathilde will take good care of you. We'll have a nice big dinner for you—look at them, Helix, they need to eat, the loves! And Helix will draw you bathwater so you can wash up. A good washing up and by the time you're done, Mathilde will have food ready for you, yes, that's right."

Mathilde bustled around the room preparing dinner and clucking to herself. The bath was a steel tub behind a curtain in the corner. Helix filled it with hot water from the stove. Maya bathed Penny first, then gave her a grain mash with milk—real milk!—that Mathilde had sent Helix out to fetch. Simon bathed next, splashing and making a racket on the other side of the curtain.

"Whoa," he called. "You should see how dirty I was, the water's practically black!"

When Simon couldn't find another speck of dirt on him to make the water dirtier he got out and emptied the water. He watched admiringly as it swilled down the drain.

After Mathilde filled the tub with fresh hot water, Maya drew the curtain and undressed and sank down in the warm, soapy bath, feeling the grime loosening from her skin. She slid all the way underwater and scrubbed her scalp. A hot bath! Civilization! She felt drowsy and content. She would have liked to luxuriate there for hours but she could hear that dinner was almost on the table and so, reluctantly, she stepped out onto the mat Helix had laid out and she dried herself with a rough towel until her skin tingled. Clean! She felt entirely human for the first time in ages. She let the water out of the tub, shuddering to see how much grit had come off of her body—there were whole bits of leaves and twigs in there! They had bathed in the sea earlier that day, but there is some dirt that only soap and hot water can do anything about. When she reached for her clothes to put back on, she found that Mathilde had taken them and replaced them with a long white shirt that was so big it went past her knees. She felt a little silly but it was so good to be in something clean that she didn't care. She combed out her hair as best as she could with her fingers and came out.

"Hello," said Mathilde cheerfully when Maya drew back the curtain. "I took those other clothes so I can give them a good washing for you. No sense getting all fresh and clean and putting on dirty clothes, is there?"

"No," murmured Maya. "Thank you so much."

She went over to check on Penny, who Mathilde had put in a wooden box with blankets in the corner. Penny was sleeping peacefully, her breath soft and her tiny hands bunched into fists.

Dinner was a feast: boiled potatoes, heaps of codfish with tomato sauce, octopus stew, and grainy yellow cassava bread. The children ate without speaking. When they were finished, Maya realized just how tired she really was. Her arms and legs felt like lead and she could barely keep her eyes open. She glanced at Simon and he was nodding off across the table. Maya badly wanted to just curl up somewhere, anywhere, even right there at the table would have been fine, but she had to make a plan.

"We need to figure out how we're going to find our father," she started to say.

"Not tonight; tonight you rest," said Mathilde, smiling.

"But . . ." Maya started. She felt as if she were speaking underwater.

"Tomorrow," said Mathilde. "It can all wait until tomorrow." She got up and helped Simon to his feet and led him, half asleep, to a mat in the corner. He lay down and she put a light blanket over him and within seconds he was breathing deeply and evenly.

"Out like a light," said Mathilde to Maya. "Come on, jewelfish, you should follow him. Here's a bed for you right over here."

Maya wanted to object but she couldn't seem to find the words. She was so tired. . . .

Mathilde had Maya's elbow and was taking her to a cane mat in the corner opposite of where Simon was sleeping. Maya mumbled something and the last thing she heard was Mathilde saying, "Sleep now, little jewelfish."

CHAPTER TWENTY - NINE

Mathilde Talks ✳ *Clues About Helix's Past*
A Sugarcane Crate ✳ *Giants' Roads*

Maya and Simon slept through the morning. When they awoke, the rest of the town was just going inside for their siestas, and the streets were empty. Shutters banged shut and then everything was drowsy and quiet. Mathilde had been washing clothes all morning and on the clothesline outside the window, a row of dresses billowed like sails in the breeze. Helix was gone, and Seagrape with him. Penny had woken and Mathilde had fed her already.

"Listen," said Simon. "It's siesta time. We nearly slept a whole day!"

"You needed it," said Mathilde. "You were exhausted, poor starfish. Now, how about some lunch for you? Helix will be out for the day. He said for you to stay put until he's back this evening—he'll be able to help you then. He's a good boy, Helix."

Maya did not want to lose a whole day, but she was nervous about running into the boys from the dock and, anyway, she knew that Helix was probably their best resource. He'd been right about the jungle—she shouldn't have doubted him before. He knew more about Port Town and Tamarind than they did and he could advise them what to do. Maya decided that they would stay put for now, and she would find out everything she could about Tamarind from Mathilde. Maybe she would learn something useful.

Mathilde dished up yams and stew, and Maya and Simon sat down happily to eat. *How wonderful,* Maya thought, *to eat real food at a real table!* A bell rang out, echoing off all the tin roofs.

The tortoise had been sleeping in the corner but now he stuck out his wrinkled head and yawned at the children, then walked slowly on pebbled feet across the room and settled next to Penny. He leaned over the side of her wooden box and she sat up and squealed and patted his wizened, tolerant old face. From where Maya sat, she could see out the window, down to the harbor below.

"Why are there so many pirates here?" she asked.

"Well, because of the war," said Mathilde. She looked at the children, perplexed. "You fishies must be from very far away, not to know about the pirates!"

"Can you tell us about them?" Maya asked.

"I can," said Mathilde, testing her iron to see if it was hot yet from the stove. It was, and she smoothed a length of fabric beneath her hand and began ironing. "Back in the beginning of the war, the Council forced all ships and fishing vessels to join war fleets. The fleets were supposed to defend coastal towns and fight ships from the North. The North had their own war fleet, of course. But then—oh, fishies, it was terrible—everything in Tamarind turned completely lawless and the fleets, they stopped answering to anyone—it was each man for himself. Crews turned into ordinary pirates, looting and pillaging anything they could get their filthy hands on. Every now and then there's a big sea battle, and all the fleets from the North will come together to fight all the fleets from the South. But mostly nowadays it's a case of fleets attacking lone ships and smaller fleets and raiding towns on the coast. Sometimes ships even attack towns on their own side—it's terrible what happens around here these days, just terrible.

"The man who runs Port Town, Senor Tecumbo, lets fleets dock here. It's supposed to keep the town safer, but if you ask me, I'd rather take my chances with ships from the North than have to walk down the street in Port Town every day with these savages running around causing havoc."

Maya thought about the rough-looking men they had seen in the tavern as she and Simon finished their breakfast.

"Mathilde," Simon asked thoughtfully. "How do you know Helix?"

Mathilde paused, lifting the iron so that steam rose from it for a moment and quickly evaporated. She looked at the children with her clear blue eyes.

"I found him," she said. Before she went on she paused, steam curling up from the iron. "He was living in a sugarcane crate at the end of this alley. He was about your age back then, Simon. He had just arrived in Port Town. In very bad shape, he was, so I took him in. He never said where he was from or what had happened to him. He never wanted to talk about it and I never tried to make him."

"A sugarcane crate," said Maya.

"Yes, yes," said Mathilde. "From the old sugarcane factory. You must have seen it, just on the edge of town. It closed down during the war. People took all the old boxes from it to use for this and that. You'll see them lying around all over the place now. The Helix Sugarcane Factory, it was called. I used to work at the factory, and I saw Helix every day, stamped on all the boxes. It's the only word I can read, you know."

So that was the story behind Helix's name and the crate they had seen in the market. Maya felt the relief of having a small mystery solved, but the deeper mystery of Helix, who he was and where he had come from, began to gather weight in her mind. She felt sure that Helix really was the boy that the children in Evondra's camp had sung about. But if he was, why hadn't he just told them the truth? Where had he come from? What was his real name, even? Her thoughts circled restlessly, and she wondered if someone with so many secrets could be trusted. Should they be relying on him to help them?

"Simon," she said. "Would you get the logbook? I want to look at the map."

Simon retrieved it from his backpack and brought it to Maya at the table. Maya opened it to the page with the map and began to study it. There they were, Port Town. Right on the southwest coast. And just a little west of them, marked promisingly by a star, was the capital, Maracairol.

"Mathilde," said Maya. "What do you know about Maracairol?"

"It's our capital!" exclaimed Mathilde. "The capital of all of Greater Tamarind. Or it used to be, anyway. I suppose now it's just the capital of the South."

"Is it bigger than Port Town?" she asked.

"Oh, much," said Mathilde, smiling. "Port Town is just a little town."

Maya liked the sound of Maracairol. Didn't it make sense that their parents would go to the capital to seek information about them? Maybe, if they couldn't find anything out in Port Town, they should go to Maracairol.

"If the fog on the bay ever clears, you can just make out the edge of Maracairol on the far point," said Mathilde, nodding out the window across the bay. The children followed her gaze. The coast was jagged, jutting in points, then disappearing into deep coves. In the distance it was swallowed by white fog.

"If you were walking, how long would it take to get there?" Maya asked.

"Oh, a few days, I'd say," said Mathilde. "But nobody goes to Maracairol anymore. Nobody goes anywhere anymore. In the old days before the war, people used to go back and forth between Port Town and Maracairol all the time. But it's too dangerous now. There are rebel soldiers from the North and you never know when they'll come down out of the jungle and attack and rob travelers on the road. Very bad times, my love. Much safer to just stay put in Port Town."

Mathilde folded a sheet and pressed it smooth with her palms. She looked over Maya's shoulder at the map.

"Oh, this is a very good map you have here," she said. "And, look, here he is!"

"Who?" the children asked.

"The giant, of course!" said Mathilde, pointing to the road between Port Town and Maracairol. Rodrigo had drawn a broad, ample figure that until then Maya had thought was just some type of ornamentation, the kind you see on old maps.

"Do you mean a *real* giant?" Maya asked.

"What is it? Ah, little starfish has never *seen* a giant before, is that it?" Mathilde asked cheerfully. "There's a giant on every main road between the towns. Though only one per road, of course. They don't like to perform together, you know. Our giant has a wonderful voice—beyond compare. People used to come from far and wide to hear him. When I was a young woman, working in the sugarcane factory, we used to go to hear him on the weekends. We'd all pile into carts and drive out there and have a picnic and not come home until nearly dawn the next day!" Mathilde paused when she saw Maya and Simon looking at her skeptically. "What—aren't there giants where you come from?"

Maya and Simon shook their heads, but they both recalled the singing giants in the story their father had told them before the storm.

🐬 🐬 🐬

Maya spent the afternoon helping Mathilde, folding sheets and holding pleats down flat while Mathilde ironed beautiful dresses that belonged to women who lived on the hill. When each dress was done it was hung from a clothesline across the ceiling. Soon Mathilde's little tin shack was full of the most elegant silk dresses, turning gently on drafts through the window.

Outside, festival preparations were under way and the streets were busy with people building stalls and stringing lights. Mathilde told the children that in a few nights there would be a great parade with people wearing sumptuous glittering masks. There would be food and games and performances by dancers and fire-eaters and magicians in the town square. The celebration would go on for a week, ending with another parade, even more spectacular than the first. There used to be festivals like it all over Tamarind, she said, but Port Town was the only place that had kept up the tradition through the war.

It rained briefly late in the afternoon, leaving Port Town steaming when it cleared. The stifling heat reminded Maya of the jungle.

"Mathilde," she asked. "Do you know anything about the interior? About the jungle?"

Mathilde was folding sheets. The sun had come out for a while, but now there was a light rain pattering on the tin roof.

"The jungle? No, love, I don't know anything about the jungle. Nobody ever goes into the jungle. Except the traders. And the soldiers."

"Why not?"

"Oh, it's not safe in there. It's full of wild animals and bloodthirsty tribes. I could tell you stories. You'd have your head chopped off if you went in there."

Maya and Simon met eyes. They wanted to say that they had lived with the peaceful Cloud Forest People and they had been imprisoned in the old ophalla mines, but Mathilde, back to ironing a pale blue evening gown, wouldn't have believed them. For her, and for most people in Port Town, Maya guessed, the green curtain of the edge of the jungle, just up the hill from Port Town, may as well have been a stone wall dividing the town from another world.

Chapter Thirty

Helix returned just as dusk was seeping down from the jungle, moving like smoke through the streets of Port Town. Seagrape flew in the window and sat on her perch in the corner. Helix had not found anything about their father, but he had not returned empty-handed. He sat down at the table and took out a folded piece of newspaper and unfolded it and smoothed it out on the table in front of them. When he took his hand away and Maya looked down at the newspaper, she gasped.

She was looking at a photograph of herself. It was her eyes, her nose, her cheekbones, her hair, long and dark and brushed neatly back behind her shoulders. How had the newspaper gotten it? Maya had never even seen it before. She squinted and looked at it more closely. But she had never worn that dress, with the bright floral pattern, and she had never worn that necklace. And wait, the eyes in the photo looked like her eyes, but not like them at the same time.

"She's Senor Tecumbo's niece," said Helix. "Her name is Isabella. She lives in Maracairol with her mother, but she's coming to Port Town for the Festival of Masks. This will be the first time her uncle has seen her in years."

Helix had spent most of the day trying to find someone in Port Town who had seen the children's father, but no one could help him. He realized that working like that, it would take weeks to talk to everyone in Port Town and then he might not find out anything, anyway. At a loss, he was on his way home when he stopped to pick up laundry from the villa. While he had waited in the magnificent grounds, the thought had crossed his mind almost idly, that it would take someone like Senor Tecumbo to find the children's parents. Senor was the most powerful man in Port Town—in the whole South. With his help, maybe they could launch a proper search for the children's parents. But even if they could somehow talk to Senor, he would never offer to help them. However . . . if it was his niece who asked him for help, how could he refuse?

Maya, disguised as Isabella, could arrive a few days before the real Isabella was scheduled to arrive. She would somehow persuade him that her mother had asked him to help launch a search for the children's parents. Hopefully Maya would find a clue to the whereabouts of her parents, and the children would be gone from Port Town before the real Isabella arrived.

Maya had had such a shock when she saw the photo that she still felt a little dazed. She looked at it again. Okay, it wasn't her, she could see that now. The other girl's face was slightly broader and her hair was thicker and a few shades darker, though it was hard to say for sure from the black-and-white photograph. If you looked closely you could see that their smiles were a slightly different shape. But at least judging from this photo, they looked to be about the same age and build and their faces bore a striking resemblance to each other.

"I went to Senor Tecumbo's villa tonight to pick up laundry for Mathilde—she washes all of their silks," said Helix. "While I was there, I overheard some of the cooks talking about Isabella. They had a newspaper with a photograph of her in it. I saw that she looked a lot like you and that you're about the same age. She's supposed to arrive here in three days.

But . . . she could get here early. . . ." He explained his plan as best he could.

Maya and Simon sat there, letting everything Helix had said sink in. It was a bold idea. Did he really think it could work?

"But look at me," she said. Mathilde had washed her clothes, but after weeks in the jungle they were practically rags. She plucked at her torn shirt and let it fall back against her body. "How would I ever convince him that I'm his niece?"

Helix waved his arm across the room, where the beautiful party dresses in blues and greens and golds, freshly washed and dried, hung swaying softly in the breeze.

"Take your pick," he said.

"But—" began Maya.

"You can borrow a dress from here to wear to the villa, and you can say that your trunk was stolen on the road from Maracairol. The road between here and there is very dangerous—he won't question you. And I'm sure he'll have a closet full of new clothes for you by the next day. Simon will stay here and he and Mathilde can take care of Penny. I can help, too. The Festival of Masks begins with Mask's Eve, in three nights from now. Senor Tecumbo has a party every year to mark the opening of the Festival. The real Isabella isn't due to arrive until the morning after Mask's Eve. We can make our getaway before that. In all the confusion of the party, we'll be able to slip away.

"Isabella hasn't been in Port Town since she was a little girl—her mother and Senor Tecumbo had a falling out, and Isabella and her uncle haven't seen each other in years. But Senor Tecumbo and Isabella's mother reconciled last year, and have decided to travel to Port Town for the later part of festival.

You will have three days to find out anything you can about your parents."

The plan was resolving itself in Maya's mind. It all depended on Senor Tecumbo believing that she was his niece, a girl that Maya had never seen. But Senor Tecumbo hadn't seen Isabella in years either, not since she had been a child. And so it seemed possible that he wouldn't know that Maya was an imposter. But still, it was terribly risky. Maya didn't know what to do.

"I need a while to think about what I'd say," she said.

"You don't have time," said Helix. "If you're going to do this, it has to be now."

"*Now*?" she asked. "Can't we wait until the morning?"

Helix shook his head.

"There's no time to waste," he said. "You only have three days."

Three days. Maya shivered. The plan seemed crazy and dangerous. If she was caught . . . who knew what would happen? It would be a disaster. What would Simon and Penny do if something happened to her? But if it worked it was the best chance they'd have of finding their parents. Twilight was creeping through the streets of Port Town, and outside the window Maya could see the last light shining on the harbor. If they left now she could be at Senor Tecumbo's villa before dark. She let her glance sweep quickly across the room and then she pointed at a simple blue dress.

"That one," she said.

✦ CHAPTER THIRTY-ONE ✦

Senor Tecumbo ✳ Lorco Is Suspicious ✳
A Conversation with Senor

Wearing a stranger's blue cotton dress that Mathilde had helped to pin in the back for her, and after a slightly tearful farewell to Simon and Penny, Maya walked through the darkening streets of Port Town with Helix.

"It's actually better this way," said Helix. "The first time he sees you it will be shadowy. By the time he sees you in daylight he'll be used to the way you look and he won't think anything of it.

"I didn't want to scare Simon," Helix went on, speaking quickly and quietly so that no one would overhear them. "But Senor Tecumbo can be a very brutal man. I wouldn't say he's a bad man, exactly. But ever since the war began the only way to keep order in Port Town is to be ruthless. He's the reason why Port Town is one of the safest towns in Greater Tamarind. Most other places are in ruins.

"Senor surrounds himself with bodyguards. The chief one, Lorco, is known to be very cruel and cunning. Senor's enemies have a way of disappearing. If he catches you you'll be in very, very bad trouble. So you have to be careful, Maya, really careful—do you understand?"

They stopped and Helix looked at Maya. The road was dark beneath a stand of low, thick palms. Beyond where they stood the road turned up to the great iron gates, on the other side of which it narrowed and continued up the hill to Senor Tecumbo's villa.

"Are you really sure you want to go?" he asked. "It isn't too late to turn back."

Maya felt like she had lost her voice, but she managed to nod stiffly.

Helix clasped her hand in his.

"Good luck," he whispered. "I'll wait here until I hear that you've gotten through."

Maya swallowed. Now she was alone to face whatever lay on the other side of the imposing iron gates. She could still feel the warmth of Helix's hand.

Two guards stopped her at the gates. Maya thought her heart would come thundering out of her chest. One guard sent word to Senor Tecumbo and the other escorted Maya up the hill. A moment later she saw two men walking swiftly down to meet her. The man in front wore a white suit and a white Panama hat that hid his eyes. A few paces behind him was a tall, broad-shouldered man in a black uniform, a gun bulging from his holster. Maya tried to ignore the man and the gun, and focused on Senor, who was standing a few steps in front of her and looking at her suspiciously. She took a deep breath.

"Uncle," she said, just as she had practiced with Helix. "It's me—it's Isabella! It's Isabella!" she repeated. "I'm here early!"

Maya watched as Senor Tecumbo's irritation turned to pure surprise.

"*Isabella?*" he asked.

"Are you surprised?" Maya asked. "Good—we wanted to surprise you."

Senor Tecumbo covered the ground between them in a couple

of strides. Maya's knees quaked and she thought she would collapse out of sheer fright. How had she ever thought she would get away with this? She closed her eyes, awaiting the worst. But then she felt herself being lifted off the ground into a great bear embrace that nearly knocked the wind out of her. Senor Tecumbo smelled of rich, bay cologne and hair oil. He put her back down and planted a kiss on her cheek and then held her at arm's length, his hands on her shoulders.

"My dear," he said. "Let me take a good look at you."

Maya held her breath, feeling faint as his eyes roved over her face. She was grateful for the shadows and the dim light from the lamps. She didn't breathe again until he straightened up and laughed.

"You look just like your mother did at your age," he said, beaming. "Speaking of whom, where *is* your mother? And why on earth are you on foot? Where is the car that brought you?"

"My mother's coming later," Maya heard herself saying. He had bought it—he believed she was his niece. She could hardly believe it. In a way the most dangerous moment had passed. If he had believed her this far, it wouldn't take much more to get him to help her with the search for her parents. And now her nervousness was making it easier to chatter on— he would think it was her excitement at seeing him. "She sent me ahead by myself because—oh, it's a long story," she said. "I have to explain it all to you later."

Senor Tecumbo frowned.

"Who is this driver who let you out to walk by yourself?"

"Oh, don't worry. He had to stop for gasoline just down the hill and I knew I was almost here and I couldn't wait any longer to see you, so I just ran up the hill by myself. It's fine. Really, I'm fine, except that the car was held up along the way and my trunk was stolen and now all my things are gone. I don't know what I'm going to do without any other clothes!"

"Clothes?" he asked. "Don't you worry about clothes, you'll have all the clothes you want by tomorrow, I'll arrange it. But I'm more concerned that the driver let you out by yourself. Tell your mother not to use him again. In fact"—he turned to the bodyguard in the black suit who had been following a little way behind them—"Lorco, find that driver and bring him to me. I'd like to have a chat with him."

Lorco—Maya knew that the man with the gun was the man Helix had warned her about. He had been looking hard at Maya ever since she had arrived. His gaze sent a chill across her skin.

"He's already on his way back to Maracairol," she said quickly, but Senor Tecumbo insisted that Lorco try to find him. Fear pierced Maya's chest as Lorco turned to leave—what if he found out the truth? She shook it off—there was no one to find.

The villa's magnificent pink stone walls loomed at the top of the hillside and great shuttered doors ran all along the front, opening onto a rectangular courtyard paved in white marble and bordered with fragrant night-blooming flowers. Maya managed to murmur responses to Senor Tecumbo's questions as they crossed the rectangle and passed through the largest of the doors into a spectacular foyer. Gleaming black-and-white tiles spread in a checker pattern across the floor, and an ornate white marble staircase swept up to the second floor.

"Why don't you freshen up and then we'll have dinner outside?" said Senor Tecumbo. "We'll meet back down here in half an hour from now."

Maya nodded and a silent maid appeared from nowhere and took her upstairs to a bedroom at the end of a long, high-ceilinged hallway. The room took Maya's breath away and for a few seconds she forgot anything other than that she had just stepped into a room fit for a princess. Long silk curtains the color of pomegranates drifted in the breeze. There was a vast, four-poster bed with a puffy ivory bedspread and fruit-colored pillows. To Maya's delight, an ivory canopy sat on top of the four posters. There was a wardrobe and a dresser made with the same rich jungle wood that the bed frame was made from. Through the doorway at the other end of the room, she could see that the bathroom was the size of the whole cabin on the *Pamela Jane*. Simon was never going to believe her when she told him about all this. Maya caught sight of her own amazed face looking back at her in a large scalloped mirror. She quickly tried to look normal so that the maid wouldn't suspect anything. The real Isabella probably wouldn't bat an eyelash at such luxury.

When Maya had washed her face and combed her hair, she left her room and descended the marble staircase. Senor Tecumbo wasn't yet there, but there were two places set at a table outside on the rectangle. While she waited for him, Maya walked to the edge of the patio and leaned on the cool marble wall, white in the moonlight. Natal plums sat brightly in the dark hedges. Above her, a spray of diamond-white stars were scattered across the great black vault of the sky. She drank in the night air—so much cooler and fresher than the fetid, briny breezes that eddied down by the dock. It was a world away up here.

Maya looked out in the direction of the sea. The lights of the boardwalk reflected on the surf on the incoming tide, but the light extended only a few yards out to sea on either side, and after that the sea fell away into swift darkness. There were no lights from passing ships in sight. Except for the evil huddle of the pirate fleet anchored in the bay, the sea was empty. And, she noticed for the first time, there was no lighthouse beam sweeping the waters around Port Town. It was as if no one ever expected—or wanted—to be found. Or expected ships to seek shelter here. She felt melancholy all of a sudden. What if the plan didn't work? What if she never saw her mother again? If they didn't find their parents soon, would there come a time when she would stop looking for them? Would she just slowly let those thoughts go, until she was like Valerie Volcano, writing letters to a sister who would never receive them? The breeze loosened blossoms and they tumbled across the marble floor past her feet.

"Aha," said Senor Tecumbo, stepping onto the rectangle behind her. "The last time you were here you were a little girl! Now I see before me a beautiful young woman! How does everything here look to you?"

"It's wonderful," said Maya, grateful that she could answer sincerely.

"It is," said Senor Tecumbo, coming to stand beside her to look out over the dark ocean. "And it's an especially beautiful night. I'm glad you got here early, it was a very happy surprise."

Maya smiled.

"One thing is odd, though," said Senor Tecumbo. "Lorco has not found that driver who brought you here. I don't like the sound of him, dropping you off and then disappearing like that. And I'm wondering if he had something to do with your trunk being stolen, too. People can be bought so easily these days. I'm going to talk to your mother about him."

"Oh," said Maya. "I told him it was okay to go home. I don't want him to get into trouble."

"Trouble?" asked Senor Tecumbo. "He *should* be in trouble. I wish your mother wasn't so stubborn about staying in Maracairol. I'd be happiest if you'd both come to live in Port Town, where I would know that you were safe. I don't know why your mother insists on staying on there when, well, when it seems clear that your brother won't be returning."

Her brother—Isabella's brother, not returning, from where? From the war? Was he a soldier? Maya's palms began to sweat. She knew hardly anything about Isabella's family. She had not had time to consider all the repercussions of the plan before Helix had whisked her from Mathilde's to the villa. How was she going to keep up her pretense? The evening stretched out long and perilous before her. She was going to have to steer the conversation to her parents as soon as possible. To her relief, a waiter arrived with their dinner, which he set at a little round table beside the house.

"Shall we?" asked Senor, offering Maya his arm.

They sat down and the servant removed silver covers from their plates. Grilled asparagus, reef fish blackened in an orange sauce, salted potatoes, jungle greens with shiny red pomegranate seeds—it was a small feast. Maya's mouth began to water. She felt guilty for a moment that Simon and Helix weren't there to enjoy it, too, but she didn't have long to think about it before Senor Tecumbo began asking her questions.

"Now," he asked. "Why did your mother send you ahead on your own? I can't think what would have made her do that, with the roads the way they are. It's not like her to be so reckless."

Maya took a sip of açai juice and swallowed it. The glass trembled a little in her hand. Here was her chance.

"She sent me early because we wanted to surprise you, but

also to ask for your help with something very important," she said. "A week ago a couple arrived in Maracairol—they were from the Outside."

Senor Tecumbo put his fork down and stared at her.

"From the Outside?" he asked.

Maya nodded.

"They had been looking for Tamarind, and they found the passage in," she said. "They know how to get back to it. They could—I mean, it would be possible—for them to take people back with them. To show them how to get there. Mami thinks they could get people from the Outside to help Tamarind."

"The passage to the Outside," said Senor Tecumbo softly. He turned his gaze to the ocean invisible in the darkness. "We used to dream of finding the way there. When the war began, many ships left to try to seek help for Tamarind, or just to save themselves. I never heard that even one made it. Days, months, even years later they would be washed back onto our shores as driftwood." He paused. "Most people said it doesn't exist, it's just fantasy."

The dreaminess left his eyes and his gaze hardened.

"Tamarind is full of charlatans," he asked. "Who are these people really? They could be from far across Tamarind—the people there are different, you know. Or, more likely, they're northern spies. How does your mother know they're really from the Outside?"

Maya spoke tremblingly. She wasn't used to lying.

"When you see people from the Outside, you just know," she said. "I promise you, they were."

"Well, is your mother going to bring them here, or do I have to go to Maracairol?" he asked. "I don't understand what she's thinking. And she sent me a letter by a messenger just a few days ago—why wouldn't she mention this then? You said the people arrived a week ago."

Maya tried to keep her breathing steady. She could feel her dress sticking to the sweat on her back.

"Perhaps it wasn't a whole week ago," she said. Maya knew she had to hurry on. "But it doesn't matter, anyway, because they've gone now."

"Gone! Gone where?"

"They were on a boat with their children, but there was a storm and they were separated, you see. So now they're somewhere in Tamarind looking for them. They have three children. Mami tried to tell them that we would help them find their children, but they were desperate and they left before she could stop them. She sent me ahead to ask for your help to find them. She's doing what she can from Maracairol, but she thought that you could do something from here. The man—we think he was on his way to Port Town. It's the only clue we have."

"Many people vanish and are never heard from again these days," Senor Tecumbo said darkly. He took a silk handkerchief out of his breast pocket and dabbed his forehead. "I had so many friends who left their homes in the morning and were never seen again. Young men—boys, orphans usually—stolen into piracy. Children captured in the jungle and never heard from again. Just think of our own family. Your father, my two brothers, killed in the fighting—it was a blessing that at least your father's body was recovered. So few are. And think about your brother—no word for a year now. It tears at my heart."

Maya fell silent. She suddenly remembered that the girl she was so recklessly impersonating was a real person. She felt pity for Isabella's family's grief and guilt that she was using Senor Tecumbo. Senor Tecumbo fell away into his own thoughts, his brooding gaze wandering restlessly to the horizon.

Reminding herself why she was there, Maya tried to steer the conversation back around to her parents.

"But we can help them," she said. "We can find them, if you just try—"

"Find them?" Senor Tecumbo asked. "Isabella, you must know that when people disappear here they don't come back. Look at what we did to try to find your brother. No, there's nothing you can do. Your mother should know that, too. It's the way it is now. These friends made enemies of the wrong people."

"But," Maya said with a sudden inspiration, "but perhaps we could, I don't know, we could put up posters about them around the town. Maybe someone saw them."

"My dear child, if we put posters up of all the people who went missing . . ."

Maya was getting desperate.

"At least we tried to find my brother. We have to *try*. If it were Mami who were lost . . ." Here Maya's voice began to quaver. "If it were Mami who were lost, or kidnapped, wouldn't you want people to help her?" Maya bowed her head, overwhelmed for a moment by genuine grief.

Senor Tecumbo was a hard man, but he was also a man of great emotions and the sight of Maya's bowed head and trembling shoulders moved him. And the thought of Margarette—his own dear sweet sister, Margarette, who had combed his hair when he was a little boy and let him bring all manner of lizards and iguanas into her bedroom without screaming at him, unlike his six other sisters—the thought of Margarette being lost to him again after they had so recently reconciled filled him with sorrow and he reached down and patted Maya's shoulder.

"Don't cry," he said.

"Please," said Maya. She wiped her hand over the back of her eyes and when she looked at him again her gaze was stern.

Suddenly Senor Tecumbo began to laugh. The sound startled Maya.

"You're just as stubborn as your mother!" he said. "The women in this family! All right, Isabella. I'll have a search begun in the morning. But I'm warning you, don't get your hopes up."

Maya raised her tearstained face to his. She took hold of one of his huge hands—more like the paw of a great animal—and clasped it tightly between her own two small hands.

"Thank you," she whispered.

Senor Tecumbo patted her head. "Go on now," he said gruffly. "You've finished your dinner and you should get some rest."

Maya bent to kiss his hand and then she turned and ran over the moonlit stones to the house.

A few minutes later she was in her bedroom. She jumped into the plush white bed and pulled the sheet up to her chin. She was relieved to be away from Senor. She didn't know how she was going to keep up this facade tomorrow, too—what if she was discovered? She took a deep breath and tried to be calm—the plan was working so far. But Maya felt very alone. She missed Simon and Penny terribly and at the thought of them together in Mathilde's safe, cozy little shack, two silent tears rolled down her cheeks and soaked the ivory pillow. Oh, she wished she were there with them!

Chapter Thirty-Two

*Missing * Exploring Villa Tecumbo *
"They're lined up down to the bay!" *
The Old Sailor Offers a Clue * Sapphire
Tooth Again * "The missing don't
return to us"*

MISSING
Peter and Marisol Nelson
Outsiders who came to Tamarind on board the
Pamela Jane. Peter Nelson was last seen alone in
Port Town. They are being searched for by
their three children, Maya, Simon, and Penny.
Generous **REWARD** for anyone with information.
Please come to Villa Tecumbo this afternoon.

True to his word, Senor Tecumbo had his servants begin a search the following morning. The light was barely on the harbor before posters were put up throughout Port Town and messengers were dispatched on foot to neighboring towns. Maya had directed what should be said on the posters. She didn't describe her parents' appearance because she knew that they may look different now than when she had seen them last—for one thing, Kate said her father had a beard. She thought that the most important details to include were themselves—her and Simon and Penny—and the *Pamela Jane*. If their parents were traveling across the island searching for them, this is what they would have talked to people about, and this is what people would be likely to remember.

After breakfast, Senor Tecumbo had business to take care of, so Maya returned to her bedroom in the villa, where the clothes that Senor Tecumbo had promised her had already been hung in her closet. It didn't seem to be getting much lighter outside and she saw with dismay that it had started to drizzle. She stood up and went to the window and as she watched the mist turned into solid, heavy rain that blurred the jungle and the town and the harbor together. She stared glumly out at it. She wondered about the others and what they were doing now.

After a while, bored, she decided to explore. She left her bedroom and tiptoed down the hallway, peering into different rooms. She had never seen anything so opulent. The rooms themselves were vast, with high ceilings and tall doors that opened onto the great marble patio that ran the length of the villa. Tall, gilt-framed mirrors rested here and there, reflecting a silvery-gray light on soft velvet couches and oiled wood dressers. Maya was caught off guard every time she glimpsed a leg (it always took a second to realize it was her own) or saw her own faintly baffled face looking back at her. There were mosaics of sea battles and mermaids with jeweled fins luring ships in storms. There were stacks of heavy oil portraits and dramatic landscapes. There was a table long enough to fit fifty people and as many chairs with red-and-gold silk seats. White sheets were thrown over some things and they loomed like ghosts. It was like treasure. Then she realized that it probably was treasure seized during the war, or paid to Senor by wealthy families in exchange for his protection.

Maya caught sight of a photograph, framed on the mantel.

It was the original of the one that Helix had found in the newspaper. She stood transfixed as Isabella's dark, piercing eyes stared down at her. Just then, she heard a noise from the hallway. She hurried to leave the room before she was caught snooping and she ran smack into Lorco. He fixed a cold, suspicious eye on her as she walked quickly back to her own room and closed the door.

The rain cleared, the posters were put up, and word traveled quickly through Port Town. By lunchtime there was a line at the gate of Senor Tecumbo's house that ran all the way down the zigzag road to the town and then coiled back on itself. Senor Tecumbo stood in a doorway leading onto the marble rectangle, smoking his pipe and looking crossly at the line.

"Every single one of them is just here after the reward, I can promise you," he said. "I'm tempted to have Lorco break the whole thing up."

He turned to summon Lorco but Maya tugged his arm.

"No," she cried. "Please, I'd like to see them all. Even if out of all of them there's only one person who has any real information, it'll be worth it. It's all we have."

Senor Tecumbo's face softened. Still, he did not want to let his niece talk to the people in the line by herself.

"But I'm the only one here who has seen the missing people," Maya said. "I'll be able to tell right away if the people who have come are telling the truth or not."

Senor Tecumbo relented, saying, "But I'm going to post Lorco at the door, just to be safe."

A maid set up a little white table and chair at the gate, and Maya went to receive the line of people. Lorco lurked broodingly in the coolness of the main doorway to the villa. Maya tried to ignore him. She sat down at the table with her back to him and the villa and beckoned to the first person in the line.

Several hours later the sun had begun its descent over the rooftops into the jungle and Maya had talked to countless people, none of whom had any useful information. Most had clearly never seen either of her parents and had invented stories in order to get the reward. However, it seemed that a handful actually had seen her father. They gave plausible descriptions of him that sounded a lot like Kate's, about a stranger searching for his three children. But they couldn't offer any information about where he had been headed or where he might be now. Maya was sweating uncomfortably at the table, but she didn't want to move into the shade closer to the villa because then she would be within earshot of Lorco. The line was down to the last few stragglers, anyway. In the end it seemed the plan had come to nothing. She felt hot, tired, and defeated.

The last person in line was an ancient-looking man with a crooked back, hands mottled with age spots, and terribly thin legs like a stork. Maya figured that it had probably taken him all day to walk up the hill from Port Town. Despite his age, he had a head of thick white hair that stuck out in tufts beneath an old green sailor's cap. He sized her up for a moment before he spoke, which was something no one else had done.

"I saw him," he said, peering with interest at Maya.

"Who did you see?" Maya asked tiredly.

"The man you're looking for," said the old man. "Not the woman, just him."

"How do I know you really saw him?" Maya asked, her voice flat. She had little hope that this scraggly little old man knew anything.

"You want proof," said the old man, a twinkle coming into his eye. "A detail to prove it was him."

"Yes," said Maya.

The old sailor chuckled softly. "All right," he said. "You."

Maya's heartbeat quickened. "What are you talking about?" she said haughtily. "I'm Senor Tecumbo's niece."

"You can't fool me," he said. "You're from the Outside. I can always tell an Outsider. I knew something was wrong here, but I didn't realize until I got close to you what it was. But now I see . . . you take after your father. Same eyes. You've all ended up here somehow and now you want to go home."

Maya's mouth dropped open.

It was true . . . she did have her father's eyes. People had always said so. She looked fearfully at the old man. He had seen right through her.

"Don't worry," said the old man, "I'm not going to give you away. I met your father some weeks ago now, when he was on his way out of Port Town. I live on the edge of town and he had come to ask for food. I had just made a stew to last for a few days, so I shared it with him. He told me his story and that he was on his way to the Ravaged Straits because he had heard that his children were there. Seeing you here now, though, it seems that he was misled."

The old man broke off and glanced over Maya's shoulder.

"We have to be quick," he said. "Your friend is watching."

Maya glanced behind her and saw Lorco eyeing her.

"Please," she said. "What are the Ravaged Straits? How do I get there?"

"It's a terrible place," the old man said. "A terrible, terrible place. The current is wicked, the sun is blinding, the rocks are treacherous. Men who go down the Straits almost never make it out alive. And if they do, they're never the same after. The place gets into them and destroys their minds. I only knew one man who returned, and until the day he died he never spoke a word again."

Maya looked in shock at the old man. A breeze came up from the sea and goose bumps rose on her skin. Behind her she could hear Lorco's footsteps getting closer.

"How do I get there?" Maya whispered urgently.

"Sail due south from the Black Cross and you'll catch the current that leads into the Straits," the old man whispered. "But don't go alone. You must—"

But the old man was interrupted by Lorco.

"Is everything all right?" he asked, stopping beside the table. His oiled mustache twitched.

"Everything is fine," snapped Maya. "I've learned all we need to, you can pay this gentleman the reward."

"No, thank you," the old man said, backing up, his hat in his hands. "I won't have any reward. Not on my soul." With that, he turned and began walking down the hill.

"What nonsense did he tell you?" Lorco asked.

"Nothing," Maya murmured.

Lorco watched her closely. "I think that Senorita should come back inside now," he said.

But before Maya could return to the villa, a new party showed up at the gates. There were three men. Stifling a gasp, Maya recognized one of them from the tavern on the day that she and Simon and Penny had fled from the bullies on the dock. He was impossible to mistake: a tall, bone-crushingly great man with a sheen of sweat shining on his bald head, and a glittering sapphire in place of a missing front tooth. His pistol sat firmly against his side.

"We're here about the *Pamela Jane*," he said. "We want to know where she is."

Maya scratched the bridge of her nose, hoping to hide her face so the pirates wouldn't recognize her. But she didn't have to worry, because Lorco pushed her back toward the house and motioned toward the trees. Several guards stepped forward, hands on their rifles.

"We have nothing to tell you," Lorco said to the pirates. "Stay on your ships or Senor will have you kicked out of Port Town for good."

The guards cocked their guns—Maya even saw a couple of them aiming from perches in the branches of trees around the gate. The pirates spat on the ground, swearing, but they were outnumbered so reluctantly they turned and left down the hill. Lorco fixed his suspicious glare on Maya. She ran quickly back to the house, heart thumping. Why did the pirates want to find the *Pamela Jane*?

～ ～ ～

Back in her room, Maya paced anxiously. Now that she knew where her father was, she wanted to run away, back to Mathilde's, so that she could get the others and they could start making their way to the Black Cross, wherever it was. But Senor Tecumbo's villa was swarming with guards, and there was no way she could slip out unnoticed. She would have to stick to Helix's plan—to leave during the opening party of the Festival, when the town was crowded and busy and everyone was in costume. She didn't know exactly how it would work, though. Helix had said that he would give her a signal—but what? And how?

She sighed and closed her eyes, trying to quiet the questions that crowded her mind. How would they find the Black Cross? And what had the pirates wanted with the *Pamela Jane*? Their unexpected visit had alarmed her. She began to feel like a prisoner in the villa.

That evening she joined Senor for dinner, her spirits leaden. She had been dreading having to see him again.

"Well," he said, "did your posters work? Did you find out anything?"

"Some people may have seen the man we were looking for, but no one could tell me where he had gone," Maya said. *Another lie,* she thought.

"I'm sorry, my dear," Senor Tecumbo said. "I know it's hard to be young and to be witness to such sad things. But in time you'll learn there are things that you don't have the power to change. The missing don't return to us."

They were interrupted by a servant. To Maya's intense alarm, she realized he was holding the logbook out before him.

"Pardon me, Senor," he said, bowing. "But a young man from Port Town brought this. He says it belongs to Senorita Isabella."

"Oh, it must have been recovered from my trunk on the road," said Maya, trying to hide her confusion. She took it quickly from the servant. "It's my diary," she said, holding it to her chest.

Simon and Helix must have sent the book to get a message to her, Maya realized. An ordinary note could have been intercepted, but a message could be concealed in the logbook. She was desperate to find out when she could get out of here, but the rest of dinner passed torturously slowly.

Finally Maya was able to excuse herself. Once she was inside she took off running up the stairs to her room with the logbook. She locked her bedroom door behind her and opened the book, turning the pages until she saw the message, written between the lines of one of her father's log entries. Simon had written:

WAIT FOR A SIGNAL FROM THE DRAGON.

Wait for a signal from the Dragon? What could that mean? Then Maya remembered that everyone would be wearing masks, even her. Her mask—a princess's—had been given to her earlier and was now hanging from the hat stand, looking at her with its empty sockets. Either Simon or Helix must be planning to disguise himself as a dragon the following night.

Maya closed the book.

All right.

She would remain Isabella one night longer.

Chapter Thirty-Three

The Festival of Masks ∗ *A Magnificent Party* ∗ *Dragon* ∗
Latecomer ∗ *A Wild Ride* ∗ *"A girl like you has plenty of beautiful
dresses in her future"*

Port Town had been busy since dawn and the villa was teeming with staff preparing for the night's party. Maya was excited because on the map in the logbook she had found a tall black X that Rodrigo had marked on a desolate part of the northwest coast of Tamarind. She believed it must be the Black Cross that the old sailor had talked about. She scrawled a quick note in the logbook to the others—PAPI IS AT BLACK CROSS. HELIX, WHAT IS THE QUICKEST WAY TO GET THERE? As an afterthought, she added, PIRATES CAME TO ASK ABOUT THE *PAMELA JANE* YESTERDAY—DON'T KNOW WHY??? She managed to slip the book in a pile of laundry going to Mathilde's. She desperately hoped they'd receive it. There was no time to waste in getting to the Black Cross. Their father's life might depend on it.

Maya spent most of the day observing the activity from her window, relieved to be away from the burden of conversation with Senor Tecumbo, and from Lorco's scrutiny.

In the evening Maya put on the dress that Senor had given her to wear that night: a lovely yellow gown made up of layers and layers of silk, with pearl-encrusted straps that crossed over her shoulders and darker yellow silk roses that gathered around her waist. She brushed her hair and then swept it up as best she could, securing it with pins. She studied herself in the mirror. She looked very grown-up, she thought. You would never know she had just spent ages in a prison in the jungle. Then she took her mask—it was beautiful, with high cheekbones and full lips and jewels studding the temples—and lifted it to her face. When she looked at herself again, a thrill ran through her. She was transformed. In this mask and dress, it was going to be so much easier to pretend to be Isabella for the last few hours of their plan. She left her bedroom and went down the hall and down the marble stairs, her dress making a lovely swishing sound. She stopped at one point and, glancing furtively around her to make sure no one was watching, ran back down the hallway and began the walk again, just so she could hear the dress swishing once more.

Outside, the marble patio and gardens had been transformed. Flowers bloomed everywhere. Tables covered in ivory cloths were being heaped with food, and uniformed waiters dashed back and forth from the tables to the kitchen. Peacocks, their throats blue as the ocean, roosted in the limbs of the Mellora trees and strutted through the servants running hither and thither with platters laden with pineapple and cupuaçu, watermelon and icy-white slivers of coconut. There were meats, too, steaming as they were lifted off the grills: wild pigano, goat, snake delicacies. And fish! Dozens of different types of fish, grilled whole and filleted by the deft knives of the white-aproned chefs. Wahoo, reef mullets, deep-sea groupers, coneys, red and yellow snappers, mako shark, and a turtle turned upside down and roasted in its own shell. Bowls of moist yellow cassava were flecked with onions and fresh wild mint. Passing a table of jungle peppers roasting in their own juices, Maya's mouth began to water. Wild mushrooms that had been gathered that day from the fringes of the jungle lay on beds of sea fennel. Stews of edible flowers bubbled gently in vats. A waiter appeared with fried sea urchins, oyster, octopus, and juicy pink crab.

Wood was being piled at the foot of the garden where later a bonfire would be lit. Dancers wearing leaves and feathers, faces stained with berries from the jungle, were set to perform old tribal dances around it for the entertainment of the guests.

The first guests were set to arrive in half an hour.

"There you are," said Senor Tecumbo, coming out onto the marble patio behind Maya. The door shut behind him and for a moment the sea, reflected in its glass, swung around the garden. He put his hand on Maya's shoulder. "Are you excited about the party, my dear?"

Maya nodded, her eyes shining.

"I've never seen anything like it," she said truthfully.

"Well, it's more than we usually do, but I wanted a real welcome for my niece," said Senor Tecumbo. "I pity you young people, growing up without music, joy, dancing! I wish you could have known Tamarind in the old days. It was a marvelous, marvelous place."

Guests from neighboring villas began to arrive, the women lifting their bright, elegant dresses off the dusty road, the men wearing shirts of vibrant greens and blues and yellows. And each person wore a dazzling, elaborate mask, made of silk and sequins and jewels and shells and painted with pigments from the jungle. There were parrots, jaguars, monkeys, and all sorts of jungle animals, as well as mermaids, pirates, rainbow fish, and ferocious visages of tribal warriors.

When the parade began in the town below, the party at

Senor Tecumbo's went to the edge of the gardens and looked down on it from the hill above as the glittering procession, shaking tambourines and maracas, snaked its way through the flower-strewn streets. More music started up throughout the town, and the crowd in Senor Tecumbo's garden drifted back toward the marble rectangle. The band beneath the Mellora tree struck up again and couples began to dance.

Maya looked through the crowd periodically for a dragon but saw none. It was dark now and the bonfire was doused in oil and lit, and the orange glow danced over the masked faces of the guests, making them mysterious. Where *was* Helix? Maya began to feel nervous—what if something had happened? What if the plan had gone awry? She lifted her mask away from her face frequently so that he would be sure to see her. Searching the crowd anxiously, she spotted someone in a green mask that looked like the face of an iguana—could that be him? She was about to walk over when the person lifted the mask to wipe his face with a handkerchief and she saw that it wasn't Helix at all. Then, at the far end of the marble rectangle, she caught sight of a great glittering dragon with jeweled red eyes, and yellow and green scales glowing in the torchlight. The dragon raised his hand—it was Helix, she was sure of it. She began to make her way to him when Senor Tecumbo tapped her shoulder.

"A dance, my dear?" he asked.

Before Maya could respond, she was swept across the dance floor with him. Senor Tecumbo was a fine dancer, and he led her all around the floor. Maya's face flushed beneath her mask and she began to enjoy herself for a moment. Her time at the magnificent villa was almost up. Soon she would be fleeing with Helix, back to Mathilde's to pick up the others and set out

283

to find the Black Cross. But right now she was dancing in the middle of a party more elegant and beautiful than any she could have ever dreamed of. She was happy that Helix could see her in her beautiful yellow dress. She swirled past him across the floor, an extra spring in her step.

The party was in full swing when a big, shiny black car came crawling up the hill—chrome gleaming—and stopped under the pavilion by the grand cedar door.

"Now who can that be?" Senor Tecumbo said, faintly annoyed, coming to a stop on the dance floor. "So late? I thought all our guests were here. Wait a moment, my dear, I'm going to see who this is." He left Maya on the dance floor and walked toward the car. Maya suddenly felt nervous, and she lifted her mask in order to better search for Helix in the dragon mask, but the marble rectangle had filled with dancers and she could not spot him. She was on one side of the crowd and he on another.

As she turned back she saw the car door open and a foot— quite a tiny foot—in polished black shoes stepped out, followed by another, and a young girl emerged. A young girl who looked surprisingly like Maya. The girl's eyes fell at once on Senor Tecumbo.

"Uncle Pedro!" she exclaimed, beaming.

She bounded over to Senor Tecumbo and flung her arms around his neck and planted a kiss on his cheek.

Senor Tecumbo was almost too stunned to speak. "What?" he stammered. "Who are you?"

The young girl's face fell and she took a step back. "Uncle Pedro, it's me. It's Isabella, your niece! I'm a day early. I know it's been a long time—I suppose I've changed a lot, haven't I? But you look exactly how I remember you!"

"My niece," Senor Tecumbo said. "Young lady," he laughed nervously. "My niece Isabella is here." He looked around for Maya, who felt as if her feet had grown roots, fixing her to the spot. "I'm not sure who you are, but I'm afraid there's been a mistake."

The girl hesitated, then smiled charmingly. "You're teasing me," she said.

Senor Tecumbo was no longer laughing. The first hints of storm clouds had begun to gather in his eyes. "I'm sorry," he said firmly. "I'm afraid there's been a mistake."

"There *has* been a mistake," said a voice from the car, and a tall, elegant woman in high heels and a cream-colored blazer and a red hat tilted to one side stepped out. "Only it looks like you're the one who's made it, little brother."

"Margarette?"

Senor Tecumbo looked like you could knock him over with a feather.

"Don't look so shocked," said the woman in the tilted hat. "We decided to come a day early to surprise you. Apparently we were successful."

Senor Tecumbo looked from Isabella to Maya and back again. The crowd had fallen silent and had turned to watch what was unfolding. The band petered out.

Just then Lorco came running up the hill.

"Senor, Senor!" he cried. He ran up to them, struggling to catch his breath. "The girl," he gasped. "The girl who's been staying here—she's not your niece."

"I can see that," Senor Tecumbo said in a low, hard voice. He turned to Maya. "Then who *are* you?"

"She's the child of the missing couple in the posters," panted Lorco.

Maya, her mouth dropped open in horror, stood still as a statue. Senor Tecumbo turned and took a long hard look at her.

"You deceived me!" he thundered finally, his face turning dark. *"Who are you?"*

Behind Maya, the figure in the dragon mask had been making his way through the crowd and now he grabbed her arm. Maya unfroze and they fled, shoving their way through the guests, who were so surprised that they opened a path to let them pass. Helix ran right into a waiter and a tray of shrimp went flying through the air into Senor Tecumbo and Lorco, who were right on their heels. An anxious murmur traveled through the crowd.

"We'll never make it," gasped Maya, who was having trouble running in her long dress.

"Yes, we will!" Helix shouted. He pulled in front of her, leaping over a low hedge. Maya followed, her dress tearing on the thorns and flying out in ribbons around her. There was a little cart on the side of the road, the kind that children wheeled their parents' produce to market in. Helix had hidden it there in case they had had to escape quickly.

"Get in," Helix hissed.

Maya scrambled into the cart, gathering her skirts around her knees. She held on to Helix's shoulders and he kicked the cart forward and down the hill. Behind her she saw one of the black-uniformed guards jump out of the bushes and begin running after them.

The wheels rumbled slowly at first and then the cart picked up speed. Soon they were careening recklessly down the dark hill so fast that the foliage on either side of the road blurred and Maya's hair streamed out behind her.

"It's too fast!" she wailed.

Whoosh! The wagon tilted on two wheels, making a sharp turn just in time to miss flying right off a steep ledge. Maya closed her eyes.

Just before the bottom of the hill, the wagon hit a rut and toppled over. Maya and Helix tumbled out of it and, without stopping to look behind them, dashed through the streets. The streets were filled with people in glittering masks and costumes, and Maya and Helix were swiftly lost in the crowd. They burst into Mathilde's little house, and Helix slammed the door behind them.

Maya embraced Simon and Penny and as quickly as she could, she told Simon and Helix about what the old fisherman had told her about the Ravaged Straits. The boys had gotten her message in the logbook, and Helix had chosen a route to get to the Black Cross that, once out of Port Town, would keep them off the main roads where Senor Tecumbo's men could find them. He would accompany them partway there.

"Come on," he said. "We have to hurry."

Maya took a shuddery breath and went behind the curtain to change into her old clothes. She picked up Penny and kissed the baby's soft downy head and felt better for a moment. Even though she was so tiny and helpless, there was something very comforting about Penny.

Helix and Mathilde had made stunning masks for the children. Simon's was a jaguar. Penny's was a rainbow fish, made from a mosaic of tiny shimmering stones. For Maya they had made a dancer's mask. It was made of pinkish-purple silk, with glitter on the cheeks, white swaths of eye shadow, long black eyelashes, and a perfectly curved red mouth.

"This is what all women wear to the Festival," Helix told her as he handed it to her.

Maya blushed and quickly put on the mask. She caught sight of the beautiful yellow dress lying in a heap on Mathilde's floor, filthy and shredded by thorns. Then she remembered that the dress she had borrowed from Mathilde was still hanging in the closet at the villa. For some reason it was the thought of the poor abandoned dress that made her feel despondent.

Mathilde seemed to know what she was thinking.

"Never mind, little petalfish," she said, lifting Maya's mask and wiping her face with her apron. "A girl like you has plenty of beautiful dresses in her future."

Then it was time for the rainbow fish, jungle cat, and dancer to say good-bye to Mathilde. Simon threw his arms around her great soft middle, and Mathilde hugged the three of them to her tightly.

"Oh, I will miss you little seashells!" Mathilde said, wringing her apron in her hands.

Simon growled from inside his mask to give himself courage. Helix snapped on his own mask—a ferocious tribal warrior—and then they were off, out the door, and being carried down the street in a sea of monkeys, pirates, sailors, dancers, sloths, witch doctors, and many other creatures and denizens of Port Town who were making their way down the streets.

❧ CHAPTER THIRTY-FOUR ❧

Escaping

Maya and Simon and Helix held on to one another so that they wouldn't be separated in the crowd. The drums were intoxicating. When the parade reached the town square a great cheer went up through the crowd and the procession dissolved into a shining, variegated sea of dancing masks. Music pulsed through the streets. On the stages in the town square the children glimpsed fire-eaters and tribal dancers and contortionists. They wove through the crowd and finally arrived on the outskirts of town, where the crowd thinned. Maya looked back over her shoulder at Port Town and felt her heart quicken with happiness—they were on their way! The plan had worked!

They had to walk along a road through steep hillside fields before they reached the trees. Then Helix would lead them secretly through the jungle on the long trek to the Black Cross. It was this first little part, when they were close to Port Town and out in the open, that was most dangerous. The noise of the Festival fading away, they walked quickly, not speaking. Maya was nervous.

"Shouldn't we stay off the road?" she whispered.

"No," said Helix. "This is much quicker. We'll be hidden in a minute, don't worry." They hurried on. The sea was on their left and up ahead was the dark fringe of the jungle. They were getting closer and closer to their father, and hopefully to their mother, too.

Just then Maya heard a sound behind her and turned to see men wearing black capes and black masks leap out from behind a boulder at the side of the road. Penny was seized from her arms. She was too stunned to scream. The moon slid behind a cloud and there was wild shuffling in the darkness. Senor Tecumbo's men—they had found them! Maya fought gamely with her bare hands. For a moment she felt Simon next to her, then a figure with hairy arms who stank of tobacco came between them. The clouds cleared and moonlight lit the road and with surprise Maya caught a glimpse of her captor. At the same time a hand struck her jaw, hard, and she tumbled backward. She started rolling down the steep embankment and couldn't stop. Her arms and legs were getting cut and scratched on sharp rocks. Then there was a sickening thud as she struck something solid and pain radiated from her head through her whole body.

Everything went black.

But as she lost consciousness, she remembered the last thing she had seen before she tumbled down the hill: in the place where a tooth should have been, a single sapphire, shining for a moment in the moonlight.

The men who had ambushed them were not Senor Tecumbo's men.

They were the pirates.

❦ CHAPTER THIRTY-FIVE ❦

*Maya Is Alone * A Sign*

Maya awoke in a hollow in the hillside, where the mist had hidden her all night. As soon as she opened her eyes a sick feeling of dread filled the pit of her stomach. Penny's sling, long empty now, hung over her shoulder. Her head was throbbing. She crawled to the edge of the hollow and peered out. Helix and Simon and Penny were nowhere in sight. Her eyes filled with tears and the landscape blurred into a wash of green vegetation and blue sky. The rocky hillside was a far cry from her soft, fluffy bed at Senor Tecumbo's. Her body was stiff and her throat felt sore from sleeping on the damp earth.

The ambush had happened too fast for her to really think, but now, in the daylight, the first thought that flashed into Maya's mind was *Helix*. He had sold them out—he had told the pirates where they would be and he had led her and Simon and Penny right into their clutches. How else would the pirates have known who they were? They had been wearing masks— masks that Helix had gotten for them. He could have easily tipped off the pirates. And that was why he had insisted that they take the open road, even when Maya hadn't thought it was wise. The pang of betrayal hurt worse than she thought it could.

Why did the pirates want them? Maya remembered how they had come to Senor Tecumbo's villa, asking about the *Pamela Jane*. But why? She was just a tiny ship, and they had a whole fleet. Maya wracked her brain to remember any detail of when the pirates had come to the gates of the villa that might be useful. But nothing about the encounter shed any light on her problem now: how to find her brother and sister. Maya sniffled and wiped her nose on her sleeve.

She began climbing back up the hill. It took a while and she had broken out in a sweat by the time she reached the road. She must have rolled for ages last night—the pirates probably couldn't find her in the darkness. But where had they taken the others? She could see the scuff marks from their shoes on the dirt road in the place where they had fought. She looked around to get her bearings. She was in farm fields just outside Port Town. Above her, terraced hills rose steeply and cassava leaves and unripe jungle fruits shone bright green. Though it was still early, the sky at the top of the hill was a deep, brilliant blue. All around her in the hollows of the earth, mist rose like steam, burning away in the sun, and butterflies began to appear above the ribbon of the road. Below her, the hill descended sharply to the dark blue sea, the surf white where it broke around the reefs. Maya looked both ways up and down the road but no one was in sight.

She leaned down to brush the rich black soil of the hills off her knees, and took a few deep breaths. Again she remembered Helix's deceit and bitter tears stung her cheeks. She wiped them away furiously and talked sternly to herself. *You have to find the others,* she told herself. *You have to stay calm and fig-ure out what to do.*

Maya began walking back toward Port Town but before she had gone a few steps her legs began to feel leaden and a vague bad feeling came over her. Closer to the town she could hear the buzzing of flies feasting on the leftover food in the stalls, and she smelled the faint odor from the flowers trampled in the streets. It felt like a sign. She saw that down in the harbor the fleet was gone—and Simon and Penny surely with it. Her heart sank. Maya suddenly felt certain that she wasn't going in the right direction. Simon and Penny weren't in Port Town. She took a few steps backward, then turned around and began running as fast as she could away from the town, her feet pounding on the dirt road.

When she couldn't breathe anymore she dropped to a walk, holding the stitch in her side. Sweat drenched her face and clothes, and rolled down her neck and the backs of her knees. She closed her eyes gratefully when a breeze lifted, rippling the foliage on the hillsides and bringing on it the first stirrings in Port Town, the sound of rakes scraping the dead flowers into piles and the smell of coffee brewing in the tin shacks. But when she turned at a bend in the road, Port Town slipped from view and she was alone, entirely alone, walking on a road that led who knew where?

Maya had been walking for about half an hour when she caught sight of something lying on the road in front of her.

She squinted.

Could it be?

A red book. And on its cover a faint gold glitter that had been nearly worn away.

The logbook from the *Pamela Jane*!

Maya ran forward on the road toward it, not even caring if it was a trap.

"Simon!" she shouted. "Penny!"

She kept calling their names but the only answer was the echo of her own voice from the steep hillsides and the sizzle of the waves on the rocks in a cove far below. When she reached the book she dropped on her knees and picked it up and squeezed it to her chest.

"Everything will be all right now," she whispered to herself. "Everything will be all right now, I've found the logbook. They were here. I'm going the right way."

Maya looked down the steep hillsides to where the little cove shone bright blue. The pirates who had kidnapped the others must have brought them along this road to meet the fleet, who would have left Port Town and come around the coast. Perhaps they hadn't wanted to drag struggling children all the way back through the town. The whole thing must have been planned with Helix's help.

She opened the logbook and looked quickly through it, desperately hoping to find a message from Simon. But there was nothing. Still, at least she had Rodrigo's map—that was something. She turned to study it. She was heading toward Maracairol. She wondered for a moment if instead she should try to make her way to the Black Cross and her father. No, she had to find Simon and Penny first. She put the logbook in her backpack and stood up. The best thing to do was to get to Maracairol. If the fleet had come by this way, that's probably where they were headed. She couldn't go back to Port Town, anyway. Maya began walking again, with new purpose in her step.

But as the morning went on, she grew thirsty and fatigued. She sang under her breath to keep her spirits up, the same songs she had sung in the jungle with Simon. She couldn't believe it, but she would give anything to be back in the swampy heat of the jungle with the ferocious insects and the threat of piganos, if she could just be with Simon and Penny again. That Helix! Maya's heart hurt so much that she had to push all thoughts of him from her mind.

She came to an abrupt stop as she heard a noise on the road ahead. *Soldiers*. They had come down out of the jungle and were walking around the corner on the next bend. They had not seen her yet. The hill was steep and there was no way that Maya could hide in the trees at the edge of the jungle before they reached her. She looked around desperately. On the hillside below her there were several empty huts. Quickly, she darted down the hillside and into the first of them, praying that the soldiers weren't headed there. She crouched, holding her breath. Between a break in the palm thatch she could see them as they passed. Their bare feet were silent on the road and their uniforms were tattered and old. What would they do if they caught her? They had armed scouts in the front and the rear. One gunner pointed his rifle down toward the palm huts. But they didn't see her and they kept walking.

Maya stayed where she was, too afraid to go back to the road. She looked through the open doorway at the neighboring huts. Most of them had been knocked down in the wind. The few that remained were sun-bleached and abandoned. Sand had blown in over the floorboards and bits of seaweed eddied in corners. The grass beds were dusty and the driftwood furniture sat motionless, as if waiting for people to return and begin using them again. Seashells had been left behind on tables and the breeze whistled through them, a hollow, lonely music. It was a sad place.

Maya found a freshwater tap around the back of the huts and drank the drizzle of rusty water from it. She picked an avocado from a tree. She looked back up at the road, but her knees still felt wobbly from fear. It had been pure luck that the soldiers hadn't spotted her.

Maya turned away from the road and looked down the hillside to see if she could make her way along the shore, and it was then that she saw the turquoise lagoon, sheltered from the ocean by a rocky ledge, sparkling prettily at the foot of the hill. It couldn't be seen from the road. Huge volcanic boulders jutted out of the water and sand around it. Maya's eye caught movement on the rocks and she saw a flash of light reflecting off the scales of what looked like a great green fish. She squinted and shaded her eyes and saw that the tail of the fish turned into the upper body of a woman. Maya was gazing at a mermaid.

✣ Chapter Thirty-Six ✣

Desmond & the Seashells ✳ *Maya Hears*
of the Sisters ✳ *A Spectacular*
Performance ✳ *"People need music"*

The mermaid lay lounging on the rocks, fiddling with shells and arranging them in patterns. Maya realized that she wasn't alone. Another mermaid was sitting nearby on the rocky ledge, fanning her tail slowly through the water. And at the far end of the lagoon, cavorting in the blue-green shallows, was a third.

Unable to resist seeing them up closer, Maya began to walk silently along a narrow, overgrown footpath down the hill to the lagoon. At the bottom of the hill, she crouched in the grasses and peered through. Two of the mermaids basked in the sun on the ledge bordering the lagoon. Their tails were supple and their scales as perfect and bright as polished emeralds. Starfish were knotted in their long hair. Scattered around them were odd bits of treasure—seashells, sand dollars, colored glass worn smooth by the waves, frayed ends of ship's rope, and a sign, the wood worn and the paint cracked and fading from the sun, which read DESMOND & THE SEASHELLS. Behind them the ocean beat dark blue and brilliant against the rocks, but the lagoon was light green and calm, its surface only ruffled by an occasional breeze that skidded in off the sea. The third mermaid lolled in the lagoon, floating on her back. With a lazy turn of her tail, she rolled over to her stomach. As she did so she caught sight of Maya. She gasped and slipped under the water. Then the other two mermaids turned and saw her, too. One slid off the ledge and beneath the surface of the lagoon and the other leaped over the ledge and disappeared into the ocean on the opposite side with a breathtaking flip of her great green tail.

It was only when all the mermaids vanished that Maya saw that what she had thought was one of the large volcanic rocks was in fact a very enormous man sitting cross-legged beside the lagoon. He wasn't just a very tall man or a very fat man, he was a gigantic man, and he cast a great gulf of shade onto the sand. Sitting down he was still twenty feet tall. He saw Maya and a grin broke out over his broad face. His teeth—several of them gold—were the size of small boulders. Maya realized that he must be the giant that Mathilde had told her about. Maya could hardly believe that he was real. When he lifted his arm a great shadow flew over the trees and sand and water, and as she watched, he picked up a fallen palm tree and, reaching behind him, used it to scratch his back. Maya noticed then that there were fallen palm trees strewn on the sand all around him.

"A visitor," he said. "How tremendous! Are you with the Peaceful Revolution?"

Maya opened her mouth to speak, but nothing but a squeak came out.

The giant—for he must be the giant—laughed, and his laughter rolled up against the steep hillside above the beach, where it startled several parrots who flew out and coasted in circles over the beach.

"Don't be afraid," he said to Maya. "Ladies," he said. "Be sociable."

A mermaid surfaced, the water streaming down from her long hair. She looked at Maya curiously. The other mermaid in the lagoon bobbed up beside her.

"I'm Desmond and these are the Seashells," said the giant.

"This is Casmeria and this is Melo Melo. Tellin is out there." The giant waved his hand toward the sea, creating a wave that rippled across the surface and buffeted the third mermaid, whose head was out of the water, watching Maya from a distance.

"She's not the friendliest," said Casmeria.

"Diva," muttered Melo Melo.

"Ladies," said the giant warningly. "Pardon us," he said to Maya. "We're not used to an audience anymore. Now, are you one of the Sisters of the Peaceful Revolution?"

"Um . . . one of what?" stuttered Maya.

Casmeria looked at Maya sharply. "She's not!" she said to Desmond.

Maya introduced herself, and frowning, Desmond changed the subject quickly.

"What brings you to us, Maya?" asked the giant. "We never have visitors anymore."

"Have you come to hear our act?" asked one of the mermaids from the lagoon. *Casmeria,* Maya thought.

"Um, not exactly," said Maya timidly.

"Well you should have," said the mermaid. "We're the best act in Greater Tamarind."

"It's true," said Desmond. "Or it used to be."

Maya studied him. His skin was dark and shiny from sitting in the sun all day. His clothes were made up of huge bolts of bright, multicolored fabric stitched together. Now that she was closer, Maya could see that the bits of fabric were actually curtains and carpets and the sails of ships, all things large enough to cover the giant's vast body. The effect was quite stunning. Sunlight flashed on his gold teeth and the rings he wore on his fingers. Something was hanging around his neck at the end of what looked to be a rope from a ship. After a minute Maya realized that the thing on the end of the rope was a ship's wheel! A huge ship's wheel, so big that in a storm it would take two men to turn, was dwarfed on this giant's chest!

"Where have you come from?" Melo Melo asked.

"Port Town," said Maya. "But I'm going to Maracairol."

"By yourself?" asked Casmeria and Melo Melo in amazement. Tellin had swum up to the rocky ledge that separated the lagoon from the sea and she hovered there, watching Maya, too.

Desmond shook his head, frowning. "Not a good idea," he said. "The road between Port Town and Maracairol is very dangerous. In the old days it was full of people, day and night. But hardly anyone dares to go on it anymore. Sometimes even from here we can see the rebels robbing people on the highway. You're lucky you made it this far without getting into trouble, but it only gets worse from here on. You can't keep going."

"You'd be sold into slavery," said Melo Melo.

"Or your head would be cut off," said Casmeria.

"You'd be doomed," said Tellin.

The giant nodded. "It's far too risky."

"But I have to get to Maracairol—I have to!" Maya cried, suddenly distressed.

"Shhh," soothed the giant. "Don't cry. It's bad for your vocal cords. Why do you need to get to Maracairol?"

"My brother and sister are there. They were kidnapped. I have to find them. We were looking for our parents when the pirates . . ."

Maya broke off. She was so tired and hungry and the sun had been beating down on her head all day, and who knew where Simon and Penny were, and it was all her fault that they had been kidnapped. She hadn't been careful enough. How would she ever explain it to her parents—if she ever even saw them again? Would she ever see anyone in her family again? Maya put her head down and wept sorrowfully.

Melo Melo hopped up on the rock beside Maya and patted her shoulder. The giant leaned forward so his big face was near Maya's and she was in cool shade for a moment, which was a relief. Even Tellin leaped over the rock divide between the sea and the lagoon and swam over to Maya.

At their prompting, Maya told them everything that had happened since the storm.

"Well," said Desmond when she finished. "That is some story."

"I did see a pirate fleet sail past last night," Tellin said.

Melo Melo tucked a starfish behind Maya's ear. "You can stay with us," she said. "We could turn your story into part of our act—we could write a song about you. People would love it."

"I could choreograph something for it," said Casmeria, dipping beneath the surface and turning a dizzying series of underwater somersaults.

"Can you sing?" asked Tellin. "If you can't sing, you can play the drums. Or something."

"Can you—" began Melo Melo.

"No," Maya whispered. "Please—stop. I have to get to Maracairol."

The mermaids fell quiet and looked at her.

"All right, child," the giant said. "We'll get you to Maracairol. Tomorrow these girls can tow you there. It's much quicker by sea and much safer. If you see pirates, you can hide in a cove or sea cave. But not until the morning. You need to rest and eat first. And I don't want these ladies out late."

Maya started to protest, but realized that the giant was not about to give in. She supposed that giants seldom had to.

"You can hear our act!" cried one of the mermaids, bursting out of the water and arching her back through the air.

"Yes," said Desmond. "It will take your mind off things. We'll give you a good meal, then you can spend the night in the old hotel—" Desmond motioned to the abandoned palm huts behind her.

Maya wiped her eyes, relieved. They would help her tomorrow—if she went by sea she would have a better chance of catching up to the pirates. The mermaids swam off and returned with an overturned turtle shell filled with green kelp and raw oysters and savory fish eggs. It was not exactly Maya's favorite meal in Tamarind so far, but she did the best she could at chewing the kelp and swallowing the jelly-like eggs. The mermaids swam in long lazy circles underwater, and Maya was left with Desmond.

"Who are the . . ." Maya began to ask. "What did you call them? The Sisters of the Revolution?"

Desmond looked wary for a moment and then he seemed to decide that Maya could be trusted.

"The Sisters of the Peaceful Revolution," he said, dropping his voice to a whisper. "You're the right age, so I thought you might be one of them. I shouldn't have jumped to conclusions and I should never have mentioned their name—it's all top secret. They've started an underground peace movement in Tamarind. They're going around the countryside now, into all the towns, trying to get girls and women to join them." Even whispering, Desmond had a deep, dramatic voice. "Something is going to happen soon, something big." He lifted his arms as he spoke, so that huge shadows flew up and down the beach and the sea.

"What?" asked Maya. She had stopped eating and was staring at him. "What's going to happen?"

Desmond lowered his arms and the shadows fell away.

"I don't know," he sighed. "I don't know. But something."

Maya wandered off down the beach so that Desmond and the mermaids could rehearse before they performed for her. Evening was falling swiftly and the lagoon glowed fiery in the sunset. The mermaids were bickering in the water about part of their routine. From the lagoon came strains of music, now starting, now stopping for the giant to call an order to the mermaids.

"Tighten the strings, Tellin. Casmeria, you're coming in too late after Mel."

The mermaids dissolved into petty squabbling. Maya heard splashing as one of their tails beat the surface of the water. The others shrieked in outrage. The skirmish was interrupted by a long, loud bellow that seemed to make the blades of grass vibrate on the hills and send a shiver over the water. It echoed off the tall hills, blue now above the beach, and when it ended, the mermaids had fallen silent and there was no sound but the gentle lap of water against the shore. Maya glanced behind her and saw the giant put down a large conch shell.

"Maya!" called Desmond. "We're ready for you."

Maya jogged back to the lagoon. Desmond motioned her to sit on a crop of rocks facing the water.

"We put together a show for you!" said Melo Melo. "It's a variation of the last act we used to do. People used to love it— that's why we'd save it for the end."

"I still can't believe we're doing all this for just one person,"

303

grumbled Tellin. "What kind of a comeback is this?" She slapped her tail viciously on the water, then sighed. She turned over in the water and looked up at Maya. "This place used to be packed," she said. "Especially for the weekend shows. People used to come from all over Tamarind to see me."

"To see *us*," corrected Melo Melo.

"*I* was the star," said Tellin, turning to glare at Melo Melo. Then she looked back up at Maya. "I was the *star*," she repeated. "They loved me. And now—no one!"

"Until tonight!" cried Casmeria.

"We're so glad you're here," said Melo Melo soothingly.

The last of the daylight was gone, the moon had risen, and the hillside above the beach was dark. Desmond began to tap on the hulls of the overturned ships, making a soft echoey thud of drums. Maya sat back from the lagoon a little and watched as the mermaids swam to the other end of the lagoon and finished fussing with the shells in their hair. As the rhythm on the ship drums picked up, they slipped back underwater and began to follow each other in a swift circle underwater.

The mermaids moved faster and faster until they became a living green ring, spinning like quicksilver in the moonlight. It was hypnotizing. Desmond beat the drums louder and louder and the circle spun faster and faster until one by one the mermaids shot out of the water and high into the air, the moonlight radiant on their green scales. Silvery droplets of water sprang off them and hung suspended in the air for a moment before splashing back into the lagoon like chimes. The mermaids arched their bodies in the air and dove soundlessly beneath the surface.

When they appeared again they began a strange, magical ballet, half in the water and half in the air. Sometimes they moved in unison, sometimes they separated into independent parts, like pieces of a clock. They snapped oyster shells together as if they were castanets and they blew through conches, adding a breathy whistling to the beating of the drums. Desmond occasionally turned from the drums for a moment to play a xylophone made from the skeleton of a whale, and he sang, his voice rich and deep as thunder.

At one point the music suddenly became soft and the mermaids vanished below the surface, and Maya held her breath. Then there was the faint shimmer of the moon on their scales from deep in the lagoon and a movement in the water and they were up in the air again, majestic and powerful. Maya, the moonlight shining on her own face, thought there was nothing so eerie and beautiful and strong as the sight of the mermaids leaping in the air. As she watched them, she temporarily forgot her troubles. And then, just like that, the music stopped and the creatures slipped back into their element. The surface of the lagoon settled and became so still that it reflected the stars and the sky.

The mermaids popped up at the other end of the lagoon a few moments later and began swimming back toward her. Maya stood and clapped as hard as she could.

"That was one of the most beautiful things I've ever seen!" she said passionately. *"Thank you."*

The mermaids were smiling, even Tellin.

"Thank *you*," said Melo Melo. "That was wonderful for us. We haven't had an audience in so many years."

"The road from Port Town to Maracairol used to be called Music Road, you know," said Desmond. "And there were other musician giants and their mermaids all over Tamarind. One day people will come back. They won't be able to help themselves.

People need music and dance and beautiful things. They forget sometimes, but never forever. You'll see. One day this will be a magical place again. With music and dance and good times and people celebrating."

Maya was very tired and her heart felt full of many things as she lay down in the palm hut that night. Through the open doorway she could see down to the lagoon, where the giant looked like one of the enormous volcanic rocks jutting up from the sea. His deep, gentle voice crooned a low, sweet song. It lulled Maya to sleep.

❦ Chapter Thirty-Seven ❦

Mermaid Chariot ✳ *A Strange New City*
Pursued by a Black Sedan ✳ *"You!"*

In the morning Maya ran down to the lagoon, the sand cool under her feet. The giant and the mermaids were already waiting. The mermaids had cobbled together a sturdy raft made of bamboo and driftwood, tied with locks of their own hair. Proudly, they pushed it out over the water for Maya to see. Maya stepped onto it and sat there, bobbing in the water.

"We have a gift for you," said Desmond.

Casmeria handed a beautiful white conch shell to Maya.

"If you ever need us you just use the conch as a horn and we'll come," Casmeria said. "Three bellows—one short and two long. Got it?"

"Got it," said Maya. "Thank you." She tucked the conch shell into her backpack with the logbook. The mermaids harnessed themselves to the raft and began to tow Maya away.

"Bring your brother and sister back here to see us one day!" Desmond called.

The giant waved farewell and a shadow flew over the water. When it lifted, Desmond was lost around a curve of the coast and the green sea was bright and sparkling.

🐬 🐬 🐬

Maya had been watching the lush coast slip by for hours when Tellin finally said, "This is as close as we can go." The mermaids brought the raft into a rocky cove. "If you walk up to the road, Maracairol is just around the bend."

Maya boosted herself onto the rocks and then turned around to face the mermaids.

"Thank you," she said sincerely. Beneath the water she could see their beautiful long tails swaying in the current. She climbed up the hill to the road. At the top she turned to wave.

Melo Melo was out by the reef line and as Maya watched, Casmeria and Tellin surfaced, too. When they saw her waving they leaped out of the water, the sun bouncing off their scales, and made a series of spectacular dives. Maya waved furiously. Then they were gone and she was alone again. The road was hard-packed coral, snaking pink around the curves of the coast. Except for the sizzle of waves breaking around the cliffs there was no noise—no birdsong or buzz of insects. The silence was unnerving and Maya felt nervous and alert.

Before long, she rounded a corner and saw the city below her. It was not like Port Town. There were a few tin roofs here and there, shining like coins dropped from a hole in a pocket, but most of the buildings were made of white stone. Ruined castles stood on the highest parts of the hills. As she got closer, Maya could see that vines hung from the open windows of the towers and blew gently in the breeze. Ragged flags were everywhere—billowing from the spires of the castles and fluttering in the garden squares in the city center. Maya made her way through the deserted streets to the harbor and saw with dismay that it was empty. The fleet was nowhere in sight. There were only a few crusty old fishing boats.

Simon and Penny weren't here.

Maya's heart dropped a little but she told herself the pirate ships probably didn't dock in plain view, but would be around the coast in some hidden cove.

There was an old woman wheeling a cart full of cabbages on the path ahead of her—the only person Maya had yet seen—and Maya ran to catch up with her and ask her if she knew where the fleet was.

"Yes," the old woman said. "The ships all set sail last night. They're going to Bembao."

Despair welled in Maya's heart. "Where is Bembao?" she asked.

"Oh, far!" the woman replied. "Far, far, far. I've never been there. I don't know anyone who has. It's in the North, just over the border. There's going to be a big battle, you know."

"A battle?" Maya asked, but the woman with the cabbages turned off onto a side street and did not look back.

For about the thousandth time since the storm, Maya wanted to sit down and just give up. But she made her legs keep going, taking her closer toward the center of town. What should she do now? How could she get to Bembao?

The city plan was orderly, the streets were swept clean and watered, and there were palm gardens everywhere with tidy patterns of flower beds. But apart from the woman with the cabbage cart, Maya hadn't seen a soul. There were still no birds or insects, which Maya attributed to the quiet, steady breeze funneling along the streets. The loudest sound was the flags beating in the wind. Maya's footsteps echoed against the stone walls. It was all eerie and strange and she felt very alone.

The buildings were almost all several stories high, and Maya noticed that all the windows at street level had been sealed with stones. She had the sensation of walking through canyons. The stone faces of the buildings were often pockmarked, as if by bullets. Every now and then a whole building had collapsed into rubble, and the windows of nearby buildings appeared to have been blown out by the explosion and were now boarded up. Maracairol was like a fortress.

On a street leading up the hillside, Maya saw a group of elegant old stone buildings set around a circular road. She walked up the hill and stood in the middle of them. They had sweeping roofs and broad, deep windows and doors that opened into grand pavilions. She recognized ophalla trimmings. Several of the buildings had ophalla window frames, others had garden ornaments made from the stone. There was a small white ophalla horse standing in one garden, but one of its legs had been blown off in an explosion. Maya caught sight of a sign outside of one building. Half of the sign had been blasted away. The half that remained read: EMBASSIES OF THE PROVINCES OF GREATER TAMARIND.

It was clear that not long ago the embassies had been grand and important, but now they were abandoned. The war had allowed moss to grow thickly on the roofs and birds to roost in the eaves and had caused their great doors to be chained shut. The few doors that had been left open now squeaked in the light breeze, and Maya peered in. Within the dimness inside, pools of rainwater were visible, faintly gleaming, along with the outlines of debris piled up against the ruined silk-covered walls.

Feeling uneasy, Maya turned and began walking quickly back down the street she had come from. As she did, she saw a shiny black sedan prowling a block behind her. The hairs on the back of her neck rose and she ducked into a windowless alley. The alley was long and deserted. Maya started to feel more and more nervous. She came out onto another main street, empty of people, but with brilliant purple hydrangeas growing in evenly spaced pots down either side. Who was tending this town, she wondered, and where were they?

Maya saw the shiny black nose of a car turning the corner toward her a block away. For a second she tried to tell herself it wasn't the same sedan, but then it began to speed up, its engine still creepily silent. It was following her. Could somebody know she was there? Could Senor Tecumbo's men have found her somehow?

She started to run. Her footsteps echoed like shots against the high walls of the buildings. She dove down the next side street as fast as she could. She kept running until she was too out of breath to run anymore. She thought that she must have shaken the car. But she was just trying to get her bearings when suddenly it appeared again from around a corner. Maya broke out in a cold sweat. She turned and slipped down another alley, but this time she stopped halfway and returned the way she had come. She peered carefully around the corner but the car was gone. She dashed across the street and stumbled down another alley. In a panic she kept twisting and turning through the streets until finally she found herself in a dead end. Hopelessly lost, she sank down to catch her breath. The only sound was the flapping of the unseen flags and the thumping of her heart.

"*Maya!*"

Maya thought her ears were playing tricks on her, but then she heard it again.

"*Maya!*" the voice whispered.

Maya held her breath.

"*Maya! It's me, look, I'm right over here.*"

Maya looked all around her but could see no one. The only windows in the buildings on either side of the alley were very high up and they were sealed shut. The voice sounded like it was coming from the street.

"Right over here, look!"

Maya looked to her right again and then she saw a hand waving from what must be some type of window just a foot above the street. She leaned out a little and saw that the hand was attached to an arm that was sticking out from between bars. It was too dark inside to see anything.

"*Who are you?*" she hissed. She wanted to get up and run but she was so exhausted from her panicked flight that she felt like she could hardly move.

"It's me—Helix!"

"HELIX!"

"Shh, yes, it's me. But you have to be quiet."

Maya crawled to the window and peered in. "Where are the others? Simon! Penny!"

Helix was there, his grime-streaked face pale in the weak light of the alley. He was in some kind of dark stone cell. Maya squinted and waited for her eyes to adjust but she couldn't see anything else. "Simon!" she shouted again. "Penny!"

"*Shh,*" Helix whispered again. "They aren't here."

"What do you mean?" she cried. "Where are they?"

"They're still on the ship. The pirates left me behind."

Maya's heart sank.

"Why? Where have they gone? Where are Simon and Penny?"

"The fleet was sailing to Bembao. The pirates threw me off the ship before they set sail. Maya, I'm so glad to see you—you have to help me get out of here."

"You betrayed us!" she whispered. "You set us up so the pirates could kidnap us."

312

"No!" said Helix. "Maya, I swear I didn't! I had no idea they were there!"

He reached through the bars for Maya's hand, but she yanked it away from him.

"You set us up and then when the pirates didn't need you anymore they got rid of you—it serves you right. I'm *glad* you're in jail—I hope you rot!"

Helix looked sad and stunned.

"How do I get to Bembao?" Maya asked in a low, hard voice.

"It's far," Helix said dully. "Almost halfway around the island."

How was she going to make it halfway around the island? Even as she sat there on the cold stones of the alley, Simon and Penny were getting farther and farther away from her. Tears welled warm in her eyes.

"It doesn't make any sense," she whispered. "Why do they want Simon and Penny?"

"They don't want them," Helix said. "They want your *boat*. Maya, I can explain everything, but you need to help me get out of here—"

"Oh, get yourself out," Maya said bitterly. "You're the one who got us into this."

She turned around and sat with her back to the wall. She didn't know where to go next. And she didn't know what to think. Maybe Helix hadn't betrayed them, after all. How could she be sure? Was he just lying so that she would help him escape? What should she believe? And why *did* the pirates want the *Pamela Jane* so badly?

Maya hadn't noticed the black sedan pulling up at the end of the alley. But suddenly she realized the shiny car had blocked her escape. She leaped to her feet and looked all around her. The walls of the alley couldn't be scaled and the sedan had sealed the only exit. Maya was desperate. The only thing she could do was get a running start and try to leap onto and over the roof of the sedan. But before she could do anything its door opened and the driver stepped into the alley.

"You!" Maya gasped.

CHAPTER THIRTY-EIGHT

Explanations ✳ *"This is a lost place"* ✳
The War Orphanage

I ndeed," said Isabella. "The question is—who are YOU?"

The two girls stood looking at each other for a moment. Their resemblance to each other was uncanny.

"We can figure everything out later," said Isabella. "Right now you have to come with me. Quickly. Come *on*, we can worry about him later."

Maya glanced down at Helix but as she did she heard the rumbling of a new vehicle approaching.

"*Hurry*," said Isabella. "We don't have time."

Isabella opened the door of the car, and Maya, after a moment's hesitation, slid into the backseat. Isabella got in on the driver's side and they had just begun driving again, the black sedan purring steadily, when an army truck appeared on the street behind them. Black guns bristled from all sides of it.

"It's okay," said Isabella. "It's just the patrol."

They turned down another street and the army truck continued past them and was gone.

"You really gave me a run for it," Isabella said, turning to smile at Maya.

Maya noticed that Isabella was sitting on a pillow in order to see over the steering wheel. *Great,* she thought.

"I'm not supposed to be driving," Isabella said cheerfully. "Girls aren't supposed to be out by themselves and I have a driver, anyway. But he's old and he sleeps half the day and doesn't even notice that I've gone. The windows are tinted, so no one can see that I'm the only one in the car. I go out every day. And, anyway, it's perfectly safe for me to be out on my own. See—" She rapped on the windshield. "Bulletproof."

"I don't know how safe it is," Maya muttered. "You almost mowed me down earlier."

Isabella laughed.

Maya eyed the door handle, wondering if she should jump out and make a run for it. They weren't going that fast. She saw Isabella watching her in the rearview mirror.

"I wouldn't do that," Isabella said. "You can't, anyway—I have everything locked from up here. Look, I'm helping you. You don't want to get caught out here. Everybody has heard about what you did in Port Town—they think you're a spy for the North. My uncle's men are looking for you."

"A spy!" Maya cried. "That's crazy!"

"*I* know that," said Isabella. "You're the daughter of the missing couple on the poster, you pretended to be me so that my uncle would help you to find them. I figured it out."

Isabella turned a corner and the car picked up speed, leaving Maracairol behind and heading into the hills.

"You disappeared and no one knew where you had gone. My uncle was furious. There are dozens of people out looking for you now. Everything happened all at once after you left—the rest of the Festival was called off because there's been new fighting on the border, and everyone thinks there's going to be a sea battle near Bembao; the ships are gathering now. My mother and I came back to Maracairol early because things were getting bad and we were afraid the road would be too dangerous if we waited any longer.

"Anyway, everyone thought you had all escaped, but I

knew the pirates were looking for you—I heard they had come to my uncle's house, asking about your boat. I suspected that they had captured you before you even left Port Town. I knew that the fleet was sailing to Maracairol first, so when we got here and I heard that a boy had been thrown off one of the ships, I thought it might be one of you. I found out he was just your friend, but I put him in jail, anyway, otherwise he would have taken off. I knew that you had been separated from the others and I figured that you'd hear that the fleet had sailed to Maracairol and you'd come here. I wanted to get both of you together."

"Listen, I'm sorry that I pretended I was you," Maya said. "But can you please just let me go? I have to get to my brother and sister!"

Isabella ignored her. "Is it true?" she asked. "Are you really from the Outside?" She looked hard at Maya. "It is true," Isabella said triumphantly. The dirt road rolled away behind them and dappled light slid across Maya's knees. Isabella grew quiet.

"Tamarind is a lost place," she said. "They always tell us that when we're children. Boats that sail past the line don't return, or they sail back without crew or cargo, just empty ghost vessels with torn sails and their hulls crusted over with barnacles. They're unlucky, so the pirates sink them. There are dozens in the waters around us. Maybe hundreds. I've never met anyone from the Outside before. People from Outside are supposed to be crazy. But I know you aren't crazy," she added.

"Gee, thanks," said Maya. "Now, please, where are you taking me?"

"To the one place where no one will think to look for you," said Isabella. "The War Orphanage. I can help you. I know what it's like to be separated from a sibling and not know where they are. My older brother is a soldier and he was taken prisoner in the North. For a long time we didn't know if he was even dead or alive. But now I do know where he is. And I'm going to get him home." Isabella's face hardened and she looked out of the windshield of the car for a moment before she turned to face Maya. "We're organizing something that will bring my brother and all the other young men back home again and end this stupid war. And you're going to help us."

"Me?" exclaimed Maya. "What can I do?"

"To start with, you can come to the meeting with me," said Isabella, turning down a narrow, rutted road overgrown with weeds. "We're already late."

"What meeting?" Maya asked. She held on to her seat as the car bounced over potholes.

"The meeting of the Sisters of the Peaceful Revolution," said Isabella. "I'm the president."

❦ CHAPTER THIRTY-NINE ❦

Sisters of the Peaceful Revolution

Isabella cut the engine in a half-moon of cleared forest. Through the trees Maya could see the peeling turquoise walls of a stone building. Through a small gate and inside the yard, children were climbing mango trees. They jumped down and began running toward Isabella when they saw her coming in the gate.

"They're all children whose parents died in the fighting or were kidnapped," whispered Isabella as they entered the grounds of the War Orphanage.

Maya followed her quickly through the yard and into the turquoise building.

The Sisters of the Peaceful Revolution turned out to be a group of about ten young women between the ages of twelve and twenty, all of who were waiting impatiently for Isabella in a schoolroom.

"You're late," said one girl who was sitting on the window ledge twirling a strand of her hair. She looked like the oldest girl there—nearly a grown-up, Maya thought—and she fixed a bored, sullen expression on Isabella. The rest of the girls were Maya and Isabella's age, and a few looked younger.

"Sorry," said Isabella as she breezed in. "But don't complain. I have good news. Everyone, meet Maya. She's going to help us."

All eyes in the room turned skeptically to Maya.

"What's she going to do?" asked the girl on the window ledge.

"Patience," said Isabella. "I'll get to all that. Let's all take our seats so this meeting can come to order."

Isabella whispered something to a tall, dark-haired girl who glanced at Maya and then disappeared out a back door. Some of the orphans had come to the windows of the schoolroom and were looking in, making faces at them and jabbering excitedly. The girl on the window ledge drew the blinds down over them.

Isabella tapped a chair and, still feeling dazed, Maya plunked down in it. Isabella went to the front of the room and clapped her hands.

"This meeting will come to order," she repeated.

"We're *in* order," said the girl on the window ledge.

"Only one person has the floor, Elouisa," said Isabella. "And right now that's me. So let me start by welcoming our new sister, Maya."

Isabella paused, pacing a few times before she cleared her throat and continued.

"Peace," she began. "We're all here because we have a vision of a peaceful Greater Tamarind. We want to bring an end to the war, to bring our fathers and brothers and cousins and friends back home to us. We are here because we can imagine this island as a happy, prosperous place again, like it was in the stories we hear about the old days, before the war. When there were no orphans, families were whole, the towns were vibrant, there was music everywhere, and you could travel from one side of the island to the other without fear and with the knowledge that you would be welcomed wherever you went. And we're here because we believe we can make this dream happen—"

"I just want a husband," said Elouisa, the girl on the window ledge. A couple of girls stifled giggles. "That's why I'm here. Isabella can have her war's end and unity of the people and all the rest of it. I just want the boys to return home so that I can get married and have my own house and not have to live with my mother anymore!"

"Isabella," said a girl in the front row. "We know all this already. And we have to go home soon, so maybe you could skip this part and just tell us what we need to do for this week?"

"I'm getting there, I'm getting there," said Isabella. "Let's go back to Elouisa's concern for a moment. Before the war the towns were full of young men! Young men everywhere—plenty of husbands for Elouisa to choose from! Now all the young men are off fighting or are dead. We're all here because we've lost family members in the war. Fathers, brothers, cousins, uncles, fiancés . . . the list is too long to count."

Maya noticed that a few girls watched Isabella as she paced but that others were not paying attention and were staring into space or picking at their fingernails. Maya got the sense they'd heard Isabella's speech before.

"So we've been meeting here for a year now to try to figure out a way to make peace with the North and reunite Greater Tamarind so that we can live again without soldiers, without rebels, without checkpoints and bombs and fear and the loss of those dear to us. And it isn't just us—from here the movement has been growing and now there's a group of women like us in every town—on both sides of this island. We've made contact with our sisters in the North. For months we've wondered what to do—how is it possible to bring peace to Tamarind? We can't fight for it with weapons. And so we've sat here for months debating. You might think it was time wasted, but while we've been meeting here, more groups like us have been forming. Our numbers have been growing. And now the time has come.

"With our sisters in the North, we've chosen a day and time for the Peace March and on that morning the Sisters of the Peaceful Revolution will leave their towns—towns all over Greater Tamarind!—and we'll begin to march along the Coastal Road until we've gone all the way around the island. And as we go, people will see how many others in Tamarind want peace and they'll feel brave and they'll join us! And soon most of Tamarind will be marching with us and we'll outnumber the soldiers and they'll be unable to attack us. Soldiers who long to stop fighting and return home to their families will have the chance— they'll throw down their weapons and leave the jungle. South and North will be one again. Our numbers as we march around the island will reveal the truth of what we all believe—Greater Tamarind is ready for peace!"

The room had fallen silent as Isabella spoke. No one hummed, no one tapped a shoe on the floor or sighed or moved so that their wooden chair squeaked. By the time she finished speaking, all eyes were on her. Maya felt goose bumps prickle her arms.

But then a girl in a seat at the back of the room spoke up.

"But how?" she asked in a small voice. "How can we make the March happen? We had established contact with Gloria in the North, it's true, but we haven't been able to get a message to her for a month—it's gotten too dangerous."

Isabella smiled patiently and waited.

"It's true that no messenger has been able to get to the North via the coast," she said. "But now all that's changed. Rather than send a messenger around the coast . . . we're going to send one over the mountains."

"Over the mountains?" cried a tiny girl in the front row incredulously.

"Yes," said Isabella triumphantly.

"But the mountains are too dangerous!" said an older girl. "There's no easy way over them. Who will go?"

And as she was saying that, the tall, dark-haired girl who Isabella had whispered to returned. And behind her, glowering, was Helix. A murmur went through the group—a boy was at the meeting!

Maya gasped when she saw him. He looked furious and was struggling with the handcuffs that were restraining him. When he caught sight of Maya he looked at her suspiciously as if she knew what was going on and was responsible for his being brought there.

"All right," said Isabella. "You can uncuff him. Were those really necessary?"

"He wouldn't come with me without them," said the dark-haired girl as she unlocked the handcuffs.

Helix stood there rubbing his wrists and glaring around the room.

"Sorry about that," said Isabella. "But we need your help." She paused. "We need you to go with Maya to carry a message to the North."

"And what makes you think I'd do that?" Helix asked.

"Because you're the only ones who have enough reason to go to the North," said Isabella. "Her brother and sister are on their way to Bembao right now. There's going to be a battle between the northern and southern fleets."

"What reason do I have to go?" asked Helix, scowling. "She thinks I betrayed them, anyway!"

"Then she'll go alone," Isabella said simply. "She's desperate, she'll have to. There's no other way to get to her brother and sister. Though she'll be far safer with you."

"What are you talking about?" said Maya. "I never said I'd go anywhere!"

Isabella went to the chalkboard and began drawing something.

"This is Greater Tamarind," she said. "This is Maracairol, where we are now. This, *all* the way around the coast and on the other side of the island, in the North, is Bembao. This road, along the coast, is impassable—any single travelers will be ambushed by soldiers. The only way to get to Bembao is to cut through the mountains, which are here."

She put the chalk down and dusted off her hands.

"It will take the fleet with your brother and sister on it three days to get to Bembao," she said to Maya. "Ships are already sailing to battle—it's supposed to be the biggest one in years. The northern fleet invaded southern waters several days ago and took several towns along the coast, and the South is going to retaliate. All the ships on either side are massing for it. If you want to rescue your brother and sister, you have to get there before that. There's no way that you can make it there without my help. It's too far to go on foot, and even if you had a boat, the seas are too dangerous. I can get a truck to take you all the way to the foot of the mountains. After that you'll have to cross on foot."

Isabella studied Maya.

"The only chance you have of getting to your family before the battle is with my help. I'll get you as far as the mountains," she went on. "On the condition that once you reach Bembao you'll deliver a message to our contact there. She's coordinating the Peace March in the North. Her name is Gloria. When my

324

brother, Lorenz, was injured fighting in the North she took him in and took care of him. She managed to get a message to us that he was safe, though not able to travel back. Anyway, that's how we were first in touch. Gloria was organizing a peace movement in the North, and we decided to coordinate our efforts.

"Anyway, our usual line of communication, through the towns, was severed a month ago because of fighting in the hills just west of here. We've decided that the Peace March will begin with the sea battle, while the soldiers are distracted. Everything is ready to be put into motion, we just need to get the message to Gloria. The March has to be coordinated perfectly or it won't work."

Isabella paused.

"You need us, we need you."

"Forget it," said Helix. "Get someone else. I don't want anything to do with this. I know how dangerous the mountains are supposed to be—no one sane would cross them."

"Fine," said Isabella. "She'll go alone."

Helix and Maya looked at each other mistrustfully. Then Helix's face softened.

"I didn't set you up," he said to Maya, emotion in his voice. "I was helping you get away. I swear. I don't know how the pirates knew it was us, except that somehow they figured out that you were one of the children from the posters. They were on the lookout for three children and a baby leaving Port Town. You wouldn't have been hard to spot, even disguised."

Maya nodded. Up until that moment she hadn't known whether Helix had betrayed them or not. She hadn't known what to believe. But looking at him now she was sure that he was telling the truth. She didn't know how she knew but she just knew.

"Will you come to Bembao with me?" she asked quietly.

Though only a moment before Helix had been ready to wring Isabella's neck and walk out of there and never see Maya again—*no way* was he going to try passing through the mountains to the North—when he looked at Maya, he knew he would go with her. He nodded. "Yes," he said.

"Meeting adjourned!" Isabella cried. "I'll meet with Maya and Helix privately to discuss the details. The rest of you—wait to hear from me."

The girls in the room stood up, chattering. They smiled at Maya and Helix as they passed, filing out of the room. In a few minutes, Maya and Helix were left alone with Isabella.

"There's one more thing," she said. She left the room and a moment later returned holding a birdcage covered in a cloth. She withdrew the cloth and there was Seagrape, looking peevish and disgruntled. Helix quickly opened the cage and she hopped out. On her way to Helix's shoulder, where she sat making grumbling noises, she pecked viciously once at Isabella.

"It wasn't until I managed to catch her, hanging around your jail cell, that I realized," Isabella said.

"Realized what?" asked Helix.

"That she's . . . you know," said Isabella. "That she's one of *their* birds."

"Whose?" asked Helix. "What are you talking about?"

"One of the Dark Women's," she said. "I'm sure of it. Didn't you know?"

Helix looked at her blankly.

"Who are you, anyway?" Isabella asked curiously.

But it seemed that Helix had no idea what she was talking about.

"Interesting," murmured Isabella. Then she changed the

subject. "I'm sorry that I had to have you locked up like that," she said brightly. "And for twisting your arm about going over the mountains. But really, it's the best way, you'll see."

Maya felt utterly confused—about everything. What did Isabella mean about Seagrape belonging to one of the Dark Women? Again she wondered, who *was* Helix, really? And how were the two of them going to make it over the mountains? She shook herself—she had to focus on the only thing that really mattered—finding Simon and Penny.

"When do we leave?" she asked.

❧ CHAPTER FORTY ❧

Catching Up ✳ *Moon Oranges* ✳
Maya Learns the Truth

Isabella showed them the room where they could sleep, and told them that she would arrange for them to depart first thing the following morning. Then she left for the night. Maya and Helix wandered outside and sat on the steps. Maya had a million questions to ask him.

"Tell me more about Simon and Penny," she said. "What kind of place are they keeping them in? Do they have enough to eat? Are they scared?" Her voice quavered. She hated to think of Simon and Penny alone and afraid.

"They were being kept in the gallows of one of the pirate ships, the *Meggie Vic*," said Helix. "After we were captured they carried us in a fishnet along the road to the cove where the ship we were going on was moored. Simon managed to shove the book through a hole in the net. He was hoping that you would find it."

"I did!" said Maya, her face lighting up. "That's how I knew you had been there, and that I was going the right way. But I don't understand why they let you go and kept Simon and Penny," Maya said.

"They threw me out as soon as they realized I was from Tamarind," said Helix. "They didn't think I could help them. The next thing I knew, Isabella had men capture me and put me in jail, hoping that I would tell her more about you."

"But it doesn't make any sense," Maya said, perplexed. "Why do the pirates want Simon and Penny and me in the first place?"

"I told you," said Helix. "It isn't you they want, it's the *Pamela Jane*."

"But *why*?" asked Maya.

"They think that she belongs to them," said Helix.

"But she's *ours*!" Maya cried. "We sailed here in her. I've lived on that boat for my whole life."

"Well, anyway," said Helix. "It doesn't matter—Simon can't take them back to her. All he knows is that you landed in the Lesser Islands—but there are dozens of them, with hundreds of tiny islands and hidden coves. It would take the pirates forever to find your boat, unless they knew exactly where to look. And I'm the only one who does. But they didn't realize that."

Maya wondered how long the pirates would keep Simon and Penny until they realized that Simon was no use to them. It was a chilling thought.

"Now, we'd better get some rest," said Helix. "Tomorrow's going to be very difficult."

Tomorrow they would be in the mountains. Maya thought of the mountains—steep and perilous, their peaks disappearing into the clouds—that she had seen in the Outside World and she felt scared. How would they manage to cross them?

Evening had come swiftly and heavily. Maya and Helix fell into silence, each giving way to their own thoughts about what lay ahead. In the yard, a few of the little girls were playing a game. They were peeling small, marbled oranges and letting the spray from their skins coat pieces of blank white paper. Then, holding the edges of the papers very carefully, they were carrying them over and lying them, faceup, on a low stone wall. It seemed such a curious thing to do that for a moment Maya stopped thinking about the journey.

"What are they doing?" she asked.

Helix looked up. "Oh, it's an old trick," he said. "Writing with ink made from zanoria pits—it's a type of fruit—the ink is invisible. But it reacts with the citrus from moon oranges. When the moon comes out in a little while, the writing will appear. But it's what people used to do in the old days when they wanted to keep special documents a secret."

The dinner bell rang and the little girls ran off inside, leaving the papers on the wall, anchored on the corners with pebbles. Maya stared at the squiggles shining on each blank white sheet, her heart beginning to beat quickly.

"Coming?" Helix asked, getting to his feet.

Maya shook her head. "In a minute," she said. "You go."

When Helix had left, Maya quickly went out into the yard and reached up and plucked a moon orange from a shaggy green branch and ran back up to her room with it. With trembling hands she took the logbook out of her backpack and opened it to the first page, where the enigmatic shiny squiggles began.

Could it be? she thought. *Could it really be that . . .*

It was dark outside now and the moon was rising in the heavy velvet sky.

She pierced the moon orange with her thumb and slowly peeled the skin. A fine citrus mist was released and hung suspended in the air for a moment before it fell down on the open page. Maya repeated this, peeling more of the orange until the facing page shone wetly. She slid the book out onto the moonlit windowsill and held her breath. Her pulse was racing. *Come on,* she whispered.

330

She waited. Seconds ticked past. Nothing happened. It had been a crazy thought—a wild hope—that was all. She leaned back a bit, shutting her eyes. She would close the book and put it away—it had no more answers to give her. But when she opened her eyes again she saw a faint shadow over the top of the first right-hand page where the citrus spray had first touched.

Maya barely breathed. As she watched, writing came into view. It grew bolder and darker on the page, rising up through her father's logbook entries, and when it was all there, she turned the page and, hands shaking, peeled more of the orange over the next two facing pages. When the writing on those pages came into view she turned back to the very first page in the book, which was empty, and peeled the last of the orange over it.

Maya watched as the logbook entries and notes receded and the new writing darkened and became clear. Was this where the answers lay, about ophalla and the Red Coral Project and Tamarind, and about how she and Simon and Penny all had come to be there? She was almost afraid to find out. Heart pounding, she began to read.

CHAPTER FORTY-ONE

The Journal

THIS IS TO BE A TRUE ACCOUNT OF THE *PAMELA JANE* ON HER VOYAGES AROUND GREATER AND LESSER TAMARIND, TOLD BY HER FIRST MATE, AND BEGINNING ON THE SPRING EQUINOX.

New Quarter Moon, Late Afternoon

We rounded the southwest coast today, taking Scarab Rocks Passage between the Lesser Islands, where all hands came above deck to watch the infamous Lesser vines swarming on the edges of the islands. They seemed to grow before our very eyes and move like snakes. While we watched, one plucked a good-sized heron in mid-flight straight out of the air and drew it into the recesses of the jungle. It can be assumed that by now the bird has already been digested and all that is left is the beak and talons and some feathers, though perhaps not even those since the vines, once they crush the life out of something, are said to devour things whole. The wind dies and the current is very slow between Scarab Rocks, so it took us nearly an hour to cross a very little distance. Our small crew was afraid, since the vines have been known to reach out and grab whole ships and drag them into the jungle, though that, of course, may just be myth. Our old captain, may he rest in peace, never made our ship take this route. Our new captain, his cousin, Captain Ademovar, was unafraid, however, and spent the whole time peering into the jungle with a spyglass, hoping to witness any carnage.

I am afraid of Captain Ademovar. He is a greedy man and loves blood. Our old captain was a wise and kind soul, who, despite my injured leg, took me to crew his ship when so many others would not, and he would never have wished the Pamela Jane *to fall into his hands. He always said that she was a rare and special ship, and that she must always be protected. He planned to leave her in my care, but the war changed all that. He was killed and Ademovar seized his ship. Though Ademovar is eager to take charge of a larger ship and be in the thick of the next battle, he holds on to the* Pamela Jane *because his cousin believed she had a secret value.*

Third Quarter Moon, Nightfall
We reached the mouth of the Nallanda River at nightfall, in time to see the barges arrive from the interior. They rode low in the water with their cargoes of ophalla, which glistened white as mountain snow. Knowing how many have been killed over ophalla in the past few years, it is quite solemn to see it there, lighting the night air with what seems to be a supernatural glow. We are here to take a quantity of it to Maracairol, to beautify the embassies. I must admit that it makes me nervous to be carrying such a cargo in these times. Men have lost their lives for a mere pebble of the stuff, and we will be in possession of nearly half

333

a ton. Our cargo will also include several cases of perfume from the cloud orchids farmed by the Amaranti tribe. No one but the traders has ever seen the Amaranti. We were supposed to carry produce—star fruit, mangoes, and eggplants—as well as cinnamon— but we received word that that barge was attacked and sunk eight miles upriver, so there will be none in the towns this week.

Our small crew is nervous. Being such a small ship, we were spared from joining the war fleet, and instead were to carry goods to towns along the coast. But as the seas grow more violent, Captain Ademovar is urging that we be allowed to join the war fleet. I pray that this will not happen, but I fear it is inevitable. It no longer seems that the Council has the power to resolve the border tensions, and the current situation does not make for a good night's sleep for any of us.

Half-Moon, Dawn

We were attacked after midnight last night, in the waters around Lafton's Pass, by two vessels from the North. They boarded us and stole our cargo and, after shredding our sail, left us tied up on the deck. We were drifting until late today, when we were discovered by a ship from our own side who, being much bigger, was able to tow us to shore, where the Pamela Jane is currently being fitted with a new sail. It now seems certain that we will join the war fleet as a fighting vessel.

It's become clear that Captain Ademovar is not concerned with fighting for his side of Tamarind, but like so many, he is interested only in his own profit and in bloodlust. All around the island, ordinary sailors conscripted into the war fleets are becoming nothing but scurrilous pirates. There isn't a night that goes by without us hearing explosions in the towns along the coast and seeing the orange glow of the fires. We hear stories about whole families who have been killed and young men who have run off to fight in the jungle. Tamarind is collapsing into anarchy with ever greater speed, and there seems now that nothing can be done to turn back the tide.

The light through the window was fading, so Maya leaned closer to the pages, squinting.

Half-Moon, Afternoon

It took until midday today before the bloodstains were washed off our deck. And as I write this I see yet another body bobbing facedown on the water, being carried to shore on the tide. There were fifty ships in battle last night. The night sky was lit by burning ships glowing furiously before they sank into the dark sea. The scent of gunpowder hung heavy in the air. Thankfully, our dear ship was spared great damage, our closest call coming when a cannonball tore clean through our mainsail and landed in the sea on the opposite side of us. An enemy vessel drew alongside us

335

at one point, and Captain Ademovar murdered the two men who tried to come aboard. He took joy in the murders. Last night was our fourth battle in as many weeks and tomorrow our captain desires to attack a tiny town on the northwest coast of the island. I can hardly bear to think that we will do this to our neighbors. We will fire on the town, then he and the others will plunder what they can—there are many who plan to be wealthy when this war ends. Because of my leg, I am allowed to remain behind.

Full Moon, Night

The moon is so bright tonight that there are hardly any shadows on the deck of the Pamela Jane and the waters around us are dazzling. In all this light I am afraid that Captain Ademovar will be able to peer into my heart and discover my plan.

The idea occurred to me when I was remembering the good days with our old captain again. I remembered all the stories he used to tell us, and how I always loved to hear about the Outside. Most people don't believe the Outside World exists, of course. But our old captain was one of the ones who did. He had a friend who had been there, who had dared to cross the Blue Line, and had returned. He said the Outside World was unimaginably vast. Our captain used to tell us stories about it on nights on the Pamela Jane. He'd ask us, jokingly, if we wanted to try to sail out to the Line.

Three nights ago I started to think that perhaps I would try to do that, to take the Pamela Jane far away from here, to where the Blue Line was, and I would try

to make it to the Outside World. Perhaps there I can
find help for Tamarind.

Clenching the logbook tightly, Maya glanced ahead. There
were only two entries left.

New Moon, night
It is my ninth day adrift.

It was more than a week ago now that we were in
port on a dark cloudy night. I left Captain Ademovar
and the rest of the crew drinking on shore and I snuck
back to the Pamela Jane. *I had been waiting for such*
a night, when the sails would not be illuminated in
the moonlight and visible to any ship that gave chase.
I set sail alone. But Captain Ademovar had sensed
that something was afoot and before I had gone far
he discovered what I had done. He came after me in
a small, fast boat. He came aboard the Pamela,
abandoning the small boat, and we fought. He
overpowered me and locked me in the cabin, but by
then we were in sight of a dark line just off the horizon.
I could just see it through the portholes, barely visible
under the moon. It was the Blue Line, and soon the
terrible storms that brew around it were upon us.

For two days we were caught in the edge of the
storm, unable to sail into or out of it. I banged on the
cabin door and shouted until I was hoarse, but Captain
Ademovar would not let me out, even to help him steer
the boat. Finally, during a lull, I took off my wooden
leg and smashed down the door with it and succeeded
in freeing myself.

Maya paused and looked up. *Wooden leg.* An idea was forming in her mind. She read on.

> *Captain Ademovar attacked me when I came on deck, but this time I was ready. We fought until we were weary. I did not mean to send him overboard, but I dodged when he ran at me—and he slipped. Suddenly he was in the water and the sharks were around him, tearing at his flesh. I untied the rowboat and cast it off toward him. He was able to grasp it and pull himself in, but I do not know what happened to him after that. The storms were gathering again and with a last look toward beloved Tamarind, I hoisted the jib and sailed into the storm. I fear that was the last I will ever see of my home.*
>
> *The compass is shattered and the sextant is broken and I must admit that I have no idea where I am. For days now I have been hovering between storms and I'm concerned about the state of the* Pamela Jane. *I am writing this in a brief period of calm, though the fog is so thick I can barely see the page I write on.*

There was only one entry left before the journal ended abruptly. A sick feeling was growing in the pit of Maya's stomach but she could not stop reading now.

> ### First Quarter Moon, night
> *I crossed the Blue Line into the Outside, but have found no one here. We are becalmed. Though the sea is peaceful now, the* Pamela Jane *has been caught in so many storms now that she has been quite badly damaged. The sails are torn and the jib mast is cracked,*

and I'm afraid that if another storm strikes, which seems inevitable, I will not be able to keep us from capsizing. The poor Pamela Jane *has been heroic, and it's for her I feel saddest. My home seems very far away now. The moonlight is eerie on the water and the creaking of the rigging may be the loneliest sound in the world.*

I, Hábil Izquierdo, First Mate of the Pamela Jane, *believe this may be my last entry in this book.*

The entries in the logbook stopped there.

Maya sat there, reeling. She could only guess what had happened after the last entry had been written. All the pieces were swirling in her mind, taking shape.

Dr. Izquierdo, Dr. Hábil Izquierdo.

The wooden leg.

The pirate ships.

The Blue Line.

The Outside World.

Their parents' discovery of an abandoned ship, its sails in tatters, that had sailed in without a crew one afternoon, and that no one had ever claimed, with the name stenciled in black letters across her hull: *Pamela Jane.*

Dr. Izquierdo's strange fascination with the boat that day in St. Alban's. The telltale clicking sound of one of his shoes on the dock that Maya had noticed as he walked away. His very name, there in the logbook of their ship, hidden until now.

The full import of her discovery struck her:

The *Pamela Jane,* their beloved *Pamela Jane,* with her crisp white sails and sunny yellow hull, had come from Tamarind.

The ship that she and Simon and Penny had all grown up on was a pirate ship.

❧ CHAPTER FORTY-TWO ❧

Thoughts on Izquierdo ✳ *Isabella's Last
Hope* ✳ *The Fateful Conch* ✳
Farewell, Isabella

"Here," said Helix. "I brought you some bread, in case you changed your mind and got hungry."

Maya jumped, startled, as he came into the room. She had been sitting alone in the dark with the logbook on her knees, absorbing the significance of her discovery.

"I know why the pirates want the *Pamela Jane*," she said. She opened the logbook again and turned it around so that Helix could see the journal that had appeared in the mist from the moon oranges.

"Here—it'll be easiest if you just read it yourself," she said, handing the book to him.

But Helix didn't take it.

"You just tell me what it says," he said.

In the moonlight, Maya noticed that the color had risen in his cheeks. Then she understood.

"You can't read!" she exclaimed.

Helix shook his head.

"Really?"

"Maya!"

"I'm sorry, it's just that . . ." Maya didn't finish the sentence, but what she meant was that she had never met anyone who couldn't read before, at least, not a person her own age. It seemed so strange, and she momentarily forgot about everything she had just read in the logbook.

"I don't know if you've noticed," said Helix. "Not too many schools around here anymore."

"Well, never mind then, I'll just tell you what's in it," she said. Helix was obviously ashamed and she felt bad for him. Helix listened quietly as she related the story in the journal.

"So," she said. "There must have been one last big storm and Hábil Izquierdo was washed overboard. He must have made it to shore somehow, though. That's why the *Pamela Jane* was drifting along on her own when my family found her, and that's why no one ever claimed her."

"It means that Hábil Izquierdo, Dr. Izquierdo, whoever he is, he's been stuck on the Outside all this time," said Helix somberly.

Maya nodded. She felt surprisingly sad. It seemed so strange that someone who had written in their logbook—whose own words and thoughts, even the ink from his quill pen, were still preserved there—had lived on the *Pamela Jane* long before Maya had even been born, and may even now have some claim over their home. She turned to the first page again and ran her finger over the red seal that she and Simon had seen before. It must have been Hábil Izquierdo's personal seal.

"But what I don't understand," she said. "Is how he knew we would be arriving at St. Alban's that day. Has he been trying to track down the *Pamela Jane* all that time? Why did he just find us then?"

Maya racked her brains but she couldn't figure anything out. She only ended up with more questions. How did Dr. Izquierdo know Dr. Fitzsimmons? Was he involved in the Red Coral Project somehow? She remembered the two figures standing on the dock as they had left the port at St. Alban's. How were all these things connected? She knew her parents mustn't have told them the whole truth about what they were doing out at sea.

"Wait until Simon hears," said Helix finally. "The *Pamela Jane* was a pirate ship."

Maya smiled. "He's going to think it's the greatest thing ever," she said.

Her eyes suddenly filled with tears.

"Don't *cry*, Maya," said Helix.

Maya sniffled. "Sorry," she said. She sighed. "I'll have to try to figure all this out later. Right now I have to concentrate on getting to Simon and Penny."

Isabella came to get Maya and Helix early the next morning. A truck was waiting for them under the mango trees. They waved to the driver and hopped into the back, which was covered by canvas.

Maya and Helix were Isabella's last desperate hope, but she could only assist them so far on their voyage. They would drive north through the valleys to the foot of the mountains. After this, Isabella couldn't help them anymore. When they reached the mountains they would leave the truck and proceed on a trail that led to the North and eventually the town of Bembao. The mountains—where the war had begun—were buckled ridges that had long been considered treacherous in Tamarind. They were riddled with ophalla mines, and after the mines dried up, the rebels hid out there and they used to fight in the hills. But it was said that avalanches happened so frequently that eventually even the rebels left and moved down into the jungle. Isabella believed that there were still a handful of very old towns in the valleys—the In-between Towns—who had little contact with the rest of Tamarind. Maya remembered what went on in the jungle that no one knew about, and she imagined the worst about the mountain pass.

Once out of the mountains, they were to deliver a note from Isabella to Gloria, who they would find in the only blue house on the hill overlooking the town of Bembao. Isabella told them nothing more about the plan after that point. She said it was best that this was all they knew.

"Good luck," said Isabella.

"Good luck to you, too," said Maya.

Maya opened her backpack and took out the conch shell. She had decided last night that she would give it to Isabella. She and Helix would be traveling all the way across the island—where the mermaids would never hear them. And Isabella needed all the help she could get if the march was going to work.

"Friends gave this to me to use if I needed it," Maya said. "A giant and three mermaids. I want you to have it. If you use it, they'll come to help you."

Isabella took the shell and held it, mesmerized, the sunlight bright on its knobs and ridges. She began to say thank you, but stopped. She looked at Maya and for a brief second Maya thought that she detected something guilty and sorrowful in Isabella's eyes. Isabella took her hand and squeezed it.

"Maya," she said, "once you get the note to Gloria, you must get your brother and sister off the ship as soon as possible. There won't be any time to waste."

She looked Maya in the eye.

"But promise me that you'll take the note to Gloria," she said urgently. "If the note doesn't reach her, everything will fall apart. All of Tamarind is counting on you, even if they don't know it. One day you'll be known for the great role you played in the history of Tamarind—the young Tamarinder and the brave Outsider who carried the message that began the great Peace March. You won't be forgotten." Isabella spoke with great emotion.

"I promise we'll get the note to Gloria," Maya said solemnly.

"Travel safely," Isabella said. "I hope we'll meet again."

Maya felt a lump in her throat as the truck drove off. She leaned out of the back to wave. Isabella stood barefoot on the gravel path, her blue dress fluttering in a breeze that had picked up. Then the lush, hungry walls of the jungle closed over the road and she was lost to sight.

CHAPTER FORTY-THREE

Journey Through the Mountains ＊
A Sad Loss ＊ *By the Waterfall* ＊
Helix's Story ＊ *Insight*

They took a winding road that immediately began to climb the hills behind the orphanage. Every now and then Maya caught sight of Seagrape following them. At one point they stopped and she flew in and spent most of the journey to Lopez-Marcanzo sitting on the floor of the truck near Maya's feet, looking seasick and disgruntled. Mumbling, she pulled peevishly at her feathers and once she nipped Helix's ankle. Maya bent down to stroke her head every now and then.

As they drove it was impossible to miss the mark the war had left. In some towns all that remained of whole streets were craters from explosions. Graveyards on the fringes of each town overflowed with headstones. Some towns had built walls around them and old men stood at the gates, rifles in hand. Fields lay fallow. They passed young children on the road, carrying buckets of water on their shoulders from village wells. They drove through orchards that one time would have been lush and bountiful, but now the aisles between the trees were clotted with weeds and the branches bore shriveled fruit. Masses of flies buzzed loudly over rotting windfall.

They were stopped at several roadblocks and at each one Maya stiffened and Seagrape fell silent, her soft feathers against Maya's bare legs, but the truck was always waved through.

They stopped in the town of Lopez-Marcanzo, the last

town before the mountains, where they were supposed to meet Lucia, one of the sisters, who would give them food for the rest of their journey and fuel for the truck. It was a very tiny, poor town. They ended up at the end of a rutted dirt lane, studded with banana plants. A young woman came out of the tin shack and ushered them furtively inside.

"I'm happy to meet another sister—and brother—of the Peaceful Revolution," said Lucia, shaking their hands warmly. "Isabella sent word late last night that you'd be coming. We were expecting you earlier—I was worried—the roads are so bad these days. I'm glad to see you made it here safely."

Lucia had prepared a meal for them, which they sat down gratefully to eat. Before they left they thanked her, and she squeezed both their hands again.

"I'm happy to do my part," she said. "Isabella is a very great woman. One day it's my dream to meet her. You're lucky you've already had the chance."

Maya looked up, startled. A very great woman! She opened her mouth, about to say that Isabella was just a girl—a girl Maya's own age!—and not even a very big girl at that. But then she stopped. If Isabella's plan did bring peace to Tamarind, she *would* be a very great woman.

They drove out of Lopez-Marcanzo, climbing into the foothills of the mountains. The tin shacks thinned out and soon they were driving along with no houses in sight. Finally the driver cut the engine.

"Well," Helix said. "I guess this is it."

They climbed out of the truck. Ahead of them the road, which had been growing narrower and rockier for some time, petered into a single dirt footpath along a ridge.

Maya gazed around at the vista. They were in the middle of

a great enormity. Miles below were vast valleys and miles above were the barren peaks of mountains frosted with snow in the thin air. Far below, Maya could see what must surely be a broad, fast-flowing river, but from this distance was merely a silver trickle flashing in the sunlight. A pair of condors coasted silently in the air over the valley. The whole scene took Maya's breath away. She and Helix stood there for a few moments gazing out at it. How would they ever cross this? The size of the mountains humbled Maya and she held back despair that she might never see her brother and sister again.

Seagrape hopped around on the ground, stretching her wings. Helix lifted their bags out of the back of the truck and tossed Maya's to her. She double-checked to make sure the logbook was still there. The sight of it was comforting and she touched its edge with her fingers before closing the bag and hoisting it onto her back. The dusty truck turned and drove back the way it had come. Maya looked back once to see its mirrors twinkling in the sun, and then it was gone. She and Helix were alone in the wild, barren mountain pass.

For long stretches there were no towns visible, no signs of human life at all. Just Helix and Maya and the pair of condors, who were so high above now that they seemed like tiny black etchings. Seagrape hung around, never getting too far away from Maya and Helix. As they climbed, the air thinned and cooled. Pearly white down bearded the plants that grew from the rocky heights. Far below was the hiss of the river, a shiny seam slipping in and out of the verdant depths of the valley. Occasionally a giant yellow bee or two, humming like airplanes, crisscrossed in front of them. Cow and donkey dung, dried in the sun, spotted the path here and there. At one point thin clouds wreathed the path in front of them and clung coldly to the folds of their clothes as they walked through it.

They walked for a few hours in silence. The air was thin at that altitude, so it was easier not to talk. The path had a metallic shine from flecks of quartz. In its middle, the stone was worn smooth by centuries of feet and hooves. Boulders as smooth as eggs sat along the edges. Sometimes in the distance they could see tiny mountain villages of three or four stucco huts—the In-between Towns, Isabella had called them—whose inhabitants belonged to neither side and had lived in the mountains for centuries. Close to these villages the hillsides were terraced and green bands of vegetation flattened in distant breezes. Soft-eared donkeys carrying sacks of onions passed them from time to time.

Sometimes on the road they passed the remnants of human skeletons still wearing soldiers' uniforms. Both bones and cloth had been bleached by the sun. Once they saw a skull with a soldier's cap still pulled firmly down over its forehead. They began to notice more bones on the slopes of the valley, reminding them of the danger that lay all around them. The war had raged for years here, and the mountains had seen much carnage.

Yet at moments the beauty of the landscape was breathtaking.

"I've never seen anything like this before," said Helix, stopping at one point to look around in awe.

"Have you ever been to the North?" Maya asked, realizing she didn't know.

He shook his head. "Nope," he said. "Never."

Maya was glad that something was new for Helix, too.

They were both seeing all of this for the first time, and neither of them really knew where they were going or what would be in store when they got there. The mountains were both eerie and humbling, and she was glad not to be alone. They passed the entrances to old mines deep in the mountains, where Isabella had told them that runaway soldiers lived as hermits. Maya looked inside the dark mouths of the cliffs but never saw anyone, though often she had the sensation that they were being watched silently.

Just when Maya was starting to think that the mountains weren't so bad after all, she heard the tinny clatter of pebbles chasing each other down the steep slope above her. She looked up and saw that high above, a waterfall of dirt and rubble was cascading down from the heights of the mountains, coming directly for them. It was an avalanche! Maya screamed and Helix reacted in an instant, seizing her hand and pulling her after him. The roar of the rocks was deafening. In moments the air was so thick with dust that they couldn't see anything and they were running blindly. Maya pulled her shirt over her mouth with one hand so she could breathe without choking on the dust, and with the other she held tightly on to Helix—she felt that if she could just hold on to him she would be all right.

But then Maya heard Seagrape squawk. She turned back and as she did so her foot slid off the path and her leg hung suspended over the miles of empty air down to the valley below. She scrambled desperately for a foothold but her foot felt only cold nothingness. She clung, panic-stricken, to Helix's hand.

Then she felt Helix haul her back to safety. They ran until they could run no more and a few minutes later they stumbled, choking, out of the thick cloud of dust and fell on their knees, fighting to get clean air in their lungs. Maya's whole body was shaking and for a while she couldn't move from where she had collapsed. As suddenly as it had begun, the avalanche had stopped, except for a few stray rocks that groaned as they rolled over each other and began a silent plunge off the cliff until they shattered in the valley below. Clouds of sand hung thickly in the air.

Maya had sand in her eyes and her legs had been scratched badly. There was a paste of dirt in her mouth and her shoes were full of dirt. The road ahead was a steep ledge above a sheer cliff face. It was miraculous that they hadn't run straight off it, Maya thought, looking down over the precarious drop. A haze of fine sand and soil settled slowly through the air, revealing the pair of condors, their wings powdered with dust, still wheeling in the air over the valley. Spitting out sand, Helix had stood up and was surveying the wash of rubble that had come to rest behind them. The path they had been on was no more.

"Seagrape!" Maya cried suddenly, looking back in dismay. Helix limped to the edge of the rockfall and Maya followed. They began to dig through the rubble. They dug until their fingers bled, but there was no sign of the bird. Not a single feather or even a feeble squawk. Helix dislodged a larger stone, which sent a gush of new debris sliding down the hill and over the cliff. They leaped back and Maya's heart plunged to her sand-filled shoes.

It was too dangerous to keep digging. Helix stood there and whistled, and the sound ricocheted around the valley and sent a new shower of pebbles plinking down from the top of the hill.

"We have to keep going," he said finally.

Maya could hear the emotion in his voice, but he didn't cry. He turned away and started walking. She had to hurry to keep up with him. She gulped down silent tears. Poor Seagrape! She had been such a good bird. She had seen them out at sea that day and landed on the mast, and then she had brought Helix to them. It was her feathers that had protected them from Evondra. It wasn't fair! She belonged to Helix—she was his *friend*. And now because Helix had helped them, he had lost her.

Soon the teetering ledge melded back onto a proper path that descended into a valley, and a rich green roof of trees closed over them. Helix didn't speak again and Maya didn't know what to say. They heard water ahead of them and suddenly the path opened out onto a majestic, foaming white falls feeding a series of green pools. They stopped to eat, unwrapping the food that Lucia had packed for them in Lopez-Maranzo. The bread was stale and the cheese had melted, and they were both so miserable about Seagrape that the food seemed tasteless, but they ate to keep up their strength. They took off their shoes and cooled their feet in the water. It was icy, and Maya was glad to feel numbness creeping up her legs. She watched as the water swirled around her feet and a single yellow leaf turned slowly across the surface.

"I'm sorry, Helix," she said miserably. "It's my fault—if you hadn't come with me, this never would have happened."

"It's not your fault," said Helix. "I wanted to come with you. It was an accident. If I hadn't come with you, something else could have happened. Really, don't blame yourself."

A tear sneaked down Maya's cheek and she wiped it away quickly. They sat in silence for a moment, listening to the jingle of water over the rocks from the tiny waterfall.

"How long did you have Seagrape?" she asked.

"As far back as I can remember," said Helix.

Maya's mother's voice came back to her from the last day before the storm. *It's a big ocean. It's lucky that we're all together on it.* Her mother had been right. Maya thought how it would have felt to have been alone—entirely alone—on the *Pamela Jane* the morning after the storm. And even though she didn't know everything, she knew that Helix *had* been that alone before. As far as she knew, Seagrape had been his most constant family.

"She was with me when I lived in the jungle with the Coboranti," Helix went on. "Maybe she was even with me in the car that day . . . She may have been our pet. I just can't remember." He paused. "Seagrape was the reason I escaped from Evondra, you know," he said. "In the end."

Maya's heart beat faster. *Evondra.* Helix *had* been in the camp—she knew it. She kept her eyes on the slowly spinning water, afraid that if she interrupted, Helix would stop talking.

"I don't really remember very much," he said slowly. "Actually, I really only remember one day. I was traveling in a car. I was with a woman. I believe she was my mother. I could see the sky through the window. We had been traveling for a long time and I was dozing, my head was in her lap. She had a ring on her finger. A little diamond. When I woke up I played with it and made it twinkle in the light. She wore some kind of perfume. It was so hot that my skin was sticking to whatever it touched. The road was very bumpy. I can remember all of that like it was yesterday.

"Then we stopped. It was sudden. There was something on the road up ahead. She was scared and she and the man in the front seat were talking to each other. They were upset. Then she opened the car door and she told me to get out. She told me to run into the trees and hide. I heard men on the road up ahead. Then I heard loud noises—now I think what I heard were gunshots. I ran as fast as I could and when I stopped I didn't know where I was. I was lost and then it was nighttime.

"I stopped and sat under a tree. And that's where a hunter found me in the morning. He was from the Coboranti tribe. They took me in and raised me, but when I was old enough I ran away. The Coboranti treated me like one of their own children, but I wasn't a Coboranti and there was a whole world outside of the Coboranti camp. Even when I was a little kid I knew I had to leave there one day."

"Your mother . . ." said Maya. "Did you look for her? When you left the Coboranti camp?"

"Where would I have looked? The only memory I had was that time in the car. I couldn't have been more than three years old—it was so long ago. And I'm not even sure that that woman was my mother—maybe she wasn't. But I feel that she was." Helix paused. "I've always believed that she was."

Maya's feet were cold and numb in the water, and the small waterfall was sending up a white mist that dampened her skin and hair.

"I never went looking for her, but I kept my eyes open," Helix said. "I had two clues. But I never found anything. Until the day I met all of you."

"What do you mean, until the day you met us?" Maya asked.

"Well, that last day in the car, my mother left me two things," said Helix. "Before she pushed me out of the car she slid her ring off her finger—it only took her a moment—and she gave it to me, along with a piece of paper that she took out of her purse. She told me to hold on to them tightly. I've carried both things with me ever since."

Helix untied a tiny cloth pouch from his belt. Maya watched as he shook out a tiny diamond ring and a folded square of paper so dirty and old that it had nearly disintegrated. Helix placed the ring in Maya's palm. It glittered faintly in the sunlight. He unfolded the paper gingerly so that Maya could read it. It was some sort of official document, but at some point it had gotten wet and the ink had blurred and was now unreadable. In the lower right-hand corner was a red wax seal. A red wax seal that bore the same insignia as the seal on the page from the logbook on the *Pamela Jane*.

"That's the same seal that's in the First Mate's journal in the logbook!" Maya exclaimed. "Why—?" She looked in astonishment at the paper Helix held, trying to piece things together.

"I don't know," said Helix. "I had never seen another one like it until I saw the one in your logbook. I noticed it when Simon was reading the book on the beach, after you had talked to Dr. Limmermor, and that night I waited until you were all asleep and I took the book so I could look at the seal properly. I don't know why they're the same—it's a mystery."

Maya looked at the seal on Helix's letter. In the low light beneath the trees it appeared dark as blood.

"It rained the first night I was by myself in the jungle and the ink smeared, so I've never known what the letter said. Nobody in the Coboranti camp could read, anyway. You can imagine how shocked I was when I saw the same seal in your book. I thought it could be a clue somehow, but I couldn't figure anything out. It's probably something I'll never know— who my mother was, why she had that paper with that seal on it, or why she gave it to me. If she was even my mother at all. What I believe now is that there are some things you just never figure out.

"After I left the Coboranti, I was working with traders from another tribe, the Zambata, carrying açai and lurdertree paste from the interior to the coast, when I was captured by the Child Stealer. The other boys I was with got away, but I stopped to fight. Not that you can fight a woman on a jaguar. She took me to the camp and I was put to work in the ophalla mines with a lot of other children. We were kept prisoner in the ark that had gotten stranded on the riverbank when the river dried up."

"I knew it," Maya murmured, remembering the ark and all the children. "Why didn't you just tell Simon and me the truth?"

Helix shrugged. "I hate talking about it. It was a horrible time. Anyway, I escaped. I got out. Why should I think about it anymore? It's in the past."

Maya sat there, absorbing everything Helix had said.

"How did you escape from Evondra?" she asked.

"Seagrape," said Helix. "When Evondra first captured me, Seagrape put up a fight. She kept swooping down and attacking Evondra. But Evondra sped off on the jaguar—me bouncing along on the side—back to her camp. Seagrape found us though, and the whole time I was there she never stopped harassing Evondra. Evondra shot at her all the time, but always missed. It was as if Seagrape couldn't be killed. I knew Evondra hated me, but somehow she was scared of me—or really of Seagrape—so she kept me alive, if just barely. I saw other children lose the will to live, or die of hunger or overwork, but I swore I would get out of there. The first time I tried to escape,

Evondra's jaguar caught me right away—that's how this happened." Helix motioned to his scarred ear.

"The second time I tried, though, I was lucky. It was near the end of the day. Seagrape had been fussing around near the mine all afternoon, and each time she landed on the overhang to the entrance, a shower of pebbles would come down. I realized the mine was about to collapse. I shouted to the rest of the children who were inside and everyone ran out. All of a sudden this colossal rumbling sound started coming from deep inside the earth and then Seagrape came flying at full speed out of the mine, screeching, her wings out and huge. All this sand and dust exploded in the air from the mine. The air was choked with dust. You could hardly see anything. The children had started running and there was confusion everywhere. I knew it was my chance. I didn't even have time to think about it, I just started running into the jungle. I ran straight into the river so that the monkeys wouldn't be able to catch my scent and track me down, and I grabbed onto an overhanging branch. I climbed across to the tree on the opposite side. I waited for a whole day and night in that tree. I wasn't very far away from the camp at all—if I had sneezed they probably could have heard me—and I could see everything that was going on. Seagrape joined me in the tree. Evondra came down to inspect the collapse. I was missing and she thought I was still down in the mine. I watched as she ordered the children to seal it up. Most of the ophalla was gone from that particular mine, anyway—it wasn't worth her opening it up again. She thought I was dead."

Helix cleared his throat before he continued.

"Once the monkeys had stopped looking for me, I climbed down from the tree and began making my way through the jungle. A few weeks later I got to Port Town. It was during the rainy season. I had nowhere to stay and so I was living in a bunch of Helix Sugarcane Factory crates on the edge of the road, which is where Mathilde found me and took me in. I didn't talk for months after I escaped from Evondra. It was like I'd lost my voice. Mathilde didn't know my name and so she called me Helix. By the time my voice came back I decided that I didn't want to go back to my old name. I stayed with Mathilde after that. I couldn't leave my old Coboranti life behind completely, though. I'd leave town every now and then and go back into the jungle to hunt. That's how I came across all of you that day, on the Lesser Islands.

"When I met all of you again in Port Town and found out that you had been in Evondra's camp it was—it was just, I don't know. I hadn't thought about that place in so long. I couldn't talk about it. I always felt guilty, because I got away and they didn't. Once I escaped I tried to never let myself think about it."

Maya's mind spun. Everything that had not made sense about Helix now did. Her heart ached. He had been so little, all on his own. She debated reaching out and taking his hand. She wanted him to know—to know what? That it was a horrible story? That she wished it hadn't happened to him? Maybe just that she was his friend. But she hesitated because she was afraid that Helix would feel embarrassed, or that she was acting like a dumb girl or something, and so she just sat there. Helix got to his feet suddenly and the moment was gone.

Taking off his shirt, he dove cleanly into the pool and swam along the bottom to the other side, where he surfaced.

"You should come in," he said. "And wash off all the dirt from the avalanche."

The water did look inviting. Maya dove into the pool. The

water was so cold that it knocked the wind out of her. She swam to warm up and then lay on her back, floating. The river was dappled with green light. A leaf and a flower bud drifted past slowly, and the jingle of water over yellow stones rang like music up into an olive tree where blue macaws shouted down to them. Now that Maya was over the initial shock, the water felt good. Helix surfaced with a pebble, which he skimmed across the water before he ducked under again. A moment later Maya felt something tug her ankles. It took her another moment to realize that it was Helix. "Don't you dare!" she managed to call out before he pulled her under. Maya struggled but Helix was stronger and when he finally let her go they popped to the surface, their faces close to each other. They looked at each other for a moment, water streaming down their faces and hair. Maya's heart beat painfully against her ribs. Then Helix swam away on his back and clambered noisily out of the water onto the rocks. Maya followed him and when she got out he tossed her his shirt.

"You can dry off with this," he said, not looking at her. "Let's rest for a few minutes before we keep going." He wandered a little way off and lay down in the grass in the sunshine and closed his eyes.

Maya wrung out her hair and dried off as best she could and then spread Helix's shirt out on the rocks to dry. A light breeze made her shiver. Her skin tingled. Her head felt like it was on the end of a balloon, floating far above her. She lay back in the grass, her heart still racing a little from the swim. High above, the glossy leaves of the rubber trees swished against the blue sky. In the distance, snow glinted on the airy tops of the mountains. She felt so strange, having finally heard

Helix's story. He lay a few feet away from her, and Maya could tell from his breathing that he had fallen asleep.

For a moment Maya felt outside herself—outside her constant worry about Simon and Penny and her parents. She forgot everything beyond this place by the waterfall in the mountains. Everything there was just as it should be—the lustrous white clouds in the tops of the trees, the mist where the falls struck the water, the gently warm sun.

Maya thought about all the things she had wanted so much before the storm. If she ever found her family again, would she still want all of those things? To be on land and go to school and live a quiet, plain, orderly existence?

She felt that she understood a little better why her parents had chosen to live on a boat and sail from place to place. She didn't know what they had been looking for. Were they really marine biologists, like they had always told Maya and Simon, or were they in search of something else? What did they know of Tamarind? What *was* Tamarind?

Whatever it was, it had led her to Netti and Helix, and to a great journey that she could still hardly believe. Whatever her parents knew or didn't know, Maya felt their restlessness, their love of adventure, in her own veins for the first time. Her old dream, to live on land, seemed so pale and ordinary after their adventures on the island. If she ever found Simon and Penny and her parents, Maya wasn't sure what she would want anymore.

It was only the faintest flicker of a thought in her mind, that perhaps she would rather be on the sea, rather be traveling from place to place, seeing new places and people, not knowing what would be in store each morning when she woke up. If she did stay on land, perhaps it wouldn't be for very long, just long enough to go to school properly, so that she could return to the sea and do the work her parents did. Or perhaps not their work exactly, but something like it. Maya wasn't sure yet. All these new thoughts were dizzying.

She suddenly remembered the night on the beach with Dr. Limmermor, when she and Helix had sat together by the tide pools. So much had happened since then. Who would have thought that they would have seen each other again, let alone have become friends? But the memory of Dr. Limmermor—half-crazy, stranded on Tamarind for all these years—brought Maya back to the present. She couldn't let that happen to her. There were still a couple of hours of daylight left, and they could cover more ground before they had to find somewhere to sleep. They only had three more days if they were going to reach Simon and Penny in time. Taking a last look around the peaceful glen, she woke Helix and they gathered their things and kept going.

❧ CHAPTER FORTY-FOUR ❧

The North ❋ *The Only Blue House in Bembao* ❋
The Fleet! ❋ *Stowaway*

T wo more days of hard hiking passed. Maya and Helix were exhausted, their feet were blistered, and food ran low and then ran out altogether. Maya despaired of ever seeing the end of the mountains and reaching Bembao before the sea battle. Early on the third morning they caught a pair of mules to ride. Once they heard an avalanche starting above them and they had to kick the mules into a gallop to escape. When the mules slowed to a walk again, Maya looked over her shoulder to see that the rock slides had kicked up great white puffs of dust and dirt that now hung suspended behind them on the trail, the dawn light just breaking through them. She thought miserably of Seagrape.

They reached the foothills while it was still early. They dismounted and Helix clapped his hand at the mules, who turned and trotted back up into the mountains. The walk down the foothills went quickly and before long they had left the smoky blue heights and were once again walking through a humid basin of earth. The sea could not be far off—Maya could smell it on the occasional breeze that crossed the red dirt road they walked along. Despite her exhaustion, a spring entered her step—Simon and Penny could not be far off now! Soon the sun was high and a paste of red dust clung to their sweaty legs.

It was not difficult to find the only blue house in Bembao. It was perched all by itself on the top of a hill overlooking the town and chalky blue sweep of the sea, just where Isabella had said it would be.

An old woman was weeding the vegetable garden and when she saw Maya and Helix approaching she shouted toward the house. A tall woman, about ten years older than Maya and Isabella, came to the open doorway and waited. She had a strong face and dark, serious eyes.

"Are you Gloria?" Maya asked.

"I am," said the woman.

"We have a message for you," Maya said. "From Isabella."

Gloria looked instantly alert.

"Isabella who?" she asked warily.

Maya found the note in her bag and handed it to her. Gloria glanced quickly at the handwriting.

"Come inside," she said. "I'm sorry to be so suspicious. But you can't be too careful these days."

They followed Gloria. Inside, the house was very spare. A kitchen opened into a main room. Vegetables were soaking in a big iron sink, and a pot was steaming on the stove. A door to what must be a bedroom was closed. There was a table on which papers, held down by sea-worn stones, fluttered in the breeze.

"It's lucky you caught me," Gloria said. "I'm mostly in town these days."

The old woman in the garden came to the door and Gloria spoke to her in a language Maya didn't understand. The woman came inside and ladled soup into two bowls and cut two thick slices of bread, placing them at the table for Maya and Helix.

Gloria sat down and read the note.

"Do you know what this means?" she asked, looking up at

them, her eyes shining. "For so long this seemed like only a dream, and now it's all about to begin."

She read the end of the note and the smile fell from her face.

"Eat quickly," she said. "Isabella says you have to get to your brother and sister on the fleet—you don't have much time."

Just then there was a sound from the bedroom door. Gloria's eyes flew to the door. She got up hastily and went into the other room. She reappeared a moment later.

"There's someone who'd like to meet you," she said.

Maya and Helix stood, confused, and walked to the door. As soon as Maya saw the young soldier sitting up in the bed she knew it must be Isabella's brother, Lorenz, who had not been seen in nearly a year. Though she knew Gloria was hiding him somewhere, she hadn't expected him to be here. Bandages covered his left eye and his left leg, what remained of it, was propped up on a pillow. Maya wondered if Isabella knew. She tried not to stare. But he was staring at her, surprised, no doubt, at how much she looked like Isabella. Gloria introduced them.

"It's not so bad," Lorenz said, smiling when he saw Maya's eye wandering to his leg again. "Anymore. Gloria's taken good care of me." He leaned forward to shake Maya's and Helix's hands. "I couldn't miss this chance to meet friends of my sister's and friends of the Peaceful Revolution."

Gloria stood in the doorway, watching Lorenz. They were in love with each other, Maya realized.

"I'm not sure if I'll see you again, so I want to thank you now for your courage and your help. It was very brave of you to come over the mountains."

Maya bowed her head, embarrassed. She couldn't accept

their thanks, her real reason was selfish—she had to find her family.

Leaving the little blue house, Maya and Helix half ran down the hill toward the town. Gloria's words rang in Maya's ears. *You don't have much time.*

With its packed dirt roads and tin shacks, Bembao was like Port Town but louder and dirtier. It was as hot as the inside of a steamed clam. The low stone buildings had been brightly painted many years before, and though mottled by the elements, the colors were still vibrant. The fronts of the buildings were decorated with shining mosaic tiles that caught the sun and each peaked rooftop was topped with a white stone ball. Plants hung from rotting ropes on porches and in doorways and on street corners were tiny shrines with colorful feathers and sea stones and other treasures laid out between candles. The candles glowed in the daylight, their flames shivering in the hot breeze. Maya and Helix wove their way between men carrying strings of herring on their shoulders, shouting their prices as they went, and people balancing trays of steaming breads on their heads. Women with brightly colored head scarves stood in line at the public wells, babies tied to their hips. The streets were narrow and confusing. Panic overcame Maya as they turned corners and went down alleys, but finally the harbor came into view.

"There!" Helix cried suddenly.

Maya followed his gaze and sure enough, anchored a half mile or so out in flat green water was the pirate fleet. Maya could see the unmistakable violent red insignia on the black flags. Her spirits lifted and for a moment she could have danced for joy right there in the street. Then the gravity of the situation struck her.

"How are we going to get out there?" she whispered.

The ships' sails were furled and a bristly nest of masts clicked together in an evil huddle. The black flags were hoisted high and beat strongly in the wind. The ships were too far away for Maya to make out which one was the *Meggie Vic*. As she stood there, she felt despair descend on her like actual physical weight. They had come so far and were so close and yet Simon and Penny seemed farther away than ever. And if she couldn't even reach her brother and sister, how would she ever find her parents?

"We'll need to get hold of a rowboat somehow," Helix said, squinting at the fleet. "And we're going to have to wait until it's dark."

"Until it's dark!" cried Maya. "Helix, we can't wait that long!"

"What do you think we can do?" he asked. "Try to head out there in broad daylight? Listen, you wait here. There's a tavern just back there, but a girl will draw too much attention. I'm going to try to find a boat for us for later. Don't move—I'll be right back. And don't worry, Maya, we're going to find them."

Maya felt as if Helix's voice were coming from very far away, or as if she were deep underwater, hearing a sound on the surface. He left, walking briskly through the throng of people toward the tavern where men sat drinking foamy pints of ale. She turned back out to gaze at the fleet. She sank deep into her own thoughts, and right now they were that all hope was lost. Her heart felt as if it was breaking. Simon and Penny were so close yet they may as well have been a million miles away for all the good it did her.

Two men passed her on their way from the tavern and

365

went down to the dock where a few rowboats were moored. They got into one and began rowing out over the harbor toward the fleet. With a start, Maya realized that they were pirates, heading back to their ships. She looked back at the dock, where several other rowboats had been left bobbing against the dock. Could they belong to other pirates who would soon be returning to the fleet?

Maya hardly thought about it. She was desperate—this could be her only chance.

She ran down the dock and, glancing quickly both ways to make sure no one was watching, jumped into one of the rowboats, hiding beneath a tarpaulin. It smelled briny and foul but she was too afraid to lift an edge of it for fresh air. Fortunately, she didn't have to wait long before she heard several drunken men returning. Maya overheard them talking about the fleet. They thudded down into the rowboat—luckily none of them landed on her—untied it from its moorings and pushed off into the harbor, drunkenly singing sea shanties in their coarse old voices. Maya was grateful that they were singing, otherwise she was sure they would hear her heart hammering.

It wasn't until they were halfway to the ships that Maya came to her senses. What had she done? What was she going to do once she reached a ship? And what was Helix going to think when he returned and found her gone? She felt a pang in her heart. Poor Helix. He wouldn't know what had happened and he'd start searching for her. . . . Oh, she couldn't think about Helix. He could take care of himself. She had to worry about how she was going to get to Simon and Penny and rescue them. Right now that was the most important thing.

A pirate shifted, kicking the tarpaulin, and suddenly Maya could see out a bit. She held her breath, terrified that the pirates would spot her. In the water she could feel sharks bumping against the hull of the rowboat. Then the pirate fleet loomed before them, rocking gently in the waves. Maya read the names of the boats. She could see *Julia Morgan, Lisa Marie, Kirsty Anne, Tara Lea, Kelly Kay, Lana Cat.* They were each named two women's names, just like the *Pamela Jane.* But she didn't have any more time to ponder why, or to see the *Meggie Vic* anywhere, because just then the pirates tossed the oars into the bottom of the rowboat—one struck her ankle and she winced—and she felt the rowboat glide a few yards through the water into the shadow of one of the ships. The pirates in the rowboat shouted back and forth with the pirates on the ship and the rowboat was hoisted to the ship's deck.

"Oi," grumbled one of the pirates as he hauled the rowboat up. "Feels like you've got another body in here—how much did you lugs eat on shore?"

"It's not the food, it's the ale," said another. "Look at 'em!"

The pirates in the rowboat returned the insults as they tumbled onto the deck. The rowboat was made fast against the side of the ship. Maya closed her eyes and held her breath and waited. She hadn't thought about what she would do at this point. She could hear pirates moving about all over the deck. She was trapped.

There was no way she could leave the rowboat until it was dark. What if other pirates decided to go to shore that afternoon and used the same rowboat that she was in? And there were so many ships in the fleet—what were the chances that she was on the same ship as Simon and Penny, anyway? If they were on another ship, how would she get from this one to the one they were on? Why hadn't she thought about all this before? Even if the rowboat stayed right where it was until nightfall, it was going to be nearly impossible to lie there silently that whole time. It was still morning! And already she was getting a cramp in her leg from the awkward position she was in. She gritted her teeth—there was nothing she could do now.

Just then there was a thundering roar as the tarpaulin was yanked back. Maya cringed as bright sunlight streamed down on her.

"I knew it!" shouted the pirate who had been grumbling about how heavy the rowboat had been. "STOWAWAY!"

↶ ↶ ↶

Maya held her head up high as she was shoved across the deck, through crowds of pirates who all turned to look at her, astonished. It was not at all a cheerful, friendly boat like the *Pamela Jane*. It was much bigger, for one, its paint was chipped and the thick coils of rope on its deck smelled rotten and fishy. It seemed dark beneath the giant masts and rigging, even in the middle of the deck. The pirates were a motley crew. Some of them were scabby, ulcerous old men with missing teeth. Others were young and brutally strong, with muscles bulging from their bare arms. They were the most terrifying. They leered at Maya and she saw with horror that the gold rings in their noses and ears were so hot in the sun that they had scalded the flesh around them. One of them grabbed her and pushed her hard down into the cabin. It smelled of mildew, and dirty, unshaven men came to doorways to smirk at her as she passed. She squealed when a rat scuttled over her foot. A pirate who had been cleaning his fingernails with a knife threw it at the creature and it whistled through the air, cutting the rat's head off cleanly. The rat's body jerked for a few seconds and its oily tail thumped on the ground and then it lay still as a murky puddle of blood seeped from it. The creature's head rolled down the floor and disappeared inside a rat hole. A pirate laughed loudly at Maya's horrified face, and then a trapdoor was opened in the floor and she was thrust down a short dark ladder. The door slammed behind her.

Maya kept very still while her eyes adjusted to the dimness. Beneath her hands and feet she could feel the boat rolling on the swells. She was down in the cargo hold, the belly of the ship, and vile-smelling bilge water was slopping over her ankles. At least they hadn't thrown her overboard, Maya thought, picturing the toothy sharks and electric eels she had seen in the greasy water at the pier. As she knelt there she had the creepy sensation that she was not alone. She decided she would feel her way around the room on her hands and knees until she found a place to hide. *Please don't let me meet a pirate, please don't let me meet a pirate,* she thought as she began to make her way around the perimeter of the room. Then she thought: *Or a rat. Please don't let me meet a pirate or a rat.*

Then Maya heard a rustling sound and something heavy that smelled strongly of fish dropped over her. She lost her balance and fell. A rope was drawn beneath her and swiftly tied, trapping her in what, given the smell, the dampness, and the bits of seaweed tangled in it, could only be a fishnet, though it was too dark for her to see anything.

"That's far enough," said a low voice.

❦ Chapter Forty-Five ❦

No Way Out

Maya froze. Whoever was standing over her stepped to one side and a beam of light fell through the porthole. From across the room she heard a familiar cry.

"Penny!" Maya shouted.

Penny started crying properly then, just as the figure standing over Maya stepped out of the shadows. Maya clenched her teeth and prepared to kick whoever it was, when she saw a face in the weak light from the porthole.

"*Simon?*"

"*Maya?*"

"I didn't recognize your voice!"

"I was trying to sound bigger!"

Simon knelt and swiftly untied the knots on the fishnet, disentangling it from his sister. The two of them stared at each other in shock for a moment. Then they threw their arms around each other, talking so happily and excitedly that neither of them could understand what the other was saying. Simon stood up and did a dance and Maya ran over and found Penny sitting up in a sugarcane box. She picked the baby up and squashed her tightly, overwhelmed with joy to feel the familiar warm weight in her arms again and to smell her sweet baby smell even through the foul stench of the gallows. Penny stopped crying and began to babble away to Maya.

"Simon, are you okay?" Maya asked. She kissed Penny's

face and hugged her close again. "Are you both okay? You weren't hurt or anything, were you?"

"No," said Simon. "They give us food and water every day. I tried to bathe Penny as often as I could with the leftover water."

Maya held Penny away from her so she could take a good look at her. Simon had done a good job—Penny was relatively clean and looked plump and healthy. Simon, on the other hand, she noted, was filthy dirty. She guessed he hadn't minded sparing any of the water for himself.

"They want me to tell them where the *Pamela Jane* is, but I haven't," said Simon. "I told them we got washed overboard in a storm and we don't know where the boat is. Helix was with us, too, but then they took him away after the first night. I don't know what they did to him. . . ."

Helix! Maya felt another pang of remorse at having run off without telling him where she was going.

"It's okay," she told Simon. "Helix is fine, I was just with him."

She took a deep breath and began to tell Simon everything that had happened since the pirates had kidnapped him and Penny and Helix.

Simon listened in awe.

"No fair!" he said. "You got to do all of that and I've been stuck down here with Penny this whole time!"

He almost cried when he saw the logbook again. He ran a hand over its gleaming red cover and then he opened it to the pages with the First Mate's journal that the moon oranges had revealed. Though Maya had told him what it said, he read it all himself, dumbstruck.

"The *Pamela Jane* is a pirate ship," he breathed, eyes wide as this new knowledge sank in. "For our entire lives we've lived on a pirate ship and we never even knew it."

Maya nodded gravely.

Simon looked down at the pages wonderingly. "And Dr. Izquierdo, the strange man we saw in St. Alban's, who was so interested in the *Pamela Jane*. He's the First Mate from the journal. He was out there on the Outside, in *our* world, looking for his ship. Our ship." Simon frowned. "Whose ship *is* it, Maya?"

"Ours," said Maya firmly.

"So Mami and Papi must have known about Tamarind—or they knew something about it, at least," said Simon. "It's too big a coincidence. . . ."

Maya agreed—there had to be some link. They were missing information. Again she remembered the last day in St. Alban's, when she had been sitting with Penny outside the Marine Station and she had overheard their parents arguing with Dr. Fitzsimmons through the laboratory window. What had been said after Dr. Fitzsimmons had come and shut the window?

"We aren't going to figure this out now," she said. "I don't know everything that Isabella and Gloria have planned, but I know that the Peace March is going to start tomorrow, during the battle at sea. There are fleets coming from all over Tamarind. I overheard the pirates talking when I was in the rowboat and this fleet will sail in the morning. We have to get out of here before then."

"There's no way out," said Simon. "I've checked every inch of the hold, there's just no way out."

Maya thought. "They must bring you food," she said. "When do they come?"

"In the mornings," said Simon. "Early."

"Well, tomorrow we'll be on the other side of the hatch and

when the pirate opens it we'll attack him and knock him out. We can take him by surprise. Then . . . then we'll just have to see what happens when we get out. We'll have to steal one of the rowboats and row to shore. We have to be off this ship before the cannons start firing."

The afternoon sun was beginning to sink in the sky, and the light through the grimy portholes was growing weaker.

"Well," Simon said. "One good thing—at least Helix is still out there. Maybe he'll save us."

Maya said nothing. But she didn't think it was likely. After she had just left him on the pier, he may have had enough of helping them, and they would never see him again. The thought of never seeing him again seemed too sad to bear, so Maya tried to push it from her mind. Penny looked up at Maya searchingly with her big dark eyes. It was all left up to Maya to save her brother and baby sister now, and more than ever before, she really didn't know if she could do it.

CHAPTER FORTY-SIX

On Board the GRETCHEN ELLA

After an uncomfortable night spent sleeping on a pile of ropes, it took Maya a few moments the next morning to realize that the squeaking sound in her dream was actually the sound of the trapdoor to the cargo hold opening, and the thudding sound was the footsteps of a huge pirate who was now just feet away from them. They were too late—there would be no surprising him now. Maya realized with a chill that it was the man with the sapphire tooth again.

"Up you get," the pirate said. "Captain Ademovar wants you on his ship."

The children looked at each other. *Captain Ademovar!*

But according to the logbook he was as good as dead!

There was no more time to wonder about this before the pirate had looped a rope around Maya's and Simon's wrists. Luckily Simon had slept with his backpack on. Maya had time only to slip the baby sling over her head, and put Penny into it. The pirate led them onto the main deck, where bleary-eyed men were moving about. The milky dawn was just lighting the sky and the town of Bembao was barely visible through the fog. Battle preparations were under way. The *Meggie Vic* was already under sail and through the fog, Maya saw that they were approaching the biggest battleship of them all—a majestic tallship called the *Gretchen Ella*. Even the name sounded terrifying. When they pulled up alongside her, the pirate pushed the children to jump from the bulwark of one ship to the other.

Fog sat heavy on the *Gretchen Ella*, and the top of her mast and the black pirate flag were invisible. The rigging creaked ominously as she swayed on a slow-rolling swell. The sapphire-toothed pirate jumped on board after the children and led them down into the cabin, where they proceeded down a narrow passageway to a closed door.

"In you go," he said, opening the door.

The door was closed and locked behind them and the children found themselves alone in a room with a figure kneeling on the floor in the shadows. Penny began to wriggle furiously in Maya's arms. The figure turned around.

"Mami!" bleated Penny.

At first Maya and Simon were too stunned to speak. Penny was right. It was their mother. Thin, pale, in clothes that weren't hers, her hair cut raggedly—but it was her.

"Mami!" Simon cried, breaking the spell. Then their mother was on her feet, rushing to them and throwing her arms around them.

Maya felt numb. She let her mother take Penny, and her mother hugged the baby tightly, tears slipping soundlessly down her cheeks. She kissed Penny's head and cradled her. After her one word—the only word she had ever spoken—Penny was curiously silent, staring up at her mother with her large, serious eyes. Simon burrowed his head against their mother's side. Maya just stared. Her mother lifted the arm that was wrapped around Simon and drew Maya to her. Maya closed her eyes and smelled her mother's scent, the powdery, sweet fragrance she always had, whether the day was broiling hot or damp and cold, whether they had been at sea for a day or a month. Nobody else in the world smelled like that. It was the smell Maya had known her whole life, since her earliest days, from a time before she

375

could even remember, and when she leaned her head on her mother's chest and smelled that fragrance, her shoulders began to shake slightly and at last she began to weep.

"Mami," she sobbed. "I missed you so much."

"My loves," said her mother. It was all she could say, and she kept repeating it, squeezing the children close to her as she cried.

Simon and Maya did not look at each other. After all they had been through together, each was lost for a time in his and her own emotion. Maya felt her mother's hand stroking her hair. When she felt she could, she lifted her face and wiped her eyes. Simon was sitting up, too, his eyes puffy and his face red and blotchy. Only Penny had not cried, and was still gazing up at their mother as if she were memorizing her face.

Their mother looked at them as if she could not believe it was really them.

"Are you alright?" she asked, her voice trembling. "You haven't been hurt, have you?"

"We're okay," said Maya. "Mami, are *you* all right?"

The children's mother managed to nod. "Have you seen your father?" she asked.

"No," said Maya quietly. Maya stared at her mother, at the familiar curve of her cheek, her hair, still the same soft, dark hair, even though it had been cut. She looked the same and yet different somehow, too, in a way that Maya could not put her finger on. Worry had left shadows in the hollows of her face. Maya looked at Simon and without speaking they both knew that they wouldn't tell their mother everything that the old man had told Maya about the Ravaged Straits. Or everything that had happened to them either. Not the worst parts, anyway, not now. Their mother looked too fragile.

"But we met people who saw him, and we know where he was headed," said Simon.

"Yes," said Maya, making her voice sound more cheerful than she felt. "So the good thing is that once we get out of here we know where to find him! But Mami, tell us what happened, after the storm—we have to know."

"We were together," said their mother. "During the storm we went on deck to fix the forestay and we were just on our way back down to the cabin when a wave washed over the deck and knocked us off our feet. We had safety harnesses on, of course, and the harnesses were tied together, but the rope holding us to the deck snapped. We went overboard. We were still tied together and through sheer luck we managed to get to the rowboat that we were towing behind the *Pamela Jane*. But that came free from the boat, too. By the time we were both safely on the rowboat, the *Pamela Jane* was already far away. We were being carried one way and you were being carried another. For a while, whenever there was a flash of lightning, we could see the *Pamela Jane* getting farther and farther away.

"We spent the night on the rowboat, hanging on until the storm had passed. In the morning we hoped that help would come soon—we knew that you would have radioed land to tell them what had happened."

"But we couldn't," said Simon. "Everything was broken."

"Keep going," said Maya.

"We sighted land the next afternoon," their mother said. "The current brought us in here. We hoped that you had made it to land—to proper land—by then, but we were afraid that the same current that brought us to this island would bring you, too. We realized very quickly that we weren't anywhere ordinary. We were desperate to find you and to figure out how to get off of this island, so we decided to split up to look for you and find out what we could in towns along the coast. We were going to meet back in the place where we started in one week. That was the last time I saw your father. In one of the towns I went to, I made the mistake of mentioning the *Pamela Jane* to some strangers, and the next thing I knew, pirates had kidnapped me. I've been on this ship ever since. The pirates think that the *Pamela Jane* is their ship. That's why they've been keeping me here. The captain—Captain Ademovar—is one of the worst pirates in Tamarind. He's the one who wants me to take him to the *Pamela Jane,* but of course I can't. . . ."

So somehow Captain Ademovar had survived after Hábil Izquierdo had tossed him into the sea, Maya thought. He had made it back to Tamarind, and now he was more powerful than ever. And he wanted his ship back. She looked at her mother, frightened.

"But if he has all of the ships in the fleet, why does he still want the *Pamela Jane*?" Simon asked. "She's just a little boat compared with all the others."

"I just don't know," said their mother.

So many questions were bubbling inside her that Maya didn't know where to start. She wanted to tell her mother about the journal in the logbook and what they knew about Hábil Izquierdo and Captain Ademovar and how they were linked to the *Pamela Jane,* but first she had to know something.

"Mami," she asked urgently. "What were we really doing out in the ocean? What is the Red Coral Project, really?"

Their mother looked at them. "Your father should be here to explain this all to you, too," she said, sighing.

Maya suddenly felt sick.

"The thing that I promise you," their mother said, pausing

to look directly at both of them. "Is that your father and I never expected to be separated from you and your brother and sister. We would never, never have put you in danger if we had known the extent of what we were involved in."

Somewhere deep inside, Maya breathed a sigh of relief. Fresh tears spilled down her cheeks. The horrible thought that her parents had abandoned them on purpose was just that: a horrible thought, with no weight or truth to it. It was so despicable and so far-fetched that she could hardly believe it had even crossed her mind. She decided that she would never, ever tell another soul about it.

"Mami," said Simon. "We read the logbook. We know what you and Papi were looking for. We know what made the sea creatures glow. It's this. . . ." Simon reached into his backpack and withdrew the ophalla stone. It glowed like a torch in the dim cabin. "Ophalla."

Their mother looked at the rock in amazement, turning it over in one hand.

"Element X," she whispered. "You found this? How?"

Before Simon could answer, she handed it back to him. "No," she said, taking a deep breath. "Wait. When we get out of here we're going to sit down and you're going to tell me every little detail of what happened to you. But put this away for now. We have to figure out how we're going to escape."

Maya became aware then that the ship had set sail and was rolling as it rode the broad swells. There was a lot of noise overhead, as footsteps pounded on the deck and orders were shouted among the crew. Then there was a loud shout that was not part of the ordinary noise, and a wild scrambling began on the deck. It sounded as if all the pirates were thundering to one end of the ship together. Maya and Simon and their mother looked up at the overhead as it shook. Feet hammered on the stairs and down the passageway toward their cabin and they were all watching the door as it flew open and someone was shoved inside.

"Helix!" Maya and Simon cried.

CHAPTER FORTY-SEVEN

Captain Ademovar ❋ *Sailing to Battle* ❋ *Friends
from the Jungle* ❋ *The Peace March* ❋ *The Conch Is
Sounded* ❋ *Into the Maelstrom*

Helix's hands were bound behind his back, and Simon immediately ran to untie the knots.

"I knew you'd come!" said Simon.

"I nearly didn't make it. I stowed away in a rowboat taking the pirates back out to the fleet. Early this morning—they just found me," said Helix. He looked at Maya. "When I came back out of the tavern and couldn't find you anywhere, I thought the pirates must have kidnapped you."

"They didn't, though. I'm so sorry, Helix," said Maya wretchedly. "I didn't think about it—really. I just saw the rowboats there and the next thing I knew I was in one of them, hiding under a tarp, and we were on our way out to the fleet."

"It's all right," said Helix. "It doesn't matter now. What matters is that this minute we're sailing to battle against the North and we need to get off this ship right away."

There was a rumble of cannon fire in the distance and they all froze.

"What are we going to do?" asked Simon.

Just then the door swung open again and the pirate with the sapphire tooth stood in the doorway.

"Captain Ademovar wants you all on deck," he said.

"Where you'll have front-row seats while the cannons come at us! Maybe that will loosen your tongues."

"Ademovar!" said Helix, looking in astonishment at Maya and Simon.

Things happened very fast. The children's mother took the sling from Maya and slotted Penny into it. The pirate knotted their hands behind their backs and led them up to the deck, where he tied them to the bulwark. The fearsome drumming of cannons was approaching—the children could see the outline of the enemy fleet. Simon estimated that they were about forty minutes away. Pirates were shouting and cursing and running back and forth across the deck as they sailed out to open waters to meet the enemy.

And there, walking from the foredeck, was Captain Ademovar. The man who, years before, was so obsessed with his lost ship that he would've killed Hábil Izquierdo to get her back. The man who had survived being left for dead to the sharks. The man who had held their mother hostage almost since she had arrived on the island. Who had kept Simon and Penny locked up in the dark bowels of the ship for days until Maya had reached them. And now he strode toward them.

The brass rings jangling on his boots grew louder as he approached, and through the hullabaloo on the deck, the children could pick out each distinct clank. The pirates dashing to and fro across the deck obscured his face until he stopped in front of them. The children drew in their breath and shrank back against the bulwark. Penny burst into tears.

Maya could see that the long-ago sharks had gouged his face with their razor-sharp teeth and when the wounds had healed they had left him disfigured. A scar, pale and lumpy as egg whites, ran diagonally across his entire face, from the left corner of his forehead, down between his eyes and across his cheek to the lower right-hand corner of his jaw. It had pushed his nose to one side, so that it was almost under his left eye, and his right eye sat a good inch higher than his left one. But the scar didn't stop at his jaw. From there it ran in a straight line across his neck, as if someone had once tried to cut his throat and part his head from the rest of his body. His skull was so scarred that hair did not grow on half of his head. The rest sat in a long, gray braid on his back. The children stared at him in horrified fascination.

His mouth had not been touched by the scar, and so while everything else on his face was not exactly where it should be, his mouth was in place and his words, when he spoke, were clear and low.

"Don't think that because we're heading to a battle that many won't return from, I've forgotten about the *Pamela Jane*," he said. "I *will* find her. She was my ship, a ship of Tamarind, and I have reason to believe she is very precious to this place. All these years—ever since I watched that thief Hábil Izquierdo sail across the Blue Line with her—I believed her to be at the bottom of the ocean. But now I know that she has returned. She's made her way back home and I'm going to have her back."

Captain Ademovar took another step forward and leaned down so that his hideous face was just inches from the children's.

"She does not belong to you," he said in a cold, deep growl. He straightened up and when he spoke again, his voice was booming. "We're sailing into battle now. If you're alive when it's over you'll tell me where she is, or I swear to you that I will load that baby in the cannon and shoot her into the side of one of our enemy vessels. I will begin with the baby, and I will move on to the children. Those of you who are too big to fit into the cannons whole will be chopped into parts. You will be able to watch as your own limbs are fired two hundred feet over the water and devoured by sharks. And I assure you, swimming with sharks is not, how shall I say it?" He paused and waved a hand over his face. "Not *pleasant*."

Captain Ademovar stood back. "You'll inform one of my crew when you wish to tell us where the *Pamela Jane* is moored," he said as he turned to walk away.

The children looked at Penny, who was in the sling in front of her mother. With all their hands tied behind their backs, a pirate could come along at any moment and pluck her from them.

Frowning with concentration, Simon began to try to figure out just how the pirate had tied them.

"I've got one," he said triumphantly. "But it's just the outside knot—he made a bunch of them." He kept his eye on the pirates milling around on the deck.

Maya yanked at her own bindings but only succeeded in chafing her wrists. With every minute that passed they were closer and closer to the enemy fleet. The closer they got, the bigger the fleet appeared. Cannons bristled from their decks and their black sails blotted out the sun. Knives and guns flashed from the holsters of the pirates.

Maya suddenly felt calm, as if she were outside her body. After everything they had been through, it seemed hard to believe that it had come to this. Were these their last moments? She looked dreamily toward land. They were about a mile off-shore. She could see Tamarind between the gentle green swells. Up ahead were the walls and ramparts of a northern city, the shells embedded in the stone glinting in the sunlight, shining cannons pointed out to sea. They fired every now and then and clouds of white smoke hung in the air. Maya saw other towns around the coast, their tin roofs flashing like mirrors sending a signal. The tops of the blue mountains were wreathed in mists and the lush cassava fields rippled gently in the breeze. Maya breathed deeply the smell of sea kelp raked up on the shores, the cassava cooking on outdoor stoves, the scents of jungle flowers and the hot, moist breath of the jungle. Squawking gulls careened in the air over the ship. The fleet passed rocks where funny, seal-like sea creatures that Maya had never seen before were sunbathing. The creatures barked joyfully, batting their flippers together as if they were applauding.

As the ship rounded the head, suddenly Maya saw a column of people marching on the coastal road. There were hundreds of them. No, thousands! The ship rushed on but Maya could see that the column stretched for miles along the road until it disappeared around a bend. It must be the Peace March! It was happening! Maya could hardly believe her eyes. Even though she was tied to the railing of a ship, a prisoner, possibly about to be shoved in a cannon and catapulted to her doom, her heart soared. The road unfolded in a coral ribbon over the hills and cliffs and shores, and all the time there seemed to be more people pouring out of coral doorways and tin shacks and hillside villas and joining the mass of people walking a circle around the island. People collecting kelp from the beaches threw down their rakes and joined. Whole tribes were arriving single file out of the jungle. Maya strained her eyes but the people were too far away to make out Isabella or Gloria.

"It's working!" Maya cried. "Look at how many people there are, it's working! They've done it!

"Helix," Maya said breathlessly. "It's the Peace March. The message—it worked!"

The pirates had also noticed what was happening on the shore and they had stopped what they were doing. An anxious murmuring seethed across the deck. They had no idea what was going on. When Captain Ademovar bellowed a command they set to work again but they were distracted. The sails of the *Gretchen Ella* were stretched taut as the mighty ship heaved through the waves toward the fleet from the North, who were now close enough that Maya could make out individual figures running around on the decks. She saw the enemy's midnight blue flags beating in the wind on the top of the masts and her knees quailed.

A distant buzzing drone sounded in the air, and Maya looked up. There was a tiny blot in the sky, growing more distinct as it grew closer. It was a two-seater propeller plane with a red snub nose. As it flew over the March, a long pink scarf fluttered from the cockpit like a festive streamer. It was Kate! Just then there was a terrific boom as the first cannon was fired from the enemy fleet. It landed inches from the *Gretchen Ella* with a giant white splash. But no one was watching because a mystical, unearthly glow had come over the fleet.

"Look!" Simon cried.

Everyone had been distracted by the plane and hadn't seen the mass of lighted insects approaching behind the fleet, but now they all squinted up at the sky. There were hundreds of thousands of fireflies, blotting out the sun. Though the lights from the creatures were faint and they twinkled on and off, together they created a shimmer in the sky. Their wings, beating faster than a hummingbird's, caused tiny currents of air to swirl beneath them. They began to descend on the fleet.

"We've been bewitched!" cried one pirate. His knees buckled beneath him and he fell to the deck, looking up in horror at the swarm of lights.

"Lower the sails!" shouted Captain Ademovar. "Lower the sails!"

But the pirates were not fast enough and the fireflies were all over the ship, smothering them.

"They're superstitious," said Helix. "They think the fireflies will steal their souls."

In his panic to get them off of him, one pirate stumbled and fell backward into the sea, where Maya was horrified to see several sharks make quick work of him. One of his arms floated off for a moment but then was snatched from below, leaving behind a bloody soup.

Captain Ademovar was suddenly in front of the children again. He pressed his hideously disfigured face against Maya's and she smelled his rotting breath. She knew he blamed them for the ghostly lights that were descending like a plague over his fleet. But then he stepped back and was halfway across the deck again, roaring orders, and the pirates began tearing the shirts off their own backs and fanning the air where the insects were as if they were beating back flames.

"Look," cried Simon. "They're like moths—they're eating the sailcloth!"

The pirates had realized this, too, but they were too late. The insects moved down the sails as swiftly as fire, devouring them.

It was happening on all the ships. Ragged sails fluttered in tatters and the fleet had come to a standstill in the water, rocking uneasily in the current. It was the same with the enemy fleet. In all the chaos, a second cannon had yet to be fired. Then the jungle fireflies rose all together in a glowing ball of light and flew back toward land, vanishing as swiftly as they had appeared.

Simon had managed to free himself and he now set to work on his mother's knots. A low bellow sounded from the shore. Maya knew that sound—it was the conch shell that she had given Isabella.

The ship rolled down a giant green swell and into a great shadow. The shore with the marching crowd was still bright but the sea had suddenly turned dark and ominous. Maya struggled to turn her head and see behind them. There was a giant towering over the sea, blotting out the sun, the ocean lapping at his knees and a cold, dark gulf of shadow pouring into the sea before him. She recognized Desmond's brightly colored patchwork tunic and her heart leaped—he was coming to rescue them!

"Desmond!" she shouted joyfully. "Desmond, we're right here!"

Maya's mother's face had drained of color and she watched speechlessly as Desmond began to walk toward them, stirring huge waves. The ships began to lurch violently, like bobbing corks.

People on the shore began pointing and cheering.

"Desmond," Maya cried again. "Desmond, we're here! Help us!"

Maya's whole body turned cold as she realized that Desmond wasn't coming to rescue them. He didn't see them on the ship at all, in fact. Isabella had sounded the conch shell and now he was coming to destroy the fleet, to do his part for peace. Maya remembered the day she had given Isabella the conch, the momentary guilt that had passed over Isabella's face as the idea must have occurred to her. She had planned right then what she would ask the giants to do. That was why she, and then Gloria, after she received Isabella's note, had told Maya and Helix that they had no time to spare in rescuing Simon and Penny. Maya looked out over the sea in shock and disbelief. Maybe Isabella had just decided to believe that they would have escaped by now? Or maybe she thought the cause was worth their lives? How could she have sacrificed them like this? Maya could have wept at how easily they had been betrayed.

"No!" she cried. "It's all gone wrong! He doesn't know we're in here! Help," she shouted. "Help!"

But the wind and the slap of the waves and the shouts of the pirates muffled her cries. The frenzied pirates raced around the decks, turning the cannons to face the giant.

"Hurry, Simon!" Maya said. "Hurry, hurry, hurry."

"I'm doing the best I can," said Simon. "Your knot is different than all the others. I'm going to do Helix's first so he can help me."

Maya's knees were shaking. Simon untied Helix's knots quickly and then both boys turned around and tried to free Maya.

Cannon fire began exploding from all the ships and it sounded as if they were in the height of a terrible thunderstorm. But the cannonballs, if they struck the giant, bounced off, barely making him flinch.

Simon and Helix were fighting with the knots that bound Maya's wrists but if anything, they seemed tighter.

"Desmond," she cried desperately. "Desmond! Stop!"

But the giant approached relentlessly. The pirates began fleeing in terror down into the cabin.

The swells rose and the ships lifted on dark green crests and plunged into the cold troughs. Electric eels flashed through the sea, shooting jolts of electricity through the water. Many of the pirates had dropped to their knees to pray. Two more giants had appeared on either side of the enemy fleet. It looked as if another was approaching in the distance. As she watched, the enemy fleet began to spin in a circle on the surface of the water, as if the ships were part of a great merry-go-round. Maya stared, transfixed, as she felt Simon tugging at the knots around her wrists.

"I can't get it!" he cried.

Maya's mother, who had hardly said a word the whole time, suddenly held Penny to one side, lunged forward, and tripped a pirate who had been fleeing toward the cabin. He sprawled facedown on the deck and in one swift motion, she unsheathed his cutlass from his belt, wheeled around, and sliced the ropes that bound Maya. The ropes slid from her wrists and dropped to the deck with a soft thud.

In the distance, the spinning ships of the enemy fleet were suddenly sucked, one by one, beneath the surface. Maya could hardly believe her eyes. But then she felt their own ship beginning to turn as Desmond dipped his arm in the water and spun it in circles, creating a whirlpool. Slowly the southern ships, helpless without their sails, were pulled along as the water turned.

"Hurry," cried their mother. "He's making a maelstrom!" She grabbed the children and pushed them toward a large wooden barrel that held freshwater on the deck. She cut the ropes binding the barrel to the railing. Helix helped her to push it over and the water gushed over the deck and into the sea. The deck was already tilting steeply.

"Get inside," their mother said. "All of you."

"There isn't room for me," said Helix but the children's mother took hold of his arm and forced him to climb into the barrel. "Squash together and we'll all fit," she said. The ship was now spinning faster and faster on the water. Captain Ademovar leaped toward them, enraged—but they crammed into the barrel just in time. It tipped on its side and rolled across the deck and Captain Ademovar was gone from sight. They were thrown from the *Gretchen Ella* into a funnel that was spinning around and around like an underwater tornado. The center of the funnel was air, surrounded by a dark wall of water. The barrel was stuck half in and half out of this wall. The force of the water and the buoyancy of the air inside the barrel meant that it lay on its side and no water came in through the open top. They were whirled around and around. Maya, Simon, Helix, and the children's mother, clutching Penny, held on to each other, too astonished to scream.

The vortex was so strong that after a few minutes there wasn't even any water touching the seafloor at the base anymore, just a pinkish crop of reefs with flattened sea fans and fish lying on their sides gasping for oxygen. The whirlpool was moving very fast but it seemed to Maya almost as if it was in slow motion. In the wall of water opposite them she watched as the flotsam and jetsam of wrecked ships and pirates flew around in a circle. One by one, the ships crashed out of the sides of the vortex and landed on the seafloor. Maya watched in astonishment as pirates climbed out of the ships and walked around, looking up in horror at the dizzyingly steep funnel of water turning all around them. Maya screamed as she felt the current slacken and she realized that the whirlpool was about to collapse. She saw the walls of water crashing down toward the pirates, who ran around in helpless terror. The sound of the ships splintering to bits filled their ears. The water struck.

❊ CHAPTER FORTY - EIGHT ❊

*The Black Cross * Going to Find Papi *
The Ravaged Straits*

The barrel was jerked from side to side in the powerful surge of water, and Maya could no longer see out of it or determine which way was up. Seawater flooded in. Maya closed her eyes and prepared for the end.

But the barrel had not been far from the surface when the walls of water collapsed and was full of enough air that it remained buoyant. It fought its way up until it burst through the surface. For a few minutes it teetered precariously in the waves and the children, their mother, and Helix held on to each other and braced themselves against the barrel's sides.

The turbulence slowly subsided. Maya stood up and peered cautiously out. The sea around them was calm, and there was no sign of either pirate fleet or of any of the giants. The maelstrom and the currents had obviously carried the barrel far away. All that surrounded them were cheery little green wavelets sparkling in the sunlight. It looked like they were about a half mile from shore. Greater Tamarind rose green and shining out of the sea, and in the distance Maya saw the tail end of the March turning a bend on the coast, after which it slipped from view. They were alone again. Simon was trying to look over the edge of the barrel, too, but Maya was taking up most of the room and all he could see was sky.

"Are we all all right?" asked the children's mother, her voice muffled inside the barrel.

"No," grumbled Simon. "I'm squashed. Mostly because of Maya."

"No," disagreed Maya. "We're squashed mostly because of *your* big feet and bony knees."

Simon tried to stand on tiptoe so he could see out.

"Just be patient," said Maya. "The current is taking us right in to shore. We'll be there in a few minutes."

"Maya, shove over," said Simon. "I want to see out, too."

"Oh, all right," said Maya, jamming herself back down in the barrel.

Simon wormed his way to the top.

Several inches of seawater sloshed back and forth as the barrel bounced on the waves.

"We're getting closer to shore," Simon called. "The tide is taking us in. We're just coming around some rocks right now."

Then Simon yelled suddenly.

"What is it?" asked Maya.

"The Black Cross!" Simon shouted. "It's here! Look!"

The barrel heaved precariously as, scrambling and twisting around uncomfortably, Maya and Helix managed to stand up and pop their heads out of the barrel. The three children fell into silence as they stared at the great cross towering forbiddingly over a rocky point on the shore. It could only be the Black Cross that the old sailor at Senor Tecumbo's had told Maya about and that Rodrigo had drawn on the map. It was easily thirty feet tall and though the sun beat down on it, it had not faded. There were no towns or people or fields in sight, no signs of civilization at all.

"This means we're near the Ravaged Straits," said Simon.

"Where?" asked their mother.

"We're near where Papi is," said Maya, sitting back down in the barrel with their mother. "Mami, we didn't want to tell you earlier, because there was nothing we could do, but we think that Papi went to a place called the Ravaged Straits. Someone told him we were there. It's a cursed place."

"What do you mean?" asked her mother.

Maya and Simon bowed their heads sorrowfully.

Helix cleared his throat. "Nobody knows exactly," he said. "Very few people have ever returned from there. I've heard stories about it before. The ones who made it back had all aged by decades and they couldn't speak, so they could never tell anyone what was there." He paused. "I'm sorry," he said. "It sounds very bad."

Maya watched her mother closely and she didn't cry or fall to pieces. Her face paled, but her dark eyes flickered as she thought quickly.

"We're near there now?" she asked.

"Yes," said Maya. "If we go to the base of the Black Cross, a current will drag us out into the Straits."

"We have to go ashore," the children's mother said. "You wait for me there, and I'll go to find your father."

"No," said Maya and Simon at the same time. Simon wriggled back down into the barrel.

"No," repeated Maya firmly. "We aren't going to be separated again."

The children's mother shook her head. "Enough is enough," she said. "I want you to go to shore. And then I'll get a proper boat and go on my own."

"We don't have time," said Simon. "Papi needs us!"

"This is our chance," said Maya seriously. She turned to Helix. "Helix, if you don't want to come you should leave now, before the current catches us."

The Black Cross loomed dark and ominous as they drew closer to it.

"Don't be ridiculous," said Helix. "I'm coming with you."

Maya was about to object when the barrel, which had been nodding happily along toward the shore, was suddenly tugged in the opposite direction.

"I think we found the current," Simon shouted. "Hold on! Here we go!"

The children's mother protested, but it was too late. The barrel had picked up speed and suddenly they were hurtling swiftly away from the coast. Maya and Simon and Helix stood up again so that they could see out. The current was like a river running right through the middle of the ocean, and once again, the barrel was jounced from side to side. Up ahead, Maya saw a thick white fog. But as they drew closer she realized that it wasn't fog at all, but salt spray.

The shore behind them had vanished and they were in an eerie world of white. Within moments, salt had crusted their eyebrows and eyelashes and frosted their hair white. It stung Maya's eyes and she blinked quickly.

The saltier the water, the more buoyant it is. The water in the Straits was so salty that the barrel sat about a foot higher in the water than it had before, and as they bobbed along in it, the children caught sight of a tiny salt island. Others appeared out of the mist, and the current guided the barrel on a bewildering passage between them. Some were small and barely grazed the surface of the water, others lifted grandly up to magnificent heights. They were all barren, sculpted smooth by the wind.

Every now and then a chunk of salt would break free and plunge into the water. The salt in the breeze made a faint sound, somewhere between the tinkling of bells and the sound of smashed glass being swept across a floor by a soft broom. Maya looked up, but the sky had been blotted out by gusts of salt and only a dull, diffused light shone through, casting a faint blue sheen on the white mounds. The salt parched the children's mouths and burned their eyes. *If this was where Papi was, how could he have survived?* Maya wondered. The air was grainy and she felt it needling her arms like fine shards of glass. Her mother had covered Penny with her shirt to protect her, and salt gathered thick as sand in the folds of the fabric. The salt mists stretched endlessly all around, like a great white blindness, and they were hopelessly lost.

And then, through the haze, on one of the tiny islands, came a spot of color.

"Look!" Simon cried, and they all turned to face where he was pointing. They kept their eyes on it and as they drew closer the spot of color turned into a human figure. Maya's heart skipped a beat. *Could it be him?* She didn't know if she wanted the motionless person, half buried in drifts of salt, to be her father. He would have been without water for too long now. . . . They neared the island and the current was about to sweep them right on past it, but Helix lunged forward so he hung half out of the barrel and he dug his fingers into the shore of the salt island.

"Get out!" he said.

Maya boosted Simon up and he scrambled onto the salt island and helped her up after him. Maya held on to the barrel so that it wouldn't be dragged off in the current, and Helix pulled himself onto the island. He helped the children's mother out with Penny, and then he lifted the barrel out so that it wouldn't float away.

Gusts of salt made it difficult to see the figure, which was sheltered in the lee of a large hill of salt.

He was wearing tattered, olive green pants.

He had a beard, and his hair was long and as white as cobwebs.

He was motionless.

Suddenly Maya felt deep down that whoever it was, he could not be alive, not here. If it was her father, they were too late. She stopped in her tracks, unable to go any closer. The salt chafed her bare arms and legs and a deep weariness began to creep over her.

But then . . . the figure moved. Slowly his head turned toward them. Maya saw that his eyes were milky—it didn't look like he could see them. But it was him.

It was her father.

"Papi!" she cried.

He showed no sign of knowing she was there.

Her mother handed Penny to the children and went to him, but Maya and Simon hung back, frightened.

"He can't hear you," Helix said. "He's been here a long time. The salt is in his eyes and ears. I've heard that's what happens."

The children watched as their mother knelt beside their father. A strong breeze shifted the salt mists and a ray of sunlight crept through and spread across the salt island. When it reached her father, Maya saw him lift his face toward it. He looked like the faces of the gods on the corners of very old maps, she thought, the ones with the long white locks blown back and the lines drawn from their mouths to show them blowing the four winds across the oceans.

Maya felt a pain in her chest. It wasn't supposed to be this way. They were supposed to find one another and get back to the *Pamela Jane* and sail home, all together, all as they were before the storm. But her father had become an old man. He was bony and frail and the salt had burned painful-looking lesions on his skin.

"Why did he come here?" Maya asked, beginning to weep.

"He was told you were here," said Helix. "I'm sure there was no stopping him."

Maya's father had sensed something, and he had turned, his face tilted up. The breeze swept his flowing hair back over his shoulders and it seemed to float there behind him as he drank in the air. A new expression flickered beneath his blind face, and he lifted his hand and held it out in front of him. He made a sound. His voice sounded un-oiled, unused. Maya remembered that the old sailor had said that people who returned from the Ravaged Straits could no longer speak. The salt must have burned her father's throat too badly.

Maya's mother leaned forward on the sand and took his hand and he reached for her face, reading it as blind people do, and they embraced. He stroked her hair silently, the saddest smile barely touching the corners of his mouth. Maya's mother wept. Gusts of salt blew over them.

Tears poured down Maya's and Simon's faces, melting tracks in the salt. Even Helix turned away and brushed the back of his hand over his cheeks. Penny was the only one not crying. Helix had taken her from Maya and she was looking curiously up at him—she knew him well by now but he had never held her before—and the wind tousled her fine baby hair.

Maya watched as her father released her mother and

looked blindly over her shoulder. He waved his hand through the air as if hoping to feel something.

Maya and Simon ran up to their father and collapsed into his arms. Drifts of salt spilled from the folds of his clothes as he hugged them. It was as if a giant hourglass had broken, and its sands were rushing all around them. Maya's mother took Penny back from Helix and brought her to her father, who reached for her. His eyes were dim, but not blind. And he was not altogether deaf. Maya was gazing at him in amazement when suddenly she was interrupted by a frightened shout from Helix. When Maya looked up she saw that the salt island they were on, no longer able to bear their weight, was breaking apart.

As they watched, a hunk of the island broke away and the barrel rolled off it, sliding away in the current. Dismayed, they watched it go.

"It's gone," said Simon in disbelief. "What do we do now?"

Beneath, the island made a crunching, grinding sound. Maya watched as little pieces of it broke free and flowed past them.

"Forget the barrel!" Maya said. "We'll float back on the island! We'll use this island like a raft and we'll push it back to land." She sat down and took off her shoes so that they wouldn't weigh her down in the water. "Papi is too weak and Mami has to hold Penny, so they'll have to stay on it, but the three of us can get in the water and kick our way back to shore! We'll be like the motor! Hurry!"

"Maya, stop! The current is too strong!" said Helix. "We can't kick our way out of it. And if you get in the water there's no way you'll be able to hang on to this island—you'll be swept away!"

But Maya had already jumped into the water and dug her fingers into the salt to hang on. She began kicking furiously. Within seconds Simon had given his backpack with the logbook in it to his mother, and he and Helix had jumped in after Maya and the three of them were side by side in the water, hanging on to the island and kicking with all their might. On the island, the children's mother and father sat in a huddle, sheltering Penny. Beneath the salt masking her mother's face, Maya could see her fear as she watched them in the water. Maya kicked harder.

At first they made little headway. There was nothing but unbroken whiteness and the low hum of the current as it bore them along, despite their efforts to kick themselves out of it. Maya's courage wavered. Salt mists came down so thickly that she could no longer see her parents and Penny on the island. But after a while the current slackened and she realized that inch by inch they were making their way out of the middle of it, to the edges where it wasn't as strong. The salt mist thinned and she could see her mother again. Maya's hands began sliding from the island. She couldn't seem to hold on to it anymore. She looked up and saw that the same thing was happening to Simon and Helix.

"It's dissolving!" cried Simon.

It was true, Maya realized. They had made their way out of the Straits and into the ordinary ocean and now the salt island was melting back into the sea. The area the children's parents and Penny were on was shrinking before their very eyes.

The island completely gone, the five of them would have to swim to land. The ghostly mists of the Straits hung behind them and they saw that they were about 600 yards away from the shore. They were all strong swimmers but they were exhausted and land seemed terribly far away. Maya felt currents tugging her ankles.

"Stick together," said the children's mother.

She swam holding Penny, Simon held the backpack with the logbook out of the water as much as he could, and Maya and Helix helped her father, since he was too weak to make it by himself.

Finally they clambered out of the water and lay on the sand of a narrow beach, exhausted.

~ ~ ~

It seemed a long time later that Maya opened her eyes, but the light was still strong. She could hardly believe that they were all there together. Had it really been that same day that she and Simon and Penny had been taken from the *Meggie Vic* to the *Gretchen Ella* where they had found their mother? Maya felt like whole lifetimes had elapsed since then. She wanted to talk to her parents, but she was so weary that she could barely keep her eyes open.

Helix filled the children's canteens at a nearby stream and they took turns drinking. Maya stared at her father. Simon couldn't take his eyes off him, and even Penny was studying him with interest. It was not just the salt that had made his hair appear white—his hair itself had turned ivory. The sight of it astonished Maya afresh each time she saw it. Maya noticed that he had a canteen tied to his belt. He must have survived in the Straits by conserving what little freshwater he had in it, refilling it when it rained. Maya could barely think about all this—it was simply too harrowing.

Simon had taken out the logbook and was looking at the map of the island that Rodrigo had drawn.

"What's the best way to get back to the *Pamela Jane*?" he asked Helix.

"We need to find a doctor for Papi first," said Maya.

"A doctor can't help," said Helix, softly so that the children's mother didn't overhear. "People who have been in the Ravaged Straits can't be cured. They've been too badly damaged."

"Then we have to get Papi home," said Maya, her voice thick. "Maybe one of our own doctors can help him. Tomorrow can you take us back to the boat?"

"All right," said Helix, nodding.

The children sat in silence, each lost in his or her own sad thoughts. Maya did not want to let the idea sink in that although they were all together again, her father was in very precarious shape. Nothing was certain. Simon was gazing down at the logbook on the ground in front of him, and Helix's eye fell on the map.

"Let me see that for a minute," he said.

Simon passed it to him and Helix studied the map intensely.

"Has everything else drawn here been accurate?" Helix asked.

Simon nodded.

"Yes, everything," said Maya. "So far."

"What is it?" asked Simon.

Helix pointed to the cluster of four palm trees that Rodrigo had drawn in the northwest of the island. Maya and Simon leaned over to look.

"He's drawn the Four Palms," said Helix. "They're supposed to just be an old story, but he's marked it here as if it's a real place. There's a myth that somewhere in Tamarind there's a sacred pool and its waters are supposed to have miraculous healing powers. The pool is in a cave, and its hidden entrance is marked by four palms in a valley. But everyone thinks the palms are somewhere different—nobody really knows where they are. The cave might not even exist at all. But if everything else on the map is accurate, maybe this is, too."

"And it might cure Papi," said Maya.

Maya turned the logbook so that she was looking at the map the right way around.

"The Four Palms aren't that far away from the Black Cross," she said. "It's just down the coast and inland a bit."

"But we might get there and find nothing—it could be just a story," said Helix.

"The myth could be true," said Simon. "We thought the island Papi told us about was just a story, but it's real."

Maya looked at the green-and-gold image Rodrigo had drawn in the middle of a long, tan valley southeast of the Black Cross. To reach it they would have to leave the coast and pass through a cluster of tiny towns. It was perhaps a day's walk away.

"What do we have to lose?" she asked.

CHAPTER FORTY-NINE

T hey spent the night camping beside the stream and set off
the next morning, moving very slowly because of the children's
father. Before long it became obvious that he could not make it
much farther. His legs had already given out twice. Helix left
the others while he went to look around the town for help. He
returned with a wooden cart, which could be rolled along almost like a wheelbarrow, and he helped the children's father into
it. Walking slowly, they pressed on. Simon and Helix took turns
pushing the cart. The wheel squeaked and the cart bounced
along the rutted road.

Town by town, it became increasingly clear that something
enormous had happened in Greater Tamarind. It was as if the
island had been under a spell and the Peace March had broken
it. They heard snatches of conversations as they passed people
in the streets and began to put together the story of the previous day.

At dawn women and children had begun marching from
Maracairol and Bembao, picking up new people in each town
they passed through, all who had been prepared by the Sisters
of the Peaceful Revolution. Columns of them marched along
the coast and into the jungle, where they had found hungry and
exhausted groups of soldiers, many who threw down their
guns and joined the marchers. Northerners and Southerners
met on the roads and marched together along the coast. The

Sisters of the Peaceful Revolution had made contacts with tribes deep in the jungle, who had captured thousands of jungle fireflies and brought them to the shores near the fleets. When the Northern and Southern fleets met that morning, the fireflies had been released to devour the sails. Isabella had blown the conch and summoned the giants, who had agreed to the plan secretly only a couple of days before. The giants had destroyed all the fleets of Tamarind, and the waters were now free from piracy. Tamarind had been liberated.

Change was evident everywhere. People were sweeping pavements and polishing ornamental shells cemented to the tops of walls. In towns like Maracairol, whose street-level windows had long ago been sealed, men with axes were punching new windows through the stone, and light was flooding into homes that had been in darkness for years. Cannons were wheeled into the jungle and abandoned. In one town, cannonballs were being dumped into the ocean. It took two men to lift each one, walking crab-ways to the edge of a cliff over the sea, where they released it and watched as it rolled, flattening sea daisies and smashing the stone white until it sailed off the edge. A few moments later the echo of a splash traveled back up the cliff.

Maya kept her eyes out for Isabella, but never saw her. Perhaps she was back in Maracairol by now, sleeping for a few hours, worn out from her long march. But, thinking about it, Maya doubted that Isabella would be sleeping at a time like this. Maya felt as though she herself could sleep for a hundred years and wake up still in need of a nap. Somehow having her parents there again made her realize how tired she was. But she pushed aside all thoughts of weariness and walked on through the countryside and the towns.

Maya had thought that once they found their parents, everything would suddenly be okay. But it wasn't, and she felt a new kind of fear and despair creeping over her. She was terrified that her father wasn't going to get better. And what if they couldn't find their way back home again? What if they were in Tamarind for the rest of their lives? Although she was with five other people, Maya did not feel safe. Around every bend in the road she expected to see Evondra astride the great jaguar, or Lorco and Senor Tecumbo coming for them, or a band of pirates chasing them with knives flashing in the sun. It didn't matter that she had watched Evondra drown in the flood, or that Senor Tecumbo and Lorco and Port Town were far away on the other end of the island, or that the pirates had all been killed in the maelstrom. Maya felt sure that danger could be anywhere at anytime, and she jumped every time she heard a lizard rustling in the undergrowth. Her fear was so great that whenever there was a break in the trees and she had a view of the sea, in her mind's eye she could *see* the fleets approaching, chasing them down. But no, a few steps farther on, the path always revealed that what she had been seeing was just the shimmer of the sun on the water. There were no boats in sight. Miserably, Maya sank deeper into her fear, and she couldn't tell anyone. She felt like she alone was in a cold shadow. Helix looked at her from time to time, and once he walked next to her on the path and put his hand on her shoulder, but Maya barely felt it.

The road narrowed to a single, overgrown track that climbed a hill. Simon consulted the map.

"The Four Palms should be in the valley on the other side of this hill," he said.

A vast field of tall grass rippled like a slow green ocean whenever a breeze rolled across it. At the top of the hill they set the legs of the cart down gently and stood up to catch their breath. Maya looked out hopefully, scanning the landscape for the Four Palms, but all that met the eye was a broad, low valley, undulating to another ridge far in the distance.

"There's nothing here," she cried in dismay. "Nothing at all!"

They gazed out before them, but there was indeed nothing in sight except for the tall green grass and the shimmering blue sky.

"We've come all this way for nothing," Maya said, unable to help herself.

"No," said Simon. "The Four Palms must be right near here. We've followed the map exactly."

Helix scanned the landscape, puzzled. "Maybe that's the problem," he said. "It's only a rough map. There's no way to tell exactly where the Four Palms would be. We could be a few miles off."

"Let's cross the valley and look out from the next ridge," said the children's mother. "Maybe the Four Palms are in the next valley."

They all looked toward the ridge in the distance. The road had gotten more and more overgrown and where they were, it had petered out almost altogether. They had been pushing the cart with their father through the tall grass, which had slowed their progress considerably.

"How about if a couple of us go ahead and see what's there?" Helix asked.

"That's a good idea," said Simon. "I'll go with you. The girls can stay here with Papi."

Maya closed her eyes and waited, listening to the soft hum of insects in the grass. When she opened them again sometime later, Simon and Helix had reappeared. Maya knew almost at once that if they had seen the Four Palms they would have been walking faster. By this point Simon probably even would have broken out in a run. But instead his shoulders were stooped. Maya didn't need to hear what they said next to know they were not in luck.

"It's just rocks and hills over the ridge for miles and miles," said Helix. "There're no palms at all."

The children's mother stood up and shaded her eyes and looked out across the valley again, lines of worry crowding her eyes.

"But this *has* to be the right valley," said Simon. He took out the logbook again and laid it on the ground and pored over the map.

"The map might be right about the valley and all the other things," said Maya. "But maybe Four Palms just doesn't exist. Maybe it really is only a myth."

Bitterly disappointed, she walked a few steps away and looked out over the valley again. The tall green grass rustled in the wind and made a lonely sound. She sat down and closed her eyes.

"We have to think about what to do now," she heard her mother saying.

Maya didn't want to think of what to do now. *Please,* she whispered to the lonely valley and the vast sky. *Please just let something work out.*

Maya had been sitting there for a few minutes when she heard the flapping of wings and heard a bird squawk. Suddenly a sharp beak pulled at a strand of her hair. She jumped up in a hurry. "Ouch," she said. Her eyes widened. There on the ground was an emerald-green parrot strutting around indignantly.

"SEAGRAPE!" Maya cried. "Helix, it's Seagrape! Look!"

The reunion was joyful. Helix ran over and Seagrape flew up to his shoulder, making a cracking sound with her beak. Speechless, Helix rubbed her under the chin. Maya and Simon were thrilled to see her, too, and they all reached in to pet her.

"*Crrrrack*!" said Seagrape.

The parrot had lost some feathers but she was otherwise unharmed. The children figured that she must have been stunned in the avalanche but had somehow escaped.

"She must have been flying around trying to find you all this time," said Simon.

Maya felt hopeful again—perhaps finding Seagrape was a good sign. After a while Seagrape sat contentedly on Helix's shoulder, pulling at bits of his hair with her beak, and they all turned their attention again to figuring out what to do next. A strong gust of wind swept up and flattened the grass for a moment. Seagrape took flight then, and soared down into the valley. Maya suddenly remembered the sensation of being on the *Pamela Jane* at sea when a strong wind would fill the sails and drive them forward through the water. The rustling of the grass sounded like the ocean to her.

Broad green wings outstretched, Seagrape flew lower, wheeling in a broad arc across the valley. Maya followed the bird with her eyes. She took a sharp breath when she saw Seagrape turn in the air, wings curved, talons thrust forward for landing, and then stop in midair. But there was nothing there. Maya couldn't understand it. Seagrape was only a hundred yards away from where Maya stood, suspended about twenty feet off the ground. The sight of her defied all logic.

Hearing Maya shout, the others looked up and saw what she was looking at.

Seagrape lifted one leg to scratch behind her ear. She lowered her leg back down, ruffled her feathers, looked in their direction, and said, "*Rrrraaaack!*"

"What the—!" cried Helix.

Then Maya knew.

"She's found them!" she cried. "Hurry, she's found them!"

Maya began charging through the grass toward the parrot.

Shocked, the others waited for a moment and then followed her.

Maya pushed the grass aside with her hands—it grew taller than her head—and ran until she struck something hard.

"Ouch!" she cried, jumping back and rubbing her forehead. She reached out and felt around in the air and sure enough, there it was, the woody trunk of a palm tree. Invisible, but there, anyway! Maya laughed in delight and hugged it. Then, slower this time, she walked around, arms outstretched, until she had found all four trunks of the Four Palms.

The others had reached her then. Helix rested the legs of the cart on the ground.

"I don't believe it," he said, looking up at Seagrape in amazement.

"They do exist!" cried Maya, laughing. "Rodrigo was right! Seagrape, you're our hero!"

The children and their mother and Helix looked up at the sky. They could hear the palm fronds rustling now, a sound distinct from the rustling of the breeze through the grass. Although the palms could not be seen, the light beneath them was green and golden and played in dappled shadows over their upturned faces. *Thank you, valley,* Maya thought, smiling and feeling the sun on her face.

After that, it did not take long to find the entrance to the cave, which was between some large rocks concealed by the tall grass. They stood outside it and listened to the mumble of an underground stream echoing inside the chamber.

Maya watched Helix as he went to help her father to his feet. Helix wasn't even part of their family, but he had come so far with them.

With a last glance at the bright day, Maya went first down into the darkness. The others followed. Maya's mother held Penny in the sling and slid down to the bottom of the slope, where a gently foaming stream flowed past. On the other side of the stream was the pale round shine of the pool. That was where they had to be. Maya realized with surprise that the pool itself appeared to be lighting up the cavern with a faint blue glow. The children's father had turned his ear to the sound of the water and was waiting.

Maya and Simon and Helix helped the children's father across the stream while their mother waited with Penny on the other bank.

The pool lay there like a turquoise jewel, a fine mist rolling over its surface. The three children half dragged and half carried the children's father to its edge.

There was a set of natural steps in the rocks, and Helix went carefully down them, letting the water lift the children's father from his arms. Maya knelt to look down into the water and gasped.

The pool was tiny—only three or four people could have fit

in it without bumping into one another, but it was extraordinarily deep. Maya had never seen to such a depth before. Usually even if the water in the sea was crystal clear, you could only look so far down before it became opaque. But here, through some trick of the water or light, you could see for miles down the sheer stone walls, and there was still no end in sight. Maya noticed then that the peculiar glow in the water seemed familiar, and then she realized that the walls of the pool were not stone, but ophalla. It was the ophalla that emitted its own radiance and lit the water. It was quite magnificent.

Her father was suspended in the middle of the pool and as Maya watched, the water seemed to be growing brighter. Though the mists made it hard to tell, Maya thought that his skin was glowing. The salt burns were vanishing before her very eyes. His form was changing from that of a stooped, withered old man and he was regaining his strength. She glanced at the others and saw that they had seen it, too. Was the ophalla doing this?

As they watched, the mist rising from the pool thickened and began to make the air white and eerie. The surface of the water began to bubble. The ophalla cast an intense blue radiance. Maya began to wonder if they should get their father out of the water. He was disappearing into the mist. Helix grabbed him and guided him to the side and the children lifted him out and pulled him away from the pool. They set him down gently.

"Papi," Maya shouted over the rushing of the stream, which suddenly seemed to be flowing faster. "Papi, can you hear me?"

But he couldn't. He seemed, in fact, to be asleep.

Up close, all of him looked healthier. His chest rose and fell with each breath. But the children couldn't wake him. The fog was very thick over the pool now and was spreading. It had nearly reached them. It had a peculiar, metallic smell. Maya wanted to get out of the cave and back into the fresh air.

Suddenly, getting back across the stream was looking much harder than it had been coming the other way. The white mist that had been rising in the air over the pool got too heavy and collapsed on itself and rolled across toward the children. The light from the pool grew brighter and brighter, and the white fog was dazzling.

They got to the stream's edge and started making their way across it. A dull roar had started—it sounded like it was coming from somewhere deep inside the earth. They scrambled as fast as they could, half swimming, half running through the water.

"Hurry!" Helix urged.

But before they could reach the other side, the roar grew suddenly terrifyingly loud. Maya looked over her shoulder to see a geyser shoot out from the ophalla pool. The water filled the cave, rushing toward the children. Maya felt herself being lifted up—her feet could no longer touch the streambed! Though they tried desperately to hang on to one another, the force of the water wrenched them apart. Maya caught a final glimpse of her mother's face just before another wall of water struck and then she was hurtling into the dark tunnel.

❦ Chapter Fifty ❦

The End?

Maya held on to her father for as long as she could before the water tore him away. She felt the current tugging at her feet and she was sucked underwater. Though she struggled, she couldn't fight her way back to the surface. Her lungs burned and felt as if they would explode. The water bore her on and then it lifted her and with a few kicks she burst to the surface, gasping. Her wet hair was pasted over her eyes, but she could just make out a cave with high ceilings, like a cathedral, and a tiny pinprick of daylight like stars far above them. She heard someone gasp beside her, but as she tried to turn to see who it was, the current suddenly swept her along and she was in darkness again, going dizzyingly fast. She felt one of the other's legs bash against her own as he slipped past her, but though she reached for whoever it was, she only grasped the frothy bubbles on the surface of the water. She called for everyone, and for a while she heard shouts echoing around her—some of them sounded like they were far ahead of her, some behind—but the cave walls were slick and she couldn't grab on to anything to stop herself, nor swim against the current, and after a while she didn't hear them anymore. It had all gone horribly wrong. This was not how it was supposed to be. She had lost everyone. Even had her father been conscious, he was too weak for this current. Simon was too small to struggle against it. What had her mother and Penny done when they had seen the river sweep the others away? And where was Helix?

Maya started crying at one point, but when her head slipped under and she got water up her nose she stopped and allowed herself to turn numb. Her arms and legs felt frozen. In the darkness, without Simon and Penny to take care of, she felt her will begin to slip away. She rode like a rag doll on the surface of the water, as the river sped her along, dragging her legs this way and that. Sometimes her ankles knocked against the cave walls, but the coldness dulled the pain. It had all been useless: the morning after the storm when she and Simon had decided to sail the *Pamela Jane,* discovering Greater Tamarind, meeting everyone they had met there, finding Simon and Penny after they had been separated, being reunited with their mother, carrying the note that had helped begin the Peace March, escaping from the pirates, rescuing their father—that had been worst of all. To see her dear father nearly blind and deaf, his hair turned white and his body ravaged and frail, all because he had tried to save them. What had been the point of any of it? Maya's heart was broken; she felt it aching inside her chest.

Then she heard something deep down in her, muffled through her black thoughts. *Swim,* the voice said. *Just swim.* Maya put her head above water and gulped in a breath of air before she put her head back down and began to kick furiously. She went along like this for a stretch, then the river that had seemed to be carrying her deeper into the earth suddenly lifted. The walls widened and after a few turns, she could smell salt in the air. Gradually the tunnel lightened and the top of the water turned white with surf. All of a sudden she was shot out into the daylight. The unexpected brightness blinded her for a moment, and when she opened her eyes and turned around, she could see the receding black mouth of the cave in the base of a steep green cliff. The current was carrying her away from it and she saw she was moving parallel to a strip of white beach with stooped palms. *How beautiful,* she thought. Without thinking further, she began to swim diagonally to the shore.

✣ CHAPTER FIFTY-ONE ✣

On the Sea Again ✳ Swapping Stories ✳ Lingering
Mysteries ✳ A Well-Known Island ✳ "Life should
always be an adventure"

As she drew closer to the beach, Maya saw a person standing there. With amazement she realized that it was her father. His back was straight and strong, his eyes were bright, but his hair was still white. It was long and streamed behind him.

He strode into the water and lifted her and carried her onto the sand. She clung to him.

"It's all right, Maya Maginot," he said as he hugged her. "I'm back now."

Maya closed her eyes and clung to him, hardly able to believe he was real.

"I've been waiting for you," her father said. "You two are the last ones."

Then behind her she heard splashing and turned to see Helix swimming to the shore.

"Helix!" she cried.

Then Maya saw the rest of her family, higher up on the shore. Simon was running down to meet her, feet silent in the sand, her mother and Penny following behind him. Simon hurled himself at her, nearly knocking her over, and then the family embraced. They were all there—Maya, Simon, Penny, their mother and father—and their father was seeing them and talking to them and his arm around Maya's shoulders was healthy and strong. Maya's heart was bursting. She thought she had never felt so happy in all her life as she did in that moment. The sea, the shore, the loamy gloom of the jungle above the beach, and the cloudless sweep of sky all seemed to fade away and there was nothing but the warm cocoon of her family, safe and together.

But something was missing. Something was . . . Maya looked up and saw Helix, standing a little apart, looking at them all. Their eyes met, but just then a flash of green appeared over the sand. Seagrape squawked, breaking the silence, and Maya and Helix looked up to see the parrot coasting past them. Helix was suddenly alert and scanned the shore quickly. Then he started to jog down the beach after Seagrape.

"Helix!" Maya called, breaking away from her family. Where was he going?

In a moment Helix stopped and waved at them to follow him.

"We're here again!" he said excitedly. "Come on, I know where we are! The cove is just around the corner!"

The family followed Helix along the sand and into the trees, where they shoved branches and leaves out of their way and stumbled over roots in their haste. Mud caked Maya's feet and brambles scratched her arms, but in only a few minutes they burst through the undergrowth and they were back at the original cove, calm and glittering blue, the white crescent of sand bright in the sun. And there she was.

The *Pamela Jane*. In the same place that Maya and Simon had anchored her. Maya nearly wept at the sight of her. There were still vines wrapped around her mast and hull but she was there. Helix withdrew a knife from his pocket and, taking careful aim, hurled it through the air. It stuck in one of the biggest of the vines. The vine recoiled as if it felt the injury, and it began to withdraw. Soon others began to follow it, falling away from the boat and drifting off across the water and sliding back into the jungle. Within moments the sunny yellow hull and tall straight mast were revealed, fresh and new. The beautiful, beautiful *Pamela Jane*. Home. Maya's heart leaped and beat painfully against her ribs. She felt like it would overflow.

Maya ran into the water and began to swim. She was the first to reach the boat and clamber onto the deck. Simon was climbing up the ladder behind her and the others were still swimming across. Maya stood there for a moment, feeling the deck rock gently beneath her feet, and then she ran down into the cabin. Everything was all there, just how they had left it. Nothing had been touched or changed. The captain's quarters, the galley, her parents' room, the bunks that she shared with Simon and Penny. Penny's crib was hanging in the middle of the room, just as it had been when they had left. Maya jumped into her bunk bed—she still fit in it!—and bounced up and down a few times. There was the half a porthole that she shared with Simon, which she looked out of every night. She heard the others on the deck and she dashed back up to meet them, beaming.

"This is our home," she said to Helix. "This is the *Pamela Jane*!"

A soft wind had risen and was funneling across the cove and they would be able to sail out on it. Maya remembered that when they had arrived the wind had not favored leaving the cove and she knew that they had to leave then, while they could. But then a terrible thought occurred to her.

"Helix," she said sadly.

No, she thought, *no*. She couldn't bear to say good-bye to him. Sorrow welled in her heart. Simon, too, was looking at him in disbelief. Helix had been quiet since they had reached the boat. Now, as the family stood there looking at him, he lifted his chin and spoke shyly but firmly.

"I want to come with you," he said. "To the Outside."

While the children's parents prepared to set sail, Helix had Simon write a note to Mathilde for him on a page in the logbook. He would not let Maya hear what he had to say to Mathilde, but she watched him curiously as he whispered to Simon. Helix, their friend. She could hardly believe he would be coming with them. She watched as he tore the page out of the book and folded it into a tiny square and tied it to Seagrape's leg with a piece of string from the hem of his pants. Mathilde would not be able to read it, but she would take it to someone who could. Seagrape cracked her beak and made grumbling noises.

"Go on," said Helix. "Get going. Take it to Mathilde."

Seagrape flapped her wings several times and lifted up into the air above them. Maya's heart hurt, seeing the parrot for the final time, and she could only imagine how Helix felt. They shaded their eyes and watched her circle a few times, her broad green wings catching the sun, before she flew straight toward the coast in the direction of Port Town.

"Well," said Helix. "That's that."

The sails were hoisted and the *Pamela Jane* began to move slowly through the water. They passed through the mouth of the cove and were out on the open sea again, where the wind picked up and they began to clip along quickly.

For the last time, Maya saw the movement of the vines on the Lesser Islands and she was sure she heard a jaguar growl from inside the jungle, but then the wind filled the mainsail and they were on their way. They passed the beach with the Limmermor turtles, but there was no sign of the doctor, so they sailed on without him. They saw peculiar bubbles rising in curtains to the surface of the sea and they watched a storm brewing in the distance, the sky around it black, lightning flashing from inside the dark clouds. The sound of the rain traveled across the water. But the storm withdrew and they sailed onward into fine weather.

Greater Tamarind had already slipped from sight when Maya caught sight of the Blue Line, stretching strong and bright from horizon to horizon. This time she braced herself before the *Pamela Jane* crossed it, lurching as if she had struck something solid. Then they were over, back on the ordinary side of the world, and when Maya looked back, the Blue Line seemed to dissolve and the sea behind them was empty.

She sighed deeply.

She went to sit by herself in her favorite old spot at the bow of the *Pamela Jane,* a hundred thoughts sifting through her mind.

There was Helix, leaning on the starboard railing, the wind tousling his hair, lost in his own thoughts. After they knew he was coming with them, bursting with excitement, Maya and Simon had shown Helix everything on the deck and in the cabin. Maya caught sight of the textbooks her mother used to teach them. *Helix will have to learn how to read,* she thought. Helix seemed strangely shy—there must be so many things going through his head right now, Maya thought. But she could tell he was happy he was there.

Maya's father was standing at the wheel of the *Pamela Jane.* The powerful waters of the cave pool had restored his health. His sight and his voice had returned, as had the hearing in one ear. The other was still deaf. Though he was thin, his body was strong. His skin had healed and his eyes were bright as he looked out to sea. He had shaved his beard, and the only visible sign of what he had been through was his hair, which remained long and white. It was still astonishing to Maya, but she was slowly getting used to it.

Her mother was in the cabin, bathing Penny, and Simon was sitting on the deck writing in the logbook. He had decided to record an account of their adventures, in case it was useful to their parents' research. Maya looked around the boat at her family.

After the flash flood in the cave and Helix and Maya and her father had been washed downriver, the river had surged and Simon and the children's mother and Penny had been swept away after them. Simon was the only one who had noticed that the river split into different tunnels. The tunnels ran separately beneath the earth before meeting up and pouring out at the base of a cliff into the sea. Maya and Helix were the last ones to shore because they had been carried down a longer series of passageways. Miraculously, they had ended up very near the cove where they'd arrived. And now they were homeward bound.

They had not been sailing for long when something quite extraordinary happened: Penny began crawling for the first time.

"Thank goodness she didn't start doing that when we had her," was all Maya could say.

When they were out at sea, sailing briskly along on course, they all sat down to talk about everything that had happened and to try to piece together the mysteries.

The children's parents had indeed seen Dr. Limmermor on their first morning in Tamarind after the storm. He had been no help at all, but they had seen the strange, glowing eggs of the turtle. Although they didn't know it then, that was their first clue that they had come to the place that was the source of the mysterious Element X that had been causing all of the sea creatures they were researching to glow.

After the children's parents had split up to look for them, the children's father told them that he had met a stranger who told him that he had heard of three children who had gone to the Ravaged Straits.

The children's father went back to meet their mother, but when she never showed up he decided that he would press on to the Ravaged Straits to find the children, and once they were safe they would try to find their mother. By this time, though he didn't know it, the children's mother had already been kidnapped by the pirates. On the outskirts of the final town before the long walk to the Black Cross, an old sailor had shared his lunch with him and tried to persuade him not to go.

"I met him, too!" said Maya. "In Port Town. That's how we knew where you were."

Not having any other clues to go on, the children's father did not feel that he could take the old sailor's advice, and so he set out for the Ravaged Straits. Once he reached the Black Cross, he cobbled a raft together and headed into the Straits and could not find his way out again.

"But why?" asked Simon, struggling to understand. "Why would somebody tell you we were there, when it wasn't true?"

"Some people enjoy leading others astray," said their father. Maya and Simon nodded, remembering the little man with the bag of skulls. "It was just bad luck that I ran into one of those people. But it doesn't matter now. All that matters is that we're safe and together." He put his hand on Simon's shoulder. "And that's entirely due to my children's bravery and strength. You've made your mother and me extremely proud."

Maya had looked down at the deck awkwardly. Her cheeks felt hot.

Their father looked at Helix.

"And to their good friend," he said. "Who we owe a great deal to, and who we all feel very happy and fortunate to have with us."

Maya's head was spinning a little as she took everything in. It was a bit of a shock to know for sure that they had been so close to their parents so many times—they had met Dr. Limmermor in the evening, their parents had been there only that morning. If they had been luckier and their timing had been just a little different, everything would have turned out another way. She tried not to think about this.

"What about the Red Coral Project?" asked Simon.

"They're a company that hired your mother and I about a year ago," said the children's father. "Dr. Fitzsimmons had become involved with them, and he brought us on board, too. Our job was supposed to be to research the growth cycle of a rare type of coral within a specific zone of the ocean—a relatively simple task. But we started to find some bizarre things— things that in our whole lives on the ocean we had never seen before."

"Basically," said the children's mother. "We were finding things that glowed that shouldn't be glowing."

"That's the simplest way to put it," said their father. "We

found unexplained bioluminescence in living creatures not usually bioluminescent, and we also discovered that much of the mineral matter—shells, mostly—were glowing, too. It simply didn't make sense. Then we began to find marine life that—well, that simply didn't exist! We were finding animals that had never been seen anywhere else before. We reported what we found, of course, but we were told that our job was to collect samples and not ask questions beyond that."

Maya glanced over at Simon. He was frowning, listening intently.

"But our findings were amazing," their father continued. "Too amazing not to study further. We believed that there must be a substance in the water that was causing the luminescence. But it was impossible to trace it to any source. We tried analyzing the creatures themselves, but whatever the substance was, it was in such trace amounts that our tests couldn't identify it. We sent several of the creatures to be analyzed at an independent laboratory. The laboratory found that the mineral compound that caused both the living creatures and the shells to glow was the same composition as the substance found in the bedrock of ancient rain forests. So we knew it came from a very old rain forest, but where?"

"That's why there are all the drawings of sea creatures in the logbook," said the children's mother. "We started drawing the creatures we found and noting the coordinates and depths we found them at, and the winds and currents they were carried on, trying to see if we could identify a pattern in their movement and, from that, trace their source. But we were never able to figure out where they were coming from—they didn't seem to be coming from *anywhere*."

426

"We went to Dr. Fitzimmons about it again—" said their father.

"The last day we were in St. Alban's, before the storm," said Maya. "I heard you arguing through the window."

Her parents nodded. Their faces were grave.

"He told us in no uncertain terms that we couldn't pursue our research any further, or we risked being dropped from not only the Red Coral Project, but we'd face being banned from all the Marine Stations," said the children's mother. "At the time, we couldn't understand it.

"After the storm, when we arrived in Tamarind, we began to put the pieces together," she went on. "What we believe now is that the Red Coral Project is really just a front for an organization investigating Greater Tamarind. It's a huge mystery—an island that isn't on any map, that can't be reliably found by ship or plane. It seems to exist simultaneously yet separately from our world. Who could believe it? Your father and I were so close to it for months—ever since Red Coral hired us last year—and we still had no idea."

"Somehow the Red Coral Project knows about Tamarind, and they want their investigation into it to be top secret," said the children's father. "We think that they've hired scientists like us to conduct tiny parts of their research. If they keep all these parts isolated, no one can put the big picture together, and their secret is safe. We think they want to find Tamarind before anyone else can."

"Why?" asked Simon.

"Ophalla," whispered Maya.

"I'm sure they have lots of reasons," said the children's father. "But even from the little we know about it from the results from the independent lab, the substance—ophalla—could have many uses. We believe it could have special healing properties. Look at what it did for me! It could be an important source of energy. We don't really know all the things it can be used for yet, but it's quite astounding. Its potential seems limitless. Your mother and I think that one of the reasons the Red Coral Project wants to find Tamarind is so they can exploit its ophalla. Whoever controls it stands to become very wealthy and powerful."

"But they can't!" exclaimed Maya. "Look at everything bad that happened in Tamarind because of ophalla—all it caused was misery. Tamarind finally has peace—the Red Coral Project can't just come in and start interfering. You have to tell Dr. Fitzsimmons that they can't do that!"

Helix had been listening silently.

Simon took out the ophalla stone and held it in his open hand and they all looked at it again as it glowed in the daylight. "Here," he said, handing it to his parents. "You should have it. We kept it for you."

Simon was a bit sad not to have the ophalla stone anymore, but it was a relief, too, ophalla was too dangerous. His father held the stone in his hand and they all looked at it, shining brightly with its own light, even as the sun streamed down.

"Thank you," said their father. "This will be tremendously important for any research that's done. It's possible that in the right hands, ophalla could make many people's lives better."

A vague, restless worry was circling in Maya's mind.

"What happens now?" she asked her parents.

"We'll be resigning from the Red Coral Project," said their

mother. "Now that we know what's really going on, it just isn't safe to have all of you involved."

"What about Dr. Fitzsimmons?" Maya asked.

Her parents met eyes over Maya's head. They looked both sad and angry. Her father cleared his throat. "We'll talk to him. He was far more involved in the RCP than we were."

Maya decided not to ask any more about this now, but the vague bad thought gnawing at the back of her mind wasn't going away.

"But what about Dr. Izquierdo?" Simon asked. "Do you think he'll find us again?"

"If he found us once, he can find us again," said Maya.

"It's weird that he was down there at the dock at St. Alban's right when we sailed in," said Simon. "How did he know that if he found Dr. Fitzsimmons, he'd find us?"

Maya stared at the horizon, puzzled. Then suddenly it clicked into place. "That's it!" she said. "You're right, it's *too* weird a coincidence. Unless . . ."

"Dr. Izquierdo didn't find Dr. Fitzsimmons, Dr. Fitzsimmons found Dr. Izquierdo," finished Simon.

The two children looked at each other.

"Somehow the people in charge of the Red Coral Project knew about the captain, Dr. Izquierdo, whoever he is—he probably isn't even a doctor at all—and they tracked him down because they think he can take them back to Greater Tamarind," said Maya. "Maybe Dr. Fitzsimmons told him that he could get the *Pamela Jane* back for him."

Maya felt ill. It was terrible to think that Dr. Fitzsimmons would betray her parents—they had all known each other for years, long before Maya had even been born. Her parents and

Dr. Fitzsimmons had been students together at the Marine Science Academy. Her father called him "Fitz." They had published hundreds of articles in marine biology journals together. If it was a betrayal, it was a staggering one. He had kept the true nature of their task from them, and he had found the man who believed the *Pamela Jane* was his—he had put their home in danger. He had put their very lives in danger. Maya looked up at her parents.

"We don't know that for sure yet," said her father. "We're going to have to wait until we can talk to him." But he looked pained.

"Maybe we need to find Dr. Izquierdo—maybe he knows something that can help stop the Red Coral Project," murmured Maya. But it wasn't clear to her—was Dr. Izquierdo the savior of the *Pamela Jane* that he seemed to be in the journal, or was he now in league with the Red Coral Project and others who didn't have Tamarind's best interests at heart? Would he want to take the *Pamela Jane* away from them?

The mysteries surrounding Helix remained unsolved, too. What was the connection between the identical red seals in the logbook and in Helix's letter? And what had Isabella meant when she said that Seagrape had belonged to one of the Dark Women? They may never know.

They sat there quietly thinking as the *Pamela Jane* plowed briskly through the sea and the sun shone warmly on the deck.

"There's something else," said Simon, turning to his father. He had just remembered something important. "You knew things about Greater Tamarind. You told us stories about it. You never told us what it was called, but the magical island in your stories *was* Greater Tamarind."

Their father smiled.

"We *didn't* know about it. It was just an old story your grandmother used to tell me when I was your age," said their father.

"Granny Pearl?" asked Simon. "What does she know about Tamarind?"

"I'd like to know that myself," said their father.

Soon after that, the conversation drifted to the problem of containing a fast-crawling baby on the deck of the boat.

🐬 🐬 🐬

Maya had many other things besides the Red Coral Project to think about.

As miles of ocean slid beneath the *Pamela Jane,* putting Greater Tamarind farther and farther behind them, she suddenly felt a pang in her heart and she missed the island. She remembered Bongo and Netti. Had they made their way back to the Cloud Forest Village? Would she ever see them again? And what would happen to Valerie Volcano, poor, sad Valerie, hiding high in the trees! For a moment Maya imagined she could smell the sweet scent of orchids and she was transported back to the lacy green light in the heights of the cloud forest, and she could imagine the nights when the jungle fireflies lit the jungle with a thousand sparks of colored lights. Maya wondered what had become of all the children who had escaped Evondra in the flood. Had they all found their way home? Maya hoped so.

She thought of Mathilde, dear Mathilde, with the crackle of soap bubbles in her washtub and the ancient tortoise that sat in the corner. Maya missed Port Town, with the blinding flash of sun off the tin roofs and the stray goats and dogs and children that wandered freely through its crooked streets. She closed her eyes and could see the rabble of the pirates and fishermen down on the docks, and then she remembered the air in the evenings, when the clouds came down from the jungle as the earth cooled.

Maya thought of Isabella, driving each day to the orphanage on the outskirts of Maracairol. Feisty Isabella! Maya had almost forgiven her betrayal—she knew it was not made without regret. Would all the soldiers return home? Would Isabella's brother come home safely? Would the Peaceful Revolution truly change life in Greater Tamarind? Maya pictured the only blue house in Bembao and Gloria and Lorenz—would everything work out for them? And there was the high mountain road and the icy pool where she had swum with Helix. Would she ever walk that road again? An ache in her heart, Maya missed it all.

She thought of how she had been before the journey: agitated, unhappy, frustrated about being trapped on the *Pamela Jane*. Everything was different now. She had felt and experienced more things than the old Maya could have even imagined. The things she had wished for so much—to be on land, to find friends—had happened, just not in a way she could have ever foreseen. She turned to look at the fast blue water rushing past, each moment bearing them farther away from Greater Tamarind. The smell of cooking filtered up from the galley and on the main deck Helix was talking to their father.

Maya thought of Dr. Limmermor and Valerie Volcano and Kate—there must be others like them, who had stumbled into Tamarind over the years. How did some people get there when most people never could? And what would happen if the Red Coral Project found Tamarind? It would all change. Tamarind as it was now would be lost. The thought made her deeply sad.

Simon came up from the cabin and sat near her on the foredeck.

"Will we ever go back?" he asked after a while.

Maya thought.

"I don't know," she said. "But it isn't someplace that you can find again easily. I don't know how we would go back."

They were quiet for a while, the water rushing over the hull as the *Pamela Jane* sliced through the ocean toward home. Evening arrived more gradually now, as they got farther away from the equator.

🐬 🐬 🐬

The following afternoon, Maya was the first to see the green curve of an island rising out of nowhere. The sea was changing beneath them. The bottomless blue was lightening, and then suddenly they came in over the reefs, and the patterns of green and turquoise, the brilliantly colored shoals of fish, and the swift flash of a barracuda took Maya's breath away. And then Bermuda came into view, with its palm trees and pink beaches and the white limestone roofs of its beloved pastel houses. The *Pamela Jane* sailed the length of the island and through an inlet, all the way up to a bobbing orange buoy where Maya's parents furled the sails and dropped anchor and they all piled into the rowboat to row to shore.

On land, Maya dashed across the lawn in the last light, red land crabs scuttling out of her way, and up the stairs to the porch of Granny Pearl's house and through the screen door.

Granny Pearl was standing in the kitchen washing potatoes from her garden. A big smile broke out over her face, and she reached for a dish towel to wipe off her hands as Maya ran toward her. Maya fell into her grandmother's soft, ample arms and buried her face in her shoulder and smelled the sun in her housedress, bleached from the clothesline. "Well, here you are

433

finally," she heard Granny Pearl saying, but then Maya closed her eyes and just held on tightly to her and let all the clatter and voices of the others fade out as they came into the house behind her. She concentrated on the feeling of the ground beneath her feet.

"I'll never leave solid land again," she murmured.

"What's that, love?" her grandmother asked, steering her to a chair at the table.

It took all evening and into the night to tell Granny Pearl about their adventures, much longer than it would have if they hadn't all kept interrupting one another and stopping to tell all the details and correcting one another and adding more details and shouting, "Remember the . . ." Somewhere during the long tale, Granny Pearl made a large dinner, which they all sat down to eat. Maya and Simon had to be reminded to keep eating since otherwise they held their forks with food speared on them and just kept talking. There was so *much* to tell. And Granny Pearl never raised an eyebrow. In fact, she seemed to accept all parts of their story—even the fantastical, incredible parts that Maya had felt sure that no one who hadn't been there would have believed. She listened with a small smile on her face and tapped their plates gently when they had paused too long between bites. And when they asked her how she had known the stories about Tamarind that she had told their father, she gave a tiny shrug and replied simply that they were just old sailors' stories she had heard many years ago. Cocking her head and gazing seriously at her grandmother, Maya had to wonder if she was telling the whole truth.

In the end Simon fell asleep at the dinner table, and Papi carried him off to bed. Maya could barely keep her eyes open and when her mother said that perhaps she should be off to bed, too, Maya nodded and excused herself. Granny Pearl came in to tuck her in.

"Well, my Maya," she said. "You had your adventure."

Maya nodded. Sleep tugged at her.

"Life should always be an adventure," Granny Pearl said softly. She stroked Maya's hair back from her face. "When it stops being an adventure, something is wrong. Remember that."

Maya wanted to talk, but when she opened her mouth, Granny Pearl put her fingers over her lips.

"Now you sleep, my love," she whispered.

When her grandmother kissed her and tiptoed out of the room, Maya lay in the little cot and forced herself to stay awake for a while to appreciate everything. She could hear the low hum of her parents' voices from the kitchen, where they were still talking to Granny Pearl. Penny was asleep in the crib in the corner, breathing deeply, her fingers twitching every now and then. A cricket landed on the edge of the crib for a moment, then clicked free and leaped into the darkness. In the next room Maya knew that Simon was asleep. She felt like the world was swaying, as if she was still on the boat. She propped herself up on her elbow for a moment to look out the window. Helix was sitting on the porch railing, looking out to where the dark ocean turned in the night. Moonlight shone on his back and she heard as he slapped a mosquito from his arm. *Helix will be restless for a while until he gets used to things,* she thought. *But that's okay.*

Maya had almost fallen asleep when a thought broke through the soft layers of sleep and brought her back to the surface, her heart racing. Somewhere in the night were Dr. Fitzsimmons and Dr. Izquierdo and countless faceless people involved with the Red Coral Project, all trying to get to Tamarind. Maya knew that they hadn't seen the last of them. They would find them. But the thought dissolved back into her mind and her fear subsided. They wouldn't find them tonight.

Sleep crept into her mind again, softening the edges of everything, and she fell back against the pillow and closed her eyes. The room still felt as though it was rocking.

ACKNOWLEDGMENTS

I would like to thank the many people who helped to bring Tamarind to life:

Kirsten Denker, Julia Holmes, Lisa Madden, and Lana Zinck, wise readers and tireless friends, whose faith in Maya, Simon, and Penny sustained the children on their journey.

Lexy Bloom, Anastacia Cavalcanti Junqueira-DeGarcia, Tara Gallagher, the Hederman family, Michelle Hudson, Eric Tyler Lindvall, Kelly Mendonca, Chris Parris-Lamb, and Nathaniel Rich, for their generosity and support on many fronts.

Patricia Hoffman, who let me skip math class in seventh grade and escape to the library to write stories, and who has been my great friend and mentor ever since. I hope that every young person who reads this book will have such a teacher.

It has been my privilege to work with talented and lovely people: my agents, Sarah Burnes and Caspian Dennis; Courtney Hammer; Jean Feiwel; the teams at Feiwel and Friends and at Puffin; and my extraordinary editor, Amanda Punter.

And with love and thanks to my mother, namer of the *Pamela Jane* and chef to hungry authors, and my father, who has made everything in my life possible, and without whom Tamarind wouldn't be.

GOFISH

NADIA AGUIAR

What did you want to be when you grew up?
When I was very young, I wanted to drive a bright pink taxi in Bermuda, the kind with the old-fashioned surrey fringe on the roof. Later I wanted to be Diane Sawyer and work for *60 Minutes*.

When did you realize you wanted to be a writer?
In the first grade. We were copying sentences from the chalkboard when I suddenly realized that I could keep the story going and take it in whatever direction I wanted. It was an electrifying moment.

What's your first childhood memory?
The daddy longlegs spiders under the bookshelf of our house on Tamarind Vale Road. Because I was small I could look up and see them, but no adults knew they were there.

What's your most embarrassing childhood memory?
My dad used to drop us off at school in his work van and shout "RAT-A-TAT-A-TAT, GO COMMANDOS!" and my younger brothers used to leap out of the side of the van while it was still moving and dash toward the school with their backpacks on. I was thirteen and it was mortifying.

What's your favorite childhood memory?
Swimming in the ocean, building forts in our living room out of sheets and furniture, climbing trees, digging in the garden. . . .

Our grocery store would deliver groceries to nearby homes, and I remember being about eleven years old and going with my dad, uncles, or grandfather to the Lightbournes' house. A whole room was devoted to their magnificent shell collection, and Mrs. Lightbourne would always let me in to look at it. There were hundreds of shells from all over the world in glass cases—deepwater murex, polished cowries, lustrous oysters—it was fascinating and beautiful. The mermaids in *The Lost Island of Tamarind* are all named after shells. The collection is now housed at the Bermuda Underwater Exploration Institute.

What was your worst subject in school?
Math . . . probably because my seventh-grade teacher used to let me skip math class to write stories in the library.

What was your best subject in school?
I enjoyed English and history the most.

What was your first job?
Sweeping under the cash registers at our grocery store—I was allowed to keep whatever coins I found. Soon after that I spent weekends and holidays as a grocery packer. I had to stand on an overturned milk crate in order to reach the counter.

Where do you write your books?
I usually work at home, at my kitchen table, where I can look out over the ocean when I need to let my thoughts drift. In

summer when the water is calm and clear I can count the parrotfish grazing on the boiler reefs, and in winter I can watch storms roll in.

Where do you find inspiration for your writing?

Art and science museums. Science books and articles. Traveling. Whenever I get stuck when I'm working, I close the laptop and go for a walk along the coast. When I return, my unconscious has usually unraveled some knots and I'm able to continue.

What's your idea of the best meal ever?

Codfish and potatoes with tomato or egg sauce, local bananas, and avocado pears. In the seventeenth and eighteenth centuries, very light, fast Bermuda sloops used to bring salt from the Turks and Caicos up the Eastern Seaboard to Newfoundland and Nova Scotia and return with salted cod. It's been the traditional Sunday morning breakfast in Bermuda ever since.

Which do you like better: cats or dogs?

My mother rescued abused and abandoned animals, and when I was growing up our house was filled with cats, dogs, ducks, terrapins, gerbils. She would even take the scraps from dinner to feed a wild rat named Templeton who lived in the hedge. In the midst of such a zoo, I always respected how independent and self-sufficient cats are, but lately dogs have begun to grow on me, largely due to a terrier my dad has named Rocket. Rocket looks like a Looney Tunes character after the firecracker has gone off—even right after a bath you can barely see his face under all the tangled fur. He's faster than a speeding bullet, takes on dogs ten times his size, snarls horrendously but would never bite, is quick and clever company, and is bosom buddies with my five-year-old daughter.

What's the best advice you have ever received about writing?
When I was fifteen I took a writing class with a British play-wright, Stuart Browne, who came to Bermuda. He said that in a story, "something happens, someone changes, or something is revealed." It's still the simplest and clearest definition of a story I've ever heard. The best advice I've received about writing is simply to read as much as possible.

What would you do if you ever stopped writing?
I'd like to be crew on a tall ship sailing around the world.

When an evil organization starts mining Tamarind's magical mineral ophalla, it's up to Simon to save the magnificent island before it's put to ruin.

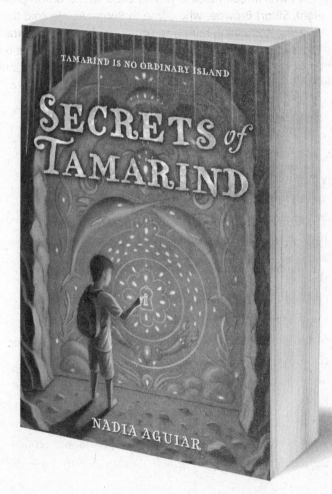

Keep reading for an excerpt.

❧ CHAPTER ONE ❧

The Watchers ❧ *Granny Pearl's House* ❧
The PAMELA JANE ❧ *A Gloomy Illumination* ❧
"It was unmistakable"

Simon's school bag bounced on his back as he ran. When he reached the bend in the road he stopped and looked back. His sisters had gotten off the bus with him but they were lagging behind. With a running leap he vaulted onto the mossy boulder that sat on the verge of the road and climbed quickly to its top. From there he could see out to the choppy winter sea around Bermuda and hear the whistle of the wind. The slate gray sky was heavy with clouds and the day was already growing dark. He wished that Maya and Penny would hurry up. Recently their parents had forbidden them to walk home alone, so Simon had no choice but to wait, even though he was impatient to get to the boatyard. He and his friends had spent the past month rebuilding an old speedboat and it was almost ready to put in the water. It was all he had thought about all day as he endured the slow crawl of the hands around the big round clock at the front of the classroom.

Through the treetops Simon could see the crisp white limestone roof of Granny Pearl's house. Even though they had lived there for nearly four years now—and it was the only real house any of them had ever lived in—they all still called it Granny Pearl's house. If he stood on his tiptoes he could just see the kitchen garden with parsley, thyme and the frothy green tops of carrots, and lettuce that grew crisp and cool deep inside the ice green heads. Around the side of the house was a milkweed patch where flocks of monarch butterflies massed in the summer. The house overlooked a small green cove, sheltered from the open ocean, with a narrow slip of sandy beach and a mat of rubbery sea daisies. The family's boat, the fifty-two-foot schooner, the *Pamela Jane*, rocked on her mooring, her yellow hull the brightest thing on this gloomy afternoon.

Something stirred in a nearby tree and Simon instantly thought of Helix, happier in trees than with his bare feet on the ground. But it was just a branch bobbing after a bird took flight. Their friend had disappeared so suddenly and had been gone for so many weeks now that Simon wondered if he was ever coming back.

Maya and Penny finally appeared—Penny hopping ponderously on one foot—and Simon slid down from the boulder and went to meet them.

"You should have waited for us," Maya said crossly

when they reached him. "What'd you need to go rushing off for?" Maya was sixteen, which meant she thought that she was in charge of Simon and Penny. Simon had just turned thirteen and he hated anyone telling him what to do, most of all Maya. Since nothing irritated her as much as being ignored, he didn't answer and instead swung five-year-old Penny up onto his shoulders so fast that she squealed. He made up a silly song that made her giggle and began walking.

"Frog!" Penny shouted, catching sight of a muddy-backed bullfrog on the side of the road, and she wriggled until Simon put her back on the ground.

Maya dawdled with Penny, who was prodding the reluctant frog to hop in front of them, and Simon turned onto the shortcut, a narrow packed-sand path between the trees to Granny Pearl's house. Old Man's Beard hung like fog from gnarled branches. The light that managed to make it through the thick clusters of stubby palm trees and the heavy climbing creepers was dim and eerie. High in the spice trees, the wind creaked ominously, a sound that reminded Simon of the wind moaning in a ship's rigging, but the air on the path was strangely still, as if it were sealed off from the rest of the day. He stopped to wait for his sisters and peered uneasily through the trees, trying to see if he could make out one of the watchers. The strange men were here all the time now.

He looked back. "Hurry up!" he shouted.

When he saw them, Maya's scowl had fallen away and her face was lost in the hazy drift of a daydream—Maya was *always* daydreaming. The frog leaped into a clump of ferns and Simon, not liking the dark stretch of the path, took Penny's hand and pulled her firmly along.

⁂ ⁂ ⁂

The house was cool when Simon came in, and the tiny television on the kitchen counter was spouting yet another news report about the mysterious glowing sea creatures that were being found dead in the waters all around the Caribbean and South America. Simon's mother wasn't home from the laboratory yet, but Granny Pearl was listening to the report as she chopped vegetables at the sink. Simon swooped down to give her a kiss—he had grown three inches in the past few months and he was doing a lot of swooping to low places, as well as stretching to high ones, reaching up nonchalantly to rap his knuckles on every door frame he went under.

"How was your day?" his grandmother asked

"Boring," he said. "But yesterday I figured out what was wrong with the boat engine. The old fuel had thickened to varnish and the jets were clogged. I'm going to take the carbs apart and clean them—I think we can have it in the water by this weekend." He glanced out of the window. "Are they still out there?"

His grandmother nodded. "They've been lurking around all afternoon."

"They can't just invade our yard," he muttered. "Why doesn't Papi get rid of them?"

"Sometimes things are more complicated than they seem," said Granny Pearl.

Simon's gaze fell on the television, where an old fisherman was holding up a dead octopus, its faint glow ebbing even as Simon watched. "*Found it in my nets,*" he said. "*Second this month—I been fishing here since I was ten years old with my father, in fifty-five years I've never seen a thing like this before . . .*"

The television still babbling tinnily, Simon went to change into his old grease-stained clothes for the boatyard, hearing the screen door bang shut as Maya came in behind him. Usually these days he breezed right by his father's study, but today he stopped and looked in.

Dr. Nelson's ear was pressed to the CB radio. With one hand he was turning the knob, listening to the series of pops and whines and static that sputtered from the speakers. With the other hand he was making notes. His beard, white since his time in the Ravaged Straits, had grown long and his skin, no longer exposed to the sun as they sailed from port to port, had faded. Frown lines deepened into grooves as he concentrated.

A year ago, the first thing Simon would have done when he got home from school would have been to head straight to Peter Nelson's study. All of them would have, Helix, too, but Simon always stayed the longest, telling his father about his day and sitting at the desk opposite his father's to do his homework. He'd browse through Papi's books, poring over the scientific illustrations. He loved the treasures on the shelves: marlin bills; exotic shells; starfish and octo-pus and coiled water snakes that floated in a solution in rows of big glass jars. Simon had a steady hand, and his father often asked him to sketch things he saw under micro-scope slides. But these days his father was preoccupied, and he rarely talked to the children except to yell at them when they were too noisy.

"Papi," said Simon. His father didn't hear him.

Messy piles of coffee-stained papers teetered precari-ously under sea stones and open books were stacked on top of each other on almost every inch of the floor. Behind his father's desk was a large map studded with colored draw-ing pins that plotted the locations of the reported sightings of dead, glowing sea life. Simon felt a sudden rush of annoy-ance at the shambles of his father's office.

"Papi!" he said, loudly this time.

His father looked up, startled. "Simon," he said. "Home already? What can I do for you?"

"I just saw that someone found another glowing sea creature," said Simon. "Did you hear about it?"

"I did," said his father, looking back down at his papers. "Very troubling business."

"What do you think is making them glow like that?" Simon asked. He had been hovering in the doorway but now he stepped inside, dropping his school bag to the ground.

"Anything I could say now would only be speculation," said his father. "And I'd rather not speculate."

Simon frowned. He wished his father would stop being

so infuriatingly vague. He looked out of the window. "You know those men are still out there," he said.

"Yes, I'm aware," said his father, sifting through the jumble on his desk in search of something.

"I could help, you know," said Simon. "We could go outside right now and tell them to get lost!"

His father looked at him. "That would be very foolish," he said seriously. "Those men are dangerous—it isn't a game. Steer clear of them, Simon. I mean it."

"What do they want?" Simon pressed.

When his father didn't answer Simon changed the subject. "What about Helix?" he asked. "It's been weeks—can't you at least tell us where he's gone, or when he'll be coming back?"

Dr. Nelson sat back, rubbing a bony knuckle over his bushy eyebrow. "I wish I did know where Helix was," he said. "I'm worried about him. He took it upon himself to— Oh, never mind. He thinks he's helping us."

"I want to help, too," said Simon.

"You're too young," said his father.

"Helix isn't that much older," argued Simon.

"Helix is different," said his father.

"That isn't a good enough reason," Simon objected in frustration. "I don't understand why no one will tell me anything!"

"Please, Simon," said Papi. "I'm very busy. Was there something specific you wanted?"

"No," mumbled Simon. He picked up his backpack and

went the rest of the way noisily to his room. He could get there now in just three long strides and—*whack*—one especially hard knock on the door frame.

※ ※ ※

When Simon got back to the kitchen his mother had returned home from the laboratory. Her lab coat hung over the back of a chair and she was helping Granny Pearl make dinner. "I'm going to the boatyard," he told them, bending down to tie his shoelace. Maya had gone to her room and just Penny was there.

"Can I come?" she asked.

"Nope," said Simon breezily.

"I won't say anything," said Penny. "You won't even know I'm there."

Simon shook his head.

"*Please.*"

"Hang on a minute, Simon," said his mother as he headed out of the door. Simon knew from the tone of her voice that she was going to say something he wouldn't like. He had almost made it. He stopped and turned around, but kept his hand on the door.

"Those men are outside again," she said. "I'd be happier if you stuck close to home, okay?"

Simon's heart plunged. He *couldn't* stay at home. He hated being there these days. The only thing he really looked forward to was the boatyard. Maybe Maya was happy to sit in her room and read a book, but he had to be out. He had to be *doing* things.

"But I have to go," he said. "If I'm not there Dennis will be the one to put the last bits of the engine back together and then he's going to act like it's *his*." It was true. That was exactly what would happen.

Mami hesitated, frowning as she wiped her hands on a tea towel. "I've had a funny feeling all afternoon," she said. "Something's in the air. I'd like you to stick nearby—just for today."

When Simon opened his mouth to argue she looked at him so seriously over her glasses that he stopped. Outside the screen door, he could see his bicycle leaning against the poinciana tree in the yard. He felt the afternoon sliding away from him, like a wave being sucked back out to sea.

"A feeling," he grumbled. "That isn't very scientific."

"Not everything is," said his mother.

🌟 🌟 🌟

Simon shuffled outside and flopped down on the porch steps. A perfectly good afternoon, ruined. Now what was he going to do? At this very moment he should have grease all over his hands and engine parts spread out on the ground around him. He scanned the garden but the men who had caused all the trouble were nowhere to be seen. It was all so stupid. The light was fading fast and the fact of the short winter days only sharpened the injustice.

The dreary day reflected Simon's thoughts.

A cool wind rustled through the trees and rattled the *Pamela Jane*'s halyards, and his gaze wandered down to her. Until four years ago, Simon, Maya, and Penny had lived on her, sailing the open seas with their parents, who were marine biologists. Back then the *Pamela Jane* had been kept in tip-top shape: Simon and his father used to dive beneath the water and scrape the barnacles from her hull, her yellow paint was fresh, her name was proud and bold, and the waters she sailed over were sometimes four thousand fathoms deep. Each day her brilliant white sails were filled by the salty Atlantic wind.

But now she sat there as if abandoned, chained on her mooring. Scummy sea moss waved around her in the current, making her appear to drift in and out of focus. Her paint was cracked and faded, her sails furled and her masts stark and lonely. Rust bloomed around her fittings, and underwater, chains of olive green barnacles plated her hull like armor. The wind drove seaweed in through the mouth of the cove and it floated over to become tangled in her anchor line. She looked like a neglected, sea-worn old hulk—bewitched and unlucky—destined for nowhere but the sea floor.

And now Simon and his family were what the old salts who hung around at every port called "landlubbers." Landlubbers—*blecch!* Simon missed the days when the family had sailed from port to port, never waking in the same place. But the best place they had ever been—the most exciting and the scariest—had been Tamarind, a mysterious island not on any map, where they had lost their parents in a storm, met Helix, and gone on a wild adventure to rescue their parents.

For a long time after they returned home and moved in

with Granny Pearl, Tamarind had been all the children could think or talk about. Simon, Maya, and Helix had formed the Tamarind Society. Sometimes, when she proved useful, Penny was brought along, too. They had played on the *Pamela Jane* or in a tree house in the garden, pretending it was in the Cloud Forest Village. Maya pretended to be Evondra or Mathilde, Simon played Rodrigo the barge captain or the pirate Captain Ademovar, Helix was always himself, and a night heron pecking for hermit crabs in the rocks of the cove would be Seagrape, Helix's green parrot that they had left behind. No other kids ever joined in these games. Simon and Maya's parents had made them solemnly swear never to breathe a word about Tamarind to another soul—*It may be the most important secret you ever keep*, Simon's father had said—and none of them ever did.

But time passed and Tamarind began to seem very far away. Simon could still remember the day when Maya had finally sighed and said to him, *Tamarind was just something that happened to us a long time ago*. She began hanging out with school friends and had little interest in Simon as he sat alone at the edge of the cove, stirring the water into a tiny maelstrom with a stick, like the giant Desmond had done, watching bits of twigs get sucked down into the whirlpool as the pirate fleet had on one of their last days in Tamarind. His parents told him that there was no way ever to go back to Tamarind, but sometimes, on days like this, Simon wished he were there again.

Though they lived in the same house and shared the same family, they didn't seem to be really *together* anymore.

Simon's parents acted weirder and weirder. They would never talk about Tamarind or the Red Coral Project or their old friend and colleague, Dr. Fitzsimmons, who was the reason they had ended up in Tamarind in the first place. Simon's parents felt Dr. Fitzsimmons had betrayed them, leading them to believe the Red Coral Project was a simple scientific study, when in fact he knew it was a dangerous investigation to find the secret island. Simon's parents had resigned from the project as soon as they had returned home, but the Red Coral had never left them alone.

In all that time, Simon had kept the secret of Tamarind faithfully, but now his parents were keeping secrets from him . . . it wasn't fair! Helix, too, had grown cagey. Before Helix disappeared a few weeks ago, Simon had several times interrupted hushed conversations between him and Simon's father, which had ceased when Simon was noticed in the doorway.

Though the Nelsons considered Helix part of their family—Simon considered him practically a brother—Helix in many ways remained a mystery. He perched on furniture, never getting too comfortable. Simon had never seen him really sink easily into an armchair or couch. He took school seriously and was a diligent student, though he had little obvious delight in learning, unlike Simon, who actually secretly liked many of his schoolbooks. Helix had been orphaned as a small child and brought up by an island tribe. The Nelson children met him on their first day in Tamarind, and from the moment Simon had seen him—when Helix had freed him from the carnivorous vines of the Lesser Islands—Simon had liked him. Helix had tattoos made of jungle pigments all over his skin, his hair was knotted and dirty, and he had carried a spear. In Tamarind he could disappear into the jungle and survive on his own for months at a stretch. Sometimes Simon thought the only surprising thing was that Helix had stayed with them as long as he had.

As he sat there on the porch steps, Simon longed for a moment to be back in Tamarind when, in spite of all the trials they'd faced, life had seemed simpler somehow, his purpose important and clear. The place he had worked so hard to escape from was now the place he desperately longed to return to.

It had already grown darker in the short time Simon had been sitting there, and the next time he looked up, to his surprise, he noticed a pale light glowing from one of the *Pamela Jane*'s portholes. At first he thought it was an illusion caused by the reflection of gray water and sky, but then he felt his heart quicken. Why was there a light in the boat and was someone on board? Everyone else was still in the house. Simon glanced around him. One of the watchers was walking around the other side of the house; the other was nowhere in sight. Simon ran quickly down the stairs, across the grass, and down to the cove, where he ducked behind the mangroves. The little rowboat was there but he wanted to get to the *Pamela Jane* unnoticed, so he stripped off his shirt and waded into the water, which lapped cold over his bare ankles. Another quick glance behind him told him no one was looking, so he began to swim out toward the schooner.

Whoever was responsible for the light could still be inside the boat, so Simon swam hidden underwater as far as he could. He popped up on the starboard side and swam along in the cool gray shadow the boat cast on the water, passing the black-stenciled letters of the *Pamela Jane*'s name, where a chiton had made its home over the N. He crouched for a moment at the top of the ladder up to the deck, making sure that no one on land was watching him, before he crept quietly to the hatch. He pressed his ear to it, but heard no one in the cabin below. He opened it and, taking a deep breath, dropped into the companionway.

To Simon's relief the main cabin was empty. He closed the hatch softly behind him. The portholes were frosted with salt and the light was dim. He waited for his eyes to adjust, listening to the familiar creaking of the boat. It felt as if an old friend were talking to him, but through a dream, the words distorted. Though he stood still, straining his ears, Simon had no sense of whether he was alone or not. He wished he had brought something more than the flimsy pocketknife he always carried, but it was too late to do anything about it.

DON'T MISS ANY OF THE
BOOK OF TAMARIND ADVENTURES!